Praise for the Shades of Magic series

"*A Darker Shade of Magic* has all the hallmarks of a classic work of fantasy. Its plot is gripping. Its characters are memorable. Its setting in four parallel, powerful Londons is otherworldly yet believable. Schwab has given us a gem of a tale that is original in its premise and compelling in its execution. This is a book to treasure." —Deborah Harkness, *New York Times* bestselling author of the All Souls trilogy

"Addictive and immersive, *A Gathering of Shadows* cements this series as a must-read. Rich details illuminate every dimension of an extravagant city flooded with magic, and intriguing personalities evolve into complex characters. . . . Between those glimpses, the vivid setting, and the climactic cliffhanger, Schwab already has us anticipating the rest of the series." —*Entertainment Weekly* (Grade A)

"An absorbing fantasy adventure . . . Impossible to put down. Fans of *A Darker Shade of Magic* will love its sequel, and fantasy fans who haven't yet read the first book in this series should hurry to catch up." —*Kirkus Reviews* on *A Gathering of Shadows*

"Filled with incident and emotion, with difficulty and heartbreak and anger . . . A lively, quick-moving fantasy." —NPR on *A Gathering of Shadows*

"Schwab is a fantastic writer—vibrant, interesting, and detailed. The world-building here is spectacular, and it's worth picking up the book for this alone." —*io9* on *A Gathering of Shadows*

"What else can I say about the wonder that is *A Gathering of Shadows*? I loved it very, very much. I cannot believe I have to wait a whole year for the next book—I don't quite know how I'll manage. . . . V. E. Schwab has done it again." —*The Book Smugglers*

A GATHERING OF SHADOWS

V. E. SCHWAB

TOR

A TOM DOHERTY ASSOCIATES BOOK
NEW YORK

This is a work of fiction. All of the characters, organizations, and events portrayed
in this novel are either products of the author's imagination
or are used fictitiously.

A GATHERING OF SHADOWS

Copyright © 2016 by Victoria Schwab

Edited by Miriam Weinberg

A Tor Book
Published by Tom Doherty Associates
175 Fifth Avenue
New York, NY 10010

www.tor-forge.com

Tor® is a registered trademark of Macmillan Publishing Group, LLC.

The Library of Congress has cataloged the hardcover edition as follows.

Schwab, Victoria, author.
    A gathering of shadows / V. E. Schwab.—1st ed.
        p. cm.
"A Tom Doherty Associates Book."
ISBN 978-0-7653-7647-3 (hardcover)
ISBN 978-0-7653-7649-7 (ebook)
1. FICTION / Fantasy / General. 2. FICTION / Fantasy / Historical. I. Title.
PS3619.C4848 G38 2016
813'.6—dc23

                                                        2015031510

ISBN 978-1-250-22206-0 (collector's edition)

Our books may be purchased in bulk for promotional, educational, or business use.
Please contact your local bookseller or the Macmillan Corporate and Premium
Sales Department at 1-800-221-7945, extension 5442, or by email at
MacmillanSpecialMarkets@macmillan.com.

First Collector's Edition: March 2019

Printed in the United States of America

0 9 8 7 6 5 4 3 2 1

For the ones who fight their way forward

Magic and magician must between them balance.
Magic itself is chaos. The magician must be calm.
A fractured self is a poor vessel for power, spilling
power without focus or measure from every crack.

—TIEREN SERENSE,
head priest of the London Sanctuary

ONE

THIEF
AT
SEA

I

The Arnesian Sea.

Delilah Bard had a way of finding trouble.

She'd always thought it was better than letting trouble find *her,* but floating in the ocean in a two-person skiff with no oars, no view of land, and no real resources save the ropes binding her wrists, she was beginning to reconsider.

The night was moonless overhead, the sea and sky mirroring the starry darkness to every side; only the ripple of water beneath the rocking boat marked the difference between up and down. That infinite reflection usually made Lila feel like she was perched at the center of the universe.

Tonight, adrift, it made her want to scream.

Instead, she squinted at the twinkle of lights in the distance, the reddish hue alone setting the craft's lanterns apart from the starlight. And she watched as the ship—*her* ship—moved slowly but decidedly *away.*

Panic crawled its way up her throat, but she held her ground.

I am Delilah Bard, she thought as the ropes cut into her skin. *I am a thief and a pirate and a traveler. I have set foot in three different worlds, and lived. I have shed the blood of royals and held magic in my hands. And a ship full of men cannot do what I can. I don't need any of you.*

I am one of a damned kind.

Feeling suitably empowered, she set her back to the ship, and gazed out at the sprawling night ahead.

It could be worse, she reasoned, just before she felt cold water licking her boots and looked down to see that there was a hole in the boat. Not a large hole by any stretch, but the size was little comfort; a small hole could sink a boat just as effectively, if not as fast.

Lila groaned and looked down at the coarse rope cinched tight around her hands, doubly grateful that the bastards had left her legs free, even if she was trapped in an abominable *dress.* A full-skirted, flimsy green contraption with too much gossamer and a waist so tight she could hardly breathe and *why in god's name* must women *do* this to themselves?

The water inched higher in the skiff, and Lila forced herself to focus. She drew what little breath her outfit would allow and took stock of her meager, quickly dampening inventory: a single cask of ale (a parting gift), three knives (all concealed), half a dozen flares (bequeathed by the men who'd set her adrift), the aforementioned dress (damn it to hell), and the contents of that dress's skirts and pockets (necessary, if she was to prevail).

Lila took up one of the flares—a device like a firework that, when struck against any surface, produced a stream of colored light. Not a burst, but a steady beam strong enough to cut the darkness like a knife. Each flare was supposed to last a quarter of an hour, and the different colors had their own code on the open water: yellow for a sinking ship, green for illness aboard, white for unnamed distress, and red for pirates.

She had one of each, and her fingers danced over their ends as she considered her options. She eyed the rising water and settled on the yellow flare, taking it up with both hands and striking it against the side of the little boat.

Light burst forth, sudden and blinding. It split the world in two, the violent gold-white of the flare and the dense black nothing around it. Lila spent half a minute cursing and blinking back tears at the brightness as she angled the flare up and away from her face. And then she began to count. Just as her eyes were finally adjusting, the flare faltered, flickered, and went out. She scanned the horizon for a ship but saw none, and the water in the boat continued its slow but steady rise up the calf of her boot. She took up a second flare—white for distress—and struck it on the wood, shielding her eyes. She counted the minutes as they ticked by, scouring the night beyond the boat for signs of life.

"Come on," she whispered. "Come on, come on, come on . . ." The words were lost beneath the hiss of the flare as it died, plunging her back into darkness.

Lila gritted her teeth.

Judging by the level of the water in the little boat, she had only a quarter of an hour—one flare's worth of time—before she was well and truly in danger of sinking.

Then something snaked along the skiff's wooden side. Something with teeth.

If there is a god, she thought, *a celestial body, a heavenly power, or anyone above—or below—who might just like to see me live another day, for pity's or entertainment's sake, now would be a good time to intercede.*

And with that, she took up the red flare—the one for pirates— and struck it, bathing the night around her in an eerie crimson light. It reminded her for an instant of the Isle River back in London. Not *her* London—if the dreary place had ever been hers—or the terrifyingly pale London responsible for Athos and Astrid and Holland, but *his* London. Kell's London.

He flashed up in her vision like a flare, auburn hair and that constant furrow between his eyes: one blue, one black. *Antari.* Magic boy. Prince.

Lila stared straight into the flare's red light until it burned the image out. She had more pressing concerns right now. The water was rising. The flare was dying. Shadows were slithering against the boat.

Just as the red light of the pirate's flare began to peter out, she saw it.

It began as nothing—a tendril of mist on the surface of the sea—but soon the fog drew itself into the phantom of a ship. The polished black hull and shining black sails reflected the night to every side, the lanterns aboard small and colorless enough to pass for starlight. Only when it drew close enough for the flare's dying red light to dance across the reflective surfaces did the ship come into focus. And by then, it was nearly on top of her.

By the flare's sputtering glow, Lila could make out the ship's name, streaked in shimmering paint along the hull. *Is Ranes Gast.*

The Copper Thief.

Lila's eyes widened in amazement and relief. She smiled a small, private smile, and then buried the look beneath something more fitting—an expression somewhere between grateful and beseeching, with a dash of wary hope.

The flare guttered and went out, but the ship was beside her now, close enough for her to see the faces of the men leaning over the rail.

"*Tosa!*" she called in Arnesian, getting to her feet, careful not to rock the tiny, sinking craft.

Help. Vulnerability had never come naturally, but she did her best to imitate it as the men looked down at her, huddled there in her little waterlogged boat with her bound wrists and her soggy green dress. She felt ridiculous.

"*Kers la?*" asked one, more to the others than to her. *What is this?*

"A gift?" said another.

"You'd have to share," muttered a third.

A few of the other men said less pleasant things, and Lila tensed, glad that their accents were too full of mud and ocean spray for her to understand all the words, even if she gleaned their meaning.

"What are you doing down there?" asked one of them, his skin so dark his edges smudged into the night.

Her Arnesian was still far from solid, but four months at sea surrounded by people who spoke no English had certainly improved it.

"*Sensan,*" answered Lila—*sinking*—which earned a laugh from the gathering crew. But they seemed in no hurry to haul her up. Lila held her hands aloft so they could see the rope. "I could use some help," she said slowly, the wording practiced.

"Can see that," said the man.

"Who throws away a pretty thing?" chimed in another.

"Maybe she's all used up."

"Nah."

"Hey, girl! You got all your bits and pieces?"

"Better let us see!"

"What's with all the shouting?" boomed a voice, and a moment later a rail-thin man with deep-set eyes and receding black hair came into sight at the side of the ship. The others shied away in deference as he took hold of the wooden rail and looked down at Lila. His eyes raked over her, the dress, the rope, the cask, the boat.

The captain, she wagered.

"You seem to be in trouble," he called down. He didn't raise his voice, but it carried nonetheless, his Arnesian accent clipped but clear.

"How perceptive," Lila called back before she could stop herself. The insolence was a gamble, but no matter where she was, the one thing she knew was how to read a mark. And sure enough, the thin man smiled.

"My ship's been taken," she continued, "and my new one won't last long, and as you can see—"

He cut her off. "Might be easier to talk if you come up here?"

Lila nodded with a wisp of relief. She was beginning to fear they'd sail on and leave her to drown. Which, judging by the crew's lewd tones and lewder looks, might actually be the better option, but down here she had nothing and up there she had a chance.

A rope was flung over the side; the weighted end landed in the rising water near her feet. She took hold and used it to guide her craft against the ship's side, where a ladder had been lowered; but before she could hoist herself up, two men came down and landed in the boat beside her, causing it to sink *considerably* faster. Neither of them seemed bothered. One proceeded to haul up the cask of ale, and the other, much to Lila's dismay, began to haul up *her*. He threw her over his shoulder, and it took every ounce of her control—which had never been plentiful—not to bury a knife in his back, especially when his hands began to wander up her skirt.

Lila dug her nails into her palms, and by the time the man finally set her down on the ship's desk beside the waiting cask ("Heavier than she looks," he muttered, "and only half as soft . . .") she'd made eight small crescents in her skin.

"Bastard," growled Lila in English under her breath. He gave her a wink and murmured something about being soft where it mattered, and Lila silently vowed to kill him. Slowly.

And then she straightened and found herself standing in a circle of sailors.

No, not sailors, of course.

Pirates.

Grimy, sea stained and sun bleached, their skin darkened and their clothes faded, each and every one of them with a knife tattooed across his throat. The mark of the pirates of the *Copper Thief.* She counted seven surrounding her, five tending to the rigging and sails, and assumed another half dozen below deck. Eighteen. Round it up to twenty.

The rail-thin man broke the circle and stepped forward.

"*Solase,*" he said, spreading his arms. "What my men have in balls, they lack in manners." He brought his hands to the shoulders of her green dress. There was blood under his nails. "You are shaking."

"I've had a bad night," said Lila, hoping, as she surveyed the rough crew, that it wasn't about to get worse.

The thin man smiled, his mouth surprisingly full of teeth. "*Anesh,*" he said, "but you are in better hands now."

Lila knew enough about the crew of the *Copper Thief* to know that was a lie, but she feigned ignorance. "Whose hands would those be?" she asked, as the skeletal figure took her fingers and pressed his cracked lips to her knuckles, ignoring the rope still wound tightly around her wrists. "Baliz Kasnov," he said. "Illustrious captain of the *Copper Thief.*"

Perfect. Kasnov was a legend on the Arnesian Sea. His crew was small but nimble, and they had a penchant for boarding ships and slitting throats in the darkest hours before dawn, slipping away with their cargo and leaving the dead behind to rot. He may have looked starved, but he was an alleged glutton for treasure, especially the consumable kind, and Lila knew that the *Copper Thief* was sailing for the northern coast of a city named Sol in hopes of ambushing the owners of a particularly large shipment of fine liquor. "Baliz Kasnov," she said, sounding out the name as if she'd never heard it.

"And you are?" he pressed.

"Delilah Bard," she said. "Formerly of the *Golden Fish.*"

"Formerly?" prompted Kasnov as his men, obviously bored by the fact she was still clothed, began to tap into the cask. "Well, Miss Bard," he said, linking his arm through hers conspiratorially. "Why don't you tell me how you came to be in that little boat? The sea is no place for a fair young lady such as yourself."

"*Vaskens,*" she said—*pirates*—as if she had no idea the word applied to present company. "They stole my ship. It was a gift, from my father, for my wedding. We were meant to sail toward Faro—we set out two nights ago—but they came out of nowhere, stormed the *Golden Fish* . . ." She'd practiced this speech, not only the words but the pauses. "They . . . they killed my husband. My captain. Most of my crew." Here Lila let herself lapse into English. "It happened so fast—" She caught herself, as if the slip were accidental.

But the captain's attention snagged, like a fish on a hook. "Where are you from?"

"London," said Lila, letting her accent show. A murmur went through the group. She pressed on, intent on finishing her story. "The *Fish* was small," she said, "but precious. Laden down with a month's supplies. Food, drink . . . money. As I said, it was a gift. And now it's gone."

But it wasn't really, not yet. She looked back over the rail. The ship was a smudge of light on the far horizon. It had stopped its retreat and seemed to be waiting. The pirates followed her gaze with hungry eyes.

"How many men?" asked Kasnov.

"Enough," she said. "Seven? Eight?"

The pirates smiled greedily, and Lila knew what they were thinking. They had more than twice that number, and a ship that hid like a shadow in the dark. If they could catch the fleeing bounty . . . she could feel Baliz Kasnov's deep-set eyes scrutinizing her. She stared back at him and wondered, absently, if he could do any magic. Most ships were warded with a handful of spells—things to make their lives safer and more convenient— but she had been surprised to find that most of the men she met at sea had little inclination for the elemental arts. Alucard said that magical proficiency was a valued skill, and that true affinity would usually land one gainful employment on land. Magicians at sea almost always focused on the elements of relevance— water and wind—but few hands could turn the tide, and in the end most still favored good old-fashioned steel. Which Lila could certainly appreciate, having several pieces currently hidden on her person.

"Why did they spare you?" asked Kasnov.

"Did they?" challenged Lila.

The captain licked his lips. He'd already decided what to do about the ship, she could tell; now he was deciding what to do about her. The Copper Thieves had no reputation for mercy.

"Baliz . . ." said one of the pirates, a man with skin darker than the rest. He clasped the captain's shoulder and whispered in his ear. Lila could only make out a few of the muttered words. *Londoners. Rich.* And *ransom.*

A slow smile spread across the captain's lips. *"Anesh,"* he said with a nod. And then, to the entire gathered crew, "Sails up! Course south by west! We have a golden fish to catch."

The men rumbled their approval.

"My lady," said Kasnov, leading Lila toward the steps. "You've had a hard night. Let me show you to my chamber, where you'll surely be more comfortable."

Behind her, she heard the sounds of the cask being opened and the ale being poured, and she smiled as the captain led her belowdecks.

Kasnov didn't linger, thank god.

He deposited her in his quarters, the rope still around her wrists, and vanished again, locking the door behind him. To her relief, she'd only seen three men belowdecks. That meant fifteen aboard the *Copper Thief.*

Lila perched on the edge of the captain's bed and counted to ten, twenty, then thirty, as the steps sounded above and the ship banked toward her own fleeing vessel. They hadn't even bothered to search her for weapons, which Lila thought a bit presumptuous as she dug a blade from her boot and, with a single practiced gesture, spun it in her grip and slashed the ropes. They fell to the floor as she rubbed her wrists, humming to herself. A shanty about the Sarows, a phantom said to haunt wayward ships at night.

How do you know when the Sarows is coming?
(Is coming is coming is coming aboard?)

Lila took the waist of her dress in two hands, and ripped; the
skirt tore away, revealing close-fitting black pants—holsters pinning a knife above each knee—that tapered into her boots. She
took the blade and slid it up the corset at her back, slicing the
ribbons so she could breathe.

When the wind dies away but still sings in your ears,
(In your ears in your head in your blood in your bones.)

She tossed the green skirt onto the bed and slit it open from
hem to tattered waist. Hidden among the gossamer were half a
dozen thin sticks that passed for boning and looked like flares,
but were neither. She slid her blade back into her boot and freed
the tapers.

When the current goes still but the ship, it drifts along,
(Drifts on drifts away drifts alone.)

Overhead, Lila heard a thud, like dead weight. And then another, and another, as the ale took effect. She took up a piece of
black cloth, rubbed charcoal on one side, and tied it over her
nose and mouth.

When the moon and the stars all hide from the dark,
(For the dark is not empty at all at all.)
(For the dark is not empty at all.)

The last thing Lila took from deep within the folds of the
green skirt was her mask. A black leather face-piece, simple but
for the horns that curled with strange and menacing grace over
the brow. Lila settled the mask on her nose and tied it in place.

How do you know when the Sarows is coming?
(Is coming is coming is coming aboard?)

A looking glass, half-silvered with age, leaned in the corner of the captain's cabin, and she caught her reflection as footsteps sounded on the stairs.

Why you don't and you don't and you won't see it coming,
(You won't see it coming at all.)

Lila smiled behind the mask. And then she turned and pressed her back against the wall. She struck a taper against the wood, the way she had the flares—but unlike flares, no light poured forth, only clouds of pale smoke.

An instant later, the captain's door burst open, but the pirates were too late. She tossed the pluming taper into the room and heard footsteps stumble, and men cough, before the drugged smoke brought them down.

Two down, thought Lila, stepping over their bodies.

Thirteen to go.

II

No one was steering the ship.

It had banked against the waves and was now breaching, being hit sidelong instead of head-on in a way that made the whole thing rock unpleasantly beneath Lila's feet.

She was halfway to the stairs before the first pirate barreled into her. He was massive, but his steps were slowed a measure and made clumsy by the drug dissolved in the ale. Lila rolled out of his grip and drove her boot into his sternum, slamming him back into the wall hard enough to crack bones. He groaned and slid down the wooden boards, half a curse across his lips before the toe of her boot met his jaw. His head snapped sideways, then lolled forward against his chest.

Twelve.

Footsteps echoed overhead. She lit another taper and threw it up against the steps just as three more men poured below-decks. The first saw the smoke and tried to backtrack, but the momentum of the second and third barred his retreat, and soon all three were coughing and gasping and crumpling on the wooden stairs.

Nine.

Lila toed the nearest with her boot, then stepped over and up the steps. She paused at the lip of the deck, hidden in the shadow of the stairs, and watched for signs of life. When she saw none, she dragged the charcoal cloth from her mouth, dragging in deep breaths of crisp winter air before stepping out into the night.

The bodies were strewn across the deck. She counted them as she walked, deducting each from the number of pirates aboard.

Eight.

Seven.

Six.

Five.

Four.

Three.

Two.

Lila paused, looking down at the men. And then, over by the rail, something moved. She drew one of the knives from its sheath against her thigh—one of her favorites, a thick blade with a grip guard shaped into metal knuckles—and strode toward the shuffling form, humming as she went.

How do you know when the Sarows is coming?

(Is coming is coming is coming aboard?)

The man was crawling on his hands and knees across the deck, his face swollen from the drugged ale. At first Lila didn't recognize him. But then he looked up, and she saw it was the man who'd carried her aboard. The one with the wandering hands. The one who'd talked about finding her soft places.

"Stupid bitch," he muttered in Arnesian. It was almost hard to understand him through the wheezing. The drug wasn't lethal, at least not in low doses (she hadn't exactly erred on the side of caution with the cask), but it swelled the veins and airways, starving the body of oxygen until the victim passed out.

Looking down at the pirate now, with his face puffy and his lips blue and his breath coming out in ragged gasps, she supposed she might have been too liberal in her measurements. The man was currently trying—and failing—to get to his feet. Lila

reached down, tangled the fingers of her free hand in the collar
of his shirt, and helped him up.

"What did you call me?" she asked.

"I said," he wheezed, "stupid . . . bitch. You'll pay . . . for this.
I'm gonna—"

He never finished. Lila gave him a sharp shove backward, and
he toppled over the rail and crashed down into the sea.

"Show the Sarows some respect," she muttered, watching him
flail briefly and then vanish beneath the surface of the tide.

One.

She heard the boards behind her groan, and she managed to
get her knife up the instant before the rope wrapped around her
throat. Coarse fibers scraped her neck before she sawed herself
free. When she did, she staggered forward and spun to find the
captain of the *Copper Thief,* his eyes sharp, his steps sure.

Baliz Kasnov had not partaken of the ale with his crew.

He tossed the pieces of rope aside, and Lila's grip tightened
on her knife as she braced for a fight, but the captain drew no
weapon. Instead, he brought his hands out before him, palms up.

Lila tilted her head, the horns of the mask tipping toward
him. "Are you surrendering?" she asked.

The captain's dark eyes glittered, and his mouth twitched. In
the lantern light the knife tattoo across his throat seemed to
glint.

"No one takes the *Copper Thief,*" he said.

His lips moved and his fingers twitched as flames leaped across
them. Lila looked down and saw the ruined marking at his feet,
and knew what he was about to do. Most ships were warded
against fire, but he'd broken the spell. He lunged for the nearest sail, and Lila spun the blade in her hand, then threw. It was
ill weighted, with the metal guard on the hilt, and it struck him
in the neck instead of the head. He toppled forward, his hands
thrown out to break his fall, the conjured fire meeting a coil of
ropes instead of sail.

It caught hold, but Kasnov's own body smothered most of it when he fell. The blood pouring from his neck extinguished more. Only a few tendrils of flame persisted, chewing their way up the ropes. Lila reached out toward the fire; when she closed her fingers into a fist, the flames died.

Lila smiled and retrieved her favorite knife from the dead captain's throat, wiping the blood from the blade on his clothes. She was sheathing it again when she heard a whistle, and she looked up to see her ship, the *Night Spire,* drawing up beside the *Copper Thief.*

Men had gathered along the rail, and she crossed the width of the *Thief* to greet them, pushing the mask up onto her brow. Most of the men were frowning, but in the center, a tall figure stood, wearing a black sash and an amused smile, his tawny brown hair swept back and a sapphire in his brow. Alucard Emery. Her captain.

"*Mas aven,*" growled the first mate, Stross, in disbelief.

"Not fucking possible," said the cook, Olo, surveying the bodies scattered across the deck.

Handsome Vasry and Tavestronask (who went simply by Tav) both applauded, Kobis watched with crossed arms, and Lenos gaped like a fish.

Lila relished the mixture of shock and approval as she went to the rail and spread her arms wide. "Captain," she said cheerfully. "It appears I have a ship for you."

Alucard smiled. "It appears you do."

A plank was laid between the two vessels, and Lila strode deftly across it, never once looking down. She landed on the deck of the *Night Spire* and turned toward the lanky young man with shadows beneath his eyes, as if he'd never slept. "Pay up, Lenos."

His brow crinkled. "Captain," he pleaded, with a nervous laugh.

Alucard shrugged. "You made the bet," he said. "You and

Stross," he added, nodding to his first mate, a brutish man with a beard. "With your own heads and your own coin."

And they had. Sure, Lila had boasted that she could take the *Copper Thief* herself, but they'd been the ones to bet she couldn't. It had taken her nearly a month to buy enough of the drug for the tapers and ale, a little every time her ship had docked. It was worth it.

"But it was a trick!" countered Lenos.

"Fools," said Olo, his voice low, thunderous.

"She clearly planned it," grumbled Stross.

"Yeah," said Lenos, "how were we supposed to know she'd been *planning* it?"

"You should have known better than to gamble with Bard in the first place." Alucard met her gaze and winked. "Rules are rules, and unless you want to be left with the bodies on that ship when we're done, I suggest you pay my thief her due."

Stross dragged the purse from his pocket. "How did you do it?" he demanded, shoving the purse into her hands.

"Doesn't matter," said Lila, taking the coin. "Only matters that I did."

Lenos went to forfeit his own purse, but she shook her head. "That's not what I bet for, and you know it." Lenos proceeded to slouch even lower than usual as he unstrapped the blade from his forearm.

"Don't you have enough knives?" he grumbled, his lip thrust forward in a pout.

Lila's smile sharpened. "No such thing," she said, wrapping her fingers around the blade. *Besides,* she thought, *this one is special.* She'd been coveting the weapon since she first saw Lenos use it, back in Korma.

"I'll win it back from you," he mumbled.

Lila patted his shoulder. "You can try."

"*Anesh!*" boomed Alucard, pounding his hand on the plank. "Enough standing around, Spires, we've got a ship to sack. Take it all. I want those bastards left waking up with nothing in their hands but their own cocks."

The men cheered, and Lila chuckled despite herself.

She'd never met a man who loved his job more than Alucard Emery. He relished it the way children relish a game, the way men and women relish acting, throwing themselves into their plays with glee and abandon. There was a measure of theatre to everything Alucard did. She wondered how many other parts he could play. Wondered which, if any, were *not* a part, but the actor beneath.

His eyes found hers in the dark. They were a storm of blue and grey, at times bright and at others almost colorless. He tipped his head wordlessly in the direction of his chambers, and she followed.

Alucard's cabin smelled as it always did, of summer wine and clean silk and dying embers. He liked nice things, that much was obvious. But unlike collectors or boasters who put their fineries on display only to be seen and envied, all of Alucard's luxuries looked thoroughly enjoyed.

"Well, Bard," he said, sliding into English as soon as they were alone. "Are you going to tell me how you managed it?"

"What fun would that be?" she challenged, sinking into one of the two high-backed chairs before his hearth, where a pale fire blazed, as it always did, and two short glasses sat on the table, waiting to be filled. "Mysteries are always more exciting than truths."

Alucard crossed to the table and took up a bottle, while his white cat, Esa, appeared and brushed against Lila's boot. "Are you made of anything *but* mysteries?"

"Were there bets?" she asked, ignoring both him and the cat.

"Of course," said Alucard, uncorking the bottle. "All kinds of small wagers. Whether you'd drown, whether the *Thief* would actually pick you up, whether we'd find anything left of you if they *did* . . ." He poured amber liquid into the glasses and held one out to Lila. She took it, and as she did, he plucked the horned mask off her head and tossed it onto the table between them. "It was an impressive performance," he said, sinking into his own chair. "Those aboard who didn't fear you before tonight surely do now."

Lila stared into the glass, the way some stared into fire. "There were some aboard who didn't fear me?" she asked archly.

"Some of them still call you the Sarows, you know," he rambled on, "when you're not around. They say it in a whisper, as if they think you can hear."

"Maybe I can." She rolled the glass between her fingers.

There was no clever retort, and she looked up from her glass and saw Alucard watching her, as he always did, searching her face the way thieves search pockets, trying to turn something out.

"Well," he said at last, raising his glass, "to what should we toast? To the Sarows? To Baliz Kasnov and his copper fools? To handsome captains and elegant ships?"

But Lila shook her head. "No," she said, raising her glass with a sharpened smile. "To the best thief."

Alucard laughed, soft and soundless. "To the best thief," he said.

And then he tipped his glass to hers, and they both drank.

III

Four Months Ago.
Red London.

Walking away had been easy.

Not looking back was harder.

Lila had felt Kell watching as she strode away, stopping only when she was out of sight. She was alone, again. *Free.* To go anywhere. Be anyone. But as the light ebbed, her bravado began to falter. Night dragged itself across the city, and she began to feel less like a conqueror and more like a girl alone in a foreign world with no grasp of the language and nothing in her pockets save for Kell's parting gift (an element set), her silver watch, and the handful of coins she'd nicked from a palace guard before she left.

She'd had less, to be sure, but she'd also had more.

And she knew enough to know she wouldn't make it far, not without a ship.

She clicked the pocket watch open and closed and watched the outlines of the crafts bob on the river, the Isle's red glow more marked in the settling dark. She had her eyes on one ship in particular, had been watching, coveting, all day. It was a gorgeous vessel, its hull and masts carved from dark wood and trimmed in silver, its sails shifting from midnight blue to black, depending on the light. A name ran along its hull—*Saren Noche*—and she would later learn that it meant *Night Spire*. For now she only knew that she wanted it. But she couldn't simply storm a fully manned craft and claim it as her own. She was good, but she wasn't *that* good. And then there was the grim fact that Lila didn't *technically* know how to sail. So she leaned against a smooth stone wall, her black attire blending into the shadows, and watched, the gentle rocking of the boat and the noise of the Night Market farther up the bank drawing her into a kind of trance.

A trance that broke when half a dozen men stomped off the ship's deck and down the plank in heavy boots, coins jingling in their pockets, raucous laughter in their throats. The ship had been preparing for sea all day, and the men had a manic enthusiasm that spoke of a last night on land. They looked eager to enjoy it. One kicked up a shanty, and the others caught it, carrying the song with them toward the taverns.

Lila snapped the pocket watch closed, pushed off the wall, and followed.

She had no disguise, only her clothes, which were a man's cut, and her dark hair, which fell into her eyes, and her own features, which she drew into sharp lines. Lowering her voice, she hoped she could pass for a slender young man. Masks could be worn in darkened alleys and to masquerade balls, but not in taverns. Not without drawing more attention than they were worth.

The men ahead disappeared into an establishment. It had no obvious name, but the sign above the door was made of metal, a shimmering copper that twisted and curled into waves around a silver compass. Lila smoothed her coat, turned up its collar, and went inside.

The smell hit her at once.

Not foul or stale, like the dockside taverns she'd known, or flower scented like the Red royal palace, but warm and simple and filling, the aroma of fresh stew mixing with tendrils of pipe smoke and the distant salt of sea.

Fires burned in corner hearths, and the bar stood not along

one wall but in the very center of the room, a curved metal circle that mimicked the compass on the door. It was an incredible piece of craftsmanship, a single piece of silver, its spokes trailing off toward the four hearth fires.

This was a sailors' tavern unlike any she'd ever seen, with hardly any bloodstains on the floors or fights threatening to spill out onto the street. The Barren Tide, back in Lila's London—no, not hers, not anymore—had serviced a far rougher crowd, but here half the men wore royal colors, clearly in the service of the crown. The rest were an assortment, but none bore the haggard look and hungry eyes of desperation. Many—like the men she'd followed in—were sea tanned and weather worn, but even their boots looked polished and their weapons well sheathed.

Lila let her hair fall in front of her blind eye, wrangled a quiet arrogance, and sauntered up to the counter.

"*Avan,*" said the bartender, a lean man with friendly eyes. A memory hit her—Barron back at the Stone's Throw, with his stern warmth and stoic calm—but she got her guard up before the blow could land. She slid onto the stool and the bartender asked her a question, and even though she didn't know the words, she could guess at their meaning. She tapped the near-empty glass of a beverage beside her, and the man turned away to fetch the drink. It appeared an instant later, a lovely, frothing ale the color of sand, and Lila took a long, steadying sip.

A quarter turn around the bar, a man was fiddling absently with his coins, and it took Lila a moment to realize he wasn't actually touching them. The metal wound its way around his fingers and under his palms as if by magic, which of course it was. Another man, around the other side, snapped his fingers and lit his pipe with the flame that hovered at the tip of his thumb. The gestures didn't startle her, and she wondered at that; only a week in this world, and it seemed more natural to her than Grey London ever had.

She turned in her seat and picked out the men from the *Night*

Spire now scattered around the room. Two talking beside a hearth, one being drawn by a well-endowed woman into the nearest shadow, and three settling in to play a card game with a couple of sailors in red and gold. One of those three caught Lila's eye, not because he was particularly good-looking—he was in fact, quite ugly, from what she could see through the forest of hair across his face—but because he was cheating.

At least, she *thought* he was cheating. She couldn't be certain, since the game seemed to have suspiciously few rules. Still, she was certain she'd seen him pocket a card and produce another. His hand was fast, but not as fast as her eye. She felt the challenge tickle her nerves as her gaze trailed from his fingers to his seat on a low stool, where his purse rested on the wood. The purse was tethered to his belt by a leather strap, and looked heavy with coins. Lila's hand drifted to her hip, where a short, sharp knife was sheathed. She drew it free.

Reckless, whispered a voice in her head, and she was rather disconcerted to find that where once the voice had sounded like Barron, it now sounded like Kell. She shoved it aside, her blood rising with the risk, only to halt sharply when the man turned and looked straight at her—no, not at her, at the barkeep just behind her. He gestured to the table in the universal signal of *more drinks.*

Lila finished her drink and dropped a few coins on the counter, watching as the barkeep loaded the round of drinks onto a tray and a second man appeared to carry the order to its table.

She saw her chance, and got to her feet.

The room swayed once in the wake of the ale, the drink stronger than she was used to, but it quickly settled. She followed the man with the tray, her eyes fixed on the door beyond him even as her boot caught his heel. He stumbled, and managed to save his own balance, but not the tray's; drinks and glasses tumbled forward onto the table, sweeping half the cards away on a crest of spilled ale. The group erupted, cursing and shouting and pushing to their feet, trying to salvage coin and cloth, and by the time the sorry servant could turn to see who'd tripped him, the hem of Lila's black coat was already vanishing through the door.

🐉

Lila ambled down the street, the gambler's stolen purse hanging from one hand. Being a good thief wasn't just about fast fingers. It was about turning situations into opportunities. She hefted the purse, smiling at its weight. Her blood sang triumphantly.

And then, behind her, someone shouted.

She turned to find herself face to face with the bearded fellow she'd just robbed. She didn't bother denying it—she didn't know enough Arnesian to try, and the purse was still hanging from her fingers. Instead, she pocketed the take and prepared for a fight. The man was twice her size across, and a foot taller, and between one step and the next a curved blade appeared in his hands, a miniature version of a scythe. He said something to her, a low grumble of an order. Perhaps he was giving her a chance to leave the stolen prize and walk away intact. But she doubted his wounded pride would allow that, and even if it did, she needed the money enough to risk it. People survived by being cautious, but they got ahead by being bold.

"Finders keepers," she said, watching surprise light up the man's features. *Hell.* Kell had warned her that English had a purpose and a place in this world. It lived among royals, not pirates. If she was going to make it at sea, she'd have to mind her tongue until she learned a new one.

The bearded man muttered something, running a hand along the curve of his knife. It looked very, very sharp.

Lila sighed and drew her own weapon, a jagged blade with a handle fitted for a fist, its metal knuckles curved into a guard. And then, after considering her opponent again, she drew a second blade. The short, sharp one she'd used to knick the purse.

"You know," she said in English, since there was no one else around to hear. "You can still walk away from this."

The bearded man spat a sentence at her that ended with *pilse*. It was one of the only Arnesian words Lila knew. And she knew it wasn't nice. She was still busy being offended when the man lunged. Lila leaped back and caught the scythe with both blades, the sound of metal on metal ringing shrilly through the street. Even with the slosh of the sea and the noise of the taverns, they wouldn't be alone for long.

She shoved off the blade, fighting to regain her balance, and jerked away as he slashed again, this time missing her throat by a hair's breadth.

Lila ducked, and spun, and rose, catching the scythe's newest slash with her main knife, the weapons sliding until his blade fetched up against her dagger's guard. She twisted the knife free and came over the top of the scythe, slamming the metal knuckles of her grip into the man's jaw. Before he could recover, she came under with the second blade and buried it between his ribs. He coughed, blood streaking his beard, and went to slash at her with his remaining strength, but Lila forced the assaulting weapon up, through organ and behind bone, and at last the man's scythe tumbled away and his body went slack.

For an instant, another death flashed in her mind, another body on her blade, a boy in a castle in a bleak, white world. Not her first kill, but the first that stuck. The first that hurt. The memory flickered and died, and she was back on the docks again, the guilt bleeding out with the man's life. It had happened so fast.

She pulled free and let him collapse to the street, her ears still ringing from the clash of blades and the thrill of the fight. She took a few steadying breaths, then turned to run, and found herself face to face with the five other men from the ship.

A murmur passed through the crew.

Weapons were drawn.

Lila swore beneath her breath, her eyes straying for an instant to the palace arcing over the river behind them, as a weak thought flickered through her—she should have stayed, *could* have stayed, would have been safe—but Lila tamped it out and clutched her knives.

She was Delilah Bard, and she would live or die on her own damn—

A fist connected with her stomach, shattering the train of thought. A second collided with her jaw. Lila went down hard in the street, one knife skittering from her grip as her vision was shattered by starbursts. She fought to her hands and knees, clutching the second blade, but a boot came down hard on her wrist. Another met her ribs. Something caught her in the side of the head, and the world slipped out of focus for several long moments, shuddering back into shape only as strong hands dragged her to her feet. A sword came to rest under her chin, and she braced herself, but her world didn't end with a bite of the blade.

Instead, a leather strap, not unlike the one she'd cut to free the purse, was wrapped around her wrists and cinched tight, and she was forced down the docks.

The men's voices filled her head like static, one word bouncing back and forth more than the rest.

Casero. She didn't know what it meant.

She tasted blood, but she couldn't tell if it was coming from her nose or her mouth or her throat. It wouldn't matter, if they were planning to dump her body in the Isle (unless that was sacrilegious, which made Lila wonder what people here did with their dead), but after several moments of heated discussion, she was marched up the plank onto the ship she'd spent all afternoon watching. She heard a thud and looked back to see a man set the bearded corpse on the plank. *Interesting,* she thought, dully. *The men didn't carry it aboard.*

All the while, Lila held her tongue, and her silence only

seemed to rattle the crew. They shouted at each other, and at her. More men appeared. More calls for *casero*. Lila wished she'd had more than a handful of days to study Arnesian. Did *casero* mean trial? Death? Murder?

And then a man strode across the deck, wearing a black sash and an elegant hat, a gleaming sword and a dangerous smile, and the shouting stopped, and Lila understood.

Casero meant *captain*.

☙

The captain of the *Night Spire* was striking. And strikingly young. His skin was sea tanned but smooth; his hair, a rich brown threaded with brass, was pinned back with an elegant clasp. His eyes, a blue so dark they were almost black, went from the body on the plank, to the crowd of gathered men, to Lila. A sapphire glittered in his left brow.

"*Kers la?*" he asked.

The five who'd dragged Lila on board broke into noise. She didn't even try to follow along and pick out words as they railed on around her. Instead she kept her eyes on the captain, and though he was obviously listening to their claims, he kept his eyes on her. When they'd burned themselves out, the captain began to interrogate her—or at least ramble at her. He didn't seem particularly angry, simply put out. He pinched the bridge of his nose and spoke very fast, obviously unaware of the fact she didn't know more than a few words of Arnesian. Lila waited for him to realize, and eventually he must have recognized the emptiness in her stare for lack of comprehension, because he trailed off.

"*Shast,*" he muttered under his breath, and then started up again, slowly, trying out several other languages, each either more guttural or more fluid than Arnesian, hoping to catch the light of understanding in her eyes, but Lila could only shake her head. She knew a few words of French, but that probably wouldn't help her in this world. There *was* no France here.

"*Anesh,*" said the captain at last, an Arnesian word that as far as Lila could tell was a general sound of assent. "*Ta . . .*" He pointed at her. "*. . . vasar . . .*" He drew a line across his throat. "*. . . mas . . .*" He pointed at himself. "*. . . eran gast.*" With that, he pointed at the body of the man she'd gutted.

Gast. She knew that word already. *Thief.*

"*Ta vasar mas eran gast.*"

You killed my best thief.

Lila smiled despite herself, adding the new words to her meager arsenal.

"*Vasar es,*" said one of the men, pointing at Lila. *Kill her.* Or perhaps, *Kill him,* since Lila was pretty sure they hadn't figured out yet that she was a girl. And she had no intention of informing them. She might have been a long way from home, but some things didn't change, and she'd rather be a man, even if that meant a dead one. And the crew seemed to be gunning for that end, as a murmur of approval went through the group, punctuated by *vasar.*

The captain ran a hand over his hair, obviously considering it. He raised a brow at Lila as if to say, *Well? What would you have me do?*

Lila had an idea. It was a very stupid idea. But a stupid idea was better than no idea, at least in theory. So she dragged the words into shape and delivered them with her sharpest smile. "*Nas,*" she said, slowly. "*An to eran gast.*"

No. I am your best thief.

She held the captain's gaze when she said it, her chin high and proud. The others grumbled and growled, but to her they didn't matter, didn't exist. The world narrowed to Lila and the captain of the ship.

His smile was almost imperceptible. The barest quirk of his lips.

Others were less amused by her show. Two of them advanced on her, and in the time it took Lila to retreat a matching step, she had another knife in hand. Which was a feat, considering the leather strap that bound her wrists. The captain whistled, and she couldn't tell if it was an order for his men, or a sound of approval. It didn't matter. A fist slammed into her back and she staggered forward into the captain, who caught her wrists and pressed a groove between her bones. Pain shot up her arm, and the knife clattered to the deck. She glared up into the captain's face. It was only inches from her own, and when his eyes bore into hers, she felt them searching.

"*Eran gast?*" he said. "*Anesh . . .*" And then, to her surprise, the captain let her go. He tapped his coat. "*Casero* Alucard Emery," he said, drawing out the syllables. Then he pointed at her with a questioning look.

"Bard," she said.

He nodded, once, thinking, and then turned to his waiting crew. He began addressing them, the words too smooth and fast for Lila to decipher. He gestured to the body on the plank, and then to her. The crew did not seem pleased, but the captain was the captain for a reason, and they listened. And when he was finished, they stood, still and sullen. Captain Emery turned and made his way back across the deck to a set of stairs that plunged down into the ship's hull.

When his boot touched the first step, he stopped and looked back with a new smile, this one sharp.

"*Nas vasar!*" he ordered. *No killing.*

And then he gave Lila a look that said, *Good luck,* and vanished belowdecks.

🐉

The men wrapped the body in canvas and set it back on the dock.

Superstition, she guessed, about bringing the dead aboard.

A gold coin was placed on the man's forehead, perhaps as payment for disposal. From what Lila could tell, Red London wasn't a particularly religious place. If these men worshipped anything, they worshipped magic, which she supposed would be heresy back in Grey London. But then again, Christians worshipped an old man in the sky, and if Lila had to say which one seemed more real at the moment, she'd have to side with magic.

Luckily, she'd never been devout. Never believed in higher powers, never attended church, never prayed before bed. In fact, the only person Lila had ever prayed to was herself.

She considered nicking the gold coin, but god or not, that seemed wrong, so she stood on the deck and watched the proceedings with resignation. It was hard to feel bad about killing the man—he would have killed her—and none of the other sailors seemed terribly broken up over the loss itself . . . but then again, Lila supposed she was in no place to judge a person's worth by who would miss them. Not with the closest thing she'd had to family rotting a world away. Who had found Barron? Who had buried him? She shoved the questions down. They wouldn't bring him back.

The huddle of men trudged back aboard. One of them walked straight up to Lila, and she recognized her knuckle-hilted dagger in his grip. He grumbled something under his breath, then raised the knife and buried its tip in a crate beside her head. To his credit, it wasn't *in* her head, and to hers, she didn't flinch. She brought her bound wrists around the blade and pulled down in a single sharp motion, freeing herself from the cord.

The ship was almost ready to set sail, and Lila appeared to have earned a place on it, though she wasn't entirely sure if it was as prisoner, cargo, or crew. A light rain began to fall, but she stayed on deck and out of the way as the *Night Spire* cast off, her heart racing as the ship drifted out into the middle of the Isle and turned its back on the glittering city. Lila gripped the rail at the *Spire*'s stern and watched Red London shrink in the distance.

She stood until her hands were stiff with cold, and the madness of what she was doing settled into her bones.

Then the captain barked her name—"Bard!"—and pointed at a group struggling with the crates, and she went to lend a hand. Just like that—only not just like that, of course, for there were many taut nights and fights won, first against and then beside the other men, and blood spilled and ships taken—Lila Bard became a member of the *Night Spire*'s crew.

IV

Once aboard the *Night Spire,* Lila barely said a word (Kell would have been thrilled). She spent every moment trying to learn Arnesian, cobbling together a vocabulary—but as fast as she was on the uptake, it was still easier to simply listen than engage.

The crew spent a fair amount of time tossing words her way, trying to figure out her native tongue, but it was Alucard Emery who found her out.

Lila had only been on board a week when the captain stumbled across her one night cussing at Caster, her flintlock, for being a waterlogged piece of shit with its last bullet jammed in the barrel.

"Well, this is a surprise."

Lila looked up and saw Alucard standing there. At first she thought her Arnesian must be improving, because she understood his words without thinking, but then she realized he wasn't speaking Arnesian. He was speaking *English.* Not only that, but his accent had the crisp enunciation and smooth execution of someone fluent in the royal tongue. Not like the court-climbers who fumbled over words, offering them up like a party trick. No, like Kell, or Rhy. Someone who had been raised with it balanced on their lips.

A world away, in the grey streets of Lila's old city, that fluency would mean little, but here, it meant neither of them were simple sailors.

In a last-ditch effort at salvaging her secret, Lila pretended not to understand him. "Oh don't go dumb on me now, Bard," he said. "You're just becoming interesting."

They were alone on the stretch of ship, tucked beneath the lip of the upper deck. Lila's fingers drifted to the knife at her waist, but Alucard held up a hand.

"Why don't we take this conversation to my chambers?" he asked, eyes glinting. "Unless you want to make a scene."

Lila supposed it would be better *not* to slit the captain's throat in plain sight.

No, it could be done in private.

❧

The moment they were alone, Lila spun on him. "You speak Eng—" she started, then caught herself. "High Royal." That was what they called it here.

"Obviously," said Alucard before sliding effortlessly into Arnesian. "But it is not *my* native tongue."

"*Tac,*" countered Lila in the same language. "Who says it is mine?"

Alucard gave her a playful grin and returned to English. "First, because your Arnesian is awful," he chided. "And second, because it's a law of the universe that all men swear in their native tongue. And I must say, your usage was quite colorful."

Lila clenched her teeth, annoyed at her mistake as Alucard led her into his cabin. It was elegant but cozy, with a bed in a nook along one wall and a hearth along the other, two high-backed chairs before a pale fire. A white cat lay curled on a dark wooden desk, like a paperweight atop the maps. It flicked its tail at their arrival and opened one lavender eye as Alucard crossed to the desk, riffling through some papers. He scratched the cat absently behind the ears.

"Esa," he said, by way of introduction. "Mistress of my ship."

His back was to Lila now, and her hand drifted once more

to the knife at her hip. But before she could reach the weapon, Alucard's fingers twitched and the blade jumped from its sheath and flew into his hand, hilt striking against palm. He hadn't even looked up. Lila's eyes narrowed. In the week she'd been aboard, she hadn't seen anyone do magic. Alucard turned toward her now with an easy grin, as if she hadn't been about to assault him. He tossed the knife casually onto the desk (the sound made Esa flick her tail again).

"You can kill me later," he said, gesturing to the two chairs before the fire. "First, let's talk."

A decanter sat on a table between the chairs, along with two glasses, and Alucard poured a drink the color of berries and held it out to Lila. She didn't take it.

"Why?" she asked.

"Because I'm fond of High Royal," he said, "and I miss having someone to speak it with." It was a sentiment Lila understood. The sheer relief of talking after so long silent was like stretching muscles after poor sleep, working the stiffness out. "I wouldn't want it to rust while I'm out at sea."

He sank into one of the chairs and downed the drink himself, the gem in his brow glinting in the hearth light. He tipped the empty glass at the other chair and Lila considered him, and her options, then lowered herself into it. The decanter of purple wine sat on the table between them. She poured herself a glass and leaned back, imitating Alucard's posture, her drink braced on the arm of the chair, legs stretched out, boots crossed at the ankle. The picture of nonchalance. He twisted one of his rings absently, a silver feather curled into a band.

For a long moment, they considered each other in silence, like two chess players before the first move. Lila had always hated chess. Never had the patience for it.

Alucard was the first to move, the first to speak. "Who are you?"

"I told you," she said simply. "My name is Bard."

"*Bard,*" he said. "There's no noble house by that name. Which family do you truly hail from? The Rosec? The Casin? The Loreni?"

Lila snorted soundlessly but didn't answer. Alucard was making an assumption, the only assumption an Arnesian *would* make: that because she spoke English, or High Royal— she must be noble. A member of the court, taught to flash English words like jewels, intent on impressing a royal, claiming a title, a crown. She pictured the prince, Rhy, with his easy charm and his flirtatious air. She could probably have kept his attention, if she'd wanted to. And then her thoughts drifted to Kell, standing like a shadow behind the flamboyant heir. Kell, with his reddish hair and his black eye and his perpetual frown.

"Fine," cut in Alucard. "An easier question. Do you have a first name, Miss Bard?" Lila raised a brow. "Yes, yes, I know you're a woman. You might actually pass for a very pretty boy back at court, but the kind of men who work on ships tend to have a bit more . . ."

"Muscle?" she ventured.

"I was going to say facial hair."

Lila smirked despite herself. "How long have you known?"

"Since you came aboard."

"But you let me stay."

"I found you curious." Alucard refilled his glass. "Tell me, what brought you to my ship?"

"Your men."

"But I saw you that day. You *wanted* to come aboard."

Lila considered him, then said, "I liked your ship. It looked expensive."

"Oh, it is."

"I was going to wait for the crew to go ashore, and then kill you and take the *Spire* as my own."

"How candid," he drawled, sipping his wine.

Lila shrugged. "I've always wanted a pirate ship."

At that, Alucard laughed. "What makes you think I'm a pirate, Miss Bard?"

Lila's face fell. She didn't understand. She'd seen them take a ship just the day before, even though she'd been confined to the *Spire,* had watched from the nest as they fought, and raided, and sailed on with a fresh bounty. "What else would you be?"

"I'm a *privateer,*" he explained, lifting his chin. "In the service of the good Arnesian crown. I sail by the permission of the Maresh. I monitor their seas and take care of any trouble I find on them. Why do you think my High Royal is so polished?"

Lila swore under her breath. No wonder the men had been welcome in that tavern with the compass. They were proper sailors. Her heart sank a little at the idea.

"But you don't fly royal colors," she said.

"I suppose I could. . . ."

"Then why don't you?" she snapped.

He shrugged. "Less fun, I suppose." He offered her a new smile, a wicked one. "And as I said, I *could* fly royal colors, *if* I wanted to be attacked at every turn, or scare away my prey. But I'm quite fond of the vessel, and I don't care to see it sunk, nor do I care to lose my post for lack of anything to show. No, the Spires prefer a more subtle form of infiltration. But we are not pirates." He must have seen Lila deflate, because he added, "Come now, don't look so disappointed, Miss Bard. It doesn't matter what you call it, *piracy* or *privateering,* it's just a difference of letters. The only thing that really matters is that I'm *captain* of this ship. And I intend to keep my post, and my life. Which begs the question of what to do with *you.*

"That man you knifed on the first night, Bels . . . the only thing that saved your skin was the fact that you killed him on land and not at sea. There are rules on ships, Bard. If you'd spilled his blood aboard mine, I'd have had no choice but to spill yours."

"You still could have," she observed. "Your men certainly wouldn't have objected. So why did you spare me?" The question had been eating at her since that first night.

"I was curious," he said, staring into the calm white light of the hearth fire. "Besides," he added, his dark eyes flicking back toward her, "I'd been looking for a way to get rid of Bels myself for months—the treacherous scum was stealing from me. So I suppose you did me a favor, and I decided to return it. Lucky for you, most of the crew hated the bastard anyhow."

Esa appeared beside his chair, her large purple eyes staring—or glaring—at Lila. She didn't blink. Lila was pretty sure cats were supposed to blink.

"So," Alucard said, straightening, "you came aboard intending to kill me and steal my ship. You've had a week, so why haven't you tried?"

Lila shrugged. "We haven't been ashore."

Alucard chuckled. "Are you always this charming?"

"Only in my native tongue. My Arnesian, as you pointed out, leaves something to be desired."

"Odd, considering that I've never met someone who could speak the court tongue, but not the common one. . . ."

He trailed off, obviously wanting an answer. Lila sipped her wine and let the silence thicken.

"I'll tell you what," he said, when it was clear she wouldn't follow him down that path. "Spend the nights with me, and I'll help improve your tongue."

Lila nearly choked on the wine at that, then glowered at Alucard. He was laughing—it was an easy, natural sound, though it made the cat ruffle her fur. "I didn't mean it like that," he said, regaining his composure. Lila felt as though she were the color of the liquor in her glass. Her face burned. It made her want to punch him.

"Come keep me company," he tried again, "and I'll keep your secret."

"And let the crew think you're *bedding* me?"

"Oh, I doubt they'll think that," he said with a wave of his hand. Lila tried not to feel insulted. "And I promise, I want only the pleasure of your conversation. I'll even help you with your Arnesian."

Lila rapped her fingers on the arm of the chair, considering. "All right," she said. She got to her feet and crossed to his desk, where her knife still sat atop the maps. She thought of the way he'd plucked it out of her grip. "But I want a favor in return."

"Funny, I thought the favor was allowing you to remain on my ship, despite the fact you're a liar, a thief, and a murderer. But please, do go on."

"Magic," she said, returning the blade to its holster.

He raised the sapphire-studded brow. "What of it?"

She hesitated, trying to choose her words. "You can do it."

"And?"

Lila pulled Kell's gift from her pocket and set it on the table. "And I want to learn." If she was going to have a chance in this new world, she needed to learn its *true* language.

"I'm not a very good teacher," said Alucard.

"But I'm a fast learner."

Alucard tipped his head, considering. Then he took up Kell's box and released the clasp, letting it fall open in his palm. "What do you want to know?"

Lila returned to the chair and leaned forward, her elbows on her knees. "Everything."

V

The Arnesian Sea.

Lila hummed as she made her way through the belly of the ship. She shoved one hand in her pocket, fingers closing around the shard of white stone she kept there. A reminder.

It was late, and the *Night Spire* had sailed on from the picked-over bones of the *Copper Thief.* The thirteen pirates she hadn't killed would be waking soon, only to find their captain dead and their ship sacked. It could be worse; their throats could have been slit along those inked blades. But Alucard preferred to let the pirates live, claiming that catch and release made the seas more interesting.

Her body was warm from wine and pleasant company, and as the ship swayed gently beneath her feet, the sea air wrapping around her shoulders, and the waves murmuring their song, that lullaby she'd wanted for so long, Lila realized she was happy.

A voice hissed in her ear.

Leave.

Lila recognized that voice, not from the sea, but from the streets of Grey London—it belonged to her, to the girl she'd been for so many years. Desperate, distrustful of anything that wasn't hers, and hers alone.

Leave, it urged. But Lila didn't want to.

And *that* scared her more than anything.

She shook her head and hummed the Sarows song as she reached her own cabin, the chords like a ward against trouble, even though she hadn't found any aboard her own ship in months. Not that it was *her* ship, not exactly, not yet.

Her cabin was small—barely big enough for a cot and a trunk—but it was the only place on the ship where she could be truly alone, and the weight of her persona slid from her shoulders like a coat as she closed the door.

A single window interrupted the wooden boards of the far wall, moonlight reflecting against the ocean swells. She lifted a lantern from the trunk's top and it lit in her hand with the same enchanted fire that filled Alucard's hearth (the spell wasn't hers, and neither was the magic). Hanging the light on a wall hook, she shucked her boots as well as her weapons, lining them up on the trunk, all save the knuckled knife, which she kept with her. Even though she now had a room of her own, she still slept with her back to the wall and the weapon on her knee, the way she had in the beginning. Old habits. She didn't mind so much. She hadn't had a good nights' sleep in years. Life on the Grey London streets had taught her how to rest without ever really sleeping.

Beside her weapons sat the small box Kell had given her that day. It smelled like him, which was to say it smelled like Red London, like flowers and freshly turned soil, and every time she opened it some small part of her was relieved that the scent was still there. A tether to the city, and to him. She took it with her onto the cot, sitting cross-legged and setting the object on the stiff blanket before her knees. Lila was tired, but this had become part of her nightly ritual, and she knew she wouldn't sleep well—if at all—until she did it.

The box was made of dark, notched wood and held shut by a small silver clasp. It was a fine thing, and she would have been able to sell it for a bit of coin, but Lila kept it close. Not out of sentimentality, she told herself—her silver pocket watch was the only thing she couldn't bring herself to sell—but because it was useful.

She slid the silver clasp, and the game board fell open in front of her, the elements in their grooves—earth and air, fire and water and bone—waiting to be moved. Lila flexed her fingers. She knew that most people could only master a single element, maybe two, and that she, being of another London, shouldn't be able to master any.

But Lila never let odds get in her way.

Besides, that old priest, Master Tieren, had told her that she had power somewhere in her bones. That it only needed to be nurtured.

Now she held her hands above either side of the drop of oil in its groove, palms in as if she could warm herself by it. She didn't know the words to summon magic. Alucard insisted that she didn't need to learn another tongue, that words were more for the user than the object, meant to help one focus, but without a proper spell, Lila felt silly. Nothing but a mad girl talking to herself in the dark. No, she needed something, and a poem, she had figured, was kind of like a spell. Or at least, it was more than just its words.

"*Tyger Tyger, burning bright . . .*" she murmured under her breath.

She didn't know many poems—stealing didn't lend itself to literary study—but she knew Blake by heart, thanks to her mother. Lila didn't remember much of the woman, who was more than a decade dead, but she remembered this—nights drawn to sleep by *Songs of Innocence and of Experience.* The gentle cadence of her mother's voice, rocking her like waves against a boat.

The words lulled Lila now, as they had back then, quieted the storm that rolled inside her head, and loosened the thief's knot of tension in her chest.

"*In the forests of the night . . .*"

Lila's palms warmed as she wove the poem through the air. She didn't know if she was doing it right, if there *was* such a thing as right—if Kell were here, he would probably insist there was, and nag her until she did it, but Kell wasn't here, and Lila figured there was more than one way to make a thing work.

"In what distant deeps or skies . . ."

Perhaps power had to be tended, like Tieren said, but not all things grew in gardens.

Plenty of plants grew wild.

And Lila had always thought of herself more as a weed than a rose bush.

"Burnt the fire of thine eyes?"

The oil in its groove sparked to life: not white like Alucard's hearth, but gold. Lila grinned triumphantly as the flame leaped from the groove into the air between her palms, dancing like molten metal, reminding her of the parade she'd seen that first day in Red London, when elementals of every kind danced through the streets, fire and water and air like ribbons in their wake.

The poem continued in her head as the heat tickled her palms. Kell would say it was impossible. What a useless word, in a world with magic.

What are you? Kell had asked her once.

What am I? She wondered now, as the fire rolled across her knuckles like a coin.

She let the fire go out, the drop of oil sinking back into its groove. The flame was gone, but Lila could feel the magic lingering in the air like smoke as she took up her newest knife, the one she'd won off Lenos. It was no ordinary weapon. A month back, when they'd taken a Faroan pirate ship called the *Serpent* off the coast of Korma, she'd seen him use it. Now she ran her hand along the blade until she found the hidden notch, where the metal met the hilt. She pushed the clasp, and it released, and the knife performed a kind of magic trick. It separated in her hands, and what had been one blade now became two, mirror images as thin as straight-edged razors. Lila touched the bead of oil and ran her finger along the backs of both knives. And then she balanced them in her hands, crossed their sharpened edges—*Tyger Tyger, burning bright*—and struck.

Fire licked along the metal, and Lila smiled.

This she hadn't seen Lenos do.

The flames spread until they coated the blades from hilt to tip, burning with golden light.

This she hadn't seen *anyone* do.

What am I? One of a kind.

They said the same thing about Kell.

The Red messenger.

The black-eyed prince.

The last *Antari*.

But as she twirled the fire-slicked knives in her fingers, she couldn't help but wonder . . .

Were they really one of a kind, or two?

She carved a fiery arc through the air, marveling at the path of light trailing like a comet's tail, and remembered the feeling of his eyes on her back as she walked away. Waiting. Lila smiled at the memory. She had no doubt their paths would cross again.

And when they did, she would *show* him what she could do.

TWO

PRINCE AT LARGE

I

Red London.

Kell knelt in the center of the Basin.

The large circular room was hollowed out of one of the bridge pillars that held up the palace. Set beneath the Isle's current, the faintest red glow from the river permeated the glassy stone walls with eerie light. A concentration circle had been etched into the stone floor, its pattern designed to channel power, and the whole space, wall and air alike, hummed with energy, a deep resonant sound like the inside of a bell.

Kell felt the power welling in him, wanting out—felt all the energy and the tension and the anger and the fear clawing for escape—but he forced himself to focus on his breathing, to find his center, to make a conscious act of the process that had become so natural. He wound back the mental clock until he was ten again, sitting on the floor of the monastic cell in the London Sanctuary, Master Tieren's steady voice in his head.

Magic is tangled, so you must be smooth.
Magic is wild, so you must be tame.
Magic is chaos, so you must be calm.
Are you calm, Kell?

Kell rose slowly to his feet, and raised his head. Beyond the concentration circle, the darkness twisted and the shadows loomed. In the flickering torchlight, sparring forms seemed to take the faces of enemies.

Tieren's soothing voice faded from his head, and Holland's cold tone took its place.

Do you know what makes you weak?

The *Antari*'s voice echoed in his head.

Kell stared into the shadows beyond the circle, imagining a flutter of cloak, a glint of steel.

You've never had to be strong.

The torchlight wavered, and Kell inhaled, exhaled, and struck.

He slammed into the first form, toppling it. By the time the shadow fell, Kell was already turning on the second one at his back.

You've never had to try.

Kell threw out his hand; water leaped to circle it and then, in one motion, sailed toward the figure, turning to ice the instant before it crashed into the form's head.

You've never had to fight.

Kell spun and found himself face to face with a shadow that took the shape of Holland.

And you've certainly never had to fight for your life.

Once he would have hesitated—once he *had* hesitated—but not this time. With a flick of his hand, metal spikes slid from the sheath at his wrist and into his palm. They rose into the air and shot forward, burying themselves in the specter's throat, his heart, his head.

But there were still more shadows. Always more.

Kell pressed himself against the Basin's curved wall and raised his hands. A small triangle of sharpened metal glinted on the back of his wrist; when he flexed his hand down it became a point, and Kell sliced his palm across with it, drawing blood. He pressed his hands together, then pulled them apart.

"*As Osoro*," he told the blood.

Darken.

The command rang out, echoing through the chamber, and between his palms the air began to thicken and swirl into shadows as thick as smoke. It billowed forth, and in moments the room was engulfed in darkness.

Kell sagged back into the cold stone wall of the room, breathless and dizzy from the force of so much magic. Sweat trickled into his eyes—one blue, the other solid black—as he let the silence of the space settle over him.

"Did you kill them all?"

The voice came from somewhere behind him, not a phantom but flesh and blood, and threaded with amusement.

"I'm not sure," said Kell. He collapsed the space between his palms, and the veil of darkness dissolved instantly, revealing the room for what it was: an empty stone cylinder clearly designed for meditation, not combat. The sparring forms were scattered, one burning merrily, another shot full of metal lances. The others—bashed, battered, broken—could hardly be called training dummies anymore. He closed his hand into a fist, and the fire on the burning dummy went out.

"Show-off," muttered Rhy. The prince was leaning in the arched entryway, his amber eyes caught like a cat's by the torchlight. Kell ran a bloody hand through his copper hair as his brother stepped forward, his boots echoing on the stone floor of the Basin.

Rhy and Kell were not actually brothers, not by blood. One year Rhy's senior, Kell had been brought to the Arnesian royal family when he was five, with no family and no memory. Indeed, with nothing but a dagger and an all-black eye: the mark of an *Antari* magician. But Rhy was the closest thing to a brother Kell had ever known. He would give his life for the prince. And— very recently—he had.

Rhy raised a brow at the remains of Kell's training. "I always thought being an *Antari* meant you didn't need to practice, that it all came"—he gestured absently—"naturally."

"The *ability* comes naturally," replied Kell. "The *proficiency* takes work. Just as I explained during every one of your lessons."

The prince shrugged. "Who needs magic when you look this good?"

Kell rolled his eyes. A table stood at the mouth of the alcove, littered with containers—some held earth, others sand and oil— and a large bowl of water; he plunged his hands into the latter and splashed his face before his blood could stain the water red.

Rhy passed him a cloth. "Better?"

"Better."

Neither was referring to the refreshing properties of the water. The truth was, Kell's blood pulsed with a restless beat, while the thing that coursed within it longed for activity. Something had been roused in him, and it didn't seem intent on going back to sleep. They both knew Kell's visits down to the Basin were increasing, both in frequency and length. The practice soothed his nerves and calmed the energy in his blood, but only for a little while. It was like a fever that broke, only to build again.

Rhy was fidgeting now, shifting his weight from foot to foot, and when Kell gave him a once-over, he noticed that the prince had traded his usual red and gold for emerald and grey, fine silk for wool and worn cotton, his gold-buckled boots replaced by a pair of black leather.

"What are you supposed to be?" he asked.

There was a glint of mischief in Rhy's eyes as he bowed with a flourish. "A commoner, of course."

Kell shook his head. It was a superficial ruse. Despite the clothing, Rhy's black hair was glossy and combed, his fingers dotted with rings, his emerald coat clasped with pearlescent buttons. Everything about him registered as royal. "You still look like a prince."

"Well, obviously," replied Rhy. "Just because I'm in disguise, doesn't mean I don't want to be recognized."

Kell sighed. "Actually," he said. "That's exactly what it means. Or *would* mean, to anyone but you." Rhy only smiled, as if it were a compliment. "Do I want to know *why* you are dressed like that?"

"Ah," said the prince. "Because we're going out."

Kell shook his head. "I'll pass." All he wanted was a bath and a drink, both of which were available in the peace of his own chambers.

"Fine," said Rhy. "*I'm* going out. And when I'm robbed and left in an alley, *you* can tell our parents what happened. Don't forget to include the part where you stayed home instead of ensuring my safety."

Kell groaned. "Rhy, the last time—"

But the prince waved off *the last time* as if it hadn't involved a broken nose, several bribes, and a thousand lin in damages.

"This will be different," he insisted. "No mischief. No mayhem. Just a drink at a place befitting our station. Come on, Kell, for me? I can't spend another minute cooped up planning tournaments while Mother second guesses my every choice, and Father worries about Faro and Vesk."

Kell didn't trust his brother to stay out of trouble, but he could see in the set of Rhy's jaw and the glint in his eyes, he was going out. Which meant *they* were going out. Kell sighed and nodded at the stairs. "Can I at least stop by my rooms and change?"

"No need," said Rhy cheerfully. "I've brought you a fresh tunic." He produced a soft shirt the color of wheat. Clearly he meant to usher Kell out of the palace before he could change his mind.

"How thoughtful," muttered Kell, shrugging out of his shirt. He saw the prince's gaze settle on the scar scrawled across his chest. The mirror image of the one over Rhy's own heart. A piece of forbidden, irreversible magic.

My life is his life. His life is mine. Bring him back.

Kell swallowed. He still wasn't used to the design—once black, now silver—that tethered them together. Their pain. Their pleasure. Their lives.

He pulled on the fresh tunic, exhaling as the mark disappeared beneath the cotton. He slicked his hair back out of his face and turned to Rhy. "Happy?"

The prince started to nod, then stopped. "Almost forgot," he said, pulling something from his pocket. "I brought hats." He placed a pale grey cap gingerly on his black curls, taking care to set it at a slight angle so the scattering of green gems shone across the brim.

"Wonderful," grumbled Kell as the prince reached out and deposited a charcoal-colored cap over Kell's reddish hair. His coat hung from a hook in the alcove, and he fetched it down and shrugged it on.

Rhy tutted. "You'll never blend in looking like that," he said, and Kell resisted the urge to point out that with his fair skin, red hair, and black eye—not to mention the word *Antari* following him wherever he went, half prayer and half curse—he would never blend in anywhere.

Instead he said, "Neither will you. I thought that was the point."

"I mean the coat," pressed Rhy. "Black isn't the fashion this winter. Haven't you got something indigo or cerulean hidden away in there?"

How many coats do you suppose there are inside that one?

The memory caught him like a blow. Lila.

"I prefer this one," he said, pushing the memory of her away, a pickpocket's hand swatted from the folds of a coat.

"Fine, fine." Rhy shifted his weight again. The prince had never been skilled at standing still, but Kell thought he'd gotten worse. There was a new restlessness to his motions, a taut energy that mirrored Kell's. And yet, Rhy's was different. Manic. Dangerous. His moods were darker and their turn sharper, cutting the span of a second. It was all Kell could do to keep up. "Are we ready, then?"

Kell glanced up the stairs. "What about the guards?"

"Yours or mine?" asked the prince. "Yours are standing by the upper doors. Helps that they don't know there's another way out of this place. As for my own men, they're probably still outside my room. My stealth really is in fine form today. Shall we?"

The Basin had its own route out of the palace, a narrow staircase that curled up one of the structure's supports and onto the bank; the two made their way up, lit only by the reddish dark and the pale lanterns that hung sparsely, burning with eternal flames.

"This is a bad idea," said Kell, not because he expected to change Rhy's mind, but simply because it was his job to say it, so that later he could tell the king and queen he'd tried.

"The best kind," said Rhy, looping his arm around Kell's shoulders.

And with that the two stepped out of the palace, and into the night.

Other cities slept away the winter months, but Red London showed no signs of retreat. As the two brothers walked the streets, elemental fires burned in every hearth, steam drifting from the chimneys, and through his clouded breath, Kell saw the haloed lights of the Night Market lining the bank, the scent of mulled wine and stew drifting on the steam, and the streets bustling with scarf-wrapped figures in jewel-toned cloaks.

Rhy was right: Kell was the only one dressed in black. He pulled the cap down over his brow, to shield him less from the cold than the inevitable looks.

A pair of young women strolled past, arm in arm, and when one cut a favoring glance at Rhy, nearly tripping over her skirts, he caught her elbow.

"*An, solase, res naster,*" she apologized.

"*Mas marist,*" replied Rhy in his effortless Arnesian.

The girl didn't seem to notice Kell, who still hung a step back, half in the bank's shadow. But her friend did. He could feel her eyes hanging on him, and when he finally met her gaze, he felt a grim satisfaction at her indrawn breath.

"*Avan,*" said Kell, his voice little more than fog.

"*Avan,*" she said, stiffly, bowing her head.

Rhy pressed his lips to the other girl's gloved fingers, but Kell didn't take his eyes off the one watching him. There had been a time when Arnesians worshipped him as blessed, fell over themselves trying to bow low enough; while he never relished that display, this was worse. There was a measure of reverence in her eyes, but also fear and, worse, distrust. She looked at him as if he were a dangerous animal. As if any sudden movement might cause him to strike. After all, as far as she knew, he was to blame for the Black Night that had swept the city, the magic that made people's eyes turn as black as his own as it ate them from the inside out. And no matter what statements the king and queen issued, no matter how many rumors Rhy tried to spread to the contrary, everyone believed it was Kell's doing. His fault.

And in a way, of course, it was.

He felt Rhy's hand on his shoulder and blinked.

The girls were walking away, arm in arm, whispering furiously.

Kell sighed and looked back at the royal palace arcing over the river. "This was a bad idea," he said again, but Rhy was already off, heading away from the Night Market and the glow of the Isle.

"Where are we going?" asked Kell, falling into step behind the prince.

"It's a surprise."

"Rhy," warned Kell, who had come to hate surprises.

"Fear not, Brother. I promised you an elegant outing, and I plan to deliver."

🐉

Kell hated the place the moment he saw it.

It was called Rachenast.

Splendor.

Ruinously loud and riotously colorful, Splendor was a leisure palace where the city's *ostra*—their elite—could stave off the coldest months by simply denying their presence. Beyond the silver-plated doors, the winter night evaporated. Inside, it was a summer day, from the fire lanterns burning sun-bright overhead to the artificial arbor, shading everyone beneath a dappled canopy of green.

Stepping from the icy night with its curtain of dark and fog into the expansive, well-lit field, Kell felt suddenly—horribly—exposed. He couldn't believe it, but he and Rhy were actually *under*dressed. He wondered if Rhy *wanted* to cause a scandal or a scene, to have his presence challenged. But the attendants at the doors either recognized the royal prince or Kell himself (and by extension Rhy, since saints knew no one else could drag the *Antari* to such a fête), because the two were welcomed in.

Kell squinted at the onslaught of activity. Banquet tables were piled with fruit and cheese and pitchers of chilled summer wine, and couples twirled across a blue stone platform made to resemble a pond, while others lounged on pillows beneath the enchanted trees. Wind chimes sang, and people laughed—the high, bright laugh of aristocrats—and toasted their companions with crystal cups, their wealth, like the landscape, on display.

Perhaps the whole charade would have been enchanting if it weren't so frivolous, so gaudy. Instead, Kell found it insufferable. Red London might have been the jewel of the Arnesian empire, but it still had poor people, and suffering—and yet, here in Splendor, the *ostra* could play pretend, craft utopias out of money and magic.

On top of it all, Rhy was right: no one else was wearing black, and Kell felt like a stain on a clean tablecloth (he thought of changing his coat, trading out the black for something brighter, but couldn't bring himself to wear any of the peacock shades so in fashion this winter) as the prince put a hand on his shoulder and ushered him forward. They passed a banquet table, and Rhy took up two flutes of summer wine. Kell kept his hat on, surveying the room from between the brim of the cap and the rim of the glass Rhy pressed into his hands.

"Do you think they've seen through my disguise yet," mused

the prince, keeping his head bowed, "or are they all too busy preening?"

Kell was surprised by the hint of judgment in his brother's tone. "Give it time," he said, "we've only just arrived." But he could feel the knowledge moving like a tremor through the room as Rhy led them toward a sofa beneath a tree.

The prince sank into the cushions and cast off his hat. His black curls shone, and even without the usual circlet of gold in his hair, everything about him—his posture, his perfect smile, his self-possession—registered as regal. Kell knew he couldn't mimic any of those things; he'd tried. Rhy tossed his hat onto the table. Kell hesitated, fingering the brim of his own, but kept it on, his only armor against prying eyes.

He sipped his drink and, having little interest in the rest of Splendor, considered his brother. He still didn't understand Rhy's half-hearted disguise. Splendor was a haunt for the elite, and the elite knew the prince's company better than anyone in the city. They spent months learning the royal tongue just so they could talk their way into his graces (even though Kell knew Rhy found that habit uncomfortable and unnecessary). But the clothes weren't the only thing that bothered him. Everything about the prince was in its place, and yet . . .

"Am I really that good-looking?" asked Rhy without meeting his gaze, while glassy laughter chimed through the room.

"You know you are," answered Kell, dragging his attention to the carpet of grass beneath their feet.

No one approached their couch save for an attendant, a young woman in a white dress, who asked if there was any-thing she could do to make their evening more enjoyable. Rhy flashed his smile and sent her in search of stronger drink and a flower.

Kell watched as the prince stretched his arms along the back of the sofa, his pale gold eyes glittering as he surveyed the room.

This was Rhy at his most understated, and it was still dreadfully conspicuous.

The attendant returned holding a decanter of ruby liquor and a single dark blue blossom; Rhy accepted the drink and tucked the flower behind her ear with a smile. Kell rolled his eyes. Some things didn't change.

As Rhy filled his glass, Kell caught a swell of whispers as more eyes wandered their way. He felt the inevitable weight as the collective gaze shifted from the prince to his companion. Kell's skin crawled under the attention, but instead of ducking his head, he forced himself to meet their eyes.

"This would be a good deal more fun," observed Rhy, "if you'd stop scowling at everyone."

Kell gave him a withering look. "They fear me."

"They worship you," said Rhy with a wave of his hand. "The majority of this city thinks you're a *god*."

Kell cringed at the word. *Antari* magicians were rare—so rare that they were seen by some as divine, chosen. "And the rest think I'm a devil."

Rhy sat forward. "Did you know that in Vesk, they believe you turn the seasons and control the tide, and bless the empire?"

"If you're appealing to my ego—"

"I'm simply reminding you that you will always be singular."

Kell stilled, thinking of Holland. He told himself that a new *Antari* would be born, or found, eventually, but he wasn't sure if he believed it. He and Holland had been two of a disappearing kind. They had always been rare, but they were rapidly approaching *extinct*. What if he really was the last one?

Kell frowned. "I would rather be normal."

Now it was Rhy's turn to wear the withering look. "Poor thing. I wonder what it feels like, to be put on a pedestal."

"The difference," said Kell, "is that the people *love* you."

"For every ten who love me," said Rhy, gesturing at the sprawling room, "one would like to see me dead."

A memory surfaced, of the Shadows, the men and women who had tried to take Rhy's life six years before, simply to send a message to the crown that they were wasting precious resources on frivolous affairs, ignoring the needs of their people. Thinking of Splendor, Kell could almost understand.

"My *point,*" continued Rhy, "is that for every ten who worship you, one wants to see you burn. Those are simply the odds when it comes to people like us."

Kell poured himself a drink. "This place is horrible," he mused.

"Well . . ." said Rhy, emptying his own glass in one swallow and setting it down with a *click* on the table, "we could always leave."

And there it was, in Rhy's eye, that glint, and Kell suddenly understood the prince's outfit. Rhy wasn't dressed for Splendor because it wasn't his true destination. "You chose this place on purpose."

A languorous smile. "I don't know what you're talking about."

"You chose it because you *knew* I would be miserable here and more likely to cave when you offered to take me someplace else."

"And?"

"And you greatly underestimate my capacity for suffering."

"Suit yourself," said the prince, rising to his feet with his usual lazy grace. "*I'm* going to take a turn around the room."

Kell glowered but did not rise. He watched Rhy go, trying to emulate the prince's practiced nonchalance as he sat back with his glass.

He watched his brother maneuver through the field of people, smiling cheerfully, clasping hands and kissing cheeks and occasionally gesturing to his outfit with a self-deprecating laugh; despite his earlier remark, the fact was, Rhy fit in effortlessly. *As he should,* Kell supposed.

And yet, Kell loathed the greedy way the *ostra* eyed the prince.

The women's batting lashes held too little warmth and too much cunning. The men's appraising looks now held too little kindness and too much hunger. One or two shot a glance toward Kell, a ghost of that same hunger, but none were brave enough to approach. Good. Let them whisper, let them look. He felt the strange and sudden urge to make a scene, to watch their amusement harden into terror at the sight of his true power.

Kell's grip tightened on his glass, and he was about to rise when he caught the edge of conversation from a nearby party.

He didn't mean to eavesdrop; the practice just came naturally. Perhaps the magic in his veins gave him strong ears, or perhaps he'd simply learned to tune them over the years. It became habit, when you were so often the topic of whispered debate.

". . . I could have entered," said a nobleman, reclining on a hill of cushions.

"Come," chided a woman at his elbow, "even if you had the skills, which you do not, you're too late by a measure. The roster has been set."

"Has it now?"

Like most of the city, they were talking of the *Essen Tasch*—the Element Games—and Kell paid them little mind at first, since the *ostra* were usually more concerned with the balls and banquets than the competitors. And when they did speak of the magicians, it was in the way people talked of exotic beasts.

"Well, of course, the list hasn't been *posted,*" continued the woman in a conspiratorial tone, "but my brother has his methods."

"Anyone we know?" asked another man in an airy, unconcerned way.

"I've heard the victor, Kisimyr, is in again."

"And what of Emery?"

At that, Kell stiffened, his grip going knuckles-white on his glass. *Surely it is a mistake,* he thought at the same time a woman said, "*Alucard* Emery?"

"Yes. *I've* heard he's coming back to compete."

Kell's pulse thudded in his ears, and the wine in his cup began to swirl.

"That's nonsense," insisted one of the men.

"You *do* have an ear for gossip. Emery hasn't set foot on London soil in three years."

"That may be," insisted the woman, "but his name is on the roster. My brother's friend has a sister who is messenger to the *Aven Essen,* and she said—"

A sudden pain lanced through Kell's shoulder, and he nearly fumbled the glass. His head snapped up, searching for the source of the attack as his hand went to his shoulder blade. It took him a moment to register that the pain wasn't actually his. It was an echo.

Rhy.

Where was Rhy?

Kell surged to his feet, upsetting the things on the table as he scanned the room for the prince's onyx hair, his blue coat. He was nowhere to be seen. Kell's heart pounded in his chest, and he resisted the urge to shout Rhy's name across the lawn. He could feel eyes shifting toward him, and he didn't care. He didn't give a damn about any of them. The only person in this place—in this *city*—he cared about was somewhere nearby, and he was in pain.

Kell squinted across the too-bright field of Splendor. The sun lanterns were glaring overhead, but in the distance, the afternoon light of the open chamber tapered off into hallways of darker forest. Kell swore and plunged across the field, ignoring the looks from the other patrons.

The pain came again, this time in his lower back, and Kell's knife was out of its sheath as he stormed into the shadowed canopy, cursing the dense trees, the star-lights in the branches the only source of light. The only other things in these woods were couples entwined.

Dammit, he cursed, his pulse raging as he doubled back.

He'd learned to keep one of Rhy's tokens on him, just in case, and he was about to draw blood and summon a finding spell when his scar throbbed in a way that told him the prince was close. He twisted around and could hear a muffled voice through the nearest copse, one that might be Rhy's; Kell shoved through, expecting a fight, and found something else entirely.

There, on a mossy slope, a half-dressed Rhy was hovering over the girl in white, the blue flower still in her hair, his face buried in her shoulder. Across his bare back, Kell could see scratch marks deep enough to draw blood, and a fresh echo of pain blossomed near Kell's hips as her nails dug into Rhy's flesh.

Kell exhaled sharply, in discomfort and relief, and the girl saw him standing there and gasped. Rhy dragged his head up, breathless, and had the audacity to smile.

"You bastard," hissed Kell.

"Lover?" wondered the girl.

Rhy sank back onto his heels, and then twisted with a languid grace, reclining on the moss. "Brother," he explained.

"Go," Kell ordered the girl. She looked disconcerted, but she gathered her dress around her and left all the same, while Rhy got unsteadily to his feet and cast about for his shirt. "I thought you were being attacked!"

"Well . . ." Rhy slipped the tunic gingerly over his head. "In a way, I was."

Kell found Rhy's coat slung over a low branch and thrust it at him. And then he led the prince back through the woods and across the field, past the silver doors, and out into the night. It was a silent procession, but the moment they were free of Splendor, Kell spun on his brother.

"What were you *thinking?*"

"Must you ask?"

Kell shook his head in disbelief. "You are an incomparable ass."

Rhy only chuckled. "How was I to know she would be so rough with me?"

"I'm going to kill you."

"You can't," said Rhy simply, spreading his arms. "You made sure of it."

And for an instant, as the words hung in the cloud of his winter breath, the prince seemed genuinely upset. But then the smile was back. "Come on," he said, slinging an arm around Kell's shoulders. "I'd had enough of Splendor anyway. Let's find somewhere more agreeable to drink."

A light snow began to fall around them, and Rhy sighed. "I don't suppose you thought to grab my hat?"

III

"Saints," cursed Rhy, "do *all* the Londons get this cold?"

"As cold," said Kell as he followed the prince away from the bright beating heart of the city, and down a series of narrower roads. "And colder still."

As they walked, Kell imagined this London ghosted against the others. Here, they would be coming upon Westminster. There, the stone courtyard where a statue of the Danes once stood.

Rhy's steps came to a halt ahead, and Kell looked up to see the prince holding open a tavern door. A wooden sign overhead read IS AVEN STRAS.

The Blessed Waters.

Kell swore under his breath. He knew enough about this place to know that they shouldn't be here. *Rhy* shouldn't be here. It wasn't as bad as the Three of Knives in the heart of the *shal,* where the black brands of limiters shone on almost every wrist, or the Jack and All, which had caused so much trouble on their last outing, but the Waters had its own rowdy reputation.

"*Tac,*" chided Kell in Arnesian, because this wasn't the kind of place to speak High Royal.

"What?" asked Rhy innocently, snatching the cap off Kell's head. "It isn't Rachenast. And I have business here."

"What kind of business?" demanded Kell as Rhy settled the

hat over his curls, but the prince only winked and went in, and Kell had no choice but to freeze or follow.

Inside, the place smelled of sea and ale. Where Splendor had been open, with bold colors and bright light, the Waters was made of dark corners and low-burning hearths, tables and booths sprawled like bodies across the room. The air was thick with smoke and loud with raucous laughter and drunken threats.

At least this place is honest with itself, thought Kell. No pretense. No illusion. It reminded him of the Stone's Throw, and the Setting Sun, and the Scorched Bone. Fixed points in the world, places where Kell had done business back when his business was less savory. When he'd traded in trinkets from faraway places, the kind only he could reach.

Rhy tugged the brim of the cap down over his light eyes as he approached the bar. He signaled to a shadow behind the barkeep, and slid a slip of paper and a single silver lish across the wood. "For the *Essen Tasch,*" said the prince under his breath.

"Competitor?" asked the shadow with a voice like stones.

"Kamerov Loste."

"To win?"

Rhy shook his head. "No. Only to the nines." The shadow gave him a wary look, but he took the bet with a flick of his fingers and retreated into the corner of the bar.

Kell shook his head in disbelief. "You came here to place a bet. On the tournament *you're* running."

There was a glint in Rhy's eye. "Indeed."

"That's hardly legal," said Kell.

"Which is why we're *here.*"

"And remind me why we couldn't have *started* the night here?"

"Because," said Rhy, flagging down the barkeep, "you were in an ornery mood when I dragged you from that palace—which is nothing unusual, but still—and you were determined to despise the first destination of the night on principle. I merely came prepared."

The barkeep came over, but he kept his gaze on the glass he was polishing. If he registered Kell's red hair, his black eye, he didn't show it.

"Two Black Sallies," said Rhy in Arnesian, and he was wise enough to pay in petty lin instead of lish or the gold rish carried by nobles. The barkeep nodded and served up two glasses of something thick and dark.

Kell lifted the glass—it was too dense to see through—and then took a cautious drink. He nearly gagged, and a handful of men down the bar chuckled. It was rough stock, syrupy but strong, and it clung to Kell's throat as it filled his head.

"That is vile," he choked out. "What's in it?"

"Trust me, Brother, you don't want to know." Rhy turned back toward the barkeep. "We'll take two winter ales as well."

"Who drinks this?" Kell coughed.

"People who want to get drunk," said Rhy, taking a long, pained sip.

Kell felt his own head swim as he shoved his glass away. "Slow down," he said, but the prince seemed determined to finish the draft, and he slammed the empty glass down with a shudder. The men at the end of the bar banged their own cups in approval, and Rhy gave an unsteady bow.

"Impressive," muttered Kell, at the same time that someone behind them spat, "If you ask me, the prince is a spoiled shit."

Kell and Rhy both tensed. The man was slumped at a table with two others, their backs to the bar.

"Watch yer tone," warned the second. "That's royalty yer smearing." But before Kell could feel any relief, they all burst into laughter.

Rhy gripped the counter, knuckles white, and Kell squeezed his brother's shoulder hard enough to feel the pain echo in his own. The last thing he needed was the crown prince involved in a brawl at the Blessed Waters. "What was it you said," he hissed in the Rhy's ear, "about the ones who wanted to watch us burn?"

"They say he hasn't got a lick of magic in him," continued the first man, obviously drunk. No sober man would speak such things so loudly.

"Figures," muttered the second.

"S'unfair," said the third. " 'Cause you know if he weren't up in that pretty palace, he'd be beggin' like a dog."

The sickening thing was, the man was probably right. This world was *ruled* by magic, but power followed no clear line or lineage; it flowed thick in some and thin in others. And yet, if magic denied a person power, the people took it as a judgment. The weak were shunned, left to fend for themselves. Sometimes they took to the sea—where elemental strength mattered less than simple muscle—but more often they stayed, and stole, and ended up with even less than they'd had to start with. It was a side of life Rhy had been spared only by his birth.

"What right's he got to sit up on that throne?" grumbled the second.

"None, that's what . . ."

Kell had had enough. He was about to turn toward the table when Rhy held out a hand. The gesture was relaxed, the touch unconcerned. "Don't bother," he said, taking up the ales and heading for the other side of the room. One of the men was leaning back in his chair, two wooden legs off the floor, and Kell tipped the balance as he passed. He didn't look back, but relished the sound of the body crashing to the floor.

"Bad dog," whispered Rhy, but Kell could hear the smile in his voice. The prince wove through the tables to a booth on the far wall, and Kell was about to follow him in when something across the tavern caught his eye. Or rather, some*one*. She stood out, not simply because she was one of the only women, but because he knew her. They had only met twice, but he recognized her instantly, from the catlike smile to the black hair twisted into coiling ropes behind her head, each woven through with gold. It was a bold thing, to wear such precious metal in a place of thugs and thieves.

But Kisimyr Vasrin was bolder than most.

She was also the reigning champion of the *Essen Tasch,* and the reason the tournament was being held in London. The Games weren't for a fortnight, but there she was, holding court in a corner of the Blessed Waters, surrounded by her usual handsome entourage. The fighter spent most of the year traveling the empire, putting on displays and mentoring young magicians, if their pockets were deep enough. She'd first earned a spot on the coveted roster when she was only sixteen, and over the last twelve years and four tournaments, she'd climbed the ranks to victor.

At only twenty-eight, she might even do it again.

Kisimyr tugged lazily at a stone earring, one of three in each ear, a wolfish smile on her face. And then her gaze drifted up, past her table and the room, and landed on Kell. Her eyes were a dozen colors, and some insisted she could see inside a person's soul. While Kell doubted her unique irises endowed her with any extraordinary powers (then again, who was he to talk, with the mark of magic drawn like ink across one eye?), the gaze was still unnerving.

He tipped his chin up and let the tavern light catch the glossy black of his right eye. Kisimyr didn't even look surprised. She simply toasted him, an almost imperceptible motion as she brought a glass of that pitch-black liquid to her lips.

"Are you going to sit," asked Rhy, "or stand sentry?"

Kell broke the gaze and turned toward his brother. Rhy was stretched across the bench, his feet up, fingering the brim of Kell's hat and muttering about how much he'd liked his own. Kell knocked the prince's boots aside so he could sit.

He wanted to ask about the tournament roster, about Alucard Emery—but even unspoken, the name left a sour taste in his mouth. He took a long sip of ale, but it did nothing to clear the bile.

"We should go on a trip," said Rhy, dragging himself upright. "Once the tournament is over."

Kell laughed.

"I'm serious," insisted the prince, his words slurring slightly.

He knew Rhy was, but he also knew it would never happen. The crown didn't let Kell travel beyond London, even when he ventured to different worlds. They claimed it was for his own safety—and maybe it was—but he and Rhy both knew that wasn't the only reason.

"I'll talk to Father. . . ." said Rhy, trailing off as if the subject were already fading from his mind. And then he was up again, sliding out of the booth.

"Where are you going?" asked Kell.

"To fetch us another round."

Kell looked down at Rhy's discarded glass, and then his own, still half-full.

"I think we've had enough," said Kell. The prince spun on him, clutching the booth.

"So now you speak for both of us?" he snapped, eyes glassy. "First body, now will?"

The barb struck, and Kell felt suddenly, horribly tired. "Fine," he growled. "Poison us both."

He rubbed his eyes and watched his brother go. Rhy had always had a penchant for consumption, but never with the sole intent of being too drunk to be useful. Too drunk to think. Saints knew, Kell had demons of his own, but he knew he couldn't drown them. Not like this. Why he kept letting Rhy try, he didn't know.

Kell felt in the pockets of his coat and found a brass clip with three slim cigars.

He'd never been much of a smoker—then again, he'd never

been much of a drinker, either—and yet, wanting to take back at least a measure of control over what he put in his body, he snapped his fingers and lit the cigar with the small flame that danced above his thumb.

Kell inhaled deeply—it wasn't tobacco, like in Grey London, or the horrible char they smoked in White, but a pleasant spiced leaf that cleared his head and calmed his nerves. Kell blew the breath out, his eyes sliding out of focus in the plume of smoke.

He heard steps and looked up, expecting Rhy, only to find a young woman. She bore the marks of Kisimyr's entourage, from the coiled dark hair to the gold tassels to the cat's-eye pendant at her throat.

"*Avan*," she said, with a voice like silk.

"*Avan*," said Kell.

The woman stepped forward, the knees of her dress brushing the edge of the booth. "Mistress Vasrin sends her regards, and wishes me to pass on a message."

"And what message is that?" he asked, taking another drag.

She smiled, and then before he could do anything—before he could even exhale—she reached out, took Kell's face in her hand, and kissed him. The breath caught in Kell's chest, heat flushed his body, and when the girl pulled back—not far, just enough to meet his gaze—she blew out a breath of smoke. He almost laughed. Her lips curled into a feline smile, and her eyes searched his, not with fear or even surprise, but with something like excitement. Awe. And Kell knew this was the part where he should feel like an impostor . . . but he didn't.

He looked past her to the prince, still standing at the bar.

"Was that all she said?" asked Kell.

Her mouth twitched. "Her instructions were vague, *mas aven vares*."

My blessed prince.

"No," he said, frowning. "Not a prince."

"What, then?"

He swallowed. "Just Kell."

She blushed. It was too intimate—societal norms dictated that even if he shed the royal title, he should be addressed as *Master* Kell. But he didn't want to be that, either. He just wanted to be himself.

"Kell," she said, testing the word on her lips.

"And your name?" he asked.

"Asana," she whispered, the word escaping like a sound of pleasure. She guided him back against the bench, the gesture somehow forward and shy at the same time. And then her mouth was upon his. Her clothes were cinched at the waist in the current fashion, and he tangled his fingers in the bodice lacings at the small of her back.

"Kell," someone whispered in his ear.

Only it wasn't Asana, but Delilah Bard. She did that, crept into his thoughts and robbed him of focus, like a thief. Which was exactly what she was. What she'd *been,* before he let her out of her world, and into his. Saints knew what—or where—she was these days, but in his mind she would always be the thief, stealing through at the most inopportune moments. *Get out,* he thought, his grip tightening on the girl's dress. Asana kissed him again, but he was being dragged somewhere else, outside, on the path in the cool October night, and another set of lips was pressing against his, there and then gone, a ghost of a kiss.

"What was that for?"

A knife's edge smile. "For luck."

He groaned in frustration, and pulled Asana against him, kissing her deeply, desperately, trying to smother Lila's intrusion as Asana's lips brushed his throat.

"Mas vares," she breathed against his skin.

"I'm not . . ." he began, but then her mouth was on his again, stealing the argument along with his air. His hand had vanished somewhere in her mane of hair. There it was now, at the nape of her neck. Her own hand splayed against his chest, and then her fingers were running down over his stomach and—

Pain.

It glanced across jaw, sudden and bright.

"What is it?" asked Asana. "What's wrong?"

Kell ground his teeth. "Nothing." *I am going to kill my brother.*

He turned his thoughts from Rhy to Asana, but just as his mouth found hers again, the pain returned, raking over his hip.

For a single, hazy moment, Kell wondered if Rhy had simply found himself another enthusiastic conquest. But then the pain came a third time, this time against his ribs, sharp enough to knock his breath away, and the possibility withered.

"*Sanct,*" he swore, dragging himself from Asana's embrace and out of the booth with murmured apologies. The room swayed as he stood too fast, and he braced himself against the booth and searched the room, wondering what kind of trouble Rhy had gotten himself into now.

And then he saw the table near the bar, where the three men had sat talking. They were gone. Two doors to the Blessed Waters: the front and the back. He chose the second set, and guessed right, bursting out into the night with a speed that quite frankly surprised him, given how much he—and Rhy—had had to drink. But pain and cold were sobering things, and as he skidded to a stop in an alley dusted with snow, he could feel the magic already rushing hotly through his veins, ready for the fight.

The first thing Kell saw was the blood.

Then the prince's knife on the cobblestones.

The three men had Rhy cornered at the end of the alley. One of them had a gash on his forearm. Another along his cheek. Rhy must have gotten in a few slashes before he'd lost the weapon, but now he was doubled over, one arm wrapped around his ribs and blood running from his nose. The men obviously didn't know who he was. It was one thing to speak ill of a royal, but to lay hands on him. . . .

"Teach you to cut up my face," growled one.

"An improvement," grumbled Rhy through gritted teeth. Kell couldn't believe it: Rhy was *goading* them on.

". . . looking for trouble."

"Sure to find it."

"Wouldn't . . . be so sure . . ." The prince coughed.

His head drifted up past the men to Kell. He smiled thinly and said through bloody teeth, "Well, hello there," as if they'd just chanced upon one another. As if he weren't getting the shit kicked out of him behind the Blessed Waters. And as if, at this moment, Kell didn't have the urge to let the men have at Rhy for being stupid and self-destructive enough to pick this fight in the first place (because Kell had no doubt that the prince had started it). The urge was compounded by the fact that, though the thugs didn't know it, they couldn't actually *kill* him. That was the thing about the spell scorched into their skin. *Nothing* could kill Rhy. Because it wasn't *Rhy's* life that held him together anymore. It was *Kell's*. And as long as Kell lived, so would the prince.

But they could hurt him, and Kell wasn't angry enough to let that happen.

"Hello, Brother," he said, crossing his arms.

Two of the men turned toward Kell.

"*Kers la?*" taunted one. "A pet dog, come to nip at our heels?"

"Don't look like he's got much bite," said the other.

The third didn't even bother turning around. Rhy had said something to insult him—Kell didn't catch the words—and now he angled a kick at the prince's stomach. It never connected. Kell clenched his teeth and the man's boot froze in midair, the bones in his leg willed still.

"What the—"

Kell wrenched with his mind, and the man went flying side-ways into the nearest wall. He collapsed to the ground, groaning, and the other two looked on with surprise and horror.

"You can't—" one grumbled, though the fact that Kell *could* was less shocking than the fact that he *had*. Bone magic was a rare and dangerous skill, forbidden because it broke the cardinal law: that none shall use magic, mental or physical, to control another person. Those who showed an affinity were strongly encouraged to *unlearn* it. Anyone caught doing it was rewarded with a full set of limiters.

An ordinary magician would never risk the punishment.

Kell wasn't an ordinary magician.

He tipped his chin up so the men could see his eyes, and took a measure of grim satisfaction as the color bled from their faces. And then footsteps sounded, and Kell turned to find more men pouring into the alley. Drunk and angry and armed. Something stirred in him.

His heart raced, and magic surged through his veins. He felt something on his face, and it took him a moment to realize that he was *smiling*.

He drew his dagger from the hidden sheath against his arm and with a single fluid motion cut his palm. Blood fell to the street in heavy red drops.

"*As Isera,*" he said, the words taking shape in his blood and on the air at the same time. They vibrated through the alley.

And then, the ground began to *freeze*.

It started at the drops of blood and spread out fast like frost over the stones and underfoot until a moment later everyone in the alley was standing atop a single solid pane of ice. One man took a step, and his feet went out from under him, arms flailing for balance even as he fell. Another must have had better boots on, because he took a sure step forward. But Kell was already moving. He crouched, pressed his bloody palm to the street stones, and said, "*As steno.*"

Break.

A cracking sound split the night, the quiet shattering with the pane of glassy ice. Cracks shot out from Kell's hand, fissuring the ground to every side, and as he stood, the shards came with him. Every piece not pinned by boot or body rose into the air and hung there, knifelike edges facing out from Kell like wicked rays of light.

Suddenly everyone in the alley grew still, not because he was willing the bones in their bodies, but because they were afraid. As they should be. He didn't feel drunk now. Didn't feel cold.

"Hey now," said one, his hands drifting up. "You don't have to do this."

"It's not fair," growled another softly, a blade of ice against his throat.

"Fair?" asked Kell, surprised by the steadiness in his voice. "Is three against one fair?"

"He started it!"

"Is eight against two fair?" continued Kell. "Looks to me like the odds are in *your* favor."

The ice began to inch forward through the air. Kell heard hisses of panic.

"We were just defending ourselves."

"We didn't know."

Against the back wall, Rhy had straightened. "Come on, Kell. . . ."

"Be still, Rhy," warned Kell. "You've caused enough trouble."

The jagged shards of ice hovered to every side, and then drifted on the air with slow precision until two or three had found each man, had charted a course for throat and heart and gut. The shards and the men that faced them waited with wide eyes and held breath to see what they would do.

What *Kell* would do.

A flick of his wrist, that's all it would take, to end every man in the alley.

Stop, a voice said, the word almost too soft to hear.

Stop.

And then suddenly, much louder, the voice was Rhy's, the words tearing from his throat. *"KELL, STOP."*

And the night snapped back into focus and he realized he was standing there holding eight lives in his hand, and he'd almost ended them. Not to punish them for attacking Rhy (the prince had probably provoked them) and not because they were bad men (though several of them might have been). But just because he *could,* because it felt good to be in control, to be the strongest, to know that when it came down to it, he would be the one left standing.

Kell exhaled and lowered his hand, letting the shards of ice crash to the cobblestones, where they shattered. The men gasped, and swore, and stumbled back as one, the spell of the moment broken.

One sank to the ground, shaking.

Another looked like he might vomit.

"Get out of here," said Kell quietly.

And the men listened. He watched them run.

They already thought he was a monster, and now he'd gone and given the fears weight, which would just make everything worse. But it didn't matter; nothing he did seemed to make it better.

His steps crackled on the broken ice as he trudged over to where Rhy was sitting on his haunches against the wall. He looked dazed, but Kell thought it had less to do with the beating and more to do with the drink. The blood had stopped falling from his nose and lip, and his face was otherwise unhurt; when Kell quested through his own body in search of echoing pain, he felt only a couple of tender ribs.

Kell held out his hand and helped Rhy to his feet. The prince took a step forward, and swayed, but Kell caught him and kept him upright.

"There you go again," murmured Rhy, leaning his head on Kell's shoulder. "You never let me fall."

"And let you take me down with you?" chided Kell, wrapping the prince's arm around his shoulders. "Come on, Brother. I think we've had enough fun for one night."

"Sorry," whispered Rhy.

"I know."

But the truth was, Kell couldn't forget the way he'd felt during the fight, the small defiant part of him that had undeniably *enjoyed* it. He couldn't forget the smile that had belonged to him and yet to someone else entirely.

Kell shivered, and helped his brother home.

IV

The guards were waiting for them in the hall.

Kell had gotten the prince all the way back to the palace and up the Basin steps before running into the men: two of them Rhy's, the other two his, and all four looking put out.

"Vis, Tolners," said Kell, feigning lightness. "Want to give me a hand?"

As if he were carrying a sack of wheat, and not the royal prince of Arnes.

Rhy's guards looked pale with anger and worry, but neither stepped forward.

"Staff, Hastra?" he said, appealing to his own men. He was met with stony silence. "Fine, get out of the way, I'll carry him myself."

He pushed past the guards.

"Is that the prince's blood?" asked Vis, pointing at Kell's sleeve, which he'd used to wipe Rhy's face clean.

"No," he lied. "Only mine."

Rhy's men relaxed considerably at that, which Kell found disconcerting. Vis was a nervous sort, hackles always raised, and Tolners was utterly humorless, with the set jaw of an officer. They had both served King Maxim himself before being assigned to guard the young royal, and they took the prince's defiance with far less nonchalance than Rhy's previous men. As for Kell's own guards, Hastra was young and eager, but Staff hardly ever said a word, either to Kell's face or in his company. For the first month, Kell hadn't been sure if the guard hated him, or feared him, or both. Then Rhy told him the truth—that Staff's sister had died in the Black Night—so Kell knew that it was likely both.

"He's a good guard," said Rhy when Kell asked why they would assign him such a man. And then added grimly, "It was Father's choice."

Now, as the party reached the royal hall the brothers shared, Tolners produced a note and held it up for Kell to read. "This isn't funny." Apparently Rhy had had the grace to pin the note to his door, in case anyone in the palace should worry.

> *Not kidnapped.*
> *Out for a drink with Kell.*
> *Sit tight.*

Rhy's room was at the end of the hall, marked by two ornate doors. Kell kicked them open.

"Too loud," muttered Rhy.

"Master Kell," warned Vis, following him in. "I must insist you cease these—"

"I didn't force him out."

"But you *allowed*—"

"I'm his brother, not his *guard*," snapped Kell. He knew he'd been raised as Rhy's protection as much as his companion, but it was proving no small task, and besides, hadn't he done enough?

Tolners scowled. "The king and queen—"

"Go away," said Rhy, rousing himself. "Giving me a headache."

"Your Highness," started Vis, reaching for Rhy's arm.

"*Out*," snapped the prince with sudden heat. The guards shied away, then looked uncertainly at Kell.

"You heard the prince," he grumbled. "Get out." His gaze went to his own men. "All of you."

As the doors closed behind him, Kell half guided, half dragged Rhy into his bed. "I think I'm growing on them," he muttered.

Rhy rolled groggily onto his back, an arm cast over his eyes.

"I'm sorry . . . sorry . . ." he said softly, and Kell shuddered, remembering that horrific night, the prince bleeding to death as he and Lila tried to drag him to safety, the soft *I'm sorry*s fading horribly into silence and stillness and—

". . . all my fault . . ." Rhy's voice dragged him back.

"Hush," said Kell, sinking into a chair beside the bed.

"I just wanted . . . like it was before."

"I know," said Kell, rubbing his eyes. "I know."

He sat there until Rhy fell quiet, safely wrapped in sleep, and then pushed himself back to his feet. The room rocked faintly, and Kell steadied himself for a moment on the carved bedpost before making his way back to his own rooms. Not via the hall and its contingent of guards, but the hidden corridor that ran between their chambers. The lanterns burned to life as Kell entered, the magic easy, effortless, but the light didn't make the room feel more like home. The space had always felt strangely foreign. Stiff, like an ill-fitting suit.

It was a room for a royal. The ceiling was lined with billowing fabric, the colors of night, and an elegant desk hugged one wall. A sofa and chairs huddled around a silver tea set, and a pair of glass doors led onto a balcony now coated with a thin layer of snow. Kell shrugged off his coat and turned it inside out a few times, returning it to its royal red before draping it over an ottoman.

Kell missed his little room at the top of the stairs in the Ruby Fields, with its rough walls and its stiff cot and its constant noise, but the room and the inn and the woman who ran it had all been burned to nothing by Holland months before, and Kell could not bring himself to seek out another. The room had been a secret, and Kell had promised the crown—and Rhy—that he would stop keeping secrets.

He missed the room, and the privacy that came with it, but there was something to the missing. He supposed he deserved it. Others had lost far more because of him.

So Kell remained in the royal chambers.

The bed waited on a raised platform, a plush mattress with a sea of pillows, but Kell slumped down into his favorite chair instead. A battered thing by comparison, dragged from one of the palace's studies, it faced the balcony doors and, beyond, the warm red glow of the Isle. He snapped his fingers, and the lanterns dimmed and then went dark.

Sitting there with only the river's light, his tired mind drifted, as it invariably did, back to Delilah Bard. When Kell thought of her, she was not one girl, but three: the too-skinny street thief who'd robbed him in an alley, the blood-streaked partner who'd fought beside him, and the impossible girl who'd walked away and never looked back.

Where are you, Lila, he mused. *And what kind of trouble are you getting into?*

Kell dragged a kerchief from his back pocket: a small square of dark fabric first given to him by a girl dressed as a boy in a darkened alley, a sleight of hand so she could rob him. He'd used it to find her more than once, and he wondered if he could do it again, or if it now belonged more to him than to her. He wondered where it would take him, if it worked.

He knew with a bone-deep certainty that she was alive—had to be alive—and he envied her, envied the fact that this Grey London girl was out there somewhere, seeing parts of the world that Kell—a Red Londoner, an *Antari*—had never glimpsed.

He put the kerchief away, closed his eyes, and waited for sleep to drag him under.

When it did, he dreamed of her. Dreamed of her standing on his balcony, goading him to come out and play. He dreamed of her hand tangling in his, a pulse of power twining them together. He dreamed of them racing through foreign streets, not the London ones they'd navigated, but crooks and bends in places he'd never been, and ones he might never see. But there she was, at his side, pulling him toward freedom.

V

White London.

Ojka had always been graceful.

Graceful when she danced. Graceful when she killed.

Sunlight spilled across the stone floor as she spun, her knives licking the air as they arced and dipped, tethered to her hands and to one another by a single length of black cord.

Her hair, once pale, now shone red, a shock of color against her still porcelain skin, bold as blood. It skimmed her shoulders as she twirled, and bowed, a bright streak at the center of a deadly circle. Ojka danced, and the metal kept pace, the perfect partner to her fluid movements, and the entire time, she kept her eyes closed. She knew the dance by heart, a dance she'd first learned as a child on the streets in Kosik, in the worst part of London. A dance she'd mastered. You didn't stay alive in this city on luck alone. Not if you had any promise of power. The scavengers would sniff it out, slit your throat so they could steal whatever dregs were in your blood. They didn't care if you were little. That only made you easier to catch and kill.

But not Ojka. She'd carved her way through Kosik. Grown up and stayed alive in a city that managed to kill off everyone. Everything.

But that was another life. That was before. This was after.

Ojka's veins traced elegant black lines over her skin as she moved. She could feel the magic thrumming through her, a second pulse twined with hers. At first it had burned, so hot she feared it would consume her, the way it had the others. But then she let go. Her body stopped fighting, and so did the power. She embraced it, and once she did, it embraced her, and they danced together, burned together, fusing like strengthened steel.

The blades sang past, extensions of her hands. The dance was almost done.

And then she felt the summons, like a flare of heat inside her skull.

She came to a stop—not suddenly, of course, but slowly—winding the black cord around her hands until the blades snapped against her palms. Only then did her eyes drift open.

One was yellow.

The other was black.

Proof that she had been chosen.

She wasn't the first, but that was all right. That didn't matter. What mattered was that the others had been too weak. The first had only lasted a few days. The second had scarcely made it through the week. But Ojka was different. Ojka was strong. She had survived. She *would* survive, so long as she was worthy.

That was the king's promise, when he had chosen her.

Ojka coiled the cord around the blades and slid the weapon back into the holster at her hip.

Sweat dripped from the ends of her crimson hair, and she wrung it out before shrugging on her jacket and fastening her cloak. Her fingers traced the scar that ran from her throat up over her jaw and across her cheek, ending just below the king's mark.

When the magic brought strength to her muscles, warmth to her blood, and color to her features, she feared it would wipe away the scar. She'd been relieved when it didn't. She'd earned this scar, and every other one she bore.

The summons flared again behind her eyes, and she stepped outside. The day was cold but not bitter, and overhead, beyond the clouds, the sky was streaked across with blue. *Blue*. Not the frosty off-white she'd grown up with, but true blue. As if the sky itself had thawed. The water of the Sijlt was thawing, too, more and more every day, ice giving way to green-grey water.

Everywhere she looked, the world was waking.

Reviving.

And Ojka's blood quickened at the sight of it. She'd been in a shop once, and had seen a chest covered in dust. She remembered running her hand across it, removing the film of grey and revealing the dark wood beneath. It was like that, she thought. The king had come and swept his hand across the city, brushed away the dust.

It would take time, he said, but that was all right. Change was coming.

Only a single road stood between her quarters and the castle walls, and as she crossed the street, her gaze flicked toward the river, and the other half of the city beyond. From the heart of Kosik to the steps of the castle. She'd come a long way.

The gates stood open, new vines climbing the stone walls to either side, and she reached out and touched a small purple bud as she stepped through onto the grounds.

Where the Krös Mejkt had once sprawled, a graveyard of stone corpses at the feet of the castle, now there was wild grass, creeping up despite the winter chill. Only two statues remained, flanking the castle stairs, both commissioned by the new king, not as a warning, but as a reminder of false promises and fallen tyrants.

They were likenesses of the old rulers, Athos and Astrid Dane, carved in white marble. Both figures were on their knees. Athos Dane stared down at the whip in his hands, which coiled like a snake around his wrists, his face twisted in pain, while Astrid clutched the handle of a dagger, its blade buried in her chest, her mouth stretched in a soundless, immortal scream.

The statues were grisly, inelegant things. Unlike the new king.

The new king was perfect.

The new king was chosen.

The new king was god.

And Ojka? She saw the way he looked at her with those beautiful eyes, and she knew he saw the beauty in her, too, now, more and more every day.

She reached the top of the stairs and passed through into the castle.

Ojka had heard tales of the hollow-eyed guards who had served under the Danes, men robbed of minds and souls, rendered nothing but shells. But they were gone now, and the castle stood open, and strangely empty. It had been raided, taken, held, and lost in the weeks after the Danes first fell, but there were no signs of the slaughter now. All was calm.

There were attendants, men and women appearing and disappearing, heads bowed, and a dozen guards, but their eyes weren't vacant. If anything, they moved with a purpose, a devotion that Ojka understood. This was the resurrection, a legend brought to life, and they were all a part of it.

No one stopped her as she moved through the castle.

In fact, some knelt as she passed, while others whispered blessings and bowed their heads. When she reached the throne room, the doors were open, and the king was waiting. The vaulted ceiling was gone, massive walls and columns now giving way to open sky.

Ojka's steps echoed on the marble floor.

Was it really once made of bones, she wondered, *or is that just a legend?* (All Ojka had were rumors; she'd been smart, kept to Kosik, and avoided the Danes at all costs during their rule. Too many stories surrounded the twins, all of them bloody.)

The king stood before his throne, gazing down into the glossy surface of the scrying pool that formed a smooth black circle before the dais. Ojka found its stillness almost as hypnotic as the man reflected in it.

Almost.

But there was something he had that the black pool lacked. Beneath the surface of his calm surged energy. She could feel it from across the room, rippling from him in waves. A source of power.

Life might have been taking root in the city, but in the king, it had already blossomed.

He was tall and strong, muscles twining over his sculpted body, his strength apparent even through his elegant clothes. Black hair swept back from his face, revealing high cheekbones and a strong jaw. The bow of his lips pursed faintly, and the faintest crease formed between his brows as he considered the pool, hands clasped behind his back. His hands. She remembered that day, when those hands had come to rest against her skin, one pressed against the nape of her neck, the other splayed over her eyes. She'd felt his power even then, before it passed between them, pulsing beneath his skin, and she wanted it, needed it, like air.

His mouth had been so close to her ear when he spoke. "Do you accept this power?"

"I accept it," she'd said. And then everything was searing heat and darkness and pain. Burning. Until his voice came again, close, and said, "Stop fighting, Ojka. Let it in."

And she had.

He had chosen her, and she would not let him down. Just like in the prophecies, their savior had come. And she would be there at his side.

"Ojka," he said now without looking up. Her name was a spell on his lips.

"Your Majesty," she said, kneeling before the pool.

His head drifted up. "You know I'm not fond of titles," he said, rounding the pool. She straightened and met his eyes: one green, the other black. "Call me Holland."

THREE

CHANGING
TIDES

I

Red London.

The nightmare started as it always did, with Kell standing in the middle of a public place—sometimes the Stone's Throw, or the statue garden in front of the Danes' fortress, or the London Sanctuary—at once surrounded and alone.

Tonight, he was in the middle of the Night Market.

It was crowded, more crowded than Kell had ever seen it, the people pressed shoulder to shoulder along the riverbank. He thought he saw Rhy at the other end, but by the time he called his brother's name, the prince had vanished into the crowd.

Nearby he glimpsed a girl with dark hair cut short along her jaw, and called out—"Lila?"—but as soon as he took a step toward her, the crowd rippled and swallowed her again. Everyone was familiar, and everyone was a stranger in the shifting mass of bodies.

And then a shock of white hair caught his eye, the pale figure of Athos Dane sliding like a serpent through the crowd. Kell growled and reached for his knife, only to be interrupted by cold fingers closing over his.

"Flower boy," cooed a voice in his ear, and he spun to find Astrid, covered in cracks as if someone had pieced her shattered body back together. Kell staggered back, but the crowd was getting even thicker now, and someone shoved him from behind. By the time he regained his balance, both the Danes were gone.

Rhy flickered again in the distance. He was looking around as if searching for someone, mouthing a word, a name Kell couldn't hear.

Another stranger bumped into Kell hard. "Sorry," he murmured. "Sorry . . ." But the words echoed and the people kept pushing past him as if they didn't see him, as if he wasn't there. And then, as soon as he thought it, everybody stopped midstride and every face turned toward him, features resolving into gruesome masks of anger and fear and disgust.

"I'm sorry," he said again, holding up his hands, only to see his veins turning black.

"No," he whispered, as the magic traced lines up his arms. "No, please, no." He could feel the darkness humming in his blood as it spread. The crowd began to move again, but instead of walking away, they were all coming toward him. "Get back," he said, and when they didn't he tried to run, only to discover that his legs wouldn't move.

"Too late," came Holland's voice from nowhere. Everywhere. "Once you let it in, you've already lost."

The magic forced its way through him with every beat of his heart. Kell tried to fight it back, but it was in his head now, whispering in *Vitari*'s voice.

Let me in.

Pain shot jaggedly through Kell's chest as the darkness hit his heart, and in the distance, Rhy collapsed.

"*No!*" Kell shouted, reaching toward his brother, uselessly, desperately, but as his hand brushed the nearest person, the darkness leaped like fire from his fingers to the man's chest. He shuddered, and then collapsed, crumbling to ash as his body struck the street stones. Before he hit the ground, the people on either side of him began to fall as well, death rippling in a wave through the crowd, silently consuming everyone. Beyond them, the buildings began to crumble too, and the bridges, and the palace, until Kell was standing alone in an empty world.

And then in the silence, he heard a sound: not a sob, or a scream, but a *laugh*.

And it took him a moment to recognize the voice.

It was his.

🜚

Kell gasped, lurching forward out of sleep.

Light was filtering through the patio doors, glinting off a fresh dusting of snow. The shards of sun made him cringe and look away as he pressed his palm to his chest and waited for his heart to slow.

He'd fallen asleep in his chair, fully clothed, his skull aching from his brother's indulgences.

"Dammit, Rhy," he muttered, pushing himself to his feet. His head was pounding, a sound matched by whatever was going on outside his window. The blows he—well, *Rhy*—had sustained the night before were a memory, but the aftereffect of the drinks was compounding, and Kell decided then and there that he vastly preferred the sharp, short pain of a wound to the dull, protracted ache of a hangover. He felt like death, and as he splashed cold water on his face and throat and got dressed, he could only hope that the prince felt worse.

Outside his door, a stiff-looking man with greying temples stood watch. Kell winced. He always hoped for Hastra. Instead he usually got Staff. The one who hated him.

"Morning," said Kell, walking past.

"*Afternoon,* sir," answered Staff—or Silver, as Rhy had nick-named the aging royal guard—as he fell in step behind him. Kell wasn't thrilled by the appearance of Staff *or* Hastra in the after-math of the Black Night, but he wasn't surprised, either. It wasn't the guards' fault that King Maxim no longer trusted his *Antari*. Just like it wasn't Kell's fault that the guards couldn't always keep track of him.

He found Rhy in the sunroom, a courtyard enclosed by glass, having lunch with the king and queen. The prince seemed to be managing his own hangover with surprising poise, though Kell could feel Rhy's headache throbbing alongside his own, and Kell noted that the prince sat with his back to the panes of glass and the glinting light beyond.

"Kell," Rhy said brightly. "I was beginning to think you'd sleep all day."

"Sorry," said Kell pointedly. "I must have indulged a little too much last night."

"Good afternoon, Kell," said Queen Emira, an elegant woman with skin like polished wood and a circlet of gold resting atop her jet-black hair. Her tone was kind but distant, and it felt like it had been weeks since she'd last reached out and touched his cheek. In truth, it had been longer. Nearly four months, since the Black Night, when Kell had let the black stone into the city, and *Vitari* had swept through the streets, and Astrid Dane had plunged a dagger into Rhy's chest, and Kell had given a piece of his life to bring him back.

Where is our son? the queen had demanded, as if she had only one.

"I hope you're well rested," said King Maxim, glancing up from the sheaf of papers in front of him.

"I am, sir." Fruit and bread were piled on the table, and as Kell slid into the empty chair a servant appeared with a silver pitcher and poured him a steaming cup of tea. He finished the cup in a single, burning swallow, and the servant considered him then left the pitcher, a small gesture for which Kell was immeasurably grateful.

Two more people were seated at the table: a man and a woman, both dressed in shades of red and each with a gold pin of the

Maresh seal—the chalice and rising sun—fastened to their shoulder. The pin marked the figures as friends of the crown; it permitted them full access to the palace and instructed any servants and guards to not only welcome but assist them.

"Parlo, Lisane," said Kell in greeting. They were the *ostra* selected to help organize the tournament, and Kell felt like he had seen more of them in the past few weeks than he had the king and queen.

"Master Kell," they said in unison, tipping their heads with practiced smiles and calculated propriety.

A map of the palace and surrounding grounds was spread across the table, one edge tucked beneath a plate of tarts, another under a tea cup, and Lisane was gesturing to the south wing. "We've arranged for Prince Col and Princess Cora to stay here, in the emerald suite. Fresh flowers will be grown there the day before they arrive."

Rhy made a face at Kell across the table. Kell was too tired to try to read it.

"Lord Sol-in-Ar, meanwhile," continued Lisane, "will be housed in the western conservatory. We've stocked it with coffee, just as you instructed, and . . ."

"And what of the Veskan queen?" grumbled Maxim. "Or the Faroan king? Why do *they* not grace us with their presence? Do they not trust us? Or do they simply have better things to do?"

Emira frowned. "The emissaries they've chosen are appropriate."

Rhy scoffed. "Queen Lastra of Vesk has *seven* children, Mother; I doubt it's much of an inconvenience for her to loan us two. As for the Faroans, Lord Sol-in-Ar is a known antagonist who's spent the last two decades stirring up discontent wherever he goes, hoping it will spark enough conflict to dethrone his brother and seize control of Faro."

"Since when are you so invested in imperial politics?" asked Kell, already on his third cup of tea.

To his surprise, Rhy shot him a scowl. "I'm invested in my *kingdom,* Brother," he snapped. "You should be, too."

"*I'm* not their prince," observed Kell. He was in no mood for Rhy's attitude. "I'm just the one who has to clean up his *messes.*"

"Oh, seeing as you've made none of your own?"

They held each other's gazes. Kell resisted the urge to stab a fork into his own leg just to watch his brother wince.

What was happening to them? They'd never been cruel to each other before. But pain and pleasure weren't the only things that seemed to transfer with the bond. Fear, annoyance, anger: all plucked at the binding spell, reverberating between them, amplifying. Rhy had always been fickle, but now Kell *felt* his brother's ever-shifting temperament, the constant oscillation, and it was maddening. Space meant nothing. They could be standing side by side or Londons apart. There was no escape.

More and more, the bond felt like a chain.

Emira cleared her throat. "I think the *eastern* conservatory would be better for Lord Sol-in-Ar. It gets better light. But what about the attendants? The Veskans always travel with a full compliment. . . ."

The queen soothed the table, guiding the conversation deftly away from the brothers' rising moods, but there were too many unspoken things in the air, making it stuffy. Kell pushed himself to his feet and turned to leave.

"Where are you going?" asked Maxim, handing his papers to an attendant.

Kell turned back. "I was going to oversee the construction on the floating arenas, Your Highness."

"Rhy can handle that," said the king. "You have an errand to run." With that, he held out an envelope. Kell didn't realize how eager he was to go—to escape not only the palace but this city, this world—until he saw that slip of paper.

It bore no address, but he knew exactly where he was meant to take it. With the White London throne empty and the city plunged into crown warfare for the first time in seven years, communication had been suspended. Kell had gone only once, in the weeks after the Dane twins fell, and had nearly lost his life to the violent masses—after which it was decided that Kell would let White London alone for a time, until things settled.

That left only Grey London. The simple, magicless realm, all coal smoke and sturdy old stone.

"I'll go now," said Kell, crossing to the king's side.

"Mind the prince regent," warned the king. "These correspondences are a matter of tradition, but the man's questions have grown prodding."

Kell nodded. He had often wanted to ask King Maxim what he thought of the Grey London leader and wondered about the contents of his letters, whether the prince regent asked as many questions of his neighboring crown as he did of Kell.

"He inquires often about magic," he told the king. "I do my best to dissuade him."

Maxim grunted. "He is a foolish man. Be careful."

Kell raised a brow. Was Maxim actually worried for his safety? But then, as he reached for the letter, he saw the flicker of distrust in the king's eyes, and his spirits sank. Maxim kept grudges like scars. They faded by degrees but always left a mark.

Kell knew he'd brought it on himself. For years, he'd used his expeditions as royal liaison to transport forbidden items between the worlds. If he hadn't developed his reputation as a smuggler, the black stone would never have found its way into his hands, would never have killed men and women and brought havoc to Red London. Or perhaps the Danes would still have found a way, but they wouldn't have used *Kell* to do it. He'd been a pawn, and a fool, and now he was paying for it—just as Rhy was forced to pay for his own part, for the possession charm that had let Astrid Dane take up residence in his body. In the end, they were both to blame. But the king still loved Rhy. The queen could still look at him.

Emira held out a second, smaller envelope. The note for King George. A courtesy more than anything else, but the fragile king clung to these correspondences, and so did Kell. The ailing king had no idea how short they were getting, and Kell had no intention of letting him know. He'd taken to elaborating, spinning intimate yarns about the Arnesian king and queen, the prince's exploits, and Kell's own life in the palace. Perhaps this time he'd tell George about the tournament. The king would love that.

He took the notes and turned to go, already pulling together what he'd say, when Maxim stopped him. "What about your point of return?"

Kell stiffened imperceptibly. The question was like a short tug, a reminder that he was now being kept on a leash. "The door will be at the mouth of Naresh Kas, just off the southern edge of the Night Market."

The king glanced at Staff, who hung back by the door, to make sure he'd heard, and the guard nodded once.

"Don't be late," ordered Maxim.

Kell turned away and left the royal family to their talk of tournament visitors and fresh linens and who preferred coffee or wine or strong tea.

At the sunroom doors, he cast a glance back, and found Rhy looking at him with an expression that might have been *I'm sorry*, but also could have been *fuck off*, or at the very least *we'll talk later*. Kell let the matter go and escaped, slipping the letters into the pocket of his coat. He walked briskly through the palace halls ,back to his chambers, and through to the smaller second room beyond, closing the door behind him. Rhy probably would have used such an alcove to hold boots, or coat pins, but Kell had transformed the space into a small but well-stocked library, holding the texts he'd collected on magic. They were as much philosophical as practical, many gifted by Master Tieren or borrowed from the royal library, as well as some journals of his own, scribbled with thoughts on *Antari* blood magic, about which so little was known. One slim black volume he'd dedicated to *Vitari*, the black magic he'd grasped—awakened—destroyed—the year before. That journal held more questions than answers.

On the back of the library's wooden door were half a dozen hand-drawn symbols, each simple but distinct, shortcuts to other places in the city, carefully drawn in blood. Some were faded from disuse, others fresh. One of the symbols—a circle with a pair of crossed lines drawn through it—led to Tieren's sanctuary on the opposite bank. As Kell traced his fingers over the mark, he vividly remembered helping Lila haul a dying Rhy through the door. Another mark had once led to Kell's private chamber at the Ruby Fields, the only place in London that had been truly his. Now it was nothing more than a smudge.

Kell scanned the door until he found the symbol he was looking for: a star made of three intersecting lines.

This mark came with its own memories, of an old king in a cell of a room, his gnarled fingers curled around a single red coin as he murmured about fading magic.

Kell drew his dagger from its place under the cuff of his coat, and grazed his wrist. Blood welled, rich and red, and he dabbed the cut and drew the mark fresh. When it was done, he pressed his hand flat against the symbol and said, *"As Tascen."* Transfer.

And then he stepped forward.

The world softened and warped around his hand, and he passed from the darkened alcove into sunlight, crisp and bright enough to revive the fading ache behind his eyes. Kell was no longer in his makeshift library, but standing in a well-appointed courtyard. He wasn't in Grey London, not yet, but in an *ostra*'s garden in an elegant village called Disan, significant not because of its fine fruit trees or glass statues, but because it occupied the same ground in Red London that Windsor Castle did in Grey.

The same *exact* ground.

Traveling magic only worked two ways. Kell could either transfer between two different places in one world, or travel between the same place in different ones. And because they kept the English king at Windsor, which sat well outside the city of London, he had to make his way first to *ostra* Paveron's garden. It was a bit of clever navigation on Kell's part . . . not that anyone knew enough of *Antari* magic to appreciate it. Holland might have, but Holland was dead, and he'd likely had a network of acrosses and betweens intricate enough to make Kell's own attempts look childish. The winter air whipped around him, and he shivered as he drew the letters out of his pocket with his unbloodied hand, then turned the coat inside out and outside in until he found the side he was looking for: a black knee-length garment with a hood and velvet lining. Fit for Grey London, where the cold always felt colder, bitter and damp in a way that seeped through cloth and skin.

Kell shrugged the new coat on and tucked the letters deep into one of the pockets (they were lined with softened wool instead of silk), blew out a plume of warm breath, and marked the icy wall with the blood from his hand. But then, as he was reaching for the cord of tokens around his neck, something tugged at his attention. He paused and looked around, considering the garden. He was alone, truly alone, and he found himself wanting to savor it. Aside from one trip north when he and Rhy were boys, this was the farthest Kell ever strayed from the city. He'd always been watched, but he'd felt more confined in the past four months than in the nearly twenty years he'd served the crown. Kell used to feel like a possession. Now he felt like a prisoner.

Perhaps he should have run when he'd had the chance.

You could still run, said a voice in his ear. It sounded suspiciously like Lila.

In the end, she had escaped. Could he? He didn't have to run to another world. What if he simply . . . walked away? Away from the garden and the village, away from the city. He could take a coach, or a boat to the ocean, and then . . . what? How far would he make it with almost no money of his own and an eye that marked him as an *Antari*?

You could take what you need, said the voice.

It was a very big world. And he'd never even seen it.

If he stayed in Arnes, he would eventually be found. And if he fled into Faro, or Vesk? The Faroans saw his eye as a mark of strength, nothing more, but Kell had heard his name paired with a Veskan word—*crat'a*—*pillar*. As if he alone held up the Arnesian empire. And if either empire got their hands on him . . .

Kell stared down at his blood-streaked hand. Saints, how could he actually consider running away?

It was madness, the idea that he could—that he *would*—abandon his city. His king and queen. His brother. He'd betrayed them once—well, one crime, albeit committed many times—and it had nearly cost him everything. He wouldn't forsake them again, no matter what restlessness had been awakened in him.

You could be free, insisted the voice.

But that was the thing. Kell would *never* be free. No matter how far he fled. He'd given up freedom with his life, when he handed it to Rhy.

"Enough," he said aloud, silencing the doubts as he dug the proper cord out from under his collar and tugged it over his head. On the strap hung a copper coin, the face rubbed smooth from years of use. *Enough,* he thought, and then he brought his bloody hand to the garden wall. He had a job to do.

"As travars."

Travel.

The world began to bend around the words and the blood and the magic, and Kell stepped forward, hoping to leave behind his troubles with his London, trade them for a few minutes with the king.

But as soon as his boots settled on the castle carpet, he realized that his problems were just beginning. Instantly, Kell knew that something was wrong.

Windsor was too quiet. Too dark.

The bowl of water that usually waited for him in the antechamber was empty, the candles to either side unlit. When he listened for the sound of steps, he heard them, distantly, in the halls behind him, but from the chamber ahead he was met with silence.

Dread crept in as he made his way into the king's sitting room, hoping to see his withered frame sleeping in his high-backed chair, or hear his frail, melodic voice. But the room was empty. The windows were fastened shut against the snow, and there was no fire going in the hearth. The room was cold and dark in a closed-up way.

Kell went to the fireplace and held out his hands, as if to warm them, and an instant later flames licked up across the empty grate. The fire wouldn't last long, fueled by nothing more than air and magic, but in its light Kell crossed through the space, searching for signs of recent occupation. Cold tea. A cast-off shawl. But the room felt abandoned, un-lived-in.

And then his gaze caught on the letter.

If it could be called a letter.

A single piece of crisp cream paper, folded and propped on the tray before the fire, with his name written on the front in the prince regent's steady, confident script.

Kell took up the note, knowing what he would find before he unfolded the page, but he still felt ill as the words danced in the enchanted fire's light.

The king is dead.

II

The four words hit him like a blow.

The king is dead.

Kell reeled; he wasn't accustomed to loss. He feared death—he always had—now more than ever, with the prince's life bound to his, but until the Black Night, Kell had never lost someone he knew. Someone he *liked*. He had always been fond of the ailing king, even in his later years, when madness and blindness stole most of his dignity and all of his power.

And now the king was gone. A sum returned to parts, as Tieren would say.

Below, the prince regent had added a postscript.

Step into the hall. Someone will bring you to my rooms.

Kell hesitated, looking around at the empty chamber. And then, reluctantly, he closed his hand into a fist, plunging the fire in the hearth back into nothing and the room back into shadow, and left. Out past the antechamber into the hallways beyond.

It was like stepping into another world.

Windsor wasn't as opulent as St. James, but it wasn't nearly so grim as the old king's chamber made it out to be. Tapestries and carpets warmed the halls. Gold and silver glinted from candlestick and plate. Lamps burned in wall sconces and voices and music carried like a draft.

Someone cleared their throat, and Kell turned to find a well-dressed attendant waiting.

"Ah, sir, very good, this way," said the man with a bow, and then, without waiting, he set off down the hall.

Kell's gaze wandered as they walked. He had never explored the halls beyond the king's rooms, but he was sure they hadn't always been like this.

Fires burned high in the hearths of every room they passed, rendering the palace uncomfortably warm. The rooms themselves were all occupied, and Kell couldn't help but feel like he was being put on display, led past murmuring ladies and curious gentlemen. He clenched his fists and lowered his gaze. By the time he was deposited in the large sitting room, his face was flushed from heat and annoyance.

"Ah. Master Kell."

The prince regent—the *king,* Kell corrected himself—was sitting on a sofa, flanked by a handful of stiff men and giggling women. He looked fatter and more arrogant than usual, his buttons straining, the points of his nose and chin thrust up. His companions fell silent at the sight of Kell, standing there in his black traveling coat.

"Your Majesty," he said, tipping his head forward in the barest show of deference. The gesture resettled the hair over his blackened eye. He knew that his next words should express condolence, but looking at the new king's face, Kell felt the more stricken of the two. "I would have come to St. James if I'd—"

George waved a hand imperiously. "I didn't come here for you," he said, getting to his feet, albeit ungracefully. "I'm spending a fortnight at Windsor, tying up odds and ends. Putting matters to rest, so to speak." He must have seen the distaste that contorted Kell's face because he added, "What is it?"

"You don't seem saddened by the loss," observed Kell.

George huffed. "My father has been dead three weeks, and should have had the decency to die years ago, when he first grew ill. For his sake, as well as mine." A grim smile spread across the new king's face like a ripple. "But I suppose for you the shock is fresh." He crossed to a side bar to pour himself a drink. "I always forget," he said, as amber liquid sloshed against crystal, "that as long as you are in your world, you hear nothing of ours."

Kell tensed, his attention flicking to the aristocrats that peppered the vast room. They were whispering, eying Kell with interest over their glasses.

Kell resisted the urge to reach out and grab the royal's sleeve. "How much do these people know?" he demanded, fighting to keep his voice low, even. "About me?"

George waved his hand. "Oh, nothing troublesome. I believe I told them you were a foreign dignitary. Which is true, in the strictest sense. But the problem is, the less they know, the more they gossip. Perhaps we should simply introduce you—"

"I would pay my respects," cut in Kell. "To the old king." He knew they buried men in this world. It struck him as strange, to put a body in a box, but it meant the king—what was left of him—would be here, somewhere.

George sighed, as if the request were both expected and terribly inconvenient. "I figured as much," he said, finishing the drink. "He's in the chapel. But first . . ." He held out a hand, heavily adorned with rings. "My letter." Kell withdrew the envelope from the pocket of his coat. "And the one for my father."

Reluctantly, Kell retrieved the second note. The old king had always taken such care with the letters, instructing Kell not to mar the seal. The new king took up a short knife from the side bar and slashed the envelope, drawing out the contents. He hated the idea of George seeing the sparse note.

"You came all the way out here to read him this?" he asked, scornfully.

"I was fond of the king."

"Well, you'll have to make do with me now."

Kell said nothing.

The second letter was significantly longer, and the new king lowered himself onto a couch to read it. Kell felt decidedly uncomfortable, standing there while George looked over the letter and the king's entourage looked over *him*. When the king had read it through three or four times, he nodded to himself, tucked the letter away, and got to his feet.

"All right," he said. "Let's get this over with."

Kell followed George out, grateful to escape the room and all the gazes in it.

"Bloody cold out," the king said, bundling himself into a lush coat with a fur collar. "Don't suppose you could do something about that?"

Kell's eyes narrowed. "The weather? No."

The king shrugged, and they stepped out onto the palace grounds, shadowed by a huddle of attendants. Kell pulled his coat close around his body; it was a bitter February day, the wind high and the air wet and biting cold. Snow fell around them, if it could be called falling. The air caught it up and twisted the drifts into spirals so that little ever touched the frozen ground. Kell pulled up his hood.

Despite the chill, his hands were bare inside their pockets; his fingertips were going numb, but *Antari* relied on their hands and their blood to do magic, and gloves were cumbersome, an obstacle to quick-drawn spells. Not that he feared an attack on Grey London soil, but he'd rather be prepared. . . .

Then again, with George, even simple conversation felt a bit like a duel, the two possessing little love and less trust for one another. Plus, the new king's fascination with magic was growing. How long before George had Kell attacked, just to see if and how he would defend himself? But then, such a move would forfeit the communication between their worlds, and Kell didn't think the king was *that* foolish. At least he hoped not; as much as Kell hated George, he didn't want to lose his one excuse to travel.

Kell's hand found the coin in his pocket, and he turned it over and over absently to keep his fingers warm. He assumed they were walking toward a graveyard, but instead the king led him to a church.

"St. George's Chapel," he explained, stepping through.

It was impressive, a towering structure, full of sharp edges. Inside, the ceiling vaulted over a checkered stone floor. George handed off his outer coat without looking; he simply assumed someone would be there to take it, and they were. Kell looked up at the light pouring in through the stained-glass windows, and thought absently that this wouldn't be such a bad place to be buried. Until he realized that George III hadn't been laid to rest up here, surround by sunlight.

He was in the vault.

The ceiling was lower, and the light was thin, and that, paired with the scent of dusty stone, made Kell's skin crawl.

George took an unlit candelabrum from a shelf. "Would you mind?" he asked. Kell frowned. There was something hungry in the way George asked. Covetous.

"Of course," said Kell. He reached out toward the candles, his fingers hovering above before continuing past them to a vase of long-stemmed matches. He took one, struck it with a small, ceremonial flourish, and lit the candles.

George pursed his lips, disappointed. "You were all too eager to perform for my father."

"Your father was a different man," said Kell, waving the match out.

George's frown deepened. He obviously wasn't used to being told no, but Kell wasn't sure if he was upset at being denied in general, or being denied magic specifically. Why was he so intent on a demonstration? Did he simply crave proof? Entertainment? Or was it more than that?

He trailed the man through the royal vault, suppressing a shudder at the thought of being buried here. Being put in a box in the ground was bad enough, but being *entombed* like this, with layers of stone between you and the world? Kell would never understand the way these Grey-worlders sealed away their dead, trapping the discarded shells in gold and wood and stone as if some remnant of who they'd been in life remained. And if it did? What a cruel punishment.

When George reached his father's tomb, he set the candelabrum down, swept the hem of his coat into his hand, and knelt, head bowed. His lips moved silently for a few seconds, and then he drew a gold cross from his collar and touched it to his lips. Finally he stood, frowning at the dust on his knees and brushing it away.

Kell reached out and rested his hand thoughtfully on the tomb, wishing he could feel something—anything—within. It was silent and cold.

"It would be proper to say a prayer," said the king.

Kell frowned, confused. "To what end?"

"For his soul, of course." Kell's confusion must have showed. "Don't you have God in your world?" He shook his head. George seemed taken aback. "No higher power?"

"I didn't say that," answered Kell. "I suppose you could say we worship magic. That is our highest power."

"That is heresy."

Kell raised a brow, his hand slipping from the tomb's lid. "Your Majesty, you worship a thing you can neither see nor touch, whereas I worship something I engage with every moment of every day. Which is the more logical path?"

George scowled. "It isn't a matter of logic. It is a matter of faith."

Faith. It seemed a shallow substitution, but Kell supposed he couldn't blame the Grey-worlders. Everyone needed to believe in *something,* and without magic, they had settled for a lesser god. One full of holes and mystery and made-up rules. The irony was that they had abandoned magic long before it abandoned them, smothered it with this almighty God of theirs.

"But what of your dead?" pressed the king.

"We burn them."

"A pagan ritual," he said scornfully.

"Better than putting their bodies in a box."

"And what of their *souls*?" pressed George, seeming genuinely disturbed. "Where do you think they go, if you don't believe in heaven and hell?"

"They go back to the source," said Kell. "Magic is in everything, Your Majesty. It is the current of life. We believe that when you die, your soul returns to that current, and your body is reduced again to elements."

"But what of *you*?"

"*You* cease to be."

"What is the point, then?" grumbled the king. "Of living a good life, if there is nothing after? Nothing earned?"

Kell had often wondered the same thing, in his own way, but it wasn't an afterlife he craved. He simply didn't want to return to nothing, as if he'd never been. But it would be a cold day in Grey London's hell before he agreed with the new king on anything. "I suppose the point is to live well."

George's complexion was turning ruddy. "But what stops one from committing sins, if they have nothing to fear?"

Kell shrugged. "I've seen people sin in the name of god, *and* in the name of magic. People misuse their higher powers, no matter what form they take."

"But no afterlife," grumbled the king. "No eternal soul? It's unnatural."

"On the contrary," said Kell. "It is the most natural thing in the world. Nature is made of cycles, and we are made of nature. What is unnatural is believing in an infallible man and a nice place waiting in the sky."

George's expression darkened. "Careful, Master Kell. That is blasphemy."

Kell frowned. "You've never struck me as a very pious man, Your Majesty."

The king crossed himself. "Better safe than sorry. Besides," he said, looking around, "I am the King of England. My legacy is divine. I rule by the grace of that God you mock. I am His servant, as this kingdom is mine at His grace." It sounded like a recitation. The king tucked the cross back beneath his collar. "Perhaps," he added, twisting up his face, "I would worship your god, if I could see and touch it as you do."

And here they were again. The old king had regarded magic with awe, a child's wonder. This new king looked at it the way he looked at everything. With lust.

"I warned you once, Your Majesty," said Kell. "Magic has no place in your world. Not anymore."

George smiled, and for an instant he looked more like a wolf than a well-fed man. "You said yourself, Master Kell, that the world is full of cycles. Perhaps our time will come again." And then the grin was gone, swallowed up by his usual expression of droll amusement. The effect was disconcerting, and it made Kell wonder if the man was really as dense and self-absorbed as his people thought, or if there was something there, beneath the shallow, self-indulgent shell.

What had Astrid Dane said?

I do not trust things unless they belong to me.

A draft cut through the vault, flickering the candlelight. "Come," said George, turning his back on Kell and the old king's tomb.

Kell hesitated, then drew the Red London lin from his pocket, the star glittering in the center of the coin. He always brought one for the king; every month, the old monarch claimed that the magic in his own was fading, like heat from dying coals, so Kell would bring him one to trade, pocket-warm and smelling of roses. Now Kell considered the coin, turning it over his fingers.

"This one's fresh, Your Majesty." He touched it to his lips, and then reached out and set the warm coin on top of the cold stone tomb.

"*Sores nast,*" he whispered. *Sleep well.*

And with that, Kell followed the new king up the stairs, and back out into the cold.

🐉

Kell fought not to fidget while he waited for the King of England to finish writing his letter.

The man was taking his time, letting the silence in the room thicken into something profoundly uncomfortable, until Kell found himself wanting to speak, if only to break it. Knowing that was probably the point, he held his tongue and stood watching the snow fall and the sky darken beyond the window.

When the letter was finally done, George sat back in his chair and took up a wine cup, staring at the pages as he drank. "Tell me something," he said, "about magic." Kell tensed, but the king continued. "Does everyone in your world possess this ability?"

Kell hesitated. "Not all," he said. "And not equally."

George tipped the glass from side to side. "So you might say that the powerful are chosen."

"Some believe that," said Kell. "Others think it is simply a matter of luck. A good hand drawn in cards."

"If that's the case, then you must have drawn a *very* good hand."

Kell considered him evenly. "If you've finished your letter, I should—"

"How many people can do what you do?" cut in the king. "Travel between worlds? I'd wager not many, or else I might have seen them instead. Really," he said, getting to his feet, "it's a wonder your king lets you out of his sight."

He could see the thoughts in George's eyes, like cogs turning. But Kell had no intention of becoming part of the man's collection.

"Your Majesty," said Kell, trying to keep his voice smooth, "if you are feeling the urge to keep me here, thinking it might gain you something, I would *strongly* discourage the attempt, and remind you that any such gesture would forfeit future communication with my world." *Please don't do this,* he wanted to add. *Don't even try it.* He couldn't bear the thought of losing his last escape. "Plus," he added for good measure, "I think you would find I am not easily kept."

Thankfully the king raised his ringed hands in mock surrender. "You mistake me," he said with a smile, even though Kell did not think he'd been at all mistaken. "I simply don't see why our two *great* kingdoms shouldn't share a closer bond."

He folded his letter, and sealed it with wax. It was long— several pages longer than usual, judging by the way the paper bulged and its weight when Kell took it.

"For years these letters have been riddled with formalities, anecdotes instead of history, warnings in place of explanation, useless bits of information when we could be sharing *real* knowledge," pressed the king.

Kell slipped the letter into the pocket of his coat. "If that's all . . ."

"Actually, it's not," said George. "I've something for you."

Kell cringed as the man set a small box on the table. He didn't reach for it. "That is kind of you, Your Majesty, but I must decline."

George's shallow smile faded. "You would refuse a gift from the *King of England*?"

"I would refuse a gift from anyone," said Kell, "especially

when I can tell it's meant as payment. Though I know not for what."

"It's simple enough," said George. "The next time you come, I would have you bring *me* something in return."

Kell grimaced inwardly. "Transference is treason," he said, reciting a rule he'd broken so many times.

"You would be well compensated."

Kell pinched the bridge of his nose. "Your Majesty, there was a time when I might have considered your request." *Well, not yours,* he thought, *but* someone's. "But that time has passed. Petition my king for knowledge if you will. Ask of *him* a gift, and if he concedes, I shall bring it to you. But I bear nothing of my own free will." The words hurt to say, a wound not quite healed, the skin still tender. He bowed and turned to go, even though the king had not dismissed him.

"Very well," said George, standing, his cheeks ruddy. "I will see you out."

"No," said Kell, turning back. "I would not inconvenience you so," he added. "You have guests to attend to." The words were cordial. Their tone was not. "I will go back the way I came."

And you will not follow.

Kell left George red-faced beside the desk, and retraced his steps to the old king's chamber. He wished he could lock the door behind him. But of course, the locks were on the outside of this room. Another reminder that this room had been more prison than palace.

He closed his eyes and tried to remember the last time he'd seen the man alive. The old king hadn't looked well. He hadn't looked well at all, but he'd still known Kell, still brightened at his presence, still smiled and brought the royal letter to his nose, inhaling its scent.

Roses, he'd murmured softly. *Always roses.*

Kell opened his eyes. Part of him—a weary, grieving part—simply wanted to go home. But the rest of him wanted to get out of this blasted castle, go someplace where he wouldn't be a royal messenger or an *Antari,* a prisoner or a prince, and wander the streets of Grey London until he became simply a shadow, one of thousands.

He crossed to the far wall, where heavy curtains framed the window. It was so cold in here that the glass hadn't frosted over. He drew the curtain back, revealing the patterned wallpaper beneath, the design marred by a faded symbol, little more than a smudge in the low light. It was a circle with a single line through it, a transfer mark leading from Windsor to St. James. He shifted the heavy curtain back even farther, revealing a mark that would have been lost long ago, if it hadn't been shielded entirely from time and light.

A six-pointed star. One of the first marks Kell had made, years ago, when the king had been brought to Windsor. He'd drawn the same mark on the stones of a garden wall that ran beside Westminster. The second mark had been long lost, washed away by rain or buried by moss, but it didn't matter. It had been drawn once, and even if the lines were no longer visible, a blood sigil didn't fade from the world as quickly as it did from sight.

Kell pushed up his sleeve and drew his knife. He carved a shallow line across the back of his arm, touched his fingers to the blood, and retraced the symbol. He pressed his palm to it and cast a last glance back at the empty room, at the light seeping beneath the door, listening to the far-off sounds of laughter.

Damned kings, thought Kell, leaving Windsor once and for all.

III

The Edge of Arnes.

Lila's boots hit land for the first time in months.

The last time they'd docked had been at Korma three weeks past, and Lila had drawn the bad lot and been forced to stay aboard with the ship. Before that, there was Sol, and Rinar, but both times Emery insisted she keep to the *Spire*. She probably wouldn't have listened, but there was something in the captain's voice that made her stay. She'd stepped off in the port town of Elon, but that had been for half a night more than two months ago.

Now she scuffed a boot, marveling at how solid the world felt beneath her feet. At sea, everything moved. Even on still days when the wind was down and the tide even, you stood on a thing that stood on the water. The world had give and sway. Sailors talked about sea legs, the way they threw you, both when you first came aboard, and then later when you disembarked.

But as Lila strode down the dock, she didn't feel off-balance. If anything, she felt centered, grounded. Like a weight hung in the middle of her being, and nothing could knock her over now.

It made her want to pick a fight.

Alucard's first mate, Stross, liked to say she had hot blood— Lila was pretty sure he meant it as a compliment—but in truth, a fight was just the easiest way to test your mettle, to see if you'd gotten stronger, or weaker. Sure, she'd been fighting at sea all winter, but land was a different beast. Like horses that were trained on sand, so they'd be faster when they ran on packed earth.

Lila cracked her knuckles and shifted her weight from foot to foot.

Looking for trouble, said a voice in her head. *You're gonna look till you find it.*

Lila cringed at the ghost of Barron's words, a memory with edges still too sharp to touch.

She looked around; the *Night Spire* had docked in a place called Sasenroche, a cluster of wood and stone at the edge of the Arnesian empire. The *very* edge.

Bells rang out the hour, their sound diffused by cliff and fog. If she squinted, she could make out three other ships, one an Arnesian vessel, the other two foreign: the first (she knew by the flags) was a Veskan trader, carved from what looked like a solid piece of black wood; the second was a Faroan glider, long and skeletal and shaped like a feather. Out at sea, canvas could be stretched over its spindly barbs in dozens of different ways to maneuver the wind.

Lila watched as men shuffled about on the deck of the Veskan ship. Four months on the *Spire,* and she had never traveled into foreign waters, never seen the people of the neighboring empires up close. She'd heard stories, of course—sailors lived on stories as much as sea air and cheap liquor—of the Faroans' dark skin, set with jewels; of the towering Veskans and their hair, which shone like burnished metal.

But it was one thing to hear tell, and another to see them with her own eyes.

It was a big world she'd stumbled into, full of rules she didn't know and races she'd never seen and languages she didn't speak. Full of *magic.* Lila had discovered that the hardest part of her charade was pretending that everything was old hat when it was all so new, being forced to feign the kind of nonchalance that only comes from a lifetime of knowing and taking for granted. Lila was a quick study, and she knew how to keep up a front; but behind the mask of disinterest, she took in *everything*. She was a sponge, soaking up the words and customs, training herself to see something once and be able to pretend she'd seen it a dozen—a hundred—times before.

Alucard's boots sounded on the wooden dock, and she let her attention slide off the foreign ships. The captain stopped beside her, took a deep breath, and rested his hand on her shoulder. Lila still tensed under the sudden touch, a reflex she doubted would ever fade, but she didn't pull away.

Alucard was dressed in his usual high style, a silvery blue coat accented with a black sash, his brassy brown hair pinned back with its black clasp beneath an elegant hat. He seemed as fond of hats as she was of knives. The only thing out of place was the satchel slung across his shoulder.

"Do you smell that, Bard?" he asked in Arnesian.

Lila sniffed. "Salt, sweat, and ale?" she ventured.

"Money," he answered brightly.

Lila looked around, taking in the port town. A winter mist swallowed the tops of the few squat buildings, and what showed through the evening fog was relatively unimpressive. Nothing about the place screamed money. Nothing about it screamed anything, for that matter. Sasenroche was the very definition of unassuming. Which was apparently the idea.

Because officially, Sasenroche didn't even exist.

It didn't appear on any land maps—Lila learned early on that there were two kinds of maps, land and sea, and they were as different as one London from another. A land map was an ordinary thing, but a sea map was a special thing, showing not only the open sea but its secrets, its hidden islands and towns, the places to avoid and the places to go, and who to find once you got there. A sea map was never to be taken off its ship. It couldn't be sold or traded, not without word getting back to a seafarer, and the punishment was steep; it was a small world, and the prize wasn't worth the risk. If any man of the waters—or any man who wished to keep his head on his shoulders—saw a sea map on land, he was to burn it before it burned him.

Thus Sasenroche was a well-guarded secret on land, and a legend at sea. Marked on the right maps (and known by the right sailors) as simply the Corner, Sasenroche was the only place where the three empires physically touched. Faro, the lands to the south and east, and Vesk, the kingdom to the north, apparently grazed Arnes right here in this small, unassuming port town. Which made it a perfect place, Alucard had explained, to find foreign things without crossing foreign waters, and to be rid of anything you couldn't take home.

"A black market?" Lila had asked, staring down at the *Spire*'s own sea map on the captain's desk.

"The blackest on land," said Alucard cheerfully.

"And what, pray tell, are we doing here?"

"Every good privateering ship," he'd explained, "comes into possession of two kinds of things; the ones it can turn over to the crown, and the ones it cannot. Certain artifacts have no business being in the kingdom, for whatever reason, but they fetch a pretty sum in a place like this."

Lila gasped in mock disapproval. "That hardly sounds legal."

Alucard flashed the kind of smile that could probably charm snakes. "We act on the crown's behalf, even when it does not know it."

"And even when we profit?" Lila challenged wryly.

Alucard's expression shifted to one of mock offense. "These services we render to keep the crown clean and the kingdom safe go unknown, and thus uncompensated. Now and then we must compensate ourselves."

"I see. . . ."

"It's dangerous work, Bard," he'd said, touching a ringed hand to his chest, "for our bodies and our souls."

Now, as the two stood together on the dock, he flashed her that coy smile again, and she felt herself starting to smile, too, right before they were interrupted by a crash. It sounded like a bag of rocks being dumped out on the docks, but really it was just the rest of the *Night Spire* disembarking. No wonder they all thought of Lila as a wraith. Sailors made an ungodly amount of noise. Alucard's hand fell from Lila's shoulder as he turned to face his men.

"You know the rules," he bellowed. "You're free to do as you please, but don't do anything dishonorable. You are, after all, men of Arnes, here in the service of your crown."

A low chuckle went through the group.

"We'll meet at the Inroads at dusk, and I've business to discuss, so don't get too deep in your cups before then."

Lila still only caught six words out of ten—Arnesian was a fluid tongue, the words running together in a serpentine way—but she was able to piece together the rest.

A skeleton crew stayed aboard the *Spire* and the rest were dismissed. Most of the men went one way, toward the shops and taverns nearest the docks, but Alucard went another, setting off alone toward the mouth of a narrow street, and quickly vanishing into the mist.

There was an unspoken rule that where Alucard went, Lila followed. Whether he invited her or not made little difference. She had become his shadow. "Do your eyes ever close?" he'd asked her back in Elon, seeing how intently she scanned the streets.

"I've found that watching is the quickest way to learn, and the safest way to stay alive."

Alucard had shaken his head, exasperated. "The accent of a royal and the sensibilities of a thief."

But Lila had only smiled. She'd said something very similar

once, to Kell. Before she knew he *was* a royal. And a thief, for that matter.

Now, the crew dispersing, she trailed the captain as he made his winding way into Sasenroche. And as she did, Sasenroche began to *change*. What seemed from the sea to be a shallow town set against the rocky cliffs turned out to be much deeper, streets spooling away into the outcropping. The town had burrowed into the cliffs; the rock—a dark marble, veined with white—arched and wound and rose and fell everywhere, swallowing up buildings and forming others, revealing alleys and stairways only when you got near. Between the town's coiled form and the shifting sea mists, it was hard to keep track of the captain. Lila misplaced him several times, but then she'd spot the tail of his coat or catch the clipped sound of his boot, and she'd find him again. She passed a handful of people, but their hoods were up against the cold, their faces lost in shadow.

And then she turned a corner, and the fog-strewn dusk gave way to something else entirely. Something that glittered and shone and smelled like magic.

The Black Market of Sasenroche.

IV

The market rose up around Lila, sudden and massive, as if she'd stepped inside the cliffs themselves and found them hollow. There were dozens upon dozens of stalls, all of them nested under the arched ceiling of rock, the surface of which seemed strangely . . . alive. She couldn't tell if the veins in the stone were actually glowing with light, or only reflecting the lanterns that hung from every shop, but either way, the effect was striking.

Alucard kept a casual, ambling pace ahead of her, but it was obvious that he had a destination. Lila followed, but it was hard to keep her attention on the captain instead of the stalls themselves. Most held things she'd never seen before, which wasn't that special, in and of itself—she hadn't seen most of what this world had to offer—but she was beginning to understand the basic order, and many of the things she saw here seemed to break it. Magic had a pulse, and here in the Black Market of Sasenroche, it felt erratic.

And yet, most of the things on display seemed, at first glance, fairly innocuous. Where, she wondered, did Sasenroche hide its truly dangerous treasures? Lila had learned firsthand what forbidden magic could do, and while she hoped to never come across a thing like the Black London stone again, she couldn't stifle her curiosity. Amazing, how quickly the magical became mundane; only months ago she hadn't known magic was real, and now she felt the urge to search for stranger things.

The market was bustling, but eerily quiet, the murmur of a dozen dialects smoothed by the rock into an ambient shuffle of sound. Ahead, Alucard finally came to a stop before an un-marked stall. It was tented, wrapped in a curtain of deep blue silk that he vanished behind. Lila would lose all pretense of sub-tlety if she followed him in, so she hung back and waited, exam-ining a table with a range of blades, from short sharp knives to large crescents of metal.

No pistols, though, she noted grimly.

Her own precious revolver, Caster, sat unused in the chest by her bed. She'd run out of bullets, only to find that they didn't use guns in this world, at least not in Arnes. She supposed she could take the weapon to a metalworker, but the truth was, the object had no place here, and transference was considered trea-son (look what had happened to Kell, smuggling items in; while one of those items had been her, another had been the black stone), so Lila was a little loath to introduce another weapon. What if it set off some kind of chain reaction? What if it changed the way magic was used? What if it made this world more like hers?

No, it wasn't worth the risk.

Instead, Caster stayed empty, a reminder of the world she'd left behind. A world she'd never see again.

Lila straightened and let her gaze wander through the mar-ket, and when it landed, it was not on weapons, or trinkets, but on herself.

The stall just to her left was filled with mirrors: different shapes and sizes, some framed and some simply panes of coated glass.

There was no vendor in sight, and Lila stepped closer to con-sider her reflection. She wore a fleece-lined short cloak against the cold, and one of Alucard's hats (he had enough to spare), a tricorne with a feather made of silver and glass. Beneath the hat, her brown eyes stared back at her, one lighter than the other and useless, though few ever noticed. Her dark hair now skimmed her shoulders, making her look more like a girl than she cared to (she'd let it grow for the con aboard the *Copper Thief*), and she made a mental note to cut it back to its usual length along her jaw.

Her eyes traveled down.

She still had no chest to speak of, thank god, but four months aboard the *Night Spire* had effected a subtle transformation. Lila had always been thin—she had no idea if it was natural, or the product of too little food and too much running for too many years—but Alucard's crew worked hard and ate well, and she'd gone from thin to lean, bony to wiry. The distinctions were small, but they made a difference.

She felt a chill prickle through her fingers, and she looked down to find her hand touching the cold surface of the mirror. Odd, she didn't remember reaching out.

Glancing up, she found her reflection's gaze. It considered her. And then, slowly, it began to shift. Her face aged several years, and her coat rippled and darkened into Kell's, the one with too many pockets and too many sides. A monstrous mask sat atop her head, like a beast with its mouth wide, and flame licked up her reflection's fingers where they met the mirror, but it did not burn. Water coiled like a snake around her other hand, turning to ice. The ground beneath her reflection's feet began to crack and split, as if under a weight, and the air around her reflection shuddered. Lila tried to pull her hand away, but she couldn't, just as she couldn't tear her gaze from her reflection's face, where her eyes—*both* of them—turned black, something swirling in their depths.

The image suddenly let go, and Lila wrenched backward, gasping. Pain scored her hand, and she looked down to see tiny cuts, drops of blood welling on each of her fingertips.

The cuts were clean, the line made by something sharp. Like glass.

She held her hand to her chest, and her reflection—now just a girl in a tricorne hat—did the same.

"The sign says *do not touch*," came a voice behind her, and she turned to find the stall's vendor. He was Faroan, with skin as black as the rock walls, his entire outfit made from a single piece of white silk. He was clean-shaven, like most Faroans, but wore only two gems set into his skin, one beneath each eye. She knew he was the stall's vendor because of the spectacles on his nose, their glass not simply glass, but mirrors, reflecting her own pale face.

"I'm sorry," she said, looking back to the glass, expecting to see the place where she'd touched it, where it had *cut* her, but the blood was gone.

"Do you know what these mirrors do?" he asked, and it took her a moment to realize that even though his voice was heavily accented, he was speaking *English*. Except that no, he wasn't, not exactly. The words he spoke didn't line up with the ones she heard. A talisman shone at his throat. At first she'd taken it as some kind of fabric pin, but now it pulsed faintly, and she understood.

The man's fingers went to the pendant. "Ah, yes, a handy thing, this, when you're a merchant at the corner of the world. Not strictly legal, of course, what with the laws against deception, but . . ." He shrugged, as if to say, *What can you do?* He seemed fascinated by the language he was speaking, as if he knew its significance.

Lila turned back to the mirrors. "What do they do?"

The vendor considered the glass, and in his spectacles she saw the mirror reflected and reflected and reflected. "Well," he said, "one side shows you what you want."

Lila thought of the black-eyed girl and suppressed a shudder. "It did not show me what I want," she said.

He tipped his head. "Are you certain? The form, perhaps not, but the idea, perhaps?"

What was the idea behind what she'd seen? The Lila in the mirror had been . . . *powerful*. As powerful as Kell. But she'd also been different. Darker.

"Ideas are well and good," continued the merchant, "but actualities can be . . . less pleasant."

"And the other side?" she asked.

"Hmm?" His mirrored spectacles were unnerving.

"You said that *one side* shows you what you want. What about the other?"

"Well, if you still want what you see, the other side shows you how to get it."

Lila tensed. Was that what made the mirrors forbidden? The Faroan merchant looked at her, as if he could see her thoughts as clearly as her reflection, and went on. "Perhaps it does not seem so rare, to look into one's own mind. Dream stones and scrying boards, these things help us see inside ourselves. The first side of the mirror is not so different; it is almost ordinary. . . ." Lila didn't think she'd ever see *this* kind of magic as ordinary. "Seeing the threads of the world is one thing. Plucking at them is another. Knowing how to make music from them, well . . . let us say this is not a simple thing at all."

"No, I suppose it's not," she said quietly, still rubbing her wounded fingers. "How much do I owe you, for using the first side?"

The vendor shrugged. "Anyone can see themselves," he said. "The mirror takes its tithe. The question now, Delilah, is do you want to see the second side?"

But Lila was already backing away from the mirrors and the mysterious vendor. "Thank you," she said, noting that he hadn't named the price, "but I'll pass."

She was halfway back to the weapons stall before she realized she'd never told the merchant her name.

Well, thought Lila, pulling her cloak tight around her shoulders, *that was unsettling.* She shoved her hands in her pockets—half to keep them from shaking, and half to make sure she didn't accidentally touch anything else—and made her way back to the weapons stall. Soon she felt someone draw up beside her, caught the familiar scent of honey and silver and spiced wine.

"Captain," she said.

"Believe it or not, Bard," he said, "I am more than capable of defending my own honor."

She gave him a sideways look and noted that the satchel was gone. "It's not your honor that concerns me."

"My health, then? No one's killed me yet."

Lila shrugged. "Everyone's immortal until they're not."

Alucard shook his head. "What a delightfully morbid outlook, Bard."

"Besides," continued Lila, "I'm not particularly worried about your honor *or* your life, Captain. I was just looking out for my cut."

Alucard sighed and swung his arm around her shoulders. "And here I was beginning to think you cared." He turned to consider the knives on the table in front of them, and chuckled.

"Most girls covet dresses."

"I am not most girls."

"Without question." He gestured at the display. "See anything you like?"

For a moment, the image in the mirror surged up in Lila mind, sinister and black-eyed and thrumming with power. Lila shook it away, looked over the blades, and nodded at a dagger with a jagged blade.

"Don't you have enough knives?"

"No such thing."

He shook his head. "You continue to be a most peculiar creature." With that, he began to lead her away. "But keep your money in your pockets. We *sell* to the Black Market of Sasenroche, Bard. We don't buy from it. *That* would be very wrong."

"You have a skewed moral compass, Alucard."

"So I've been told."

"What if I stole it?" she asked casually. "Surely it can't be wrong to *steal* an item from an illegal market?"

Alucard choked on a laugh. "You could try, but you'd fail. And you'd probably lose a hand for your effort."

"You have too little faith in me."

"Faith has nothing to do with it. Notice how the vendors don't seem particularly concerned about guarding their wares? That's because the market has been warded." They were at the edge of the cavern now, and Lila turned back to consider it. She squinted at the stalls. "It's strong magic," he continued. "If an object were to leave its stall without permission, the result would be . . . unpleasant."

"What, did you try to steal something once?"

"I'm not that foolish."

"Maybe it's just a rumor then, meant to scare off thieves."

"It's not," said Alucard, stepping out of the cavern and into the night. The fog had thickened, and night had fallen in a blanket of cold.

"How do you know?" pressed Lila, folding her arms in beneath her cloak.

The captain shrugged. "I suppose . . ." He hesitated. "I suppose I've got a knack for it."

"For what?"

The sapphire glinted in his brow. "Seeing magic."

Lila frowned. People spoke of *feeling* magic, of *smelling* it, but never of *seeing* it. Sure, one could see the effects it had on things, the elements it possessed, but never the magic itself. It was like the soul in a body, she supposed. You could see the flesh, the blood, but not the thing it contained.

Come to think of it, the only time Lila had ever *seen* magic was the river in Red London, the glow of power emanating from it with a constant crimson light. A source, that's what Kell had called it. People seemed to believe that that power coursed through everyone and everything. It had never occurred to her that someone could see it out in the world.

"Huh," she said.

"Mm," he said. He didn't offer more.

They moved in silence through the stone maze of streets, and soon all signs of the market were swallowed by the mist. The dark stone of the tunnels tapered into wood as the heart of Sasenroche gave way again to its facade.

"What about me?" she asked as they reached the port.

Alucard glanced back. "What about you?"

"What do you see," she asked, "when you look at me?"

She wanted to know the truth. Who was Delilah Bard? *What* was she? The first was a question she thought she knew the answer to, but the second . . . she'd tried not to bother with it, but as Kell had pointed out so many times, she shouldn't be here. Shouldn't be alive, for that matter. She bent most of the rules. She broke the rest. And she wanted to know why. How. If she was just a blip in the universe, an anomaly, or something *more*.

"Well?" she pressed.

She half expected Alucard to ignore the question, but at last he turned, squaring himself to her.

For an instant, his face crinkled. He so rarely frowned that the expression looked wrong on him. There was a long silence, filled only by the thud of Lila's pulse, as the captain's dark eyes considered her.

"Secrets," he said at last. And then he winked. "Why do you think I let you stay?"

And Lila knew that if she wanted to know the truth, she'd have to give it, and she wasn't ready to do that yet, so she forced herself to smile and shrug. "You like the sound of your own voice. I assumed it was so you'd have someone to talk to."

He laughed and put an arm around her shoulders. "That, too, Bard. That, too."

V

Grey London.

The city looked positively bleak, shrouded in the dying light, as if everything had been painted over with only black and white, an entire palette dampened to shades of grey. Chimneys sent up plumes of smoke and huddled forms hurried past, shoulders bent against the cold.

And Kell had never been so happy to be there.

To be invisible.

Standing on the narrow road in the shadow of Westminster, he drew a deep breath, despite the hazy, smoke-and-cold-filled air, and relished the feeling. A chill wind cut through and he thrust his hands in his pockets and began to walk. He didn't know where he was going. It didn't matter.

There was no place to hide in Red London, not anymore, but he could still carve out space for himself here. He passed a few people on the streets, but no one knew him. No one balked or cringed away. Sure, there had been rumors once, in certain circles, but to most passersby, he was just another stranger. A shadow. A ghost in a city filled with—

"It's *you.*"

Kell tensed at the voice. He slowed, but didn't stop, assuming that the words weren't meant for him, or if they were, then said by mistake.

"Sir!" the voice called again, and Kell glanced around—not for the source, but for anyone else it might be speaking to. But there was no one nearby, and the word was said with recognition, with *knowing*.

His rising mood shuddered and died as he dragged himself to a stop and turned to find a lanky man clutching an armful of papers and staring directly at him, eyes as large as coins. A dark scarf hung around the man's shoulders, and his clothes weren't shabby, but they didn't fit him well; he looked like he'd been stretched out, his face and limbs too long for his suit. His wrists protruded from the cuffs, and on the back of one Kell saw the tail edge of a tattoo.

A power rune.

The first time Kell had seen it, he remembered thinking two things. The first was that it was inaccurate, distorted the way a copy of a copy of a copy might be. The second was that it belonged to an Enthusiast, a Grey-worlder who fancied himself a magician.

Kell *hated* Enthusiasts.

"Edward Archibald Tuttle, the third," said Kell drily.

The man—Ned—burst into an awkward grin, as if Kell had just delivered the most spectacular news. "You remember me!"

Kell did. He remembered everyone he did business (or chose *not* to do business) with. "I don't have your dirt," he said, recalling his half-sarcastic promise to bring the man a bag of earth, if he waited for Kell.

Ned waved it away. "You came back," he said, hurrying forward. "I was beginning to think you wouldn't, after everything, that is to say, after the horrible business with the pub's owner—dreadful business—I waited, you know, before it happened, and then after, of course, and still, and I was beginning to wonder, which isn't the same thing as doubting, mind you, I hadn't begun to doubt, but no one had seen you, not in months and months, and now, well, you're back. . . ."

Ned finally trailed off, breathless. Kell didn't know what to say. The man had done enough talking for both of them. A sharp wind cut through, and Ned nearly lost his papers. "Bloody hell, it's cold," he said. "Let me get you a drink."

He nodded at something behind Kell when he said it, and Kell turned to see a tavern. His eyes widened as he realized where his treacherous feet had taken him. He should have known. The feeling was there, in the ground itself, the subtle pull that only belonged to a fixed point.

The Stone's Throw.

Kell was standing only a few strides from the place where he'd done business, the place where Lila had lived and Barron had died. (He had been back once, when it was all over, but the doors were locked. He'd broken in, but Barron's body was already gone. He climbed the narrow stairs to Lila's room at the top, found nothing left but a dark stain on the floor and a map with no markings. He'd taken the map with him, the last trinket he'd ever smuggle. He hadn't been back since.)

Kell's chest ached at the sight of the place. It wasn't *called* the Stone's Throw anymore. It looked the same—*felt* the same, now that Kell was paying attention—but the sign that hung above the door said THE FIVE POINTS.

"I really shouldn't . . ." he said, frowning at the name.

"The tavern doesn't open for another hour," insisted Ned. "And there's something I want to show you." He pulled a key from his pocket, fumbling one of his scrolls in the process. Kell reached out and caught it, but his attention was on the key as Ned slid it into the lock.

"You *own* this place?" he said incredulously.

Ned nodded. "Well, I mean, I didn't always, but I bought it up, after all that nasty business went down. There was talk of razing it, and it just didn't seem right, so when it came up for sale, well, I mean, you and I, we both know this place isn't *just* a tavern,

that's to say it's special, got that aura of"—he lowered his voice—
"*magic . . .*"—and then spoke up again—"about it. And besides,
I knew you'd come back. I just *knew. . . .*"

Ned went inside as he rambled, and Kell didn't have much
choice but to follow—he could have walked away and left the
man prattling, but Ned had waited, had bought the whole damn
tavern so he could *keep* waiting, and there was something to be
said for stubborn resolve, so he followed the man in.

The place was impenetrably dark, and Ned set his scrolls on
the nearest table and made his way, half by feel, to the hearth to
stoke a fire.

"The hours are different here now," he said, piling a few logs
into the grate, "because my family doesn't know, you see, that I've
taken up the Points, they just wouldn't understand, they'd say it
wasn't a fitting profession for someone in my position, but they
don't know me, not really. Always been a bit of a stray cat, I suppose. But you don't care about that, sorry, I just wanted to explain
why it was closed up. Different crowd nowadays, too. . . ."

Ned trailed off, struggling with a piece of flint, and Kell's gaze
drifted from the half-charred logs in the hearth to the unlit
lanterns scattered on tabletops and hung from ceiling beams.
He sighed, and then, either because he was feeling cold or
indulgent, he snapped his fingers; the fire in the hearth burst to
life, and Ned staggered back as it crackled with the bluish-white
light of enchanted flames before settling into the yellows and
reds of more ordinary fire.

One by one, the lanterns began to glow as well, and Ned
straightened and turned, taking in the spreading light of the self-
igniting lamps as if Kell had summoned the stars themselves
into his tavern.

He made a sound, a sharp intake of breath, and his eyes went
wide: not with fear, or even surprise, but with adoration. With
awe. There was something to the man's unguarded fascination,
his unbridled delight at the display, that reminded Kell of the

old king. His heart ached. He'd once taken the Enthusiast's interest as hunger, greed, but perhaps he'd been mistaken. He was nothing like the new King George. No, Ned had the childlike intensity of someone who *wanted* the world to be stranger than it was, someone who thought they could *believe* magic into being.

Ned reached out and rested his hand on one of the lanterns. "It's warm," he whispered.

"Fire generally is," said Kell, surveying the place. With the infusion of light, he could see that while the outside had stayed the same, inside the Five Points was a different place entirely.

Curtains had been draped from the ceiling in dark swaths, rising and falling above the tables, which were arranged like spokes on a wheel. Black patterns had been drawn—no, *burned*—into the wooden tabletops, and Kell guessed they were meant to be symbols of power—though some looked like Ned's tattoo, vaguely distorted, while others looked entirely made up.

The Stone's Throw had always been a place of magic, but the Five Points *looked* like one. Or at least, like a child's idea of one.

There was an air of mystery, of performance, and as Ned shrugged out of his overcoat, Kell saw that he was wearing a black high-collared shirt with glossy onyx buttons. A necklace at his throat bore a five-pointed star, and Kell wondered if that was where the tavern had gotten its name, until he saw the drawing framed on the wall. It was a schematic of the box Kell had had with him when he and Ned first met. The element game with its five grooves.

Fire, water, earth, air, bone.

Kell frowned. The diagram was shockingly accurate, down to the grain in the wood. He heard the sound of clinking glasses and saw Ned behind the counter, pulling bottles from the wall. He poured two draughts of something dark, and held one out in offering.

For a moment, Kell thought of Barron. The bartender had

been as broad as Ned was narrow, as gruff as the youth was exuberant. But he'd been as much a part of this place as the wood and stone, and he was dead because of Holland. Because of Kell.

"Master Kell?" pressed Ned, still holding out the glass.

He knew he should be going, but he found himself approaching the counter, willing the stool out a few inches before he sat down.

Show-off, said a voice in his head, and maybe it was right, but the truth was, it had been so long since anyone had looked at him the way Ned did now.

Kell took up the drink. "What is it you want to show me, Ned?"

The man beamed at the use of the nickname. "Well, you see," he said, drawing a box from beneath the bar, "I've been *practicing.*" He set the box on the counter, flicked open the lid, and drew out a smaller parcel from within. Kell had his glass halfway to his lips when he saw what Ned was holding, and promptly set the drink down. It was an element set, just like the one Kell had traded here four months ago. No, it was the same *exact* element set, from the dark wood sides down to the little bronze clasp.

"Where did you get that?" he asked.

"Well, I bought it." Ned set the magician's board reverently on the counter between them, and slid the clasp, letting the board unfold to reveal the five elements in their grooves. "From that gentleman you sold it to. Wasn't easy, but we came to an agreement."

Great, thought Kell, his mood suddenly cooling. The only thing worse than an ordinary Enthusiast was a wealthy one.

"I tried to make my own," Ned continued. "But it wasn't the same, I've never been much good with that kind of thing, you should have seen the chicken scratch of that drawing, before I hired—"

"Focus," said Kell, sensing that Ned could wander down mental paths all night.

"Right," he said, "so, what I wanted to show you"—he cracked his knuckles dramatically—"was this."

Ned tapped the groove containing water, and then brought his hands down flat on the counter. He squinted down at the board, and Kell relaxed as he realized where this was going: nowhere.

Still, something was different. The last time Ned had tried this, he'd gestured in the air, and spoken some nonsense over the water, as if the words themselves had any power. This time his lips moved, but Kell couldn't hear what he was saying. His hands stayed flat, splayed on the counter to either side of the board.

For a moment, as predicted, nothing happened.

And then, right as Kell was losing his patience, the water *moved*. Not much, but a bead seemed to rise slightly from the pool before falling back, sending tiny ripples through the water. *Sanct.*

Ned stepped back, triumphant, and while he managed to keep his composure, it was clear he wanted to thrust his arms in the air and cheer.

"Did you see it? Did you see it?" he chanted. And Kell had. It was hardly a dangerous capacity for magic, but it was far more than he had expected. It should have been impossible—for Ned, for *any* Grey-worlder—but the past few months made him wonder if anything was truly out of bounds. After all, Lila had come from Grey London, and she was . . . well, but then she was something else entirely.

Magic has no place in your world, he'd told the king. *Not anymore.*

The world is full of cycles. Perhaps our time will come again.

What was happening? He'd always thought of magic as a fire, each London sitting farther and farther from its heat. Black London had burned up, so near it was to the flame, but Grey London had gone to coals long ago. Was there still somehow a spark? Something to be kindled? Had he accidently blown on the dying flames? Or had Lila?

"That's all I've been able to manage," said Ned excitedly. "But with proper training . . ." He looked at Kell expectantly as he said that, and then quickly down again. "That is, with the right teacher, or at least some guidance . . ."

"Ned," Kell started.

"Of course, I know you must be busy, in demand, and time is precious . . ."

"Edward—" he tried again.

"But I have something for you," pressed the man.

Kell sighed. Why was everyone suddenly so keen to give him gifts?

"I tried to think about what you said, last time, about how you were only interested in things that mattered, and it took me some time but I think I've found something worthy. I'll go get it."

Before Kell could tell him to stop, could explain that whatever it was, he couldn't take it, the man was out from behind the bar and hurrying into the hall, taking the steps upstairs two at a time.

Kell watched him go, wishing he could stay.

He missed the Stone's Throw, no matter its name, missed the simple solidity of this place, this city. Did he have to go home? And that was the problem, right there. Red London was *home*. Kell didn't belong here, in this world. He was a creature of magic—Arnesian, not English. And even if this world still had any power (for Tieren said no place was truly without it), Kell couldn't afford to stoke it, not for Ned, or the king, or himself. He'd already disrupted two worlds. He wouldn't be to blame for a third.

He raked a hand through his hair and pushed up from the stool, the footsteps overhead growing fainter.

The game board still sat open on the counter. Kell knew he should take it back, but then what? He'd just have to explain its presence to Staff and Hastra. No, let the foolish boy keep it. He set the empty glass down and turned to leave, shoving his hands in his pockets.

His fingers brushed something in the very bottom of his coat.

His hand closed over it, and he drew out a second Red London lin. It was old, the gold star worn smooth by hands and time, and Kell didn't know how long it had languished in his pocket. It might have been one of the coins he'd taken from the old king, exchanged for one new and pocket-worn. Or it might have been a stray piece of change, lost in the wool-lined pocket. He considered it for a moment, then heard the sound of a door shutting overhead, and footsteps on the stairs.

Kell set the coin on the counter by his empty glass, and left.

VI

Sasenroche.

Growing up, Lila had always hated taverns.

She seemed bound to them by some kind of tether; she would run as hard as she could, and then at some point she'd reach the end of the line and be wrenched back. She'd spent years trying to cut that tie. She never could.

The Inroads stood at the end of the docks, its lanterns haloed by the tendrils of the sea fog that crept into the port. A sign above the door was written in three languages, only one of which Lila recognized.

The familiar sounds reached her from within, the ambient noise of scraping chairs and clinking glass, of laughter and threats and fights about to break out. They were the same sounds she'd heard a hundred times at the Stone's Throw, and it struck her as odd that those sounds could exist here, in a black market town at the edge of an empire in a magical world. There was, she supposed, a comfort to these places, to the fabric that made them, the way that two taverns, cities apart—*worlds* apart—could feel the same, look the same, sound the same.

Alucard was holding the door open for her. "*Tas enol*," he said, sliding back into Arnesian. *After you.*

Lila nodded and went in.

Inside, the Inroads looked familiar enough; it was the *people*

who were different. Unlike the black market, here the hoods and
hats had all been cast off, and Lila got her first good look at the
crews from the other ships along the dock. A towering Veskan
pushed past them, nearly filling the doorway as he went, a massive blond braid falling down his back. He was bare-armed as
he stepped out into the winter cold.

A huddle of men stood just inside the door, talking in low
voices with smooth foreign tongues. One glanced at her, and she
was startled to see that his eyes were gold. Not amber, like the
prince's, but bright, almost reflective, their metallic centers flecked
with black. Those eyes shone out from skin as dark as the ocean
at night, and unlike the Faroan she'd seen in the market, this
man's face was studded with dozens of pieces of pale green glass.
The fragments traced lines over his brows, followed the curve
of his cheek, trailed down his throat. The effect was haunting.

"Close your mouth," Alucard hissed in her ear. "You look like
a fish."

The light in the tavern was low, shining up from tables and
hearths instead of down from the ceiling and walls, casting faces
in odd shadow as the candles glanced off cheeks and brows.

It wasn't terribly crowded—she'd only seen four ships in the
port—and she could make out the *Spire*'s men, scattered about
and chatting in groups of two or three.

Stross and Lenos had snagged a table by the bar and were
playing cards with a handful of Veskans; Olo watched, and
broad-shouldered Tav was deep in conversation with an Arnesian from another ship.

Handsome Vasry was flirting with a Faroan-looking barmaid—
nothing unusual there—and a wiry crewman named Kobis sat
at the end of a couch, reading a book in the low light, clearly
relishing the closest thing he ever found to peace and quiet.

A dozen faces turned as Lila and Alucard moved through the
room, and she felt herself shrink toward the nearest shadow
before she realized none of them were looking at her. It was the

captain of the *Night Spire* who held their attention. Some nodded, others raised a hand or a glass, a few called out a greeting. He'd obviously made a few friends during his years at sea. Come to think of it, if Alucard Emery had made *enemies,* she hadn't met one yet.

An Arnesian from the other rig waved him over, and rather than trail after, Lila made her way to the bar and ordered some kind of cider that smelled of apple and spice and strong liquor. She was several sips along before she turned her attention to the Veskan man a few feet down the bar.

The *Spire* crew called Veskans *"choser"*—giants—and she was beginning to understand why.

Lila tried not to stare—that is, she tried to stare without looking like she was staring—but the man was *massive,* even taller than Barron had been, with a face like a block of stone circled by a rope of blond hair. Not the bleached whitish blond of the Dane twins, but a honey color, rich in a way that matched his skin, as though he'd never spent a day in the shade.

His arms, one of which leaned on the counter, were each the size of her head; his smile was wider than her knife, but not nearly as wicked; and his eyes, when they shifted toward her, were a cloudless blue. The Veskan's hair and beard grew together around his face, parting only for his wide eyes and straight nose, and made his expression hard to read. She couldn't tell if she was merely being sized up, or challenged.

Lila's fingers drifted toward the dagger at her hip, even though she honestly didn't want to try her hand against a man who looked more likely to *dent* her knife than be impaled on it.

And then, to her surprise, the Veskan held up his glass.

"Is aven," she said, lifting her own drink. *Cheers.*

The man winked, and then began to down his ale in a single, continuous gulp, and Lila, sensing the challenge, did the same. Her cup was half the size of his, but to be fair, he was more than twice the size of her, so it seemed an even match. When her empty mug struck the counter an instant before his own, the Veskan laughed and knocked the table twice with his closed fist while murmuring appreciatively.

Lila set a coin on the bar and stood up. The cider hit her like a pitching deck, as if she were no longer on solid ground but back on the *Spire* in a storm.

"Easy now." Alucard caught her elbow, then swung his arm around her shoulders to hide her unsteadiness. "That's what you get for making friends."

He led her to a booth where most of the men had gathered, and she sank gratefully into a chair on the end. As the captain took his seat, the rest of the crew drifted over, as if drawn by an invisible current. But of course, the current was Alucard himself.

Men laughed. Glasses clanked. Chairs scraped.

Lenos cheated a glance at her down the table. He was the one who'd started the rumors, about her being the Sarows. Was he still afraid of her, after all this time?

She drew his knife—now hers—from her belt and polished it on the corner of her shirt.

Her head spun from that first drink, and she let her ears and attention drift through the crew like smoke, let the Arnesian words dissolve back into the highs and lows, the melodies of a foreign tongue.

At the other end of the table, Alucard boasted and cheered and drank with his crew, and Lila marveled at the way the man shifted to fit his environment. She knew how to adapt well enough, but Alucard knew how to *transform*. Back on the *Spire,* he was not only captain but king. Here at this table, surrounded by his men, he was one of them. Still the boss, always the boss, but not so far above the rest. This Alucard took pains to laugh as loud as Tav and flirt almost as much as Vasry, and slosh his ale like Olo, even though Lila had seen him fuss whenever she spilled water or wine in his cabin.

It was a performance, one that was entertaining to watch. Lila wondered for perhaps the hundredth time which version of Alucard was the real one, or if, somehow, they were all real, each in its own way.

She also wondered where Alucard had found such an odd group of men, when and how they'd been collected. Here, on land, they seemed to have so little in common. But on the *Spire,* they functioned like friends, like *family.* Or at least, how Lila imagined family would act. Sure they bickered, and now and then even came to blows, but they were also fiercely loyal.

And Lila? Was she loyal, too?

She thought back to those first nights, when she'd slept with her back to the wall and her knife at hand, waiting to be attacked. When she'd had to face the fact that she knew almost nothing about life aboard a ship, and grappled every day to stay on her feet, clutching at scraps of skill and language and, on the occasion it was offered, help. It seemed like a lifetime ago. Now they treated her more or less as if she was one of them. As if she *belonged.* A small, defiant part of her, the part she'd done her best to smother on the streets of London, fluttered at the thought.

But the rest of her felt ill.

She wanted to push away from the table and walk out, walk away, break the cords that tied her to this ship and this crew and this life, and start over. Whenever she felt the weight of those bonds, she wished she could take her sharpest knife and cut them free, carve out the part of her that wanted, that cared, that warmed at the feeling of Alucard's hand on her shoulder, Tav's smile, Stross's nod.

Weak, warned a voice in her head.

Run, said another.

"All right, Bard?" asked Vasry, looking genuinely concerned.

Lila nodded, fixing a sliver of a smile back on her face.

Stross slid a fresh drink her way, as if it was nothing.

Run.

Alucard caught her eye and winked.

Christ, she should have killed him when she had the chance.

"All right, Captain," shouted Stross over the noise. "You've got us waiting. What's the big news?"

The table began to quiet, and Alucard brought his stein down. "Listen up, you shabby lot," he said, his voice carrying in a wave. The group fell to murmurs and then silence. "You can have the night on land. But we sail at first light."

"Where to next?" asked Tav.

Alucard looked right at Lila when he said it. "To London."

Lila stiffened in her seat.

"What for?" asked Vasry.

"Business."

"Funny thing," called Stross, scratching his cheek. "Isn't it about time for the tournament?"

"It might be," said Alucard with a smirk.

"You *didn't*," gasped Lenos.

"Didn't what?" asked Lila.

Tav chuckled. "He's gone and entered the *Essen Tasch*."

Essen Tasch, thought Lila, trying to translate the phrase. *Element . . . something.* What was it? Everyone else at the table seemed to know. Only Kobis said nothing, simply frowned down into his drink, but he didn't look confused, only concerned.

"I don't know, Captain," said Olo. "You think you're good enough to play that game?"

Alucard chuckled and shook his head. He brought his glass to his lips, took a swig, and then slammed the stein down on the table. It shattered, but before the cider could spill, it sprang into the air, along with the contents in every other glass at the table, liquid freezing as it surged upward. The frozen drinks hung for a moment, then tumbled to the wooden table, some lodging sharp-end down, others rolling about. Lila watched the frozen spear that had once been her cider fetch up against her glass. Only the icicle that had been Alucard's drink stayed up, hovering suspended above his ruined glass.

The crew whooped and applauded.

"Hey," growled a man behind the bar. "You pay for everything you break."

Alucard smiled and lifted his hands, as if in surrender. And then, as he flexed his fingers, the shards of glass strewn across the table trembled and drew themselves back together into the shape of a stein, as if time itself were beginning to reverse. The stein formed in one of Alucard's hands, the cracks blurring and then vanishing as the glass re-fused. He held it up, as if to inspect it, and the shard of frozen cider still hovering in the air above his head liquefied and spilled back into the unbroken glass. He took a sip and toasted the man behind the bar, and the crew burst into a raucous cheer, hammering the table, their own drinks forgotten.

Only Lila sat motionless, stunned by the display.

She'd seen Alucard do magic, of course—he'd been teaching her for months. But there was a difference—a chasm, a world—between levitating a knife and *this*. She hadn't seen anyone handle magic like this. Not since Kell.

Vasry must have read her surprise, because he tipped his head toward hers. "Captain's one of the best in Arnes," he said. "Most magicians only got a handle on one element. A few are duals. But Alucard? He's a *triad*." He said the word with awe. "Doesn't go around flashing his power, because great magicians are rare out on the water, rarer than a bounty, so they're likely to be caught and sold. Of course that wouldn't be the first coin on his head, but still. Most don't leave the cities."

Then why did he? she wondered.

When she looked up, she saw Alucard's gaze leveled on her, sapphire winking above one storm-dark eye.

"You ever been to an *Essen Tasch,* Vasry?" she asked.

"Once," said the handsome sailor. "Last time the Games were in London."

Games, thought Lila. So that's what *Tasch* meant.

The Element Games.

"Only runs every three years," continued Vasry, "in the city of the last victor."

"What's it like?" she pried, fighting to keep her interest casual.

"Never been? Well you're in for a treat." Lila liked Vasry. He wasn't the sharpest man, not by a long stretch; he didn't read too much into the questions, didn't wonder how or why she didn't know the answers. "The *Essen Tasch* has been going for more than sixty years now, since the last imperial war. Every three years they get together—Arnes and Faro and Vesk—and put up their best magicians. Shame it only lasts a week."

"S'the empires' way of shaking hands and smiling and showing that all is well," chimed in Tav, who had leaned in conspiratorially.

"*Tac,* politics are boring," said Vasry, waving his hand. "But the duels are fun to watch. And the *parties.* The drinking, the betting, the beautiful women . . ."

Tav snorted. "Don't listen to Vasry, Bard," he said. "The duels are the best part. A dozen of the greatest magicians from each empire going head to head." *Duels.*

"Oh, and the masks are pretty, too," mused Vasry, eyes glassy.

"Masks?" asked Lila, interest piqued.

Tav leaned forward with excitement. "In the beginning," he said, "the competitors wore helmets, to protect themselves. But over time they began to embellish them. Set themselves apart. Eventually, the masks just became part of the tournament." Tav frowned slightly. "I'm surprised you've never been to an *Essen Tasch,* Bard."

Lila shrugged. "Never been in the right place at the right time."

He nodded, as if that answer was good enough, and let the

matter lie. "Well, if Alucard's in the ranks, it'll be a tournament to remember."

"Why do men do it?" she asked. "Just to show off?"

"Not just men," said Vasry. "Women, too."

"It's an honor, being chosen to compete for your crown—"

"Glory's well and good," said Vasry, "but this game is winner take all. Not that the captain needs the money."

Tav shot him a warning look.

"A pot that large," said Olo, chiming in, "even the king himself is sore to part with it."

Lila traced her finger through the cider that was beginning to melt on the table, half listening to the crew as they chatted. Magic, masks, money . . . the *Essen Tasch* was becoming more and more interesting.

"Can anyone compete?" she wondered idly.

"Sure," said Tav, "if they're good enough to get a spot."

Lila stopped drawing her finger through the cider, and no one noticed that the spilled liquid kept moving, tracing patterns across the wood.

Someone set a fresh drink in front of her.

Alucard was calling for attention.

"To London," he said, raising his glass.

Lila raised her own.

"To London," she said, smiling like a knife.

FOUR

LONDONS CALLING

I

Red London.

The city was under siege.

Rhy stood on the uppermost balcony of the palace and watched the forces assemble. The cold air bit at his cheeks and tugged on his half cloak, catching it up like a golden flag behind him.

Far below, structures collided, walls rose, and the sounds of stoked fires and hammer on steel echoed like weapons struck together in a barrage of wood and metal and glass.

It would surprise most to know that when Rhy thought of himself as king, he saw himself like this: not on a throne, or toasting friends at lavish dinners, but overseeing armies. And while he had never seen an *actual* battlefront—the last true war was more than sixty years past, and his father's forces always smothered the border flares and civil skirmishes before they could escalate—Rhy was blessed with enough imagination to compensate. And at first glance, London *did* appear to be under attack, though the forces were all his own.

Everywhere Rhy looked, the city was being overtaken, not by enemy soldiers but by masons and magicians, hard at work constructing the platforms and stages, the floating arenas and bankside tents that would house the *Essen Tasch* and its competitors.

"The view from up here," said a man behind him, "it is . . . magnificent." The words were High Royal, but their edges were smoothed out by the *ostra*'s Arnesian accent.

"It is indeed, Master Parlo," said Rhy, turning toward the man. He had to bite back a smile. Parlo looked positively miserable, half frozen and obviously uncomfortable with the distance between the balcony and the red river far below, clutching the scrolls to the flowery pattern of his vest as if they were a rope. Almost as bad as Vis; the guard stood with his armored back pressed against the wall, looking pale.

Rhy was tempted to lean back against the railing, just to make the *ostra* and the guard nervous. It was something Kell would do. Instead he stepped away from the edge, and Parlo gratefully mirrored his action by retreating a pace into the doorway.

"What brings you to the roof?" asked Rhy.

Parlo drew a roll of parchment from under his arm. "The arrangements for the opening ceremonies, Your Highness."

"Of course." He accepted the plans but didn't unroll them. Parlo still stood there, as if waiting for something—a tip? a treat?—and Rhy finally said, "You can go now."

The *ostra* looked wounded, so Rhy dredged up his most princely smile. "Come now, Master Parlo, you've been excused, not banished. The view up here may be magnificent, but the weather is not, and you look in need of tea and a fire. You'll find both in the gallery downstairs."

"I suppose that does sound nice . . . but the plans . . ."

"Hopefully I won't need help deciphering a scheme I made myself. And if I do, I know where to find you."

After a moment, Parlo finally nodded and retreated. Rhy sighed and set the plans on a small glass table by the door. He unrolled the parchment, wincing as sunlight made the page glow white, his head still throbbing dully from the night before. The nights had grown harder for Rhy. He'd never been afraid of the dark—even after the Shadows came and tried to kill him in the night—but that was because the dark itself *used* to be empty. Now it was not. He could feel it, whatever *it* was, hovering in the air around him, waiting until the sun went down and the world got quiet. Quiet enough to *think*. Thoughts, those were the waiting things, and once they started up, he couldn't seem to silence them.

Saints, how he tried.

He poured himself a glass of tea and dragged his attention back to the plans, setting weights at the corners against the wind. And there it was, laid out before him, the thing he focused on in a desperate attempt to keep the thoughts at bay.

Is Essen Tasch.

The Element Games.

An international tournament between the three empires— Vesk, Faro, and, of course, Arnes. It was no modest affair. The *Essen Tasch* was made up of thirty-six magicians, a thousand wealthy spectators willing to make the journey, and of course, the royal guests. The prince and princess from Vesk. The king's brother from Faro. By tradition, the tournament was hosted by the capital of the previous winner. And thanks to Kisimyr Vasrin's prowess, and Rhy's vision, London would be the dazzling centerpiece of this year's games.

And at the center, Rhy's crowning achievements: the first ever floating arenas.

Tents and stages blossomed all across the city, but Rhy's deepest pride was reserved for those three stages being erected not on the banks, but on the river itself. They were temporary, yes, and would be torn down again when the tournament was over. But they were also *glorious,* works of art, statues on the scale of stadiums. Rhy had commissioned the best metal- and earthworkers in the kingdom to build his magnificent arenas. Bridges and walkways were being crafted around the palace, and from above they resembled golden ripples across the Isle's red water. Each stadium was an octagon, canvas stretched like sails over a skeleton of stone. On top of this body, the arenas were covered: the first in sculpted scales, the second in fabric feathers, the third in grassy fur.

As Rhy watched, massive dragons carved of ice were being lowered into the river to circle the eastern arena, while canvas birds flew like kites above the central one, caught in a perpetual wind. And to the west, eight magnificent stone lions marked the stadium's posts, each caught in a different pose, a captured moment in the narrative of predator and prey.

He could have simply numbered the platforms, Rhy supposed, but that would have been woefully predictable. No, the *Essen Tasch* demanded more.

Spectacle.

That's what everyone expected. And spectacle was certainly something Rhy knew how to deliver. But this wasn't just about putting on a show. Kell could tease all he liked, but Rhy *did* care about his kingdom's future. When his father put him in charge of the tournament, he'd been insulted. He'd thought the *Essen Tasch* a glorified party, and as good as Rhy was at entertaining, he'd wanted more. More responsibility. More power. And he'd told the king as much.

"Ruling is a delicate affair," his father had chided. "Every gesture carries purpose and meaning. This tournament is not only a game. It helps to maintain peace with our neighboring empires, and it allows us to show them our resources without implying any threat." The king had laced his fingers. "Politics is a dance until the moment it becomes a war. And we control the music."

And the more Rhy thought on it, the more he understood.

The Maresh had been in power for more than a hundred years. Since before the War of the Empires. The *ostra* elite loved them, and none of the royal *vestra* were bold enough to challenge their reign, solid as it was. That was the benefit of ruling for more than a century; none could remember what life was like before the Maresh came to power. It was easy to believe the dynasty would never end.

But what of the other empires? No one spoke of war—no one ever spoke of war—but whispers of discontent reached like fog across the borders. With seven children, the Veskans were reaching for power, and the king's brother was hungry; it was only a matter of time before Lord Sol-in-Ar muscled his way onto the Faroan throne, and even if Vesk and Faro had their sights on each other, the fact remained that Arnes sat squarely between them.

And then there was Kell.

As much as Rhy joked with his brother about his reputation, it was no joke to Faro or Vesk. Some were convinced Kell was the keystone of the Arnesian empire, that it would crumble and fall without him at its center.

It didn't matter if it was true—their neighbors were always searching for a weakness, because ruling an empire was about *strength*. Which was really the *image* of strength. The *Essen Tasch* was the perfect pedestal for such a display.

A chance for Arnes to shine.

A chance for *Rhy* to shine, not only as a jewel, but as a sword. He had always been a symbol of wealth. He wanted to be a symbol of *power*. Magic was power, of course, but it wasn't the *only* kind. Rhy told himself he could still be strong without it.

His fingers tightened on the balcony's rail.

The memory of Holland's gift flickered through his mind. Months ago he had done something foolish—so foolish, it had nearly cost him and his city everything—just to be strong in the way Kell was. His people would never know how close he'd come to failing them. And more than anything else, Rhy Maresh wanted to be what his people needed. For a long time he thought they needed the cheerful, rakish royal. He wasn't ignorant enough to think that his city was free of suffering, but he used to think—or perhaps he only *wanted* to think—that he could bring a measure of happiness to his people by being happy himself. After all, they loved him. But what befitted a prince would not befit a king.

Don't be morbid, he thought. His parents were both in good health. But people lived and died. That was the nature of the world. Or at least, that was how it should be.

The memories rose like bile in his throat. The pain, the blood, the fear, and finally the quiet and the dark. The surrender of letting go, and being dragged back, the force of it like falling, a terrible, jarring pain when he hit the ground. Only he wasn't falling down. He was falling up. Surging back to the surface of himself, and—

"Prince Rhy."

He blinked and saw his guard, Tolners, standing in the door-way, tall and stiff and official.

Rhy's fingers ached as he pried them from the icy railing. He opened his mouth to speak, and tasted blood. He must have bitten his tongue. *Sorry, Kell,* he thought. It was such a peculiar thing, to know your pain was tethered to someone else's, that every time you hurt, they felt it, and every time they hurt, it was because of you. These days, Rhy always seemed to be the source of Kell's suffering, while Kell himself walked around as if the world were suddenly made of glass, all because of Rhy. It wasn't even in the end, wasn't balanced, wasn't fair. Rhy held Kell's *pain* in his hands, while Kell held Rhy's *life* in his.

"Are you all right?" pressed the guard. "You look pale."

Rhy took up a glass of tea—now cold—and rinsed the metallic taste from his mouth, setting the cup aside with shaking fingers.

"Tell me, Tolners," he said, feigning lightness. "Am I in so much danger that I need not one but *two* men guarding my life?" Rhy gestured to the first guard, who still stood pressed against the cold stone exterior. "Or have you come to relieve poor Vis before he faints on us?"

Tolners looked to Vis, and jerked his head. The other guard gratefully ducked back through the patio doors and into the safety of the room. Tolners didn't take up a spot along the wall, but stood before Rhy at attention. He was dressed, as he always was, in full armor, his red cape billowing behind him in the cold wind, gold helmet tucked under his arm. He looked more like a statue than a man, and in that moment—as in many moments—Rhy missed his old guards, Gen and Parrish. Missed their humor and their casual banter and the way he could make them forget that he was a prince. And sometimes, the way they could make *him* forget, too.

Don't be contrary, thought Rhy. *You cannot be the symbol of power and an ordinary man at the same time. You have to choose. Choose right.*

The balcony suddenly felt crowded. Rhy freed the blueprints from the table and retreated into the warmth of his chambers. He dumped the papers on a sofa, and he was crossing to the sideboard for a stronger drink when he noticed the letter sitting on the table. How long had it been there?

Rhy's gaze flicked to his guards. Vis was standing by the dark wood doors, busying himself with a loose thread on his cape. Tolners was still on the balcony, looking down at the tournament construction with a faint crease between his brows.

Rhy took up the paper and unfolded it. The message scrawled in small black script wasn't in English or Arnesian, but Kas-Avnes, a rare border dialect Rhy had been taught several years before.

He'd always had a way with languages, as long as they belonged to men and not magic.

Rhy smiled at the sight of the dialect. As clever as using code, and far less noticeable.

The note read:

Prince Rhy,

I disapprove wholeheartedly, and maintain the hope, however thin, that you will both regain your senses. In the event that you do not, I've made the necessary arrangements— may they not come to haunt me. We will discuss the cost of your endeavors this afternoon. Maybe the steams will prove clarifying. Regardless of your decision, I expect a substantial donation will be made to the London Sanctuary when this is over.

Your servant, elder, and Aven Essen,
Tieren Serense

Rhy smiled and set the note aside as bells chimed through the city, ringing out from the sanctuary itself across the river.

Maybe the steams will prove clarifying.

Rhy clapped his hands, startling the guards.

"Gentlemen," he said, taking up a robe. "I think I'm in the mood for a bath."

II

The world beneath the water was warm and still.

Rhy stayed under as long as he could, until his head swam, and his pulse thudded, and his chest began to ache, and then, and only then, he surfaced, filling his lungs with air.

He loved the royal baths, had spent many languorous afternoons—evenings, mornings—in them, but rarely alone. He was used to the laughter of boisterous company echoing off the stones, the playful embrace of a companion, kisses splashing on skin, but today the baths were silent save for the gentle drip of water. His guards stood on either side of the door, and a pair of attendants perched, waiting with pitchers of soap and oil, brushes, robes, and towels while Rhy strode through the waist-high water of the basin.

It took up half the room, a wide, deep pool of polished black rock, its edges trimmed in glass and gold. Light danced across the arched ceilings and the outer wall broken only by high, thin windows filled with colored glass.

The water around him was still sloshing from his ascent, and he splayed his fingers across the surface, waiting for the ripples to smooth again.

It was a game he used to play when he was young, trying to see if he could still the surface of the water. Not with magic, just with patience. Growing up, he'd been even worse at waiting than he was at summoning elements, but these days, he was getting better. He stood in the very center of the bath and slowed his breathing, watched the water go still and smooth as glass. Soon his reflection resolved in its surface, mirror-clear, and Rhy considered his black hair and amber eyes before his gaze invariably drifted down over his brown shoulders to the mark on his chest.

The circles wound together in a way that was both intuitive and foreign. A symbol of death and life. He focused and became aware of the pulse in his ears, the echo of Kell's own, both beats growing louder and louder, until Rhy expected the sound to ruin the glassy stillness of the water.

A subtle aura of peace broke the mounting pulse.

"Your Highness," said Vis from his place at the door. "You have a—"

"Let him pass," said the prince, his back to the guard. He closed his eyes and listened to the hushed tread of bare feet, the whisper of robes against stone: quiet, and yet loud enough to drown out his brother's heart.

"Good afternoon, Prince Rhy." The *Aven Essen*'s voice was a low thrum, softer than the king's but just as strong. Sonorous.

Rhy turned in a slow circle to face the priest, a smile alighting on his face. "Tieren. What a pleasant surprise."

The head priest of the London Sanctuary was not a large man, but his white robes hardly swallowed him. If anything, he grew to fill them, the fabric swishing faintly around him, even when he stood still. The air in the room changed with his presence, a calm settling over everything like snow. Which was good, because it counteracted the visible discomfort most seemed to feel around the man himself, shying away as if Tieren could see through them, straight past skin and bone to thought and want and soul. Which was probably why Vis was now studying his boots.

The *Aven Essen* was an intimidating figure to most—much

like Kell, Rhy supposed—but to him, Master Serense had always been *Tieren*.

"If this is a bad time . . ." the priest began, folding his hands into his sleeves.

"Not at all," said Rhy, ascending the glass stairs that lined the bath on every side. He could feel the eyes in the room drift to his chest: not only the symbol seared into the bronze skin, but the scar between his ribs, where his knife—Astrid's knife—had gone in. But before the cool air could settle or the eyes could linger, an attendant was there, draping him in a plush red robe. "Please leave us," he said, addressing the rest of the room. The attendants instantly began to withdraw, but the guard lingered. "You too, Vis."

"Prince Rhy," he began, "I'm not supposed to . . ."

"It's all right," said Rhy drolly. "I don't think the *Aven Essen* means me any harm."

Tieren's silver brows inched up a fraction. "That remains to be seen," said the priest evenly.

Vis was halfway through a step back, but stopped again at the words. Rhy sighed. Ever since the Black Night, the royal guards had been given strict instructions when it came to their kingdom's heir. And its *Antari*. He didn't know the exact words his father had used, but he was fairly sure they included *don't let them* and *out of your sight* and possibly *on pain of death*.

"Vis," he said slowly, trying to summon a semblance of his father's stony command. "You insult me, and the head priest, with your enduring presence. There is one door in and out of this room. Stand on the other side with Tolners, and *guard it*."

The impression must have been convincing, because Vis nodded and reluctantly withdrew.

Tieren lowered himself onto a broad stone bench against the wall, his white robes pooling around him, and Rhy came to sit beside him, slumping back against the stones.

"Not much humor in this bunch," said Tieren when they were alone.

"None at all," complained Rhy, rolling his shoulders. "I swear, sincerity is its own form of punishment."

"The tournament preparations are coming along?"

"Indeed," said Rhy. "The arenas are almost ready, and the empire tents are positively decadent. I almost envy the magicians."

"Please tell me *you're* not thinking of competing, too."

"After all the trouble Kell went to, to keep me alive? That would be sore thanks."

The smallest frown formed between Tieren's eyes. On anyone else it would have been imperceptible, but on the *Aven Essen*'s calm face, it registered as discontent (though he claimed that Kell and Rhy were the only ones who managed to draw out that particular forehead crease).

"Speaking of Kell . . ." said Rhy.

Tieren's gaze sharpened. "Have you reconsidered?"

"Did you really think I would?"

"A man can hope."

Rhy shook his head. "Anything we should be worried about?"

"Besides your own foolish plans? I don't believe so."

"And the helmet?"

"It will be ready." The *Aven Essen* closed his eyes. "I'm getting too old for subterfuge."

"He needs this, Tieren," pressed Rhy. And then, with a coy smile, "How old *are* you?"

"Old enough," answered Tieren. "Why?" One eye opened. "Are my grey hairs showing?"

Rhy smiled. Tieren's head had been silver for as long as he could remember. Rhy loved the old man, and he suspected that, against Tieren's better judgment, he loved Rhy, too. As the *Aven Essen,* he was the protector of the city, a gifted healer, and a very close friend to the crown. He'd mentored Kell as he came into his powers, and nursed Rhy back to health whenever he was sick, or when he'd done something foolish and didn't want to get caught. He and Kell had certainly kept the old man busy over the years.

"You know," said Tieren slowly, "you really should be more careful about who sees your mark."

Rhy flashed him a look of mock affront. "You can't expect me to remain clothed *all* the time, Master Tieren."

"I do suppose that would be too much to ask."

Rhy tipped his head back against the stones. "People assume it's just a scar from that night," he said, "which is exactly what it is, and as long as *Kell* remains clothed—which, let's be honest, is a *much* easier demand—no one will realize it's anything more."

Tieren sighed, his universal signal for discontent. The truth was that the mark unsettled Rhy, more than he wanted to admit, and hiding it only made it feel more like a curse. And, strangely, it was all he had. Looking down at his arms, his chest, Rhy saw that aside from the silvery burst of spell work, and the knife wound that looked so small and pale beneath, he bore very few scars. The seal wasn't pleasant, but it was a scar he'd earned. And one he needed to live with.

"People whisper," observed Tieren.

"If I make a point of hiding it any more than I do, they will just whisper *more*."

What would have happened, wondered Rhy, *if I had gone to Tieren with my fears of weakness, instead of accepting Holland's gift for strength? Would the priest have known what to say? How to help?* Rhy had confessed to Tieren, in the weeks after the incident. Told him about accepting the talisman—the possession charm—expecting one of the old man's reprimands. Instead Tieren had listened, speaking only when Rhy was out of words.

"Strength and weakness are tangled things," the *Aven Essen* had said. "They look so much alike, we often confuse them, the way we confuse magic and power."

Rhy had found the response flip, but in the months that

followed, Tieren had been there, at Rhy's side, a reminder and a support.

When he looked over at Tieren now, the man was staring at the water, past it, as if he could see something there, reflected in the surface, or the steam.

Maybe Rhy could learn to do that. Scry. But Tieren told him once it wasn't so much about looking out as looking in, and Rhy wasn't sure he wanted to spend any more time than necessary doing that. Still, he couldn't shake the feeling—the hope—that everyone was born with the ability to do *something,* that if he just searched hard enough he would find it. His gift. His *purpose.*

"Well," said Rhy, breaking the silence, "do you find the waters to your liking?"

"Why won't you leave me in peace?"

"There's too much to do."

Tieren sighed. "As it seems you will not be dissuaded . . ." He drew a scroll from the folded sleeves of his robes. "The final list of competitors."

Rhy straightened and took the paper.

"It will be posted in the next day or two," explained the priest, "once we receive the lists from Faro and Vesk. But I thought you'd want to see it first." There was something in his tone, a gentle caution, and Rhy undid the ribbon and uncoiled the scroll with nervous fingers, unsure of what he'd find. As the city's *Aven Essen,* it was Master Tieren's task to select the twelve representatives of Arnes.

Rhy scanned the list, his attention first landing on *Kamerov Loste*—he felt a thrill at seeing the name, an invention, a fiction made real—before a name farther down snagged his gaze, a thorn hidden among roses.

Alucard Emery.

Rhy winced, recoiled, but not before the name drew blood. "How?" he asked, his voice low, almost hollow.

"Apparently," said Tieren, "you're not the only one capable of pulling strings. And before you get upset, you should know that Emery broke *far* fewer rules than you have. In fact, he technically broke none. He auditioned for me in the fall, when the *Spire* was docked, and as far as I'm concerned, he's the strongest one in the ranks. Two weeks ago his sister came to me, to refresh my memory and to petition his place, though I think she simply wants him to come home. If that's not enough, there's the matter of the loophole."

Rhy tried to keep himself from crumpling the paper. "What loophole?"

"Emery was formally invited to compete three years ago, but . . ." Tieren hesitated, looking uncomfortable. "Well, we both know that certain circumstances prevented that. He's entitled to a spot."

Rhy wanted to climb back into the bath and vanish beneath the water. Instead he slowly, methodically rolled the paper up and retied it with string.

"And here I thought you might be happy," said Tieren. "The mystery and madness of youth is clearly lost on me."

Rhy folded forward, rubbing his neck, and then his shoulder. His fingers found the scar over his heart, and he traced the lines absently, a recent habit. The skin was silvery and smooth, just barely raised, but he knew that the seal went all the way through, flesh and bone and soul.

"Let me see," said Tieren, standing.

Rhy was grateful for the change of focus. He tipped his head out of the way and let the man examine his shoulder, pressing one cool, dry hand to the front, and one to the back. Rhy felt a strange warmth spreading through him along the lines of the spell. "Has the bond weakened?"

Rhy shook his head. "If anything, it seems to be growing stronger. At first, the echoes were dull, but now . . . it's not just pain, either, Tieren. Pleasure, fatigue. But also anger, restlessness. Like right now, if I clear my head, I can feel Kell's"—he hesitated, reaching for his brother—"weariness. It's exhausting."

"That makes sense," said Tieren, hands falling away. "This isn't simply a physical bond. You and Kell are sharing a life force."

"You mean I'm sharing *his*," corrected Rhy. His own life had been cut off by the dagger driven into his chest. What he had, he was siphoning off Kell. The heat of the bath had vanished, and Rhy was left feeling tired and cold.

"Self-pity is not a good look on you, Your Highness," said Tieren, shuffling toward the door.

"Thank you," Rhy called after him, holding up the scroll. "For this."

Tieren said nothing, only crinkled his brow faintly—there it was again, that line—and vanished.

Rhy sank back against the bench, and considered the list again, Kamerov's name so close to Alucard's.

One thing was certain.

It was going to be one hell of a tournament.

III

The guards met Kell at the mouth of the Naresh Kas, as planned.

Staff with his barrel chest and silvering temples and beard, and Hastra, young and cheerful, with a sun-warmed complexion and a crown of dark curls. *At least he's pretty,* Rhy had said months ago, on seeing the new guards. The prince had been sulking because his own set, Tolners and Vis, had neither looks nor humor.

"Gentlemen," said Kell as his coat settled around him in the alley. The guards looked cold, and he wondered how long they'd been waiting for him.

"I would have brought you a hot drink, but . . ." He held up his empty hands as if to say, *rules.*

"S'okay, Master Kell," said Hastra through clenched teeth, missing the jab. Staff, on the other hand, said nothing.

They had the decency not to search him then and there, but rather turned and fell silently in step behind him as he set off in the direction of the palace. He could feel the eyes drifting toward their small procession, any chance at blending in ruined by the presence of the royal guards flanking him in their gleaming armor and red cloaks.

Kell would have preferred subterfuge, the suspicion of being followed, to the actuality, but he straightened his shoulders and held his head high and tried to remind himself that he looked like a royal, even if he felt like prisoner.

He hadn't even done anything wrong, not today, and saints knew he'd had the chance. *Several* chances.

At last they reached the palace steps, strewn even now with frost-dusted flowers.

"The king?" Kell asked as they strode through the entryway.

Staff led the way to a chamber where King Maxim stood near a blazing hearth, in conversation with several *ostra*. When he saw Kell, he dismissed them. Kell kept his head up, but none of the attendants met his gaze. When they were gone, the king nodded him forward.

Kell continued into middle of the room before spreading his arms for Staff and Hastra in a gesture that was as much challenge as invitation.

"Don't be dramatic," said Maxim.

The guards had the decency to look uncertain as they came forward.

"Rhy must be rubbing off on me, Your Majesty," said Kell grimly as Staff helped him out of his coat, and Hastra patted down his shirt and trousers, and ran a hand around the lip of his boots. He didn't have anything on his person, and they wouldn't be able to find anything in his coat, not unless he wanted it to be found. He sometimes worried that the coat had a mind of its own. The only other person who'd ever managed to find what they wanted in its pockets was Lila. He'd never found out how she'd done that. Traitorous coat.

Staff withdrew the Grey London letter from one of the pockets, and delivered it to the king before handing the coat back to Kell.

"How was the king?" asked Maxim, taking the letter.

"Dead," said Kell. That caught the man off guard. He recounted his visit, and the Prince Regent's—now George IV's—renewed interest in magic. He even mentioned that the new king had tried to bribe him, taking care to emphasize the fact that he'd *declined* the offer.

Maxim stroked his beard and looked troubled, but he said nothing, only waved a hand to show Kell that he was dismissed. He turned, feeling his mood darken, but as Staff and Hastra moved to follow, Maxim called them back.

"Leave him be," he said, and Kell was grateful for that small kindness as he escaped to his rooms.

His relief didn't last. When he reached the doors to his chamber, he found two more guards standing outside them. The men were Rhy's.

"Saints, I swear you just keep multiplying," he muttered.

"Sir?" said Tolners.

"Nothing," grumbled Kell, pushing past them. There was only one reason Tolners and Vis would be stationed outside *his* door.

He found Rhy standing in the middle of his room, his back to Kell as he considered himself in a full-length mirror. From this angle, Kell couldn't see Rhy's face, and for a moment, a memory surged into his mind, of Rhy waiting for him to wake—only it hadn't been Rhy, of course, but Astrid wearing his skin, and they were in Rhy's chambers then, not his. But for an instant the details blurred and he found himself searching Rhy for any pendants or charms, searching his floor for blood, before the past crumbled back into memory.

"About time," said Rhy, and Kell was secretly relieved when the voice that came from Rhy's lips was undoubtedly his brother's.

"What brings you to my room?" he asked, relief bleeding into annoyance.

"Adventure. Intrigue. Brotherly concern. Or," continued the prince lazily, "perhaps I'm just giving your mirror something to look at besides your constant pout."

Kell frowned, and Rhy smiled. "Ah, there it is! That famous scowl."

"I don't scowl," grumbled Kell.

Rhy shot a conspiratorial look at his own reflection. Kell sighed and tossed his coat onto the nearest couch before heading for the alcove off his chamber.

"What are you doing?" Rhy called after.

"Hold on," Kell called back, shutting the door between them. A single candle flickered to life, and by its light he saw the symbols drawn on the wood. There, amid the other marks and fresh with blood, was the doorway to Disan. The way to Windsor Castle. Kell reached out and rubbed at the mark until it was obscured, and then gone.

When Kell returned, Rhy was sitting in Kell's favorite chair, which he'd dragged around so it was facing the room instead of the balcony doors. "What was that about?" he asked, head resting in his hand.

"That's my chair," said Kell flatly.

"Battered old thing," said Rhy, knowing how fond Kell was of it. The prince had mischief in his pale gold eyes as he got to his feet.

"I'm still nursing a headache," said Kell. "So if you're here to force me on another outing—"

"That's not why I'm here," said Rhy, crossing to the sideboard. He started to pour himself a drink, and Kell was about to say something very unkind when he saw that it was simply tea.

He nodded at one of the sofas. "Sit down."

Kell would have stood out of spite, but he was weary from the trip, and he sank onto the nearest sofa. Rhy finished fixing his tea and sat down opposite.

"Well?" prompted Kell.

"I thought Tieren was supposed to teach you patience," chided Rhy. He set the tea on the table and drew a wooden box from underneath. "I wanted to apologize."

"For what?" asked Kell. "The lying? The drinking? The fighting? The relentless—" But something in Rhy's expression made him stop.

The prince raked the black curls from his face, and Kell realized that he looked older. Not *old*—Rhy was only twenty, a year and a half younger than Kell—but the edges of his face had sharpened, and his bright eyes were less amazed, more intense. He'd grown up, and Kell couldn't help but wonder if it was all natural, the simple, inevitable progression of time, or if the last dregs of his youth had been stripped away by what had happened.

"Look," said the prince, "I know things have been hard. Harder these past months than ever. And I know I've only made it worse."

"Rhy—"

The prince held up his hand to silence him. "I've been difficult."

"So have I," admitted Kell.

"You really have."

Kell found himself chuckling, but shook his head. "One life is a hard thing to keep hold of, Rhy. Two is . . ."

"We'll find our stride," insisted the prince. And then he shrugged. "Or you'll get us both killed."

"How can you say that with such levity?" snapped Kell, straightening.

"Kell." Rhy sat forward, elbows on his knees. "I was dead."

The words hung in the air between them.

"I was *dead*," he said again, "and you brought me back. You have already given me something I shouldn't have." A shadow flashed across his face when he said it, there and then gone. "If it were lost again," he went on, "I would still have lived twice. This is all borrowed."

"No," said Kell sternly, "it is bought and paid for."

"For how long?" countered Rhy. "You cannot measure out what you have purchased. I am grateful for the life you've bought me, though I hate the cost. But what do you plan to do, Kell? Live forever? I don't want that."

Kell frowned. "You would rather die?"

Rhy looked tired. "Death comes for us all, Brother. You cannot hide from it forever. We *will* die one day, you and I."

"And that doesn't frighten you?"

Rhy shrugged. "Not nearly as much as the idea of wasting a perfectly good life in fear of it. And to that end . . ." He nudged the box toward Kell.

"What is it?"

"A peace offering. A present. Happy birthday."

Kell frowned. "My birthday's not for another month."

Rhy took up his tea. "Don't be ungrateful. Just take it."

Kell drew the box onto his knees and lifted the lid. Inside, a face stared up at him.

It was a helmet, made of a single piece of metal that curved from the chin over the top of the head and down to the base of the skull. A break formed the mouth, an arch the nose, and a browlike visor hid the wearer's eyes. Aside from this subtle shaping, the mask's only markings were a pair of decorative wings, one above each ear.

"Am I going into battle?" asked Kell, confused.

"Of a sort," said Rhy. "It's your mask, for the tournament."

Kell nearly dropped the helmet. "The *Essen Tasch*? Have you lost your mind?"

Rhy shrugged. "I don't think so. Not unless you've lost yours . . ." He paused. "Do you think it works that way? I mean, I suppose it—"

"I'm an *Antari*!" Kell cut in, struggling to keep his voice down. "I'm the adopted son of the Maresh crown, the strongest magician in the Arnesian empire, possibly in the *world*—"

"Careful, Kell, your ego is showing."

"—and you want me to compete in an inter-empire tournament."

"Obviously the great and powerful *Kell* can't compete," said Rhy. "That would be like rigging the game. It could start a war."

"*Exactly.*"

"Which is why you'll be in disguise."

Kell groaned, shaking his head. "This is insane, Rhy. And even if you were crazy enough to think it could work, Tieren would never allow it."

"Oh, he didn't. Not at first. He fought me tooth and nail. Called it madness. Called us fools—"

"It wasn't even my idea!"

"—but in the end he understood that approving of something and allowing it are not always the same thing."

Kell's eyes narrowed. "Why would Tieren change his mind?"

Rhy swallowed. "Because I told him the truth."

"And what's that?"

"That you needed it."

"Rhy—"

"That *we* needed it." He grimaced a little when he said it.

Kell hesitated, meeting his brother's gaze. "What do you mean?"

Rhy shoved himself up from the chair. "You're not the only one who wants to crawl out of their skin, Kell," he said, pacing. "I see the way this confinement is wearing on you." He tapped his chest. "I *feel* it. You spend hours training in the Basin with no one to fight, and you have not been at peace a single day since Holland, since the Danes, since the Black Night. And if you want the honest truth, unless you find some release"—Rhy stopped pacing—"I'll end up strangling you myself."

Kell winced, and looked down at the mask in his lap. He ran his fingers over the smooth silver. It was simple and elegant, the silver polished to such a shine that it was nearly a mirror. His reflection stared back at him, distorted. It was madness, and it frightened him, how badly he wanted to agree to it. But he couldn't.

He set the mask on the sofa. "It's too dangerous."

"Not if we're careful," insisted his brother.

"We're tethered to each other, Rhy. My pain becomes your pain."

"I'm well aware of our condition."

"Then you know I can't. I *won't*."

"I am not only your brother," said Rhy. "I am your prince. And I command it. You will compete in the *Essen Tasch.* You will burn off some of this fire before it spreads."

"And what about our bond? If I get hurt—"

"Then I will share your pain," said Rhy levelly.

"You say that now, but—"

"Kell. My greatest fear in life isn't dying. It's being the source of someone else's suffering. I know you feel trapped. I know I'm your cage. And I can't—" His voice broke, and Kell could feel his brother's pain, everything he tried to smother until dark and drown until morning. "You *will* do this," said Rhy. "For me. For both of us."

Kell held his brother's gaze. "All right," he said.

Rhy's features faltered, and then he broke into a smile. Unlike the rest of his face, his grin was as boyish as ever. "You will?"

Kell felt a thrill go through him as he took up the mask again. "I will. But if I'm not competing as myself," he said, "then who will I be?"

Rhy reached into the box and withdrew from among the wrappings a scroll of paper Kell hadn't noticed. He held it out, and when Kell unfurled it he saw the Arnesian roster. Twelve names. The men and women representing their empire.

There was Kisimyr, of course, as well as Alucard (a thrill ran through Kell at the thought of having an excuse to fight him). He skimmed past them, searching.

"I picked out your name myself," said Rhy. "You'll be competing as—"

"Kamerov Loste," answered Kell, reading the seventh name aloud.

Of course.

K. L.

The letters carved into the knife he wore on his forearm. The only things that had come with him from his previous life, whatever it was. Those letters had become his name—*KL, Ka-El, Kell*—but how many nights had he spent wondering what they stood for? How many nights had he dreamed up names for himself?

"Oh, come on," chided Rhy, misreading Kell's tension for annoyance. "It's a good name! Rather princely, if I do say so."

"It'll do," said Kell, fighting back a smile as he set the scroll aside.

"Well," said Rhy, taking up the helmet and holding it out to Kell. "Try it on."

Kell hesitated. The prince's voice was light, the invitation casual, but there was more to the gesture, and they both knew it. If Kell put on the mask, this would cease to be a stupid, harmless idea and become something more. Something real. He reached out and took the helmet.

"I hope it fits," said Rhy. "You've always had a big head."

Kell slipped the helmet on, standing as he did. The inside was soft, the fit made snug by the padding. The visor cut all the way from ear to ear, so his vision and hearing were both clear.

"How do I look?" he asked, his voice muffled slightly by the metal.

"See for yourself," said Rhy, nodding at the mirror. Kell turned toward the glass. It was eerie, the polished metal creating an almost tunneling reflection, and the cut of the visor hid his gaze so that even though he could see fine, no one would be able to see that one of his eyes was blue and the other black.

"I'm going to stand out," he said.

"It's the *Essen Tasch,*" said Rhy. "Everyone stands out."

And while it was true that everyone wore *masks* and it was part of the drama, the tradition, this wasn't just a mask. "Most competitors don't dress as though they're going to war."

Rhy crossed his arms and gave him an appraising look. "Yes, well, most competitors don't truly *need* to maintain their anonymity, but your features are . . . unique."

"Are you calling me ugly?"

Rhy snorted. "We both know you're the prettiest boy at the ball."

Kell couldn't stop cheating glances in the mirror. The silver helmet hovered over his simple black clothes, but something was missing. . . .

His coat was still draped on the back of the couch. He took it up and shook it slightly as he turned it inside out, and as he did, his usual black jacket with silver buttons became something else. Something new.

"I've never seen that one before," said Rhy. Neither had Kell, not until a few days earlier, when he'd gotten bored and decided to see what other sides the coat had tucked away (now and then, unused outfits seemed to disappear, new ones turning up in their place).

Kell had wondered at the sudden appearance of this one, so unlike the others, but now, as he shrugged it on, he realized that was because this coat didn't belong to him.

It belonged to *Kamerov.*

The coat was knee-length and silver, trimmed in a patterned border of black and lined with bloodred silk. The sleeves were narrow and the bottom flared, the collar high enough to reach the base of his skull.

Kell slipped the coat on, fastening the clasps, which cut an asymmetrical line from shoulder to hip. Rhy had gone rooting around in Kell's closet, and now he reemerged with a silver walking stick. He tossed it, and Kell plucked it out of the air, his fingers curled around the black lion's head that shaped the handle.

And then he turned back to his reflection.

"Well, Master Loste," said Rhy, stepping back, "you do look splendid."

Kell didn't recognize the man in the mirror, and not simply because the mask hid his face. No, it was his posture, too, shoulders straight and head up, his gaze level behind the visor.

Kamerov Loste was an impressive figure.

A breeze wove gently around him, ruffling his coat. Kell smiled.

"About that," said Rhy, referring to the swirling air. "For obvious reasons, Kamerov can't be an *Antari*. I suggest you pick an element and stick with it. Two if you must—I've heard there are quite a few duals this year—but triads are rare enough to draw attention. . . ."

"Mmhmm," said Kell, adjusting his pose.

"While I'm sympathetic to your sudden bout of narcissism," said Rhy, "this is important, Kell. When you're wearing that mask, you cannot be the most powerful magician in Arnes."

"I understand." Kell tugged the helmet back off and struggled to smooth his hair. "Rhy," he said, "are you certain . . . ?" His heart was racing. He wanted this. He shouldn't want this. It was a terrible idea. But he wanted it all the same. Kell's blood sang at the idea of a fight. A good fight.

Rhy nodded.

"All right, then."

"So you've come to your senses?"

Kell shook his head, dazed. "Or lost my mind." But he was smiling now, so hard he felt his face might crack.

He turned the helmet over and over in his hands.

And then, as suddenly as his spirits had soared, they sank.

"*Sanct,*" he cursed, sagging back onto the couch. "What about my guards?"

"Silver and Gold?" asked Rhy, his pet names for the men. "What about them?"

"I can't exactly ditch Staff and Hastra for the entire length of the tournament. Nor can I conveniently misplace them for each and every bout."

"I'm sorry, I thought you were a master magician."

Kell threw up his hands. "It has nothing to do with my skill, Rhy. There's suspicious, and then there's obvious."

"Well, then," said the prince, "we'll just have to tell them."

"And they'll tell the king. And do you want to guess what the king will do? Because I'm willing to bet he won't risk the stability of the kingdom so I can let off some steam."

Rhy pinched the bridge of his nose. Kell frowned. That gesture, it didn't suit the prince; it was something *he* would do, had done a hundred times.

"Leave it to me," he said. He crossed to Kell's doors and swung them open, leaning against the frame. Kell hoped the guards had truly stayed behind when he left King Maxim, but they must have only granted him a berth, because Rhy called them in, closing the door before his own guards could follow.

Kell rose to his feet, unsure what his brother meant to do.

"Staff," said Rhy, addressing the man with silver temples. "When my father assigned you to shadow Kell, what did he say?"

Staff looked from Kell to Rhy, as if it were a trap, a trick question. "Well . . . he said we were to watch, and to keep him from harm, and to report to His Majesty if we saw Master Kell doing anything . . . suspicious."

Kell scowled, but Rhy flashed an encouraging smile. "Is that so, Hastra?"

The guard with dark gold hair bowed his head. "Yes, Your Highness."

"But if you were informed about something in advance, then it wouldn't be suspicious, would it?"

Hastra looked up. "Um . . . no, Your Highness?"

"Rhy," protested Kell, but the prince held his hand up.

"You both swore your lives to this family, this crown, and this empire. Does your oath hold?"

Both men bowed their heads and brought their hands to their

chests. "Of course, Your Highness," they said, almost in unison. *What on earth is Rhy getting at?* wondered Kell.

And then, the prince's countenance changed. The easiness fell away, as did his cheerful smile. His posture straightened and his jaw clenched, and in that moment he looked less like a prince than a future king. He looked like *Maxim.*

"Then understand this," he said, his voice now low and stern. "What I'm about to tell you regards the safety and security of not only our family, but of the Arnesian empire."

The men's eyes went wide with concern. Kell's narrowed.

"We believe there is a threat in the tournament." Rhy shot Kell a knowing look, though Kell honestly had no idea where he was going with this. "In order to determine the nature of this threat, Kell will be competing in the *Essen Tasch,* disguised as an ordinary entrant, Kamerov Loste."

The guards frowned, cheating looks toward Kell, who managed a stiff nod. "The secrecy of my identity," he cut in, "is paramount. If either Faro or Vesk discovers my involvement, they'll assume we've rigged the game."

"My father already knows of Kell's inclusion," added Rhy. "He has his own matters to attend to. If you see anything during the tournament, you will tell Kell himself, or me."

"But how are we supposed to guard him?" asked Staff. "If he's pretending to be someone else?"

Rhy didn't miss a beat. "One of you will pose as his second— every competitor needs an attendant—and the other will continue to guard him from a safe distance."

"I've always wanted to be in a plot," whispered Hastra. And then, raising his voice, "Your Highness, could I be the one in disguise?" His eagerness was a barely contained thing.

Rhy looked to Kell, who nodded. Hastra beamed, and Rhy brought his hands together in a soft, decisive clap. "So it's settled. As long as Kell is Kell, you will guard him with your usual attentiveness. But when dealing with Kamerov, the illusion must be flawless, the secret held."

The two guards nodded solemnly and were dismissed. *Saints,* thought Kell as the doors swung shut. *He's actually done it.*

"There," said Rhy, slouching onto the couch. "That wasn't so hard."

Kell looked at his brother with a mixture of surprise and awe. "You know," he said, taking up the mask, "if you can rule half as well as you can lie, you're going to make an incredible king."

Rhy's smile was a dazzling thing. "Thank you."

IV

Sasenroche.

It was late by the time Lila made her way back to the *Night Spire*. Sasenroche had quieted, and it had started to sleet, an icy mix that turned to slush on the deck and had to be swept away before it froze solid.

Back in her London—*old* London—Lila had always hated winter.

Longer nights meant more hours in which to steal, but the people who ventured out usually didn't have a choice, which made them poor marks. Worse than that, in winter, everything was damp and grey and bitter cold.

So many nights in her past life, she had gone to bed shivering. Nights she couldn't afford wood or coal, so she'd put on every piece of clothing she owned and huddled down and froze. Heat cost money, but so did food and shelter and every other blasted thing you needed to survive, and sometimes you had to choose.

But here, if Lila practiced, she could summon fire with her fingertips, could keep it burning on nothing but magic and will. She was determined to master it, not just because fire was useful or dangerous, but because it was *warm,* and no matter what happened, Lila Bard never wanted to be cold again.

That was why Lila favored fire.

She blew out a puff of air. Most of the men stayed behind to enjoy the night on land, but Lila preferred her room on the ship, and she wanted to be alone so she could think.

London. Her pulse lifted at the thought. It had been four months since she first boarded the *Night Spire.* Four months since she said good-bye to a city she didn't even know, its name the only tether to her old life. She'd planned to go back, of course. Eventually. What would Kell say, when he saw her? Not that *that* was her first thought. It wasn't. It was sixth, or maybe seventh, somewhere below all the ones about Alucard and the *Essen Tasch.* But it was still *there,* swimming in her head.

Lila sighed, her breath clouding as she leaned her elbows on the ship's slush-covered rail and looked down at the tide as it sloshed up against the hull. Lila favored fire, but it wasn't her only trick.

Her focus narrowed on the water below, and as it did, she tried to push the current back, away. The nearest wave stuttered, but the rest kept coming. Lila's head had begun to hurt, pounding in time with the waves, but she gripped the splintered rail, determined. She imagined she could *feel* the water— not only the shudder traveling up the boat, but the energy coursing through it. Wasn't magic supposed to be the thing in all things? If that was true, then it wasn't about moving the water, it was about moving the *magic.*

She thought of "The Tyger," the poem she used to focus her mind, with its strong and steady beat . . . but it was a song for fire. No, she wanted something else. Something that flowed.

"Sweet dreams," she murmured, summoning a line from another Blake poem, trying to get the feeling right. *"Of pleasant streams . . . "* She said the line over and over again until the water filled her vision, until the sound of the sloshing waves was all she could hear, and the beat of them matched the beat of her pulse and she could feel the current in her veins, and the water up and down the dock began to still, and . . .

A dark drop hit the rail between her hands.

Lila lifted her fingers to her nose; they came away stained with blood.

Someone *tsk*ed, and Lila's head snapped up. How long had Alucard been standing at her back?

"Please tell me you didn't just try to exert your will on the *ocean*," he said, offering her a kerchief.

"I almost did it," she insisted, holding the cloth to her face. It smelled like him. His magic, a strange mixture of sea air and honey, silver and spice.

"Not that I doubt your potential, Bard, but that's not possible."

"Maybe not for *you*," she jabbed, even though in truth she was still unnerved by what she'd seen him do back in the tavern.

"Not for *anyone*," said Alucard, slipping into his teacher's voice. "I've told you: when you control an element, your will has to be able to encompass it. It has to be able to reach, to surround. That's how you shape an element, and that's how you command it. No one can stretch their mind around an ocean. Not without tearing. Next time, aim sma—"

He cut off as a clod of icy slush struck the shoulder of his coat. "Agh!" he said, as bits slipped down his collar. "I know where you sleep, Bard."

She smirked. "Then you know I sleep with knives."

His smile faltered. "Still?"

She shrugged and turned back to the water. "The way they treat me—"

"I've made my orders very clear," he said, obviously assuming she'd been misused. But that wasn't it.

"—like I'm one of them," she finished.

Alucard blinked, confused. "Why shouldn't they? You're part of the crew."

Lila cringed. *Crew.* The very word referred to more than one. But belonging meant caring, and caring was a dangerous thing. At best, it complicated everything. At worst, it got people killed. People like Barron.

"Would you rather they try to knife you in the dark?" asked the captain. "Toss you overboard and pretend it was an accident?"

"Of course not," said Lila. But at least then she'd know how to react. Fights she recognized. Friendship? She didn't know what to do with that. "They're probably too scared to try it."

"Some of them may fear you, but all of them respect you. And don't let on," he added, nudging her shoulder with his, "but a few may even *like* you."

Lila groaned, and Alucard chuckled.

"Who are you?" he asked.

"I'm Delilah Bard," she said calmly. "The best thief aboard the *Night Spire*."

Normally Alucard left it at that, but not tonight. "But who *was* Delilah Bard before she came aboard my ship?"

Lila kept her eyes on the water. "Someone else," she said. "And she'll be someone else again when she leaves."

Alucard blew out a puff of air, and the two stood there, side by side on deck, staring out into the fog. It sat above the water, blurring the line between sea and sky, but it wasn't entirely still. It shifted and twisted and curled, the motions as faint and fluid as the rocking of the water.

The sailors called it scrying fog—supposedly, if you stared at it long enough, you began to see things. Whether they were visions or just a trick of the eye depended on who you asked.

Lila squinted at the coiling mist, expecting nothing—she'd never had a particularly vivid imagination—but after a moment she thought she saw the fog began to shift, begin to *change*. The effect was strangely entrancing, and Lila found she couldn't look away as tendrils of ghostly mist became fingers, and then a hand, reaching toward her through the dark.

"So." Alucard's voice was like a rock crashing through the vision. "London."

She exhaled, the cloud of breath devouring the view. "What about it?"

"I thought you'd be happy. Or sad. Or angry. In truth, I thought you'd be *something*."

Lila cocked her head. "And why would you think that?"

"It's been four months. I figured you left for a reason."

She gave him a hard look. "Why did *you* leave?"

A pause, the briefest shadow, and then he shrugged. "To see the world."

Lila shrugged. "Me, too."

They were both lies, or at best, partial truths, but for once, neither challenged the other, and they turned away from the water and crossed the deck in silence, guarding their secrets against the cold.

V

White London.

Even the stars burned in color now.

What he'd always taken for white had become an icy blue, and the night sky, once black, now registered as a velvet purple, the deepest edge of a bruise.

Holland sat on the throne, gazing up past the vaulting walls at the wide expanse of sky, straining to pick out the colors of his world. Had they always been there, buried beneath the film of failing magic, or were they new? Forest-green vines crept, dark and luscious, around the pale stone pillars that circled the throne room, their emerald leaves reaching toward silver moonlight as their roots trailed across the floor and into the still, black surface of the scrying pool.

How many times had Holland dreamed of sitting on this throne? Of slitting Athos's throat, driving a blade into Astrid's heart, and taking back his life. How many times . . . and yet it hadn't been his hand at all, in the end.

It had been Kell's.

The same hand that had driven a metal bar through Holland's chest, and pushed his dying body into the abyss.

Holland rose to his feet, the rich folds of his cape settling around him as he descended the steps of the dais, coming to a stop before the black reflective pool. The throne room stood empty around him. He'd dismissed them all, the servants and the guards, craving solitude. But there was no such thing, not anymore. His reflection stared up from the glassy surface of the water, like a window in the dark, his green eye a gem floating on the water, his black eye vanishing into the depths. He looked younger, but of course even in youth, Holland had never looked like *this*. The blush of health, the softness of a life without pain.

Holland stood perfectly still, but his reflection moved.

A tip of the head, the edge of a smile, the green eye devoured in black.

We make a fine king, said the reflection, words echoing in Holland's head.

"Yes," said Holland, his voice even. "We do."

Black London.
Three months ago.

Darkness.

Everywhere.

The kind that stretched.

For seconds and hours and days.

And then.

Slowly.

The darkness lightened into dusk.

The nothing gave way to something, pulled itself together until there was ground, and air, and a world between.

A world that was impossibly, unnaturally still.

Holland lay on the cold earth, blood matted to his front and back where the metal bar had passed through. Around his body, the dusk had a strange permanence to it, no lingering tendrils of daylight, no edge of approaching night. There was a heavy quiet to this place, like shelves beneath long-settled dust. An abandoned house. A body without breath.

Until Holland gasped.

The dusty world shuddered around him in response, as if by breathing, he breathed life into it, set the time stuttering forward into motion. Flecks of dirt—or ash, or something else—that had been hanging in the air above him, the way motes seemed to do when caught in threads of sunlight, now drifted down, settling like snow on his hair, his cheeks, his clothes.

Pain. Everything was pain.

But he was alive.

Somehow—impossibly—he was alive.

His whole body hurt—not just the wound in his chest, but his muscles and bones—as if he'd been lying on the ground for days, weeks, and every shallow breath sent spikes through his lungs. He should be dead. Instead he braced himself, and sat up.

His vision swam for a moment, but to his relief, the pain in his chest didn't worsen. It remained a heavy ache, pulsing in time with his heart. He looked around and discovered he was sitting in a walled garden, or at least, what might have once been a garden; the plants had long since withered, and what still stood of vine and stem looked ready to crumble to ash at a touch.

Where was he?

Holland searched his memory, but the last image he had was of Kell's face, set in grim determination even as he struggled against the water Holland had used to bind him, Kell's eyes narrowing in focus, followed by the spike of pain in Holland's back, the metal rod tearing through flesh and muscle, shattering ribs and rending the scar on his chest. So much pain, and then surrender, and then nothing.

But that fight had been in another London. This place held none of that city's floral odor, none of its pulsing magic. Nor was it *his* London—this Holland knew with equal certainty, for though it shared the barren atmosphere, the colorless palette, it lacked the bitter cold, the scent of ash and metal.

Vaguely, Holland recalled lying in the Stone Forest, numb to everything but the slow fading of his pulse. And after, the drag of the abyss. A darkness he assumed was death. But death had rejected him, delivering him to this place.

And it could only be one place.

Black London.

Holland had stopped bleeding and his fingers drifted absently, automatically, not to the wound but to the silver circle that had fastened his cloak—the mark of the Danes' control—only to discover it was gone, as was the cloak itself. His shirt was ripped, and the skin beneath, once scarred silver by Athos's seal, was now a mess of torn flesh and dried blood. Only then, with his fingers hovering over the wound, did Holland feel the change. It had been overshadowed by the shock and pain and strange surroundings, but now it prickled across his skin and through his veins, a lightness he hadn't felt in seven years.

Freedom.

Athos's spell had been broken, the binding shattered. But how? The magic was bound to soul, not skin—Holland knew, had tried to cut it away a dozen times—and could only be broken by its caster.

Which could only mean one thing.

Athos Dane was *dead*.

The knowledge shuddered through Holland with unexpected intensity, and he gasped, and gripped the desiccated ground beneath him. Only it wasn't desiccated anymore. While the world to every side had the bleak stillness of a winter landscape, the ground beneath Holland, the place where his blood had soaked into the soil, was a rich and waking green.

Beside him on the grass sat the black stone—*Vitari*—and he tensed before he realized it was hollow. Empty.

He patted himself down for weapons. He'd never been particularly concerned with them, preferring his own sharp talents to the clumsier edge of a blade, but his head was swimming and, considering how much strength it was taking just to stay upright, he honestly wasn't sure he had any magic to summon at the moment. He'd lost his curved blade back in the other London, but he found a dagger against his shin. He pressed the tip to the hard ground and used it to help push himself to his knees, then his feet.

Once he was up—he bit back a wave of dizziness and a swell of pain—Holland saw that the greenery wasn't entirely confined to his impression on the ground. It trailed away from him, forging a kind of path. It was little more than a thread of green, woven through the barren earth, a narrow strip of grass and weed and wildflower, disappearing through the walled arch at the far end of the garden.

Haltingly, Holland followed.

His chest throbbed and his body ached, his veins still starved of blood, but the ribs he knew were broken had begun to heal, and the muscles held, and slowly Holland found a semblance of his old stride.

Years under the cruelty of Athos Dane had taught him to bear his pain in silence, and now he gritted his teeth and followed the ribbon of life as it led him beyond the garden wall and into the road.

Holland's breath caught in his chest, sending a fresh spike through his shoulder. The city sprawled around him, a version of London at once familiar and entirely *other*. The buildings were elegant, impossible structures, carved out of glassy stone, their shapes drifting toward the sky like smoke. They reflected what little light was left as the dusk thickened into twilight, but there was no other source of light. No lanterns on hooks or fires in hearths. Holland had keen eyes, so it wasn't the pressing dark that bothered him, but what it meant. Either there was no one here to *need* the light, or what remained preferred the darkness.

Everyone assumed Black London had consumed itself, destroyed itself, like a fire starved of fuel and air. And while that seemed to be true, Holland knew that assumptions were made to take the place of facts, and the stretch of green at Holland's feet made him wonder if the world was truly dead, or merely *waiting.*

After all, you can kill people, but you cannot kill magic.

Not truly.

He followed the thread of new growth as it wove through the ghostly streets, reaching out here and there to brace himself against the smooth stone walls, peering as he did into windows, and finding nothing. No one.

He reached the river, the one that went by several names but ran through every London. It was black as ink, but that disturbed Holland less than the fact that it wasn't flowing. It wasn't frozen, like the Isle; being made of water, it couldn't have decayed, petrified with the rest of the city. And yet, there was no current. The impossible stillness only added to the unnerving sensation that Holland was standing in a piece of time rather than a place.

Eventually, the green path led him to the palace.

Much like the other buildings, it rose like smoke to the sky, its black spires disappearing into the haze of twilight. The gates hung open, their weight sagging on rusted hinges, the great steps cracked. The grassy thread continued, undeterred by the landscape. If anything, it seemed to thicken, braiding into a rope of vine and blossom as it climbed the broken stairs. Holland climbed with it, one hand pressed to his aching ribs.

The palace doors swung open beneath his touch, the air inside still and stagnant as a tomb, the vaulted ceilings reminiscent of White London's churchlike castle, but with smoother edges. The way the glassy stone continued inside and out, without sign of forge or seam, made it seem ethereal, impossible. This entire place had been made with magic.

The path of green persisted in front of him, winding over stone floors and beneath another pair of doors, massive panes of tinted glass with withered flowers trapped inside. Holland pushed the doors open, and found himself staring at a king.

His breath caught, before he realized the man before him,

cast in shadows, wasn't made of flesh and blood, but glassy black stone.

Just a statue seated on a throne.

But unlike the statues that filled the Stone Forest in front of the Danes' palace, this one was *clothed*. And the clothes seemed to *move*. The cloak around the king's shoulders fluttered, as if caught by a wind, and the king's hair, though *carved*, seemed to rustle gently in the breeze (even though there *was* no breeze in the room). A crown sat atop the king's head, and a wisp of grey a shade lighter than the stone itself swirled in the statue's open eyes. At first Holland thought it was simply part of the rock, but then the swirl of grey twitched, and moved. It coiled into pupils that drifted until they found Holland, and stopped.

Holland tensed.

The statue was *alive*.

Not in the way of men, perhaps, but alive all the same, in a simple, enduring way, like the grass at his feet. Natural. And yet entirely unnatural.

"*Oshoc*," murmured Holland. A word for a piece of magic that broke away, became something more, something with a mind of its own. A will.

The statue said nothing. The wisps of grey smoke watched him from the king's face, and the thread of green trailed up the dais, wound itself around the *oshoc*'s throne and over one sculpted boot. Holland found himself stepping forward, until his shoes grazed the bottom of the throne's platform.

And then, at last, the statue spoke.

Not out loud, but in Holland's mind.

Antari.

"Who are you?" asked Holland.

I am king.

"Do you have a name?"

Again, the illusion of movement. The faintest gesture: a tightening of fingers on the throne, a tipping of the head, as if this were a riddle. *All things have names.*

"There was a stone found in my city," continued Holland, "and it called itself *Vitari.*"

A smile seemed to flicker like light against the creature's petrified face. *I am not* Vitari, he said smoothly. *But* Vitari *was me.* Holland frowned, and the creature seemed to relish his confusion. *A leaf to a tree,* he said, indulgently.

Holland stiffened. The idea that the stone's power was a mere leaf compared to the thing that sat before him—the *thing* with its stone face and its calm manner and its eyes as old as the world . . .

My name, said the creature, *is Osaron.*

It was an old word, an *Antari* word, meaning *shadow.*

Holland opened his mouth to speak, but his air was cut off as another spasm of pain lurched through his chest. The grey smoke twisted.

Your body is weak.

Sweat slid down Holland's cheek, but he forced himself to straighten.

I saved you.

Holland didn't know if the *oshoc* meant that he'd saved his life once, or that he was still saving it. "Why?" he choked.

I was alone. Now we are together.

A shiver went through him. This was the *thing* that had feasted on an entire world of magicians. And now, somehow, Holland had woken it.

Another spasm of pain, and he felt one knee threaten to buckle.

You live because of me. But you are still dying.

Holland's vision slid in and out of focus. He swallowed, and tasted blood. "What happened to this world?" he asked.

The statue looked at him levelly. *It died.*

"Did you kill it?" Holland had always assumed that the Black London plague was something vast and un-fightable, that it was born from weakness and greed and hunger. It had never occurred to him that it could be a thing, an entity. An *oshoc*.

It died, repeated the shadow. *As all things do.*

"*How*?" demanded Holland. "*How* did it die?"

I . . . did not know, it said, *that humans were such fragile things. I have learned . . . how to be more careful. But . . .*

But it was too late, thought Holland. *There was no one left.*

I saved you, it said again, as if making a point.

"What do you want?"

To make a deal. The invisible wind around Holland picked up, and the statue of Osaron seemed to lean forward. *What do you want, Antari?*

He tried to steel his mind against the question, but answers poured through like smoke. To live. To be free. And then he thought of his world, starving for power, for life. Thought of it dying—not like this place, but slowly, painfully.

What do you want, Holland?

He wanted to save his world. Behind his eyes, the image began to change as London—*his* London—came back to life. He saw himself on the throne, staring up through a roofless palace at a bright blue sky, the warmth of the sun against his skin, and—

"No," he snapped, digging his hand into his wounded shoulder, the pain shocking him out of the vision. It was a trick, a trap.

All things come with a cost, said Osaron. *That is the nature of the world. Give and take. You can stay here and die for nothing while your world dies, too. Or you can save it. The choice is yours.*

"What do *you* want?" asked Holland.

To live, said the shadow. *I can save your life. I can save your world. It is a simple deal, Antari. My power for your body.*

"And whose mind?" challenged Holland. "Whose *will*?"

Ours, purred the king.

Holland's chest ached. Another binding. Would he never be free?

He closed his eyes, and he was back on that throne, gazing up at that wondrous sky.

Well, asked the shadow king. *Do we have a deal?*

FIVE

ROYAL
WELCOME

I

The Arnesian Sea.

"Dammit, Bard, you're going to set the cat on fire."

Lila's head snapped up. She was perched on the edge of a chair in Alucard's cabin, holding a flame between her palms. Her attention must have slipped, because she'd lowered her hands without thinking, letting the fire between them sink toward the floor, and Esa, who'd been sitting there watching with feline intensity.

She sucked in a breath and brought her palms together quickly, extinguishing the flame in time to spare the tip of Esa's fluffy white tail.

"Sorry," she muttered, slouching back in the chair. "Must have gotten bored."

In truth, Lila was exhausted. She had slept even less than usual since Alucard's announcement, spending every spare moment practicing everything he'd taught her, and a few things he hadn't. And when she actually *tried* to sleep, her thoughts invariably turned to London. And the tournament. And Kell.

"Must have," grumbled Alucard, hoisting Esa up under his arm and depositing her safely on his desk.

"What do you expect?" She yawned. "I was holding that flame for ages."

"Forty-three minutes by the clock," he said. "And the whole *point* of the exercise is to keep your mind from drifting."

"Well then," she said, pouring herself a drink, "I suppose I'm just distracted."

"By my intoxicating presence, or our impending arrival?"

Lila swirled the wine and took a sip. It was rich and sweet, heavier than the usual sort he kept decanted on the table. "Have you ever fought a Veskan before?" she asked, dodging his question.

Alucard took up his own glass. "Behind a tavern, yes. In a tournament, no."

"What about a Faroan?"

"Well," he said, lowering himself into the opposite chair, "if their battle manner is anything like their bed manner . . ."

"You jest," she said, sitting forward, "but won't you have to fight both, in the *Essen Tasch*?"

"Assuming I don't lose in the first round, yes."

"Then what do you know about them?" she pressed. "Their skill? Their fighting style?"

The sapphire glittered as he raised his brow. "You're awfully inquisitive."

"I'm naturally curious," she countered. "And believe it or not, I'd rather not have to go looking for a new captain when this is over."

"Oh, don't worry, few competitors actually *die*." She gave him a hard look. "As for what I know? Well, let's see. Aside from Veskans growing like trees and Faroans taking my facial fashion choices to an extreme, they're both rather fascinating when it comes to magic."

Lila set the drink aside. "How so?"

"Well, we Arnesians have the Isle as a source. We believe that magic runs through the world the way that river runs through our capital, like a vein. Similarly, the Veskans have their mountains, which they claim bring them closer to their gods, each of which embodies an element. They are strong people, but they rely on physical force, believing that the more like mountains they are, the closer to power."

"And the Faroans? What is their source?"

Alucard sipped. "That's the thing. They don't have one. The Faroans believe instead that magic is everywhere. And in a sense they're right. Magic is technically in everything, but they claim they can tap into the heart of the world simply by walking on it. The Faroans consider themselves a blessed race. A bit on the arrogant side, but they're *powerful*. Perhaps they *have* found a way to make themselves into vessels. Or perhaps they use those jewels to bind magic to them." His voice colored with distaste when he said this, and Lila remembered Kell telling her about White Londoners, the way they used tattoos to bind power, and the way Red Londoners saw the practice as disgraceful. "Or maybe it's all for show."

"It doesn't bother you, that everyone believes different things?"

"Why should it?" he asked. "We all believe the same thing really, we simply give it different names. Hardly a crime."

Lila snorted. If only people in her world took such a forgiving stance. "The *Essen Tasch* is itself a kind of lesson," continued Alucard, "that it doesn't matter what you call magic, so long as you can believe."

"Do you really think you can win the tournament?" she asked.

He scoffed. "Probably not."

"Then why bother?"

"Because fighting's half the fun," he said, and then, reading her skepticism, "don't pretend that's a concept lost on you, Bard. I've seen the way you lunge into trouble."

"It's not that. . . ."

And it wasn't. She was just trying to picture Alucard in a magical duel. It was hard, because Lila had never seen the captain *fight*. Sure, she'd seen him hold a sword and make grand gestures with it, but he usually stood around looking pretty; before his display back in Sasenroche, she'd had no idea how good he was at magic. But the effortless way he'd performed at the Inroads . . . She couldn't help but wonder what he'd look like fighting. Would he be a torrent of energy, or a breeze, or would he be like Kell, who was somehow both at once?

"I'm surprised," said Alucard, "that you've never seen the tournament yourself."

"Who says I haven't?"

"You've been questioning my men for days. Did you think I wouldn't notice?"

Obviously, she thought.

"So I've never been." Lila shrugged, taking up her drink again. "Not everyone spends their winters in the city."

His smug expression faltered. "You could have simply asked *me.*"

"And endured your speculation, your answers that are questions, your constant probing?"

"I've been told my probing is quite pleasant." Lila snorted into her cup at this. "You cannot fault a captain for wanting to know about his crew."

"And you cannot fault a thief for keeping secrets out of reach."

"You have trouble with trust, Delilah Bard."

"Your powers of observation are astonishing." She smiled and finished her drink. Her lips tingled and her throat burned. It really was stronger than usual. Lila didn't usually drink much; she'd spent too many years needing every faculty she had to stay alive. But here, in Alucard Emery's cabin, she realized something: she wasn't afraid. She wasn't running. Sure, it was a balancing act every time they spoke, but she knew how to keep her footing.

Alucard offered her a lazy, inebriated smile. Drunk or sober, he was always smiling. So unlike Kell, who always frowned.

Alucard sighed, and closed his eyes, tipping his head back

against the plush chair. He had a nice face, soft and sharp at the same time. She had the strangest urge to reach out and trace the lines of it with her fingers.

Lila really should have killed him, back when they first met. Back before she could know him. Back before she could like him so much.

His eyes drifted open. "Silver and gold for your thoughts," he said softly, lifting his glass to his lips.

Esa brushed against Lila's chair, and she twined the cat's tail around her fingers. "I was just wishing I'd killed you months ago," she said with easy cheer, relishing the way Alucard nearly choked on his wine.

"Oh, Bard," he teased, "does that mean you've since developed a fondness for me?"

"Fondness is weakness," she said automatically.

At that, Alucard stopped smiling, and set his glass aside. He leaned forward and considered her for a long moment, and then he said, "I'm sorry." He sounded so . . . earnest, which made Lila instantly suspicious. Alucard was many things, but genuine wasn't usually one of them.

"For growing on me?" she asked.

He shook his head. "For whatever happened to you. For whoever hurt you so deeply that you see things like friends and fondness as weapons instead of shields." Lila felt the heat rising to her cheeks.

"It's kept me alive, hasn't it?"

"Perhaps. But life is pointless without pleasure."

Lila's bristled at that, and got to her feet. "Who says I don't feel pleasure? I feel pleasure when I win a bet. Pleasure when I conjure fire. Pleasure when—"

Alucard cut her off. Not with a word, but with a kiss. He closed the space between them in one single, fluid motion, and then one of his hands was on her arm, the other against the nape of her neck, and his mouth was on hers. Lila didn't pull away.

She told herself after that it was surprise that stopped her, but that might have been a lie. Maybe it was the wine. Maybe it was the warmth of the room. Maybe it was the fear that he was right about her, about pleasure, about life. Maybe, but in that moment all she knew was that Alucard was kissing her, and then she was kissing him back. And then, suddenly, his mouth was gone from hers, his smile floating in front of her face.

"Tell me," he whispered, "was that better than winning a bet?"

She was breathless. "You make a valid argument."

"I'd love to press the point," he said, "but first . . ." He cleared his throat, and looked down at the knife she had resting against the inside of his leg.

"Reflex," she said with a smirk, returning the weapon to its sheath.

Neither one of them moved. Their faces were so close, nose to nose, lip to lip, and lash to lash, and all she could see were his eyes, storm blue, and the faint laugh lines that creased their corners, the way Kell's creased the space between. Opposites. Alucard's thumb brushed her cheek, and then he kissed her again, and this time there was no attack in the gesture, no surprise, only slow precision. His mouth grazed hers, and as she leaned forward into it, he drew playfully back. Measure for measure, like a dance. He wanted her to want him, wanted to prove himself right—the logical part of her knew all that, but the logical part was getting lost beneath her pounding heart. Bodies were traitorous things, she realized, as Alucard's lips grazed her jaw, and began to trail down her throat, causing her to shiver.

He must have felt the tremor, because he smiled against her skin, that perfect, serpent-charming smile. Her back arched. His hand was at the base of her spine, pulling her against him as he teased his way along her collarbone. Heat blossomed across her body where his hands found her skin. Lila knotted her fingers in his hair and pulled his mouth back to hers. They were a tangle

of limbs and want, and she didn't think it was *better* than freedom or money or magic, but it was certainly close.

Alucard was the first to come up for air.

"Lila," he whispered against her, breath jagged.

"Yes," she said, the word half answer and half question.

Alucard's half-lidded eyes were dancing. "What are you running from?"

The words were like cold water, jarring her out of the moment.
She shoved him away. His chair caught him behind the knees
and he tumbled gracefully into it with something half laugh,
half sigh.

"You are a *bastard*," she snapped, blushing fiercely.

He tilted his head lazily. "Without question."

"All that, whatever *that* was"—she waved her hand—"just so
I'd tell you the truth."

"I wouldn't say that. I'm more than capable of multitasking."

Lila took up her wine glass and threw it at him. Both wine
and cup hurtled through the air, but before they reached his
head they just . . . stopped. The glass hung in the air between
them, beads of purple wine floating, as if weightless.

"That," he said, reaching out to pluck the goblet from the air,
"is a *very* expensive vintage."

The fingers of his other hand made a swirling motion, and the
wine became a ribbon, spilling back into his glass. He smiled.
And so did Lila, just before she snatched the bottle from the
table and hurled it into the fire. This time Alucard wasn't fast
enough, and the hearth crackled and flared as it devoured the
wine.

Alucard let out an exasperated sound, but Lila was already
storming out, and the captain had enough sense not to follow.

II

Red London.

The bells were ringing, and Rhy was late.

He could hear the distant sounds of music and laughter, the clatter of carriages and dancing. People were waiting for him. They'd had a fight, he and his father, about how he didn't take things seriously. How he *never* took things seriously. How could he be king when he couldn't even be bothered to arrive on time?

The bells stopped ringing and Rhy cursed, trying to fasten his tunic. He kept fumbling with the top button.

"Where *is* he?" he could hear his father grumbling.

The button slipped again, and Rhy groaned and crossed to his mirror, but when he stepped in front of it, he froze.

The world got quiet in his ears.

He stared into the glass, but *Kell* stared back.

His brother's eyes were wide with alarm. Rhy's room was reflected behind him, but Kell acted as though he were trapped in a box, his chest rising and falling with panic.

Rhy reached out, but a horrible chill went through him when he touched the glass. He wrenched back.

"Kell," he said. "Can you hear me?"

Kell's lips moved, and Rhy thought for an instant that the

impossible reflection was just repeating his own words, but the shapes Kell's mouth made were different.

Kell pressed his hands against the mirror, and raised his voice, and a single muffled word came through.

"Rhy . . ."

"Where are you?" demanded Rhy, as the room behind Kell began to darken and swirl with shadows, the chamber dissolving into black. *"What's going on?"*

And then, on the other side of the glass, Kell clutched his chest and *screamed.*

A horrible, gut-wrenching sound that tore through the room and raised every hair on Rhy's body.

He shouted Kell's name and beat his fists against the mirror, trying to break the spell, or the glass, trying to reach his brother, but the surface didn't even crack. Rhy didn't know what was wrong. He couldn't feel Kell's pain. He couldn't feel *anything.*

Beyond the glass, Kell let out another sobbing cry, and doubled over before crumpling to his knees.

And then Rhy saw the blood. Kell was pressing his hands to his chest, and Rhy watched, horrified and helpless, as blood poured between his brother's fingers. So much. Too much. A life's worth. *No, no, no,* he thought, *not this.*

He looked down and saw the knife buried between his ribs, his own fingers curled around the golden hilt.

Rhy gasped and tried to pull the blade free, but it was stuck.

Beyond the glass, Kell coughed blood.

"Hold on," cried Rhy.

Kell was kneeling in a pool of red. A room. A sea. So much red. His hands fell away.

"Hold on," pleaded Rhy, pulling at the knife with all his strength. It didn't move.

Kell's head slumped forward.

"Hold on."

His body crumpled.

The knife came free.

⚘

Rhy wrenched forward out of sleep.

His heart was pounding, and the sheets were soaked with sweat. He pulled a pillow into his lap and buried his face in it, dragging in ragged breaths as he waited for his body to realize the dream wasn't real. Sweat ran down his cheek. His muscles twitched. His breath hitched, and he looked up, hoping to find morning light spilling in through the balcony doors, but was met with darkness, tempered only by the Isle's pale red glow.

He bit back a sob of frustration.

A glass of water sat beside his bed, and he gulped it down with shaking fingers while he waited to see if his brother would come barging in, convinced the prince was under attack, the way he had those first few nights.

But when it came to nights and mornings and the dreams between, Rhy and Kell had quickly developed a silent under-standing. After a bad night, one would give the other a small, consoling look, but it seemed crucially important that nothing actually be *said* about the nightmares that plagued them both.

Rhy pressed his palm flat against his chest, lessening the pressure with the inhalation, increasing with the exhalation, just as Tieren had taught him to do years before, after he'd been taken by the Shadows. It wasn't the abduction that gave him nightmares in the months that followed, but the sight of Kell crouched over him, eyes wide and skin pale, the knife in his hand and the rivers of blood streaming from his severed veins.

It's all right, Rhy told himself now. *You're all right. Everything's all right.*

Feeling steadier, he threw off the sheets and stumbled up.

His hands itched to pour a drink, but he couldn't bear the

thought of going back to sleep. Besides, it was closer to dawn than dusk. Better to just wait it out.

Rhy pulled on a pair of silk trousers and a robe—the latter plush and heavy in a simple, comforting way—and threw open the balcony, letting the night's icy chill dispel any dregs of sleep.

Below, the floating arenas were nothing more than shadows blotting out the river's glow. The city was speckled here and there with lights, but his attention drifted to the docks, where even now ships were sailing sleepily into port.

Rhy squinted, straining to pick out one ship in particular.

A dark-wood vessel with silver trim and blue-black sails.

But there was no sign of the *Night Spire*.

Not yet.

III

The Arnesian Sea.

Lila stormed across the *Spire*'s deck, glaring at anyone who chanced to look her way. She'd left her coat in Alucard's cabin, and the night wind hit her like a wall, piercing sleeves and skin. It bit and burned, but Lila didn't turn back; instead she welcomed the sobering shock of the cold air as she crossed to the ship's stern, and slumped against the rail.

Bastard, she grumbled at the water below.

She was used to being the thief, not the mark. And she'd nearly fallen for it, focused on the hand in front of her face while the other tried to pick her pocket. She gripped the rail with bare fingers and stared out at the open sea, furious: at Alucard, at herself, at this stupid ship, the edges of which were so fixed, and so small.

What are you running from? he'd asked.

Nothing.

Everything.

Us. This.

Magic.

The truth was, there had been an instant, staring into the hissing fire, when it had stared back, hot and fierce, and listening, and she knew she could have made it grow, could have torched the whole cabin in a moment's temper, burned the ship, and herself and everyone on it.

She was starting to understand that magic wasn't just something to be accessed, tapped into when needed. It was always there, ready and waiting. And that frightened her. Almost as much as the way Alucard had been able to play her, toy with her, twist her distraction to his advantage. She'd let her guard slip, a mistake she wouldn't make again.

Bastard.

The cold air helped cool the fire in her cheeks, but the energy still surged beneath her skin. She glared at the sea, and imagined reaching out and shoving the water with all her strength. Like a child in a bath.

She didn't bother summoning any poems, didn't expect the desire to actually take shape, but a second later she felt energy flood through her, and the water bucked and surged, the ship tilting violently on a sudden wave.

Cries of concern went up across the *Spire* as the men tried to figure out what had happened, and Lila smirked viciously, hoping that down below she'd toppled a few more of Alucard's finest wines. And then it hit her, what she'd done. She'd moved the ocean—or at least a ship-sized piece of it. She touched a hand to her nose, expecting to find blood, but there was none. She was fine. Unharmed. She let out a small, dazed chuckle.

What are you?

Lila shivered, the cold having finally reached her bones. She was suddenly tired, and she didn't know if it was the backlash of expended magic or simply her frustration burning out.

What was it Barron used to say?

Something about tempers and candles and powder kegs.

The fact that she couldn't remember the exact words hit her like a dull blow to the chest. Barron was one of her only tethers, and he was gone now. And what right did she have to mourn? She'd wanted to be free of him, hadn't she? And this was why. People could only hurt you if you cared enough to let them.

Lila was about to turn away from the rail when she heard a muffled sniff, and realized she wasn't alone. Of course, no one was ever truly alone, not on a ship, but someone was standing against the rigging nearby, holding their breath. She squinted at the shadows, and then, when the figure looked more willing to collapse than step forward, she snapped her fingers and summoned a small, vibrant flame—a gesture managed with nonchalance, even though she'd been practicing it for weeks.

The light, which struggled against the sea breeze, illuminated the scarecrow shape of Lenos, Alucard's second mate. He squeaked, and she sighed and extinguished the fire, plunging them both back into comfortable darkness.

"Lenos," she said, trying to sound friendly. Had he seen what she'd done with the ship and the sea? The look on his face was one of caution, if not outright fear, but that was his usual expression around her. After all, he'd been the one to start the rumor that she was the Sarows, haunting the *Spire*.

The man stepped forward, and she saw that he was holding something out for her. His coat.

A refusal rose to her lips, automatic, but then good sense made her reach out and take it. She'd survived magic doors and evil queens; she'd be damned if she died of catching cold.

He let go of the coat the instant her fingers found purchase, as if afraid of being burned, and she shrugged it on, the lining still warm from Lenos's body. She turned up the collar and shoved her hands into the pockets, flexing her fingers for warmth.

"Are you afraid of me?" she asked in Arnesian.

"A little," he admitted, looking away.

"Because you don't trust me?"

He shook his head. "Not that," he mumbled. "You're just different from us. . . ."

She gave him a crooked smile. "So I've been told."

"Not cause you're a, well, you know, a girl. S'not that."

"Because I'm the Sarows, then? You really think that?"

He shrugged. "S'not that, not exactly. But you're *aven*."

Lila frowned. The word he used was *blessed*. But Lila had learned that there was no English equivalent. In Arnesian *blessed* wasn't always a good thing. Some said it meant *chosen*. Others said *favored*. But some said *cursed*. *Other*. *Apart*.

"*Aven* can be a good thing, too," she said, "so long as they're on your side."

"Are you on our side?" he asked quietly.

Lila was on her own side. But she supposed she was on the *Spire*'s side, too. "Sure."

He wrapped his arms around himself and turned his attention past her to the water. A fog was rolling in, and as he stared intently at it, Lila wondered what he saw in the mist.

"I grew up in this little place called Casta," he said. "On the southern cliffs. Castans think that sometimes magic chooses people."

"Like Master Kell," she said, adding, "the black-eyed prince."

Lenos nodded. "Yes, magic chose Master Kell. But what he is—*Antari*—that's only one kind of *aven*. Maybe the strongest, but it depends on your definition of strong. The priests are another. Some people think that *they're* the strongest, because they have just enough of every element to use them all in balance, so they can heal and grow and make life. There used to be all kinds of *aven*. Ones who could master all the elements. Ones who could only master one, but were so powerful, they could change the tides, or the wind, or the seasons. Ones who could hear what magic had to say. *Aven* isn't just one thing, because magic isn't just one thing. It's everything, old and new and always changing. The Castans think that when someone *aven* appears, it's for a reason. It's because the magic is trying to tell us something. . . ."

He trailed off. Lila stared at him. It was the most Lenos had ever

said to her. The most she'd ever heard him say to *anyone,* for
that matter.

"So you think I'm here for a reason?" she asked.

Lenos rocked from heel to toe. "We're all here for a reason,
Bard. Some reasons are just bigger than others. So I guess I'm
not scared of who you are, or even what you are. I'm scared of
why you are."

He shivered and turned away.

"Wait," she said, shrugging out of his coat. "Here."

He reached for it, and to Lila's relief, when their hands nearly
brushed, he didn't jerk back. She watched the man retreat across
the dock, then rolled her neck and made her way below.

She found her own coat hanging on her cabin door, along
with an unopened bottle of purple wine, and a note that read
Solase.

Sorry.

Lila sighed and took up the bottle, her thoughts churning and
her body aching for sleep.

And then she heard the call go up overhead.

"*Hals!*" shouted a voice from the deck above.

Land.

IV

The bells rang out a dozen times, and then a dozen more. They went on and on until Kell lost count, far past the hours in a day, a week, a month.

The persistent sound could only mean one thing: the royals had arrived.

Kell stood on his balcony and watched them come. It had been six years since London last played host to the *Essen Tasch,* but he still remembered watching the procession of ships and people, trying to imagine where they'd come from, what they'd seen. He couldn't go to the world, but on these rare occasions, it seemed to come to him.

Now, as he watched the ships drift up the Isle (as far as Rhy's floating stadiums would allow), he found himself wondering which one Lila would choose for herself. There were a handful of smaller, private crafts, but most were massive vessels, luxury boats designed to transport wealthy merchants and nobles from Faro and Vesk to the festivities in the Arnesian capital. All ships bore a mark of origin, on either sail or side, the painted symbol of their crown. That, along with a scroll of approval, would grant them access to the docks for the length of the *Essen Tasch.*

Would Lila prefer an elegant silver wood ship, like the one bearing the Faroan mark? Or something bolder, like the vibrantly painted Veskan vessel now approaching? Or a proud

Arnesian craft, with dark polished wood and crisp sails? Come to think of it, did Lila even know *how* to sail? Probably not, but if anyone could make the strange seem ordinary, the impossible look easy, it was Delilah Bard.

"What are you smirking at?" asked Rhy, appearing beside him.

"Your stadiums are making a mess of the river."

"Nonsense," said Rhy. "I've had temporary docks erected on the northern and southern banks on both sides of the city. There's plenty of room."

Kell nodded at the Isle. "Tell that to our guests."

Below, the other vessels had parted to make way for the Veskan fleet as it came up the river, stopping only when it reached the barricade. The Veskan royal barge, a splendid rig made of redwood with dark sails bearing the royal emblem of the crow in flight against a white moon, was flanked by two military ships.

Minutes later the Faroans' imperial vessel followed, its ships all skeletal and silver-white, the crest of the black tree scorched into their sails.

"We should get going," said the prince. "We'll have to be there to welcome them."

"*We*?" echoed Kell, even though the king had already made it clear that his presence was required. Not because Kell was family, he thought bitterly, but because he was *aven*. A symbol of Arnesian power.

"They'll want to see you," the king had said, and Kell had understood. When Maxim said *you* he didn't mean Kell the *person*. He meant Kell the *Antari*. He bristled. Why did he feel like a trophy? Or worse, a trinket—

"Stop that," chided Rhy.

"Stop what?"

"Whatever's going through your head that has you frowning even more than usual. You'll give us both wrinkles." Kell sighed.

"Come," pressed Rhy. "There's no way I'm facing them on my own."

"Which one are you afraid of? Lord Sol-in-Ar?"

"Cora."

"The Veskan princess?" Kell laughed. "She's just a child."

"She *was* just a child—and a nightmarish one at that—but I've heard she's grown into something truly fearsome."

Kell shook his head. "Come on, then," he said, slinging his arm around the prince's shoulder. "I'll defend you."

"My hero."

The Red Palace had five halls: the Grand, an extravagant three-story ballroom made of polished wood and sculpted crystal; the Gold, a sprawling reception hall, all stone and precious metal; the Jewel, seated at the palace heart and made entirely of glass; the Sky on the roof, its mosaic floor glittering under the sun and stars; and the Rose. The last of these, positioned near the front of the palace and accessed through its own hall and doors, possessed a stately elegance. It had been built in a wing of the palace with nothing overhead, and light shone through windows set into the ceiling. The walls and floor were royal marble, pale stone threaded with garnet and gold, crafted by mineral mages for the crown's use alone. In place of columns, bouquets of flowers in massive urns cut parallel lines through the chamber. Between these columns, a gold runner ran from doorway to dais and throne.

The Rose Hall was where the crown held court with its people, and where it intended to greet its neighboring royals.

If they ever showed up.

Kell and Rhy stood on either side of the thrones, Rhy leaning against his father's chair, Kell at attention beside the queen's.

Master Tieren stood at the foot of the dais, but he wouldn't meet Kell's gaze. Was it his imagination, or had the *Aven Essen* been avoiding him? The royal guards stood statuesque in their gleaming armor, while a select assembly of *ostra* and *vestra* milled about, having drifted into clusters to chat. It had been more than an hour since the royal ships had docked and an escort had been sent to accompany them to the palace. Sparkling wine sat on trays, going flat with the wait.

Rhy shifted from foot to foot, clearly tense. This was, after all, his first time at the helm of a royal affair, and while he'd always been one for details, they usually centered around his clothing, or his hair. The *Essen Tasch* was on another scale entirely. Kell watched him fidget with the gleaming gold seal of the Maresh—a chalice and rising sun—over his heart. He'd produced a second one, for Kell, which he had reluctantly pinned on the breast of his red coat.

King Maxim fiddled with a coin, something Kell only saw him do when he couldn't sit still. Like his father before him, Maxim Maresh was a metalworker, a strong magician in his own right, though he had little need of it now. Still, Kell had heard the stories of Maxim's youth, tales of the "steel prince" who forged armies and melted hearts, and he knew that even now the king traveled twice a year to the borders to stoke the fires of his men.

"I hope nothing has happened to our guests," said King Maxim.

"Perhaps they got lost," mused Rhy.

"We could only be so lucky," murmured Kell.

Queen Emira shot them both a look, and Kell almost laughed. It was such simple, motherly scorn.

At last, the trumpets sounded, and the doors swung open.

"Finally," muttered Rhy.

"Prince Col and Princess Cora," announced a servant, his voice echoing through the hall, "of the House Taskon, ruling family of Vesk."

The Taskon siblings entered, flanked by a dozen attendants.

They were striking, dressed loosely in green and silver, with elegant cloaks trailing behind. Col was eighteen now, Cora two years his junior.

"Your Majesties," said Prince Col, a burly youth, in heavily accented Arnesian.

"We are welcomed to your city," added Princess Cora with a curtsy and a cherubic smile.

Kell shot Rhy a look that said, *Honestly? This is the girl you're so afraid of?*

Rhy shot him one back that said, *You should be, too.*

Kell gave Princess Cora another, more appraising glance. The princess hardly looked strong enough to hold a wine flute. Her cascades of honey-blond hair were done up in an elaborate braid that circled her head like a crown, woven through with emeralds.

She was slight for a Veskan—tall, yes, but narrow-waisted, willowy in a way that would have better suited the Arnesian court. Rhy had been allowed to accompany his mother to the *Essen Tasch* in Vesk three years before, so he'd seen her grow. But Kell, confined to the city, had only seen the tournament on years when Arnes was called to host. When the Games were held there six years ago, Prince Col had come, along with one of his other brothers.

The last time Kell had seen *Cora,* twelve years ago, she'd been a small child.

Now her pale blue eyes traveled up, landed on his two-toned gaze, and stuck. He was so accustomed to people avoiding his eyes, their own glancing off, finding safer ground, that the intensity caught him off guard, and he fought the sudden urge to look away.

Meanwhile an attendant carried a large object, shrouded in heavy green cloth, to the throne dais, and set it down on the step. Whisking the cloth away with a dramatic flair, the attendant revealed a bird inside a cage—not a multicolored mimic, or a

songbird, both favored by the Arnesian court, but something
more . . . *predatory*. It was massive and silvery grey, save for its
head, which had a plume and collar of black. Its beak looked
razor sharp.

"A thank you," announced Prince Col, "for inviting us into
your home." Col shared Cora's coloring, but nothing else. Where
she was tall, he was taller. Where she was narrow, he was built
like an ox. A handsome one, but still, there was something
bullish about his attitude and expression.

"Gratitude," said the king, nodding to Master Tieren, who
strode forward and lifted the cage. It would go to the sanctuary, Kell supposed, or be set free. A palace was no place for wild
animals.

Kell tracked the exchange out of the corner of his eye, his
attention still leveled on the princess, whose gaze was still
leveled on him, too, as if transfixed by his black eye. She
looked like the kind of girl who would point to something—or
some*one*—and say, "I want one of those." The thought was almost amusing until he remembered Astrid's words—*I would
own you, flower boy*—and then the humor turned cold. Kell
took a slight, almost imperceptible step back.

"Our home shall be yours," King Maxim was saying. It all felt
like a script.

"And if the gods favor us," said Prince Col with a grin, "so
shall your tournament."

Rhy bristled, but the king simply laughed. "We shall see
about that," he said with a hearty smile that Kell knew was
false. The king didn't care for Prince Col, or any of the Veskan
royal family for that matter. But the real danger lay with Faro.
With Lord Sol-in-Ar.

As if on cue, the trumpets sounded again, and the Veskan
entourage took up their glasses of wine and stepped aside.

"Lord Sol-in-Ar, Regent of Faro," announced the attendant
as the doors opened.

Unlike the Veskans, whose entourage surrounded them, Sol-in-Ar strode in at the front, his men filing behind him in formation. They were all dressed in Faroan style, a single piece of fabric intricately folded around them, the tail end cast back over one shoulder like a cape. His men all wore rich purple, accented in black and white, while Sol-in-Ar wore white, the very edges of the fabric trimmed in indigo.

Like all ranking Faroans, he was clean-shaven, affording a full view of the beads set into his face, but unlike most, who favored glass or precious gems, Lord Sol-in-Ar's ornamentation appeared to be white gold, diamond-shaped slivers that traced curved paths from temples to throat. His black hair was trimmed short, and a single larger teardrop of white gold stood out against his forehead, just above his brows, marking him as royal.

"How do they choose?" Rhy had wondered aloud, years before, holding a ruby to his forehead. "I mean, Father says the *number* of gems is a social signifier, but apparently the color is a mystery. I doubt it's arbitrary—if it were the Veskans, maybe, but nothing about the Faroans seems arbitrary—which means the colors must mean *something*."

"Does it matter?" Kell had asked wearily.

"Of course it matters," snapped Rhy. "It's like knowing there's a language you don't speak, and having no one willing to teach it to you."

"Maybe it's private."

Rhy tipped his head and furrowed his brow to keep the ruby from falling. "How do I look?"

Kell had snorted. "Ridiculous."

But there was nothing ridiculous about Lord Sol-in-Ar. He was tall—several inches taller than the men of his guard—with a chiseled jaw and rigid gate. His skin was the color of charcoal, his eyes pale green, and sharp as cut glass. Older brother to the king of Faro, commander of the Faroan fleet, responsible for the unification of the once dispersed territories, and considered to be the majority of the actual thinking behind the throne.

And unable to rule, for lack of magic. He more than made up for it with his military prowess and keen eye for order, but Kell knew the fact made Rhy uneasy.

"Welcome, Lord Sol-in-Ar," said King Maxim.

The Faroan regent nodded, but did not smile. "Your city shines," he said simply. His accent was heavy and smooth, like a river stone. He flicked his hand, and two attendants carried forward a pair of potted saplings, their bark an inky black. The same trees that marked the Faroan royal seal, just as the bird was the symbol of Vesk. Kell had heard of the Faroan birch, rare trees said to have medicinal—even magical—properties.

"A gift," he said smoothly. "So that good things may grow."

The king and queen bowed their heads in thanks, and Lord Sol-in-Ar's gaze swept across the dais, passing Rhy and landing for only a moment on Kell before he bowed and stepped back. With that, the king and queen descended their thrones, taking up glasses of sparkling wine as they did. The rest of the room moved to echo the motion, and Kell sighed.

Standing there on display was painful enough.

Now came the truly unfortunate task of socializing.

Rhy was clearly steeling himself against the princess, who had apparently spent their last encounter trying to steal kisses and weave flowers in his hair. But Rhy's worrying turned out to be for nothing—she had her sights set on other prey. *Kings*, swore Kell in his head, gripping his wine flute as she approached.

"Prince Kell," she said, flashing a childlike grin. He didn't bother to point out that she should address him as *Master*, not *Prince*. "You will dance with me, at the evening balls."

He wasn't sure if her Arnesian was simply limited, or if she meant to be so direct. But Rhy shot him a look that said he'd spent months preparing for this tournament, that it was a display of politics and diplomacy, that they would all be making sacrifices, and that he'd rather stab himself than let Kell put the empire's peace in jeopardy by denying the princess a dance.

Kell managed a smile, and bowed. "Of course, Your Highness," he answered, adding in Veskan, *"Gradaich an'ach."*

It is my pleasure.

Her smile magnified as she bobbed away to one of her attendants.

Rhy leaned over. "Looks like I'm not the one who needs protecting after all. You know . . ." He sipped his wine. "It would be an interesting match. . . ."

Kell kept his smile fixed. "I will stab you with this pin."

"You would suffer."

"It would be worth—" He was cut off by the approach of Lord Sol-in-Ar.

"Prince Rhy," said the regent, nodding his head. Rhy straightened, and then bowed deeply.

"Lord Sol-in-Ar," he said. *"Hasanal rasnavoras ahas."*

Your presence honors our kingdom.

The regent's eyes widened in pleased surprise. *"Amun shahar,"* he said before shifting back to Arnesian. "Your Faroan is excellent."

The prince blushed. He had always had an ear for languages. Kell knew a fair amount of Faroan, too, thanks to Rhy preferring to have someone to practice on, but he said nothing.

"You make the effort to learn our tongue," said Rhy. "It is only respectful to reciprocate." And then, with a disarming smile, he added, "Besides, I've always found the Faroan language to be beautiful."

Sol-in-Ar nodded, his gaze shifting toward Kell.

"And you," said the regent. "You must be the Arnesian *Antari.*"

Kell bowed his head, but when he looked up, Sol-in-Ar was still examining him, head to toe, as if the mark of his magic were drawn not only in his eye, but across every inch of his being.

When at last his attention settled on Kell's face, he frowned faintly, the drop of metal on his forehead glinting.

"*Namunast,*" he murmured. *Fascinating.*

The moment Sol-in-Ar was gone, Kell finished his wine in a single gulp, and then retreated through the open doors of the Rose Hall before anyone could stop him.

He'd had more than enough royals for one day.

V

The river was turning red.

When the *Night Spire* first hit the mouth of the Isle, Lila could make out only the slightest tint to the water, and that only visible at night. Now, with the city fast approaching, the water glowed like a ruby lit from within, the red light visible even at midday. It was like a beacon, leading them into London.

At first, she'd thought the river's light was steady, even, but she noticed now—after months of training herself to see and feel and think about magic as a living thing—that it pulsed beneath the surface, like lightning behind layers of clouds.

She leaned on the rail and turned the shard of pale stone between her fingers. She'd only had it since facing the Dane twins in White London, but the edges were starting to wear smooth. She willed her hands to still, but there was too much nervous energy, and nowhere for it to go.

"We'll be there by dusk," said Alucard beside her. Lila's pulse fluttered. "If there's anything you want to tell me about your departure from the city, now's the time. Well, actually, any time over the last four months would have been the time, now is really up against a wall, but—"

"Don't start," she grumbled, tucking the stone shard back into her pocket.

"We all have demons, Bard. But if yours are waiting there—"

"My demons are all dead."

"Then I envy you." Silence fell between them. "You're still mad at me."

She straightened. "You tried to seduce me, for *information*."

"You can't hold that against me forever."

"It was *last night*."

"Well I was running out of options, and I figured it was worth a shot."

Lila rolled her eyes. "You really know how to make a girl feel special."

"I thought I was in trouble precisely for making you feel special."

Lila huffed, blowing the hair out of her eyes. She returned to watching the river, and was surprised when Alucard stayed, leaning his elbows on the rail beside her.

"Are *you* excited to go back?" she asked.

"I quite like London," he said. Lila waited for him to go on, but he didn't. Instead, he began to rub his wrists.

"You do that," said Lila, nodding at his hands, "whenever you're thinking."

He stopped. "Good thing I don't make a habit of deep thought." Elbows still resting on the rail, he turned his hands palm up, the cuffs of his tunic riding up so Lila could see the marks across his wrists. The first time she'd noticed them, she thought they were only shadows, but up close she realized they were *scars*.

He folded his arms in and drew a flask from inside his coat. It was made of glass, the pale-pink liquid sloshing inside. Alucard had never seemed all that fond of sobriety, but the closer they got to the city, the more he drank.

"I'll be sober again by the time we dock," he said, reading her look. His free hand drifted toward his wrist again.

"It's a tell," she said. "Your wrists. That's why I brought it up. People should always know their tells."

"And what is yours, Bard?" he asked, offering her the flask.

Lila took it but didn't drink. Instead she cocked her head. "You tell me."

Alucard twisted toward her and squinted, as if he could see the answer in the air around her. His blue eyes widened in mock revelation. "You tuck your hair behind your ear," he said. "But only on the right side. Whenever you're nervous. I'm guessing it's to keep yourself from fidgeting."

Lila gave him a grudging smile. "You got the gesture, but missed the motive."

"Enlighten me."

"People have a tendency to hide behind their features when they're nervous," she said. "I tuck my hair behind my ear to show my opponent—mark, adversary, what have you—that I'm not hiding. I look them in the eyes, and I let them look *me* in the eyes."

Alucard raised a brow at that. "Well, *eye*."

The flask shattered in Lila's hand. She hissed, first in shock, and then in pain as the liquor burned her palm. She dropped the flask and it fell in pieces to the deck.

"What did you say?" she whispered.

Alucard ignored the question. He tutted and flicked his wrist, the broken shards rising into the air above his fingers. Lila brought her bloody palm to her chest, but Alucard held out his other hand.

"Let me," he said, taking her wrist and turning it over gently to expose the shallow cuts. Glass glittered in her palm, but as his lips moved, the flecks and fragments rose to join the larger pieces in the air. With a twitch of his fingers, he brushed the shards away, and they fell soundless over the side of the boat.

"Alucard," she growled. "What did you say?"

Her hand was still resting upturned in his. "Your tell," he said, inspecting the cuts. "It's slight. You try to pass it off by cocking your head, steadying your gaze, but you're really doing it to make up for the gap in sight." He drew a black swatch of fabric from his sleeve, and began to wrap her hand. She let him. "And the hair," he added, tying the makeshift bandage in a knot. "You only tuck it behind your ear on the *right* side, to mislead people." He let go of her hand. "It's so subtle, I doubt many notice."

"You did," she muttered.

Alucard reached out, tipped her chin up with his knuckle, and looked her in the eyes. Eye.

"I'm extraordinarily perceptive," he said.

Lila clenched her fists, focusing on the pain that blossomed there.

"You're an incredible thief, Lila," he said, "especially con—"

"Don't you dare say *considering*," she snapped, pulling out of his grip. He respected her enough not to look away. "I am an incredible thief, Alucard. This," she said, gesturing to her eye, "is not a weakness. It hasn't been for a very long time. And even if it were, I more than make up for it."

Alucard smiled. A small, genuine smile. "We all have scars," he said, and before she could stop herself, she glanced at his wrists. "Yes," he said, catching the look, "even charming captains." He pushed up his cuffs again, revealing smooth, tan skin interrupted only by the silvered bands around both wrists. They were strangely uniform. In fact, they almost looked like—

"Manacles," he confirmed.

Lila frowned. "From what?"

Alucard shrugged. "A bad day." He took a step away, and leaned back against a stack of crates. "Do you know what Arnesians do to the pirates they catch?" he asked casually. "The ones who try to escape?"

Lila crossed her arms. "I thought you said you weren't a pirate."

"I'm not." He waved his hand. "Not anymore. But youth makes fools of us all. Let's just say I was in the wrong place at the wrong time on the wrong side."

"What do they do . . . ?" asked Lila, curious despite herself.

Alucard's gaze drifted toward the river. "The jailers use an efficient system of dissuasion. They keep all the prisoners in manacles, put them on before even hearing your plea. They're heavy things, fused together at the wrist, but not so bad, as irons go. But if you make too much of a fuss, or put up a fight, then they simply heat the metal up. Not too much. The first time it's really just a warning. But if it's your second or third offense, or if you're foolish enough to try to escape, it's much worse." Alucard's eyes had somehow gone sharp and empty at the same time, as if he were focusing, just on something else, something far away. His voice had a strangely even quality as he spoke. "It's a simple enough method. They take a metal bar from the fires, and touch it to the iron cuff until it gets hot. The worse the offense, the longer they hold the rod to the cuffs. Most of the time they stop when you start screaming, or when they see the skin begin to burn. . . ."

In Lila's mind, she saw Alucard Emery, not in his polished captain's coat, but bruised and beaten, his brown hair plastered to his face with sweat, hands bound as he tried to pull back from the heated iron. Tried to charm his way out of the mess. But it obviously hadn't worked, and she imagined the sound of him begging, the smell of charred flesh, the scream. . . .

"The trouble is," Alucard was saying, "that metal heats much faster than it cools, so the punishment doesn't end when they take away the rod."

Lila felt ill. "I'm sorry," she said, even though she hated those words, hated the pity that went with them.

"I'm not," he said, simply. "Every good captain needs his scars. Keeps the men in line."

He said it so casually, but she could see the strains of memory on his face. She had the strangest urge to reach out and touch his wrist, as if heat might still be rising from the skin.

Instead she asked, "Why did you become a pirate?"

He shot her that coy smile. "Well, it seemed like the best of several bad ideas."

"But it didn't work."

"How perceptive."

"Then how did you escape?"

The sapphire winked above his eye. "Who says I did?"

Just then, the call went through the crew.

"London!"

Lila twisted, and saw the city rising like a fire in the fading light.

Her heart raced, and Alucard stood up straight, the tunic sleeves sliding down over his wrists.

"Well then," he said, his rakish smile back in place. "It seems we have arrived."

VI

The *Night Spire* docked at dusk.

Lila helped tie off the lines and settle the ramps, her attention straying to the dozens of elegant ships that filled the Isle's banks. The Red London berths were a tangle of energy and people, chaos and magic, laughter and twilight. Despite the February chill, the city radiated warmth. In the distance, the royal palace rose like a second sun over the settling dark.

"Welcome back," said Alucard, brushing his shoulder against hers as he hauled a chest onto the dock. She started when she saw Esa sitting on top, purple eyes wide, tail flicking.

"Shouldn't she stay on the boat?" The cat's ear twitched, and Lila felt that whatever pleasant inclinations the cat was forming toward her, she'd just lost them.

"Don't be ridiculous," said Alucard. "The ship's no place for a cat." Lila was about to point out that the cat had been aboard the ship as long as she had when he added, "I believe in keeping my valuables with me."

Lila perked up. Were cats so precious here? Or rare? She hadn't ever seen another one, but in the little time she was ashore, she hadn't exactly been looking. "Oh yeah?"

"I don't like that look," Alucard said, twisting chest and cat away.

"What look?" asked Lila innocently.

"The look that says Esa might conveniently go missing if I tell you what she's worth." Lila snorted. "But if you must know, she's only priceless because I keep my heart inside her, so no one can steal it." He smiled when he said it, but Esa didn't even blink.

"Is that so?"

"In truth," he said, setting the chest onto a cart, "she was a gift."

"From who?" asked Lila before she could catch herself.

Alucard smirked. "Oh, are you suddenly ready to share? Shall we begin trading questions and answers?"

Lila rolled her eyes and went to help the men haul more chests ashore. A couple of hands would stay with the *Spire,* while the rest took up at an inn. The cart loaded, Alucard presented his papers to a guard in gleaming armor, and Lila let her gaze wander over the other ships. Some were intricate, others simple, but all were, in their way, impressive.

And then, two boats down, she saw a figure descend from an Arnesian rig. A *woman.* And not the kind Lila knew to frequent ships. She was dressed in trousers and a collarless coat, a sword slung on a belt at her waist.

The woman began to make her way down the dock toward the *Spire,* and there was something animal about the way she moved. *Prowled.* She was taller than Lila, taller than Alucard for that matter, with features as pointed as a fox's and a mane—there was no better word for it—of wild auburn hair, large chunks not braided exactly but twisted around themselves so she looked half lion and half snake. Perhaps Lila should have felt threatened, but she was too busy being awestruck.

"Now *there's* a captain not to cross," Alucard whispered in her ear.

"Alucard Emery," said the woman when she reached them. Her voice had a slight sea rasp, and her Arnesian was full of edges. "Haven't seen you on London land in quite a while. Here for the tournament, I assume."

"You know me, Jasta. Can't turn down the chance to make a fool of myself."

She chuckled, a sound like rusted bells. "Some things never change."

He flashed a mock frown. "Does that mean you won't be betting on me?"

"I'll see if I can spare a few coins," she said. And with that, Jasta continued on, weapons chiming like coins.

Alucard leaned on Lila. "Word of advice, Bard. Never challenge that one to a drinking contest. Or a sword fight. Or anything you might lose. Because you will."

But Lila was barely listening. She couldn't tear her gaze from Jasta as the woman stalked away down the docks, a handful of wolfish men falling in step behind her.

"I've never seen a female captain."

"Not many in Arnes proper, but it's a big world," said Alucard. "It's more common where she's from."

"And where's that?"

"Jasta? She's from Sonal. Eastern side of the empire. Up against the Veskan edge, which is why she looks . . ."

"Larger than life."

"Exactly. And don't you go looking for a new rig. If you'd pulled the stunt you did to get onto *her* ship, she would have cut your throat and dumped you overboard."

Lila smiled. "Sounds like my kind of captain."

❧

"Here we are," said Alucard when they reached the inn.

The name of the place was Is Vesnara Shast, which translated to *The Wandering Road*. What Lila didn't know, not until she saw Lenos's unease, was that the Arnesian word for *road—shast—* was the same as the word for *soul*. She found the alternate name a bit unsettling, and the inn's atmosphere did nothing to ease the feeling.

· It was a crooked old structure—she hadn't noticed, in her short time in Red London last fall, that most of the buildings felt new—that looked like boxes stacked rather haphazardly on top of each other. It actually reminded her a bit of her haunts back in Grey London. Old stones beginning to settle, floors beginning to slouch.

The main room was crammed with tables, each of which in turn was crammed with Arnesian sailors, and most appeared well in their cups, despite the fact it was barely sundown. A single hearth burned on the far wall, a wolfhound stretched in front, but the room was stuffy from bodies.

"Living the life of luxury, aren't we?" grumbled Stross.

"We've got beds," said Tav, ever the optimist.

"Are we sure about that?" asked Vasry.

"Did someone replace my hardened crew with a bunch of whining children?" chided Alucard. "Shall I go find you a teat to gnaw on, Stross?"

The first mate grumbled but said nothing more as the captain handed out the keys. Four men to a room. But despite the cramped quarters, and the fact that the inn looked like it was far exceeding capacity, Alucard had managed to snare a room of his own.

"Captain's privilege," he said.

As for Lila, she was bunked with Vasry, Tav, and Lenos.

The group dispersed, hauling their chests up to their chambers. The Wandering Road was, as the name suggested, wandering, a tangled mess of halls and stairs that seemed to defy several laws of nature at once. Lila wondered if there was some kind of spell on the inn, or if it was simply peculiar. It was the kind of place where you could easily get lost, and she could only imagine it got more confusing as the night and drink wore on. Alucard called it *eccentric*.

Her room had four bodies, but only two beds.

"This'll be cozy," said Tav.

"No," said Lila in decisive, if broken, Arnesian. "I don't share beds—"

"*Tac?*" teased Vasry, dropping his chest on the floor. "Surely we can work something ou—"

"—because I have a habit of stabbing people in my sleep," she finished coolly.

Vasry had the decency to pale a little.

"Bard can have a bed," said Tav. "I'll take the floor. And Vasry, what are the odds of you actually spending your nights here with us?"

Vasry batted his long, black lashes. "A point."

So far, Lenos had said nothing. Not when they got their key, not when they climbed the stairs. He hugged the wall, obviously unnerved to be sharing quarters with the Sarows. Tav was the most resilient, but if she played her cards right, she could probably have the room to herself by tomorrow.

It wasn't a bad room. It was roughly the same size as her cabin, which was roughly the same size as a closet, but when she looked out the narrow window, she could see the city, and the river, and the palace arcing over it.

And the truth was, it felt good to be back.

She pulled on her gloves, and a cap, and dug a parcel out of her chest before heading out. She closed the door just as Alucard stepped out of a room across the hall. Esa's white tail curled around his boot.

"Where are you off to?" he asked.

"Night Market."

He raised a sapphire-studded brow. "Barely back on London soil, and already off to spend your coins?"

"What can I say?" said Lila evenly. "I'm in need of a new dress."

Alucard snorted but didn't press the issue, and though he trailed her down to the stairs, he didn't follow her out.

For the first time in months, Lila was truly alone. She drew a breath and felt her chest loosen as she cast off Bard, the best thief aboard the *Night Spire,* and became simply a stranger in the thickening dark.

She passed several scrying boards advertising the *Essen Tasch,* white chalk dancing across the black surface as it spelled out details about the various ceremonies and celebrations. A couple of children hovered around the edges of a puddle, freezing and unfreezing it. A Veskan man lit a pipe with a snap of his fingers. A Faroan woman somehow changed the color of her scarf simply by running it through her fingers.

Wherever Lila looked, she saw signs of magic.

Out on the water, it was a strange enough sight—not as strange as it would have been in Grey London, of course—but here, it was everywhere. Lila had forgotten the way Red London glittered with it, and the more time she spent here, the more she realized that Kell really *didn't* belong. He didn't fit in with the clashes of color, the laughter and jostle and sparkle of magic. He was too understated.

This was a place for performers. And that suited Lila just fine.

It wasn't late, but winter darkness had settled over the city by the time she neared the Night Market. The stretch of stalls along the bank seemed to *glow,* lit not only by the usual lanterns and torches, but by pale spheres of light that followed the market-goers wherever they went. At first, it looked like they themselves were glowing, not head to toe, but from their core, as if their very life force had suddenly become visible. The effect was unsettling, hundreds of tiny lights burning against cloak fronts. But as she drew closer, she realized the light was coming from something in their hands.

"Palm fire?" asked a man at the mouth of the market, holding up a glass sphere filled with pale light. It was just warm enough to fog the air around its edges.

"How much?"

"Four lin."

It wasn't cheap, but her fingers were chilled, even with the gloves, and she was fascinated by the sphere, so she paid the man and took the orb, marveling at the soft, diffuse heat that spread through her hands and up her arms.

She cradled the palm fire, smiling despite herself. The market air still smelled of flowers, but also of burning wood, and cinnamon, and fruit. She'd been such an outsider last fall—she was still an outsider, of course, but now she knew enough to cover it. Jumbled letters that had meant nothing to her months before now began to form words. When the merchants called out their wares, she could glean their meaning, and when the music seemed to take shape on the air, as if by magic, she knew that was exactly what it was, and the thought didn't set her off balance. If anything, she'd felt off balance all her life, and now her feet were firmly planted.

Most people wandered from stall to stall, sampling mulled wine and skewered meat, fondling velvet-lined hoods and magical tokens, but Lila walked with her head up, humming to herself as she wove between the tents and stalls toward the other end of the market. There would be time to wander later, but right now, she had an errand.

Down the bank, the palace loomed like a low red moon. And there, sandwiched between two other tents at the far edge of the market, near the palace steps, she found the stall she was looking for.

The last time she'd been here, she hadn't been able to read the sign mounted above the entrance. Now she knew enough Arnesian to decipher it.

IS POSTRAN.

The Wardrobe.

Simple, but clever—just as in English, the word *postran* referred both to clothing and the place where it was kept.

Tiny bells had been threaded through the curtain of fabric that served as a door, and they rang softly as Lila pushed the cloth aside. Stepping into the stall was like crossing the threshold into a well-warmed house. Lanterns burned in the corners, emitting not only rosy light, but a glorious amount of heat. Lila scanned the tent. Once the back wall had been covered with faces, but now it was lined with winter things—hats, scarves, hoods, and a few accessories that seemed to merge all three.

A round woman, her brown hair wrestled into a braided bun, knelt before one of the tables, reaching for something beneath.

"*An esto,*" she called at the sound of the bells, then muttered quiet curses at whatever had escaped. "Aha!" she said at last, shoving a bauble back into her pocket before pushing to her feet. "*Solase,*" she said, brushing herself off as she turned. "*Kers . . .*" But then she trailed off, and burst into a smile.

It had been four months since Lila had stepped into Calla's tent to admire the masks along the wall. Four months since the merchant woman had given her a devil's face, and a coat, and a pair of boots, the beginnings of a new identity. A new life.

Four months, but Calla's eyes lit up instantly with recognition. "Lila," she said, stretching out the *i* into several *e*s.

"Calla," said Lila. "*As esher tan ves.*"

I hope you are well.

The woman smiled. "Your Arnesian," she said in English, "it is improving."

"Not fast enough," said Lila. "Your High Royal is impeccable as always."

"*Tac,*" she chided, smoothing the front of her dark apron.

Lila felt a peculiar warmth toward the woman, a fondness that should have made her nervous, but she couldn't bring herself to smother the feeling.

"You have been gone."

"At sea," answered Lila.

"You have docked along with half the world, it seems," said Calla, crossing to the front of her stall and fastening the curtain shut. "And just in time for the *Essen Tasch.*"

"It's not a coincidence."

"You come to watch, then," she said.

"My captain is competing," answered Lila.

Calla's eyes widened. "You sail with Alucard Emery?"

"You know of him?"

Calla shrugged. "Reputations, they are loud things." She waved her hand in the air, as if dismissing smoke. "What brings you to my stall? Time for a new coat? Green perhaps, or blue. Black is out of fashion this winter."

"I hardly care," said Lila. "You'll never part me from my coat."

Calla chuckled and ran a questing finger along Lila's sleeve. "It's held up well enough." And then she tutted. "Saints only know what you've been doing in it. Is that a *knife* tear?"

"I snagged it on a nail," she lied.

"*Tac,* Lila, my work is not so fragile."

"Well," she conceded, "it might have been a small knife."

Calla shook her head. "First storming castles, and now fighting on the seas. You are a very peculiar girl. *Anesh,* Master Kell is a peculiar boy, so what do I know."

Lila colored at the implication. "I have not forgotten my debt," she said. "I've come to pay it." With that, she produced a small wooden box. It was an elegant thing, inlaid with glass. Inside, the box was lined with black silk, and divided into basins. One held fire pearls, another a spool of silver wire, violet stone clasps and tiny gold feathers, delicate as down. Calla drew in a small, sharp breath at the treasure.

"*Mas aven,*" she whispered. And then she looked up. "Forgive me for asking, but I trust no one will come looking for these?" There was surprisingly little judgment in the question. Lila smiled.

"If you know of Alucard Emery, then you know he sails a royal ship. These were confiscated from a vessel on our waters. They were mine, and now they are yours."

Calla's short fingers trailed over the trinkets. And then she closed the lid, and tucked the box away. "They are too much," she said. "You will have a credit."

"I'm glad to hear that," said Lila. "Because I've come to ask a favor."

"It's not a favor if you've purchased and paid. What can I do?"

Lila reached into her coat and pulled out the black mask Calla had given her months before, the one that had solidified her nickname of Sarows. It was worn by salt air and months of use; cracks traced across the black leather, the horns had lost some of their upward thrust, and the cords that fastened it were in danger of breaking.

"What on earth have you been doing with this?" chided Calla, her lips pursing with something like motherly disapproval.

"Will you mend it?"

Calla shook her head. "Better to start fresh," she said, setting the mask aside.

"No," insisted Lila, reaching for it. "I'm fond of this one. Surely you can reinforce it."

"For what?" asked Calla archly. "Battle?"

Lila chewed her lip, and the merchant seemed to read the answer. "*Tac,* Lila, there is eccentricity, and there is *madness.* You cannot mean to compete in the *Essen Tasch.*"

"What?" teased Lila. "Is it *unladylike?*"

Calla sighed. "Lila, when we first met, I gave you your pick of all my wares, and you chose a devil's mask and a man's coat. This has nothing to do with what is proper, it's only that it's dangerous. *Anesh,* so are you." She said it as though it were a compliment, albeit a grudging one. "But you are not on the roster."

"Don't worry about that," said Lila with a smirk.

Calla started to protest, and then stopped herself and shook her head. "No, I do not want to know." She stared down at the devil's mask. "I should not help you with this."

"You don't have to," said Lila. "I could find someone else."

"You *could,*" said Calla, "but they wouldn't be as good."

"Nowhere *near* as good," insisted Lila.

Calla sighed. "*Stas reskon,*" she murmured. It was a phrase Lila had heard before. *Chasing danger.*

Lila smiled, thinking of Barron. "A friend once told me that if there was trouble to be found, I'd find it."

"We would be friends, then, your friend and I."

"I think you would," said Lila, her smile faltering. "But he is gone."

Calla set the mask aside. "Come back in two days. I will see what I can do."

"*Rensa tav,* Calla."

"Do not thank me yet, strange girl."

Lila turned to go, but hesitated when she reached the curtain. "I have only just returned," she said carefully, "so I've not had time to ask after the princes." She glanced back. "How are they?"

"Surely you can go and see for yourself."

"I can't," said Lila. "That is, I shouldn't. Kell and I, what we had . . . it was a temporary arrangement."

The woman gave her a look that said she didn't believe that, not as far as she could throw it. Lila assumed that was the end of things, so she turned again, but Calla said, "He came to me, after you were gone. Master Kell."

Lila's eyes widened. "What for?"

"To pay the debt for your clothes."

Her mood darkened. "I can pay my own debts," she snapped, "and Kell knows it."

Calla smiled. "That is what I told him. And he went away. But a week later, he came back, and made the same offer. He comes every week."

"Bastard," mumbled Lila, but the merchant shook her head.

"Don't you see?" said Calla. "He wasn't coming to pay your debt. He was coming to see if you'd returned to pay it yourself." Lila felt her face go hot. "I do not know why you two are circling each other like stars. It is not *my* cosmic dance. But I do know that you come asking after one another, when only a few strides and a handful of stairs divide you."

"It's complicated," said Lila.

"*As esta narash*," she murmured to herself, and Lila now knew enough to know what she said. *All things are.*

VII

Kell strolled the Night Market for the first time in weeks.

He'd taken to avoiding such public appearances, his moments of defiance too rare compared to those of self-consciousness. *Let them think what they want* was a thought that visited him with far less frequency and force than *They see you as a monster.*

But he was in need of air and Rhy, for once in his life, was too busy to entertain him. Which was fine. In the growing madness of the approaching games, Kell simply wanted to move, to wander, and so he found himself strolling through the market under the heavy cover of the crowds. The influx of strangers in the city afforded him shelter. There were so many foreigners here for the locals to look at, they were far less likely to notice him. Especially as Kell had taken Rhy's advice and traded his stark black high coat for a dusty blue one more in fashion, and pulled a winter hood up over his reddish hair.

Hastra walked beside him in common clothes. He hadn't tried to ditch his guard tonight, and in return, the young man had agreed to change his red and gold cloak and armor for something less conspicuous, even if the royal sword still hung sheathed at his side.

Now, as initial hesitation gave way to relief, Kell found himself *enjoying* the market for the first time in ages, moving through the crowd with a blissful degree of anonymity. It made him impatient to don the competitor's mask, to become someone else entirely.

Kamerov.

Hastra vanished and reappeared a few minutes later with a cup of spiced wine, offering it to Kell.

"Where is yours?" asked Kell, taking the cup.

Hastra shook his head. "Isn't proper, sir, to drink on guard."

Kell sighed. He didn't care for the idea of drinking alone, but he was in dire need of the wine. His first stop hadn't been to the market. It had been to the docks.

And there he'd found the inevitable: dark hull, silver trim, blue sails.

The *Night Spire* had returned to London.

Which meant that Alucard Emery was here. Somewhere.

Kell had half a mind to sink the ship, but that would only cause trouble, and if Rhy found out, he'd probably throw a tantrum or stab himself out of spite.

So he had settled for glaring at the *Spire,* and letting his imagination do the rest.

"Are we on a mission, sir?" Hastra had whispered (the young guard was taking his new role as confidant and accomplice very seriously).

"We are," muttered Kell, feigning severity.

He'd lingered in the shadowed overhang of a shop and scowled at the ship for several long and uneventful minutes before announcing that he needed a drink.

Which was how Kell ended up in the market, sipping his wine and absently scanning the crowds.

"Where's Staff?" he asked. "Did he get tired of being left behind?"

"Actually, I think he's been sent to see to Lord Sol-in-Ar."

See to? thought Kell. Was the king that nervous about the Faroan lord?

He set off again through the market, with Hastra a few strides behind.

The crowds grew thicker as Kell walked, swirling around him

like a tide. Faroans with their bright, intricately folded fabrics and jeweled skin. Veskans adorned by silver and gold bands, tall and made taller by their manes of hair. And of course, Arnesians, in their rich cowls and cloaks.

And then, some Kell couldn't place. A few fair enough to be Veskans, but in Arnesian clothes. A dark-skinned figure with a coil of Veskan braids.

The nightmare floated to the surface of his mind—so many strange faces, so many almost familiar ones—but he forced it down. A stranger brushed his arm as they crossed paths, and Kell found his hands going into his pockets to check for missing things, even though there was nothing there to steal.

So many people, he thought. Lila would pick every pocket here.

Just as he thought it, he caught sight of a shadow amid the color and light.

A thin figure.

A black coat.

A sharp smile.

Kell caught his breath, but by the time he blinked, the shadow was gone. Just another phantom made by the crowd. A trick of the eye.

Still, the glimpse, even false, made him feel unsteady, and his pace slowed enough to interrupt the foot traffic around him.

Hastra was there again at his side. "Are you all right, sir?"

Kell waved off his concern. "I'm fine," he said. "But we'd better head back."

He set off toward the palace end of the market, stopping only when he reached Calla's stall. "Wait here," he told Hastra before ducking inside.

Calla's shop was always changing, it seemed, to suit the city's festive needs. His gaze wandered over the various winter accessories that now lined the walls and covered the tables.

"Avan!" called the merchant as she appeared from a curtained

area near the back of the tent, holding a piece of black leather in one hand. Calla was short and round, with the shrewd eye of a businesswoman and the warmth of a wood fire. Her face lit up when she saw him. "Master Kell!" she said, folding herself into deep curtsy.

"Come now, Calla," he said, guiding her up, "there's no need for that."

Her eyes danced with even more mischief than usual. "What brings you to my shop tonight, *mas vares*?"

She said the words—*my prince*—with such kindness that he didn't bother correcting her. Instead he fidgeted with a box on the table, a pretty inlaid thing. "Oh, I found myself in the market, and thought I would come and see that you are well."

"You do me too much honor," she said, smile widening. "And if you were coming to see about that debt," she went on, eyes bright, "you should know that it has recently been paid."

Kell's chest tightened. "What? *When*?"

"Indeed," continued Calla. "Only a few minutes ago."

Kell didn't even say good-bye.

He lunged out of the tent and into the churning market, scanning the currents of people streaming past.

"Sir," asked Hastra, clearly worried. "What's wrong?"

Kell didn't answer. He turned in a slow circle, scouring the crowd for the thin shadow, the black coat, the sharp smile.

She'd been real. She'd been *here*. And of course, she was already gone.

Kell knew he was beginning to draw attention, even with the cover of the masses. A few Arnesians started to whisper. He could feel their gazes.

"Let's go," he said, forcing himself back toward the palace. But as he walked, heart pounding, he replayed the moment in his mind, the glimpse of a ghost.

But it *hadn't* been a ghost. Or a trick of the eye.

Delilah Bard was back in London.

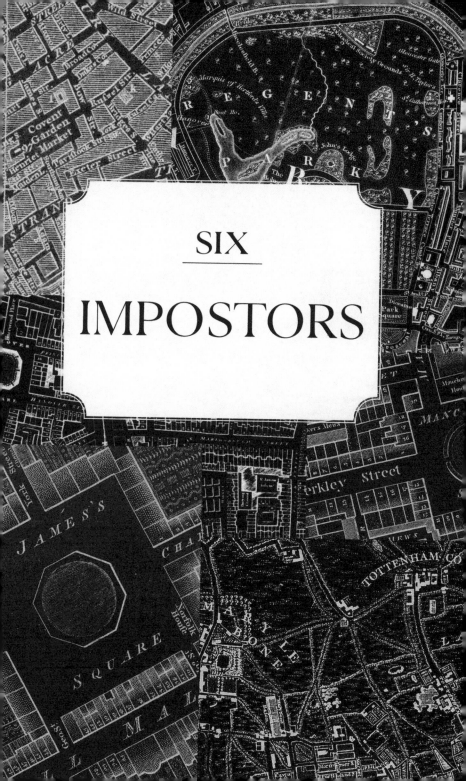

SIX

IMPOSTORS

I

White London.

Holland knew the stories by heart.

He'd grown up with them—stories of a bad king, a mad king, a curse; of a good king, a strong king, a savior. Stories of why the magic went away, and who would bring it back. And every time a new ruler the throne with blood and the dregs of power in their veins, the people would say *now*. Now the magic will come back. Now the world will wake. Now it will get better, now we will get stronger.

The stories ran in the veins of every Londoner. Even when the people grew thin and pale, even when they began to rot inside and out, even when they had no food, no strength, no power, the stories survived. And when Holland was young, he believed them, too. Even believed, when his eye went black, that *he* might be the hero. The good king. The strong king. The savior.

But on his knees before Athos Dane, Holland had seen the stories for what they were: desperate tales for starving souls.

And yet.

And yet.

Now he stood in the square at the heart of the city, with his name on every tongue and a god's power running in his veins. Everywhere he stepped, the frost withdrew. Everything he touched regained its color. All around him, the city was thawing (the day the Siljt unfroze, the people went mad. Holland had led uprisings, had witnessed riots, but never in his life had he seen *celebration*). Of course, there was tension. The people had starved too long, survived only on violence and greed. He couldn't blame them. But they would learn. Would see. Hope, faith, change: these were fragile things, and they had to be tended.

"*Køt!*" they called out—*King*—while the voice in his head, that constant companion, hummed with pleasure.

The day was bright, the air alive, and the people crowded to see Holland's latest feat, held at bay by the Iron Guard. Ojka stood beside him, her hair on fire in the sun, a knife in hand.

King! King! King!

It was called the Blood Square, where they stood. An execution site, the stones beneath his boots stained black and streaked where desperate fingers had scrounged at the spilled life in case it held a taste of magic. Eight years ago, the Danes had dragged him from a fast death here, and granted him a slow one.

The Blood Square.

It was time to give the name another meaning.

Holland held out his hands, and Ojka brought the blade to rest against his palms. The crowd quieted in anticipation.

"My king?" said Ojka, her yellow eye asking for permission. So many times the hand had been his, but not the will. This time the hand was his servant's, the will his own.

Holland nodded, and the blade bit down. Blood welled and spilled to the ruined stones, and where it struck, it broke the surface of the world, like a stone cast in a pool. The ground rippled, and behind his eyes Holland saw the square reborn. Clean, and whole. As the ripples spread, they swallowed the stains, mended the cracks, turned the broken pavers to polished marble, the abandoned basin of a well to a fountain, the fallen columns to vaulting archways.

We can do more, said the god in his head.

And before Holland could sort the *oshoc*'s thoughts from his own, the magic was spreading.

The archways of the Blood Square rippled and reformed, melting from stone into water before hardening to glass. Beyond them, the streets shuddered, and the ground beneath the crowd's feet dissolved from rock into rich, dark soil. The people fell to their knees, sinking to the loamy earth and digging their fingers in up to the wrists.

Enough, Osaron, thought Holland. He closed his bloody hands, but the ripples went on, the shells of ruined buildings collapsing into sand, the fountain overflowing not with water but with amber-colored wine.

The pillars morphed into apple trees, their trunks still marbled stone, and Holland's chest began to ache, his heart pounding as the magic poured like blood from his veins, each beat forcing more power into the world.

Enough!

The ripples died.

The world fell still.

The magic tapered off, the square a shimmering monstrosity of elements, the edges a wavering shore. The people were caked with earth, and wet from the fountain's rain, their faces bright, their eyes wide—not with hunger, but with awe.

"King! King! King!" they all called, while in his head, Osaron's own word echoed.

More. More. More.

II

Red London.

Back at the Wandering Road, the crowd had thinned, but the wolfhound was still sprawled in the exact same position by fire. Lila couldn't help but wonder if it was alive. She crossed to the hearth, and knelt slowly, hand hovering over the creature's chest.

"I already checked," said a voice behind her. Lila looked up to see Lenos fidgeting nervously. "He's okay."

Lila straightened. "Where is everybody?"

Lenos cocked his head toward a corner table. "Stross and Tav have got a game going."

The men were playing Sanct, and from what she could tell, they hadn't been playing long, because neither looked that angry and both still had all their weapons and most of their clothes. Lila wasn't a fan of the game, mostly because after four months of watching the sailors win and lose, she felt no closer to understanding the rules well enough to play, let alone cheat.

"Vasry went out," Lenos continued as Lila ambled toward the table. "Kobis went to bed."

"And Alucard?" she asked, trying to keep her tone flat with disinterest. She took up Stross's drink and downed it, ignoring the first mate's muttered protests.

Stross threw down a card with a hooded figure holding two

chalices. "Too late," he said to her, keeping his eyes on the table and the cards. "Captain said he was retiring."

"Awfully early," mused Lila.

Tav chuckled and mumbled something, but she couldn't decipher it. He was from somewhere at the edge of the empire, and the more he drank, the less intelligible his accent became. And since Lila's default when she didn't understand something was to keep her mouth shut, she simply walked away. After a few steps she stopped and turned back to Lenos, drawing the palm fire from her coat. The light was already fading, and she hadn't thought to ask if there was a way to restore it, or if it was a one-time-use kind of charm, which seemed wasteful.

"Here," she said, tossing Lenos the orb.

"What's this for?" he asked, surprised.

"Keeps the shadows at bay," she said, heading for the stairs. Lenos stood there, staring down at the orb, perplexed by either the sphere itself or the fact that the Sarows had just given him a gift.

Why *had* she given it to him?

Getting soft, grumbled a voice in her head. Not Kell's, or Barron's. No, this voice was all hers.

As Lila climbed the stairs, she produced a narrow bottle of wine she'd nicked, not from the inn or the market—she knew better than to steal from warded tents—but from Alucard's own stash aboard the *Spire.*

The captain's room sat across from hers, the doors facing like duelers. Which seemed fitting. But when she reached the doors, she paused between them, presented with the question of which she'd come for, and which she planned to open.

Lila hovered there in the hall.

She wasn't sure *why* she was drawn to his room more than hers. Perhaps because she was restless, being back in this city for the first time, a place at once strange and familiar. Perhaps because she wanted to slip back into the comfort of English. Perhaps because she wanted to learn more about the tournament, and Alucard's participation. Or perhaps out of simple habit. This was how they spent most nights at sea, after all, a bottle of wine and a magical fire, each trying to pry secrets from the other without giving up any of their own. Had Lila become so accustomed to the dance that she actually missed it?

Hang this, she thought. What a waste of life, to stand around and think so much on every little thing. What did it matter why she wanted to see the captain? She simply did.

And so, casting motive aside, she reached out to knock, only to stop when she heard footsteps from within, coming briskly toward the door.

Her thief's sense twitched, and her body moved before her mind, boots silently retreating one stride, then two, before sliding smoothly behind the corner of the hallway's nearest bend. She had no reason to hide, but she'd been doing it so long, the gesture came naturally. Besides, hiding was simply seeing without being seen, and that gave her the upper hand. Nothing to be lost by it, and often something to be gained.

An instant later, the door swung open and Alucard Emery stepped into the hall.

The first thing she noticed was his silence. The captain of the *Night Spire* normally made a certain amount of noise. His jewelry jangled and his weapons clanked, his steel-heeled boots announced every step, and even when his attire was quiet, Alucard himself usually hummed. Lila had mentioned it once, and he simply said he'd never been a fan of quiet. She'd thought him incapable of it, but as he made his way down the hall, his steps marked only by the gentle creak of the floorboards, she realized that, before, he'd always *meant* to be loud.

Another aspect of the role he was playing, now cast aside, replaced by . . . what?

He was fully dressed, but not in his usual clothes. Alucard had always favored fine, flashy things, but now he looked less like a pirate captain and more like an elegant shadow. He'd traded the blue coat he'd worn ashore for a charcoal half cloak, a simple silver scarf at his throat. He wore no obvious weapons and the sapphire was gone from his brow, along with all the rings from his fingers save one, the thick silver band shaped like a feather. His brassy brown hair was combed back beneath a black cap, and Lila's first thought was that, pared down, he looked younger, almost boyish.

But where was he going? And why was he going in disguise?

Lila trailed him down the stairs of the inn and out into the night, close enough to keep track and far enough away to avoid notice. She might have spent the last four months as a privateer, but she had spent *years* as a shadow. She knew how to blend into the dark, how to tail a mark, how to breathe and move with the current of the night instead of against it, and Alucard's steps might have been light, but hers were silent.

She'd expected him to head for the market, overflowing with people, or the web of streets that traced lines of light away from the river. Instead he hugged its banks, following the red glow of the Isle and the main concourse past the palace to a bridge on the far side. It was made of pale stone and accented with copper: copper railings, and copper pillars, and sculpted copper canopies. The whole thing formed a kind of shining tunnel. Lila hesitated at its base—the entire length of the bridge beneath the canopies was well lit, the metal reflecting and magnifying the light, and though people were strewn along it, mostly in pairs and groups, collars turned up against the cold, few actually seemed to be making their way across to the opposite bank. Blending in would be nearly impossible.

A few merchants had set up stalls beneath the lanterns, haloed by mist and candlelight, and Lila hung back to see if Alucard was heading for one of those, but he made his way briskly across, eyes ahead, and Lila was forced to either follow or be left behind. She set off after him, fighting to keep her pace leisurely, ignoring the glittering stalls and the patterned metal ceiling, but not so pointedly as to give away her purpose. It was a wasted effort in the end—Alucard never once looked back.

Walking beneath the copper canopies, she saw that they were dappled to look like trees, starlight shining through the leaves, and Lila thought, once more, what a strange world she'd stumbled into, and how glad she was to be there.

Alucard crossed the entire length of the bridge and descended a grand set of stairs to the southern bank of the Isle. Lila had only been on this side once, when she and Kell took Rhy to the sanctuary, and she'd never given much thought to what else lined this other, darker half of the city. Shops and taverns, she would have guessed, perhaps a shadier version of the northern bank. She would have been wrong. This half of London was quiet by comparison; the sanctuary rose solemnly from a bend in the river, and beyond a boundary of bank-side shops and inns, the city gave way to gardens and orchards and, beyond these, to manor homes.

Lila's old stomping grounds in Mayfair and Regent Park paled in comparison to this London's southern bank. Elegant carriages pulled by magnificent steeds dotted street after street of grand estates, high-walled and furnished with marble and glass and gleaming metal. The evening mist itself seemed to glitter with wealth.

Ahead, Alucard had quickened his pace, and Lila picked hers up to match. Far fewer people were on these streets, which made tailing him a good deal harder, but his attention was fixed on the road ahead. As far as Lila could tell, there was nothing to see here. No deals to do. No trouble to get into. Nothing but houses, half the windows dark.

Finally Alucard turned off the road, stepping through an intricate gate and into a courtyard lined with shrubbery and bordered by trees, their branches winter-bare.

When Lila caught up, she saw that the curling metalwork of

the gate formed an ornate *E*. And then she looked inside, and caught her breath. The floor of the courtyard was a mosaic of glittering blue and silver stone. She hovered in the shadow of the gate as Alucard made his way up the walk, and watched as, halfway to the door, he paused to collect himself. He dragged his cap from his head and shoved it into the satchel on his shoulder, tousled his hair, flexed his hands, muttered something she couldn't hear, and then picked up again, his stride calm and confident as he hopped up a short set of steps, then rang a bell.

A moment later, one of the two front doors swung open, and a steward appeared. On seeing Alucard, he bowed. "Lord Emery," he said, stepping aside. "Welcome home."

Lila stared in disbelief.

Alucard wasn't visiting the master of the house.

He *was* the master of the house.

Before he could step inside, a girl appeared in the doorway, squealed with delight, and threw her arms around his neck.

"Luc!" she cried as he swung her into the air. The girl couldn't be more than twelve or thirteen, and she had his wavy brown curls and dark eyes.

"Anisa." He broke into a smile Lila had never seen before, not on him. It wasn't the proud grin of a captain or the mischievous smirk of a rake, but the absolute adoration of an older brother. She'd never had any siblings, so she didn't *understand* the look, but she recognized the simple, blind love, and it twisted something in her.

And then, as suddenly as the girl had launched herself forward, she pulled away, affecting the mock frown Lila had seen on Alucard's own mouth so many times.

"Where is Esa?" demanded the girl, and Lila tensed, not at the question itself, but the fact she'd asked it in *English*. No one spoke that tongue in Red London, not unless they were trying to impress the royalty. Or they *were* royalty.

Alucard chuckled. "Of course," he said, crossing the threshold.

"Three years away from home, and your first question is about the cat. . . ." They disappeared inside, and Lila found herself staring at the front door as it closed.

Alucard Emery, captain of the *Night Spire,* tournament magician, and . . . Red London royal? Did anyone know? Did *everyone* know? Lila knew she should be surprised, but she wasn't. She'd known from the moment she met Alucard aboard the *Night Spire* that he was playing a part; it was just a matter of uncovering the man behind it. Now she knew the truth, and the truth gave her a card to play. And when it came to men like Alucard Emery, any advantage was worth taking.

A decorative wall circled the house, and Lila managed to hoist herself up with the help of a low branch. Perched on top, she could see through the great glass windows, many of which were unshuttered. Her silhouette blended into the tracery of trees at her back as she skirted the house, following the glimpses of Alucard and his sister as they made their way into a grand room with tall windows and a blazing hearth, and a pair of glass doors on the far wall leading to an expansive garden. She dropped into a crouch atop the wall as a man came into view. He had Alucard's coloring, and his jaw was the same square cut, but it looked hard without Alucard's smile. The man looked older by several years.

"Berras," said Alucard by way of greeting. The windows were cracked open, and the word reached Lila through the parted glass.

The man, Berras, strode forward, and for an instant it looked as though he might strike Alucard, but before he could, the girl lunged in front of her brother like a shield—there was something terribly practiced about the gesture, as if she'd done it many times before—and Berras stilled his hand in midair. On one of his fingers Lila saw a duplicate of Alucard's feather ring before his hand fell back to his side.

"Go, Anisa," he ordered.

The girl hesitated, but Alucard gave her a gentle smile and a nod, and she backed out of the room. The moment they were alone, Berras snapped.

"Where is Kobis?"

"I pushed him overboard," said Alucard. Disgust spilled across the man's face, and Alucard rolled his eyes. "Saints, Berras, it was a joke. Your moody little spy is safely housed at an inn with the rest of my crew."

Berras sneered faintly at the mention of the *Spire*'s men.

"That look does nothing for you, Brother," said the captain. "And the *Night Spire* sails for the crown. To insult my post is to insult House Maresh, and we wouldn't want to do *that*."

"Why are you *here*?" growled Berras, taking up a goblet. But before he could drink, Alucard flicked his wrist and the wine abandoned its cup, rising in a ribbon, coiling in on itself as it did. Between one instant and the next, it had hardened into a block of ruby-colored ice.

Alucard plucked the crystal from the air and considered it absently. "I'm in town for the tournament. I only came to make sure my family was well. How foolish of me to think I'd find a welcome." He tossed the frozen cube into the hearth, and turned to go.

Berras didn't speak, not until Alucard was at the garden doors.

"I would have let you rot in that jail."

A small, bitter smile touched the edge of Alucard's mouth. "Good thing it wasn't up to you."

With that, he stormed out. Lila straightened atop the wall, and rounded the perimeter to find Alucard standing on a broad balcony overlooking the grounds. Beyond the wall she could make out the arc of the palace, the diffused glow of the river.

Alucard's face was a mask of icy calm, bordering on disinterest, but his fingers gripped the balcony's edge, knuckles white.

Lila didn't make a sound, and yet Alucard sighed and said, "It isn't polite to spy."

Dammit. She'd forgotten about his gift for seeing the magic in people. It would make a handy skill for a thief, and Lila wondered, not for the first time, if there was a way to steal talents the way one did trinkets.

She stepped off the low wall onto the edge of the patio rail before dropping soundlessly to the terrace beside him.

"Captain," she said, half greeting and half apology.

"Still simply looking after your interests?" he asked. But he didn't sound angry.

"You're not upset," she observed.

Alucard raised a brow, and she found herself missing the familiar wink of blue. "I suppose not. Besides, my excursions were fairly innocuous compared to yours."

"You followed me?" snapped Lila.

Alucard chuckled. "You hardly have a right to sound affronted."

Lila shook her head, silently grateful she hadn't decided to march into the palace and surprise Kell. Truth be told, she still hadn't decided when she would see him. *If* she would see him. But when—and if—she did, she certainly didn't want Alucard there spying on them. Kell was somebody here, a royal, a saint, even if she could only think of him as the silly smuggler who frowned too much and nearly got them both killed.

"What are you grinning about?"

"Nothing," said Lila, leveling her expression. "So . . . *Luc,* huh?"

"It's a nickname. Surely they have those, wherever you're from. And for the record, I prefer Alucard. Or Captain Emery."

"Does the crew know?"

"Know what?"

"That you're . . ." She gestured to the estate, searching for the word.

"It's hardly a secret, Bard. Most Arnesians have heard of the House of Emery."

He gave her a look that said, *Odd, isn't it, that you haven't.*

"Haven't you heard them calling me *vestra*?"

Lila had. "I just assumed it was a slur. Like *pilse*."

Alucard laughed soundlessly. "Maybe it is, to them. It means *royal*."

"Like a *prince*?"

He gave a humorless laugh. "What a disappointment I must be to you. I know you wanted a pirate. You should have conned your way aboard a different ship. But don't worry. There are many doors between my person and the throne. And I have no desire to see them opened."

Lila chewed her lip. "But if everyone knows, then why sneak about like a thief?"

His gaze drifted back to the garden wall. "Because there are other people in this city, Bard. Some I don't care to see. And some I'd rather not see me."

"What's this?" she teased. "The great Alucard Emery has enemies?"

"Comes with the trade, I fear."

"It's hard to imagine you meeting someone you couldn't charm."

His eyes narrowed. "You say that like it's not a compliment."

"Perhaps it's not."

An uncomfortable silence began to settle.

"Nice house," said Lila.

It was the wrong thing to have said. His expression hardened. "I hope you'll forgive me for not inviting you in and introducing you to my esteemed family. It might be tricky to explain the sudden presence of a girl in a man's suit with the ability to speak the royal tongue but not the grace to use the front door."

Lila bit back a reply. She felt dismissed, but as she stepped up onto the balcony's edge, Alucard said, "Wait," and there was something in his voice that she barely recognized, because she'd never heard it from him before. Sincerity. She twisted back, and she saw him haloed by the light from the room behind, framed by the doorway. He was little more than a silhouette, a simplified portrait of a nobleman.

A picture of what someone should be, not what they were.

Then Alucard stepped forward, away from the light and into the shadows with her. This version of him looked real. Looked right. And Lila understood—when he said *Wait,* what he meant was, *Wait for me.*

"I suppose we should both be getting back," he added, aiming for indifference but falling short.

"Shouldn't you say good-bye?"

"I've never been a fan of farewells. Or hellos, for that matter. Unnecessary punctuation. Besides, they'll see me again."

Lila looked back at the house. "Won't Anisa be upset?"

"Oh, I imagine so. I'm afraid I'm accustomed to her disappointment."

"But what about—"

"No more questions, Lila," he said. "I'm tired."

The last protests cooled to ash on her tongue as Alucard stepped up onto the banister beside her, and then, in a single, effortless stride, onto the low wall.

It was narrow, but he moved with sure-footed ease atop it. He didn't even look down to check his steps.

"I grew up here," he said, reading her surprise. "If there's a way in or out, I've tried it."

They slipped along the garden wall and down into the courtyard, hugging the shadows until they were safely beyond the gate.

Alucard set off down the street without looking back, but Lila cast a glance at the grand estate.

The truth was, Lila understood why Alucard did it. Why he traded safety and boredom for adventure. She didn't know what it felt like to be safe, and she'd never had the luxury of being bored, but it was like she'd once told Kell. People either stole to stay alive or to feel alive. She had to imagine that they ran away for the same reasons.

Lila jogged to catch up, and fell in step beside the captain, the street quiet save for the sounds of their boots. She cheated a sideways glance, but Alucard's gaze was straight ahead, and far away.

She used to hate people like him, people who gave up something good, shucked warm meals and solid roofs as if they didn't matter.

But then Barron died and Lila realized that in a way she'd done the same thing. Run away from what could have been a good life. Or at least a happy one. Because it wasn't enough to be happy, not for Lila. She wanted *more*. Wanted an adventure. She used to think that if she stole enough, the want would fade, the hunger would go away, but maybe it wasn't that simple. Maybe it wasn't a matter of what she didn't have, of what she wasn't, but what she *was*. Maybe she wasn't the kind of person who stole to *stay* alive. Maybe she just did it for the thrill. And that scared her, because it meant she didn't need to do it, couldn't justify it, could have stayed at the Stone's Throw, could have saved Barron's life. . . . It was a slippery slope, that kind of thinking, one that ended in a cliff, so Lila backed away.

She was who she was.

And Alucard Emery?

Well, he was a man with secrets of his own.

And she couldn't fault him that.

III

Kell ducked and dodged, moving like shadow and light across the Basin.

He relished his burning muscles, his pounding heart; he'd slept poorly and woken worse, his thoughts still churning around the news of Lila's return. It made sense, didn't it? If she'd taken up with an Arnesian crew, most of them had docked back in London for the tournament.

Only two days until the *Essen Tasch*.

A blade swung high, and Kell lunged back out of its reach.

Two days, and still no sign of her. Some small, irrational part had been convinced that he'd be able to *feel* her return, be tuned to it the way he'd been to the Stone's Throw, and the Setting Sun, and the Scorched Bone. The fixed points in the worlds. Then again, maybe he *was* tuned to her. Maybe she was the small, invisible force that had drawn him out into the city in the first place.

But he'd missed her, and with the city so overrun, how was he supposed to find her again?

Just follow the knives, said a voice in his head. *And the bodies they're lodged in.*

He smiled to himself. And then, with a small pang, he wondered how long she'd been in London. And why she hadn't come to see him sooner. Their paths had only crossed for a few days, but he and Rhy and Tieren, they were the only people she knew in this world, or at least, the only people she'd known four months ago. Perhaps she'd gone off and made a wealth of friends—but he doubted it.

The next blow nearly found skin, and Kell jerked away just in time.

Focus, he chided himself. *Breathe.*

The silver mask was perfectly contoured to his face, shielding everything but air and sight. He'd put it on, wanting to get used to its size and weight, and quickly found himself relishing the difference, slipping into the comfort of anonymity, persona. So long as he wore the mask, Kell wasn't Kell.

He was *Kamerov.*

What would Lila think about that? Lila, Lila, he'd even considered using blood magic to find her—he still had her kerchief—but stopped himself before he drew the knife. He'd gone months without stooping so low. Besides, he wasn't some pup, chasing after a master or a bone. Let her come to him. But why *hadn't* she come to—

Metal flashed, too close, and he swore and rolled, regaining his feet.

He'd traded a dozen enemies for only one, but unlike the dummies he'd trained against, this one was very much alive. Hastra shifted back and forth, in full armor, trying to avoid Kell's blows. The young guard had been surprisingly willing to run around the Basin armed with only a small shield and a dull blade while Kell honed his agility and practiced turning elements into weapons.

The armor . . . he thought, wind whipping around him, *is designed to crack . . .* He leaped, pushed off a wall, slammed a gust of air into Hastra's back. *. . . when struck.* Hastra stumbled forward and spun to face him. *The first to ten hits . . .* He continued reciting the rules as water swirled around his hand. *. . . wins the match . . .* The water split, circling both hands. *. . . unless one of the competitors . . .* Both streams shot forward, freezing before they hit. . . . *is unable to continue . . .* Hastra could only block one shard, and the second caught him in the armored thigh and shattered into drops of ice. *. . . or admits defeat.*

Kell broke into a smile behind his mask, and when the breathless guard pulled off his helmet, he was grinning, too. Kell tugged off his silver mask, his damp hair standing on end.

"Is this what you've been doing down here all these weeks, Master Kell?" asked Hastra breathlessly. "Practicing for the tournament?"

Kell hesitated, and then said, "I suppose." After all, he had been training; he simply hadn't known what he was training *for*.

"Well it's paying off, sir," said the guard. "You make it look easy."

Kell laughed. The truth was, his whole body ached, and even while his blood sang for a fight, his power felt thin. Drained. He'd grown too used to the efficiency of blood magic, but elements took more will to wield. The fatigue from using blood spells hit him all at once, but this kind of fighting wore him down. Perhaps he'd actually get a sound night's sleep before the tournament.

Hastra crossed the training room gingerly, as if treading on hallowed ground, and stood by the Basin's archway, considering the equipment table with its bowl of water, its containers of earth and sand and oil.

"Do *you* have an element?" asked Kell, slicking back his hair.

Hastra's smile softened. "Little of this, little of that, sir."

Kell frowned. "What do you mean?"

"Parents wanted me to be a priest," said the young guard, scratching his head. "But I thought that didn't sound like nearly as much fun. Spend all day meditating in that musty stone structure—"

"You can *balance*?" cut in Kell, amazed. Priests were chosen not for their strength in one element, but for their tempered ability to manage all, not as Kell did, with sheer power, but with the evenness needed to nurture life. Balancing the elements was a sacred skill. Even Kell struggled with balance; just as a strong wind could uproot a sapling, an *Antari*'s power held too much force for the subtle arts. He could impact things already grown, but life was fragile at the start, and required a gentle touch.

The young guard shrugged, and then brightened a little. "You want to see?" he asked, almost bashful.

Kell looked around "Right now?"

Hastra grinned and dug a hand in his pocket, fetching out a small seed. When Kell raised a brow, the guard chuckled. "You never know when you might need to impress a lady," he said. "Lots of people puff up their chest and go for the flash and the bang. But I can't tell you how many nights have started with a seed and ended, well . . ." Hastra seemed to ramble whenever he got nervous, and Kell apparently made him very nervous. "Then again I doubt you'd have to try as hard to impress them, sir."

Hastra scanned the elements on the table. In one small bowl was some loose dirt: not the rich soil of the orchards and gardens, but the rocky kind found beneath pavers in the street. It wasn't the most elegant thing to train with—and when given the choice, Kell would go for rocks over dirt—but it was abundant. Kell watched as Hastra scooped up a palmful of earth, and made a small indent with his finger before dropping in the seed. He then dipped his other hand into the bowl of water, and pressed it down over the dirt, packing the seed and soil between his palms into a ball. Hastra closed his eyes, and his lips began to move. Kell felt a subtle warmth in the air between them, a sensation he knew well from his time with Tieren.

And then, still murmuring, Hastra began to slowly open his hands, the mound of damp earth cupped like an egg between them.

Kell watched, transfixed, as a pale green stem crept up through the moistened earth. The stem grew an inch, then two, twisting up into the air. Leaves began to unfurl, their surface a dark purple, before a white spherical bloom emerged.

Hastra trailed off, looking pleased.

"What is it?" asked Kell.

"Acina," said the guard. "Its leaves are good for pain."

"That's amazing."

The young guard shrugged. "My mum and dad were not happy when I chose to be a guard instead."

"I can imagine." Kell wanted to tell Hastra that he was wasted here. That his talent was far too precious to be thrown away in favor of a sword and some armor. But then, if a person's value alone should determine their place, what argument did Kell have for wanting more?

"But that's just because they don't know," continued Hastra sunnily. "They probably think I'm doing street patrol in the *sha*. They'll be proud, when they hear I'm guarding you, sir. Besides, I made a deal with my father," he added. "I'll join the sanctuary, eventually. But I've wanted to be a royal guard as long as I can remember. I knew I wouldn't be happy, not until I tried. Can't think of a worse thing, than wondering what would have been. So I thought, why not have both? The sanctuary will still have me, when I'm good and ready."

"And if you die before then?"

Hastra's cheery mood didn't dampen. "Then someone else will get my gift. And hopefully they'll be less stubborn. That's what my mother says." He leaned in conspiratorially. "I tend the courtyards, though, when no one's looking."

Kell smiled. The palace grounds *had* looked suspiciously lush, for this time of year. Hastra straightened, his gaze flicking to the stairs. "We should go—"

"We still have time," Kell assured him, getting to his feet.

"How do you know?" asked Hastra. "We can't hear the bells down here, and there are no windows to gauge the light."

"Magic," said Kell, and then, when Hastra's eyes widened, he gestured to the hourglass sitting on the table with his other tools. "And that."

There was still sand in the glass, and Kell wasn't ready to face the world above just yet. "Let's go again."

Hastra took up his position. "Yes, sir."

"Call me Kamerov," said Kell, slipping the helmet back over his head.

IV

Sessa Av!

The words ran across the tops of the scrying boards throughout London.

Two days!

The city was counting down.

Two days until the Essen Tasch!

Two days, and Lila Bard had a problem.

She'd hoped there'd be an obvious chink in the system, a way to threaten or bribe her way onto the tournament roster, or snag a wild card spot, but apparently the champions had all been chosen *weeks* ago. There were twelve names on that list, and two alternates, which meant if Lila Bard wanted a chance to play— and she *did*—she was going to have to steal a name.

Lila had nicked plenty of things in her time, but an identity wasn't one of them. Sure, she'd taken up pseudonyms, played a variety of made-up parts, but she'd never impersonated anyone *real*.

And of course, she couldn't simply impersonate them. She'd have to *replace* them.

Not worth it, warned a voice in her head, that pesky, pragmatic one that sounded too much like Kell. Maybe it was madness. Maybe she should just take her place in the stands and cheer for her captain, earn a few extra coins in the betting pools. It wouldn't be an unpleasant way to spend the week. And after all, what place did she have in the ring? She'd only been practicing a few months.

But.

There was that one word, lodged in her skin like a splinter.

But.

But she was restless.

But she wanted a thrill.

But it would be a challenge.

And when it came to magic, Lila wasn't just a quick study. She was a *natural*.

Master Tieren had told her months ago that something powerful lay inside her, waiting to be woken. Well, Lila had poked it with a stick, and it was wide awake—a living, humming thing as restless as she was.

And restlessness had always made her reckless.

Still, there was that pesky matter of the roster.

Lila had spent the day wandering Red London, learning everything she could about the *Essen Tasch* and its competitors. She'd passed enough time in taverns and brothels and public houses to know where you were most likely to find answers to questions without ever asking. Sure, you could always garnish pockets, but often if you sat in one place long enough, you'd learn more than anyone you paid would tell you. And everyone seemed to be talking about the tournament.

Alucard, apparently, was one of the Arnesian favorites, along with a woman named Kisimyr, the tournament's previous victor, and a man named Jinnar. But names were names. She needed to *see* the lineup before they took the stage. If there were no good marks, she told herself, she would let it go, stick to the stands with the rest of the crew. If there were no good marks. But she had to see. Had to know.

Frustrated, Lila finished her drink and pushed off her stool and headed back to the inn.

Somewhere on the way, her feet changed course, and by the

time she focused on where she was, she found herself standing across the main road from the royal palace, staring up. She wasn't surprised. All day her legs had been tugging her here. All day she'd found her gaze drifting to the gleaming structure.

Go in, said a voice.

Lila snorted. What would she do? Walk up the front steps? She'd done it once before, but that had been as a guest, with a stolen invitation. The doors had been cast open then, but now they were closed, a dozen guards in polished armor and red capes standing sentinel.

What would she say to them? *I'm here to see the black-eyed prince.* Her English might get her through the front door, but then what? Would the king and queen recognize her as the scrawny girl who'd helped Kell save their city? Lila suspected *Rhy* would remember her. She found herself warming at the thought of the prince—not as he was under the control of Astrid Dane, or bleeding to death on a sanctuary cot, but after, surrounded by pillows, dark circles below his amber eyes. Tired and kind and flirting through the pain.

And Kell?

How fared the black-eyed prince? Would he welcome her in? Hand her a drink and ask after her travels, or frown and ask if she was ready to leave, return to her own world where she belonged?

Lila squinted up in the dusk—the high balconies of the palace reduced to haloes of light in the cold evening—and thought she could make out a shadow standing on one of the tallest patios. It was too far to tell, that distance where everything was reduced to vague shapes, and the mind could twist them into anything. Still, the shadow seemed to curl over before her eyes, as if leaning on the rail, and in that moment the smudge of darkness became a magician in a high-collared coat. Lila stood and watched until the shape dissolved, swallowed up by the thickening night.

Her attention drifted down and landed on a pair of elegant black scrying boards that rose like columns before the palace steps. Months ago, Kell's face had shown up on these, first with the word *missing* at the top, and later with the word *wanted*. Now the ghostly chalk announced a variety of events in the hours leading up to the tournament itself—damn, there were a lot of parties—but one in particular caught her eye. Something called *Is Gosar Noche.*

The Banner Night.

She caught sight of the notice just before the board erased itself, and had to stand there for ten minutes waiting for the message to cycle back around. When it did, she read as quickly as she could, trying to make sense of the Arnesian script.

From what she could tell, competitors from all three empires were being summoned to the palace the following night—the night before the tournament—for a royal reception. And to select their banner, whatever that meant.

Wasn't this what she'd wanted?

An excuse to walk right into the Red Palace.

All she needed was a name.

The bells rang, and Lila swore under her breath. A whole day gone, she thought grimly as she trudged back to the Wandering Road, and no closer to her goal.

"There you are," said the captain's voice as soon as she stepped inside.

A handful of Alucard's men were gathered in the front room. They weren't dressed for the ship or the dock or the tavern inn. Tav, Stross, and Vasry wore fine hooded half-cloaks that gathered at the wrists, collar and cuff fastened with polished silver clasps. Alucard himself was dressed in an elegant coat, midnight blue with silver lining, his curls clasped back beneath a hat that dipped and curved like the sea. One hand rested on the hilt of his short sword, the silver feather ring glinting in the low light. Aside from the sapphire still sparkling in his right brow, he

280 ·   V. E. SCHWAB

didn't look like the *casero* of the *Night Spire*. And yet, if he didn't look like a pirate, he didn't look entirely like a princeling, either. He looked polished, but also sharp, like a well-kept knife.

"Where have you been, Bard?"

She shrugged. "Exploring."

"We nearly left without you."

Her brow crinkled. "Where are you going?"

Alucard flashed a grin. "To a party," he said. Only the word for *party* in Arnesian wasn't that simple. Lila was learning that so many Arnesian words had meanings that shifted to fit their context. The word Alucard used was the broadest: *tasura,* which meant *party,* or *event,* or *function,* or *gathering,* and whose meaning ranged from celebratory to nefarious.

"I hate parties," she said, heading for the stairs.

But Alucard wasn't so easily dissuaded. He caught up, and took her elbow—gingerly, and only for an instant, as he knew how dangerous it was to touch Lila when she didn't want to be touched. "This one I think you'll enjoy," he murmured in English.

"Why's that?"

"Because I know how fascinated you are by the upcoming games."

"And?"

"And it's an unofficial tradition," he said, "for the local competitors to share a drink before the tournament begins." Lila's interest sharpened. "It's a bit of posturing, I admit," he added, gesturing to the others, "but I was hoping you would come."

"Why me?"

"Because it's a chance to size up the competition," said Alucard. "And you've got the sharpest eyes," he added with a wink.

Lila tried to hide her excitement. "Well," she said. "If you insist."

Alucard smiled and produced a silver scarf from his pocket.

"What's this for?" she asked as he tied it loosely around her throat.

"Tonight you're part of my entourage."

Lila laughed outright, a biting sound that stung the other men. "Your *entourage*." *What next?* She wondered. *Squire?*

"Think of it as the name for a crew on land."

"I hope you don't expect me to call you *Master*," she said, adjusting the knot.

"Saints, no, that word has no place except in bed. And *Lord* makes my skin crawl. *Captain* will do." He gestured at the waiting men. "Shall we?"

Lila's smile sharpened as she nodded at the door. "Lead the way, Captain."

🜂

The sign above the tavern door said *Is Casnor Ast*.

The Setting Sun.

Lila's steps slowed, then stopped. It was the strangest thing, but she couldn't shake the feeling she'd been there before. She hadn't, of course. She'd only stayed in Red London a few days after the ordeal with the Danes before taking up with the *Spire*'s crew—just long enough to heal and answer questions—and been confined to the palace the entire time.

But standing there, on the threshold, the place felt so *familiar*. When she closed her eyes, she almost felt like she was at . . . it couldn't be. Lila blinked, and looked around at the surrounding streets, trying to layer the image of this city on top of another, the one she'd lived in her entire life. And as the images merged, she realized that she knew exactly where she was. Where she would be. On this corner, back in Grey London, the exact same distance from the river, stood another tavern, one she knew too well.

The Stone's Throw.

What were the odds? Taverns were as plentiful as problems,

but two occupying the same exact place? Even from the outside, they looked nothing alike, and yet this place tugged on her bones with the same peculiar gravity she'd always felt back home. *Home.* She'd never thought of the Stone's Throw that way when she was there, but now it was the only word that fit. Only it wasn't the *building* she longed for. Not really.

She thrust her hand into her pocket, and curled her fingers around the silver pocket watch that hung like a weight in the bottom of the silk-lined fold.

"*Kers la,* Bard?"

She looked up, and realized that Alucard was holding the door open for her. She shook her head.

"*Skan,*" she said. *Nothing.*

Stepping inside, the power hit her in a wave. She couldn't see magic as Alucard did, but she could still feel it, filling the air like steam as it wafted off the gathered magicians. Not all the competitors traveled with a full entourage. Some—like the tan woman on the back wall, her black hair twisted into ropes and studded with gold—were the center of their own universe, while others sat in small groups or wandered the room alone, an aura of power drifting in their wake.

Meanwhile, the déjà vu continued. She did her best to shake it off and focus. After all, she wasn't just here to be part of Alucard's tableau. There was the issue of finding a mark, of performing her own little magic trick. The tavern was full of magicians, and Delilah Bard was going to make one of them disappear.

Someone boomed a greeting to Alucard, and the entourage came to a halt as the two clasped wrists. Tav went to round up drinks, while Stross surveyed the room with keen appraisal. She guessed he'd been brought along for the same reason she had, to size up the competition.

Vasry, meanwhile, eyed the room as if it were a feast.

"That's the reigning champion, Kisimyr," he whispered to

Lila in Arnesian as the woman with the roped hair strode toward Alucard, boots ringing out on the worn wood floor. The man who'd greeted Alucard retreated a few steps as she approached.

"Emery," she said with a feline grin and a heady accent. "You really don't know how to stay out of trouble." She wasn't from London. She was speaking Royal, but her words all ran together—not in the serpentine way of the Faroan tongue, more like she'd hacked off all the edges and taken out the space between. She had a low, resonant voice, and when she spoke, it sounded like rumbling thunder.

"Not when trouble is more fun," said Alucard with a bow. Kisimyr's grin widened as the two fell to quiet conversation—there was something sharp about that grin, and paired with the rest of her face, the slanted brow and straight-on gaze, it read like a taunt. A challenge. The woman exuded confidence. Not arrogance, exactly—that was usually unfounded, and everything about Kisimyr said she'd just *love* an excuse to show you what she could do.

Lila liked that, found herself mimicking the features, wondering what kind of whole they'd add up to on her own face.

She didn't know if she wanted to fight the woman or be her friend, but she certainly wouldn't be *replacing* her. Lila's attention shifted, trailing across a pair of brawny figures, and a very pretty girl in blue with cascades of dark hair, not to mention a fair number of curves. No good matches there. She continued to scan the room as Alucard's entourage made its way toward a corner booth.

Kisimyr had retreated into the folds of her own group, and she was talking to a young, dark-skinned man beside her. He was fine-boned and wiry, with bare arms and gold earrings running the length of both ears to match the ones in Kisimyr's.

"Losen," said Alucard softly. "Her protégé."

"Will they have to compete against each other?"

He shrugged. "Depends on the draw."

A man with a stack of paper appeared at Kisimyr's elbow.

"Works for the Scryer, that one," said Stross. "Best avoid him, unless you want to find yourself on the boards."

Just then, the tavern doors flung open, and a young man blew in—quite literally—on a gust of wind. It swirled around him and through the tavern, shuddering candle flames and rocking lanterns. Alucard twisted in his seat, then rolled his eyes with a smile. "Jinnar!" he said, and Lila couldn't tell by the way he said it if that was a name or a curse.

Even next to the broad Veskans and the jewel-marked Faroans she'd met in Sasenroche, the newcomer was one of the most striking men Lila had ever seen. Wisp-thin, like a late shadow, his skin had the rich tan of an Arnesian and his black hair shot up in a vertical shock. Below black brows, his eyes were *silver*, shining like a cat's in the low tavern light and scored only by the beads of black at their center. A fringe of thick black lashes framed both silver pools, and he had a jackal's grin, not sharp but wide. It only got wider when he saw Alucard.

"Emery!" he called, tugging the cloak from his shoulders and crossing the room, the two gestures wound together in a seam-less motion. Beneath the cloak, his clothes weren't just close fit-ting; they were molded to his body, ornamented by silver cuffs that circled his throat and ran the lengths of his forearms.

Alucard stood. "They let you out in public?"

The young man threw his arm around the captain's shoulder. "Only for the *Essen Tasch*. You know that old Tieren has a soft spot for me."

He spoke so fast Lila could barely follow, but her attention prickled at the mention of London's head priest.

"Jin, meet my crew. At least, the ones I like best."

The man's eyes danced over the table, flitting across Lila for only a moment—it felt like a cool breeze—before returning to Alucard. Up close, his metallic gaze was even more unsettling.

"What are we calling you these days?"

"Captain will do."

"How very official. Though I suppose it's not as bad as a *vestra* title." He dipped into an elaborate gesture that vaguely resembled a bow, if a bow were paired with a rude hand gesture. "His Eminence Alucard, second son of the Royal House of Emery."

"You're embarrassing yourself."

"No, I'm embarrassing *you,*" said Jin, straightening. "There's a difference."

Alucard offered him a seat, but Jin declined, perching instead on the shoulder of Alucard's own chair, light as a feather. "What have I missed?"

"Nothing, yet."

Jin looked around. "Going to be a strange one."

"Oh?"

"Air of mystery around it all this year."

"Is that an element joke?"

"Hah," said Jin, "I didn't even think about that."

"I thought you kept a list of wind jokes," teased Alucard. "I certainly do, just for you. I've broken them down into chills, gales, steam. . . ."

"Just like your sails," jabbed Jin, hopping down from the chair. "So full of air. But I'm serious," he said, leaning in. "I haven't even seen half the competition. Hidden away for effect perhaps. And the pomp surrounding everything! I was at Faro three years back, and you know how much they like their gold, but it was a pauper's haunt compared to this affair. I'm telling you, the air of spectacle's run away with it. Blame the prince. Always had a flare for drama."

"Says the man floating three inches off the ground."

Lila looked down, and started slightly when she saw that Jinnar was, in fact, hovering. Not constantly, but every time he moved, he took a fraction too long to settle, as if gravity didn't have the same hold on him as it did on everyone else. Or maybe, as if something else were lifting him up.

"Yes, well," Jin said with a shrug, "I suppose I'll fit in splendidly. As will you," he added, flicking the silver feather on Alucard's hat. "Now if you'll excuse me, I should make the rounds and the welcomes. I'll be back."

And with that, he was gone. Lila turned to Alucard, bemused. "Is he always like that?"

"Jinnar? He's always been a bit . . . enthusiastic. But don't let his childish humor fool you. He is the best wind mage I've ever met."

"He was *levitating*," said Lila. She'd seen plenty of magicians *doing* magic. But Jinnar *was* magic.

"Jinnar belongs to a particular school of magic, one that believes not only in using an element, but in becoming one with it." Alucard scratched his head. "It's like when children are learning to play renna and they have to carry the ball with them everywhere, to get comfortable with it. Well, Jin never set the ball down."

Lila watched the wind mage flit around the room, greeting Kisimyr and Losen, as well as the girl in blue. And then he stopped to perch on the edge of a couch, and began talking to a man she hadn't noticed yet. Or rather, she *had* noticed him, but she'd taken him for the cast-off member of someone else's entourage, dressed as he was in a simple black coat with an iridescent pin shaped like an *S* at his throat. He'd made his way through the gathering earlier, hugging the edges of the room and clutching a glass of white ale. The actions held more discomfort than stealth, and he'd eventually retreated to a couch to sip his drink in peace.

Now Lila squinted through the smoke and shadow-filled room as Jin shook his hand. The man's skin was fair, his hair dark—darker than Lila's—and shorter, but his bones were sharp. *How tall is he?* she wondered, sizing up the cut of his shoulders, the length of his arms. A touch of cool air brushed her cheek, and she blinked, realizing Jin had returned.

He was sitting again on the back of Alucard's chair, having appeared without so much as a greeting.

"Well," asked Alucard, tipping his head back, "is everyone here?"

"Nearly." Jinnar pulled the competition roster from his pocket. "No sign of Brost. Or the Kamerov fellow. Or Zenisra."

"Praise the saints," muttered Alucard at this last name.

Jin chuckled. "You make more enemies than most make bed-fellows."

The sapphire in Alucard's brow twinkled. "Oh, I make plenty of those, too." He nodded at the man on the couch. "And the shadow?"

"Tall, dark, and quiet? Name's Stasion Elsor. Nice enough fellow. Shy, I think."

*Stasion Elso*r, thought Lila, turning the name over on her tongue.

"Or smart enough to keep his cards close to his chest."

"Maybe," said Jin. "Anyhow, he's a first-timer, comes from Besa Nal, on the coast."

"My man Stross hails from that region."

"Yes, well, hopefully Stasion's stage manner is stronger than his tavern one."

"It's not always about putting on a show," chided Alucard.

Jin cackled. "You're one to talk, Emery." With that, he dismounted the chair, and blew away.

Alucard got to his feet. He looked at the drink in his hand, as if he wasn't sure how it had gotten there. Then he finished it in a single swallow. "I suppose I better say my hellos," he said, setting down the empty glass. "I'll be back."

Lila nodded absently, her attention already returning to the man on the couch. Only he wasn't there anymore. She searched the room, eyes landing on the door just in time to see Stasion Elsor vanishing through it. Lila finished her own drink, and shoved herself up to her feet.

"Where are you going?" asked Stross.

She flashed him a sharp-edged smile and turned up the collar of her coat. "To find some trouble."

V

They were nearly the same height. That was the first thing she noticed as she fell in step behind him. Elsor was a touch taller, and a fraction broader in the shoulders, but he had a narrow waist and long legs. As Lila followed, she first matched his stride, and then began to mimic it.

So close to the river, the streets were crowded enough to cloak her pursuit, and she began to feel less like a thief with a mark and more like a cat with its prey.

There were so many chances to turn back. But she kept going.

Lila had never really bought into fate, but like most people who disavowed religion, she could summon a measure of belief when it was necessary.

Elsor wasn't from London. He didn't have an entourage. As she closed the gap, she wondered how many people had even noticed him back at the tavern, besides Jinnar. The light in the Sun had been low. Had anyone gotten a good look at his face?

Once the tournament began, they'd have no faces anyway.

Madness, warned a voice, but what did she have to lose? Alucard and the *Spire*? Caring, belonging, it was all so overrated.

Elsor put his hands in his pockets.

Lila put her hands in her pockets.

He rolled his neck.

She rolled her neck.

She had a variety of knives on her, but she didn't plan on killing him, not if it could be helped. Stealing an identity was one thing; stealing a life was another, and though she'd certainly killed her fair share, she didn't take it lightly. Still, for her plan to work, *something* had to happen to Stasion Elsor.

He rounded a corner onto a narrow street that led to the docks. The street was jagged and empty, dotted only by darkened shops and a scattering of bins and crates.

Elsor was no doubt an excellent magician, but Lila had the element of surprise and no problem playing dirty.

A metal bar leaned against a door, winking in the lantern light.

It scraped the stones as Lila lifted it, and Elsor spun around. He was fast, but she was faster, pressed into the doorway by the time his eyes found the place she'd been.

Flame sparked in the man's palm, and he held the light aloft, shadows dancing down the street. A fireworker.

It was the last sign Lila needed.

Her lips moved, magic prickling through her as she summoned a couplet of Blake. Not a song of fire, or water, but earth. A planter on the windowsill above him slid off the edge and came crashing down. It missed him by inches, shattering against the street, and Elsor spun to face the sound a second time. As he did, Lila closed the gap and raised the pipe, feeling a little less guilty.

Fool me twice, she thought, swinging the bar.

His hands came up, too slow to stop the blow, but fast enough to graze the front of her jacket before he collapsed to the street with the sound of dead weight and the hiss of doused flame.

Lila patted the drops of fire on her coat and frowned. Calla wouldn't be happy.

She set the bar against the wall, and knelt to consider Stasion Elsor—up close, the angles of his face were even sharper. Blood ran from his forehead, but his chest was rising and falling, and Lila felt rather proud of her restraint as she dragged his arm around her shoulders and struggled to her feet under the load. With his head lolling forward, and his dark hair covering the wound at his temple, he almost looked like a man too deep in his cups.

Now what? she thought, and at the same exact moment a voice behind her said, "What now?"

Lila spun, dropping Elsor and drawing her dagger at the same time. With a flick of her wrist the dagger became two, and as she struck metal against metal, the two blades lit, fire licking up their edges.

Alucard stood at the mouth of the narrow road, arms crossed. "Impressive," he said, sounding decidedly *unimpressed*. "Tell me, are you planning to burn me, or stab me, or both?"

"What are you doing here?" she hissed.

"I really think I should be the one asking that."

She gestured to the body. "Isn't it obvious?"

Alucard's gaze flicked from the knives down to the metal bar and the crumpled form at Lila's feet. "No, not really. Because you couldn't *possibly* be foolish enough to kill a competitor."

Lila snapped the knives back together, putting out the flames. "I didn't kill him."

Alucard let out a low groan. "Saints, you actually have a death wish." He gripped his hat. "What were you *thinking*?"

Lila looked around. "There're plenty of transports coming and going. I was going to stash him away on one of them."

"And what do you plan to do when he wakes up, turns the boat around, and makes it back in time to have you arrested and still compete?" When Lila didn't answer—she hadn't exactly gotten that far—Alucard shook his head. "You've got a real gift for taking things, Bard. You're not nearly as good at getting rid of them."

Lila held her ground. "I'll figure it out." Alucard was muttering curses in a variety of languages under his breath. "And were you *following* me?"

Alucard threw up his hands. "You've assaulted a competitor—I can only imagine with the daft notion of taking his place—and you honestly have the gall to be affronted at *my* actions? Did you even *think* what this would mean for *me*?" He sounded vaguely hysterical.

"This has nothing to do with you."

"This has everything to do with me!" he snapped. "I am your captain! You are my crew." The barb struck with unexpected force. "When the authorities find out a sailor aboard my ship sabotaged a competitor, what do you think they'll assume? That you were mad enough to do something so stupid on your own, or that *I* put you up to it?" He was pale with fury, and the air around them hummed. Indignation flickered through Lila, followed swiftly by guilt. The combination turned her stomach.

"Alucard—" she started.

"Did he see your face?"

Lila crossed her arms. "I don't think so."

Alucard paced, muttering, and then dropped to his knee beside Elsor. He rolled the man over and began digging through his pockets.

"Are you *robbing* him?" she asked, incredulous.

Alucard said nothing as he spread the contents of Elsor's coat across the frozen stones. An inn key. A few coins. A handful of folded pages. Tucked in the center of these, Lila saw, was his formal invitation to the *Essen Tasch*. Alucard plucked the iridescent pin from the collar of the man's coat, then shook his head and gathered up the items. He got to his feet, shoving the articles into Lila's hands. "When this goes badly, and it *will*, you won't take the *Spire* with you. Do you understand, Bard?"

Lila nodded tightly.

"And for the record," he said, "this is a terrible idea. You *will* get caught. Maybe not right away. But eventually. And when you do, I won't protect you."

Lila raised a brow. "I'm not asking you to. Believe it or not, Alucard, I can protect myself."

He looked down at the unconscious man between them. "Does that mean you *don't* need my help disposing of this man?"

Lila tucked her hair behind her ear. "I'm not sure I *need* it, but I'd certainly appreciate it." She knelt to take one of Elsor's arms, and Alucard reached for the other, but halfway there, he stopped and seemed to reconsider. He folded his arms, his eyes dark and his mouth a grim line.

"What is it now?" asked Lila, straightening.

"This is an expensive secret Bard," he said. "I'll keep it, in trade for another."

Dammit, thought Lila. She'd made it months at sea without sharing a thing she didn't want to. "I'll give you one question," she said at last. "One answer."

Alucard had asked the same ones over and over and over: *Who are you,* and *What are you,* and *Where did you come from?* And the answers she'd told him over and over and over weren't even lies. *Delilah Bard. One of a kind. London.*

But standing there on the docks that night, Alucard didn't ask any of those questions.

"You say you're from London . . ." He looked her in the eyes. "But you don't mean *this* one, do you?"

Lila's heart lurched, and she felt herself smile, even though this was the one question she couldn't answer with a lie. "No," she said. "Now help me with this body."

🜂

Alucard proved disturbingly adept at making someone disappear.

Lila leaned against a set of boxes at the transport end of the docks—devoted to the ships coming and going instead of the ones set in for the length of the tournament—and turned Elsor's *S* pin over in her fingers. Elsor himself sat on the ground, slumped against the crates, while Alucard tried to convince a pair of rough-looking men to take on a last-minute piece of cargo. She only caught snippets of the conversation, most of them Alucard's, tuned as she was to his Arnesian.

"Where do you put in . . . that's what, a fortnight this time of year . . . ?"

Lila pocketed the pin and sifted through Elsor's papers, holding them up to the nearest lantern light. The man liked to draw. Small pictures lined the edges of every scrap of paper, save the formal invitation. That was a lovely thing, edged in gold—it reminded her of the invite to Prince Rhy's birthday ball—marred only by a single fold down the center. Elsor had also been carrying a half-written letter, and a few sparse notes on the other competitors. Lila smiled when she saw his one-word note on Alucard Emery:

Performer.

She folded the pages and tucked them into her coat. Speaking of coats—she crouched and began to peel the unconscious man out of his. It was fine, a dark charcoal grey with a low, stiff collar and a belted waist. For a moment she considered trading, but couldn't bring herself to part with Calla's masterpiece, so instead she took a wool blanket from a cart and wrapped it around Elsor so he wouldn't freeze.

Lastly she produced a knife and cut a lock of hair from the man's head, tying it in a knot before dropping it in her pocket.

"I don't want to know," muttered Alucard, who was suddenly standing over her, the sailors a step behind. He nodded to the man on the ground. "*Ker tas naster,*" he grumbled. *There's your man.*

One of the sailors toed Elsor with his boot. "Drunk?"

The other sailor knelt, and clapped a pair of irons around Elsor's wrists, and Lila saw Alucard flinch reflexively.

"Mind him," he said as they hauled the man to his feet.

The sailor shrugged and mumbled something so garbled Lila couldn't tell where one word ended and the next began. Alucard only nodded as they turned and began to haul him toward the ship.

"That's it?" asked Lila.

Alucard frowned. "You know the most valuable currency in life, Bard?"

"What?"

"A favor." His eyes narrowed. "I now owe those men. And you owe me." He kept his eyes trained on the sailors as they hauled the unconscious Elsor aboard. "I've gotten rid of your problem, but it won't *stay* gone. That's a criminal transport. Once it sets out, it's not authorized to turn around until it reaches Delonar. And he's not on the charter, so by the time it docks, they'll know they're carrying an innocent man. So no matter what happens, you better not be here when he gets back."

The meaning in the words was clear, but she still had to ask. "And the *Spire*?"

Alucard looked at her, jaw set. "It only has room for one criminal." He let out a low breath, which turned to fog before his mouth. "But I wouldn't worry."

"Why's that?"

"Because you'll get caught long before we sail away."

Lila managed a grim smirk as Stasion Elsor and the sailors vanished below deck. "Have a little faith, Captain."

But the truth was, she had no idea what she was going to do when this fell apart, no idea if she'd just damned herself by accident, or worse, on purpose. Sabotaged another life. Just like at the Stone's Throw.

"Let's get something straight," said Alucard as they walked

away from the docks. "My help ends here. Alucard Emery and Stasion Elsor have no business with each other. And if we chance to meet in the ring, I won't spare you."

Lila snorted. "I should hope not. Besides, I still have a few tricks up my sleeve."

"I suppose you do," he said, finally glancing toward her. "After all, if you run far enough, no one can catch you."

She frowned, remembering his question, her answer.

"How long have you known?" she asked.

Alucard managed a ghost of a smile, framed by the doorway of their inn. "Why do you think I let you on my ship?"

"Because I was the best thief?"

"Certainly the strangest."

⋟

Lila didn't bother with sleep; there was too much to do. She and Alucard vanished into their respective rooms without even so much as a *good night,* and when she left a few hours later with Elsor's things bundled under her arm, Alucard didn't follow, even though she *knew* he was awake.

One problem at a time, she told herself as she climbed the stairs of the Coach and Castle Inn, the room key hanging from her fingers. A brass tag on the end held the name of the place and the room—*3.*

She found Elsor's room and let herself in.

She'd raided the man's pockets and studied his papers, but if there was anything else to learn before she donned the role at nightfall, she figured she'd find it here.

The room was simple. The bed was made. A looking glass leaned by the window and a silver folding frame sat on the narrow sill, a portrait of Elsor on one side, and a young woman on the other.

Rifling through a trunk at the foot of the bed, she found a few more pieces of clothing, a notebook, a short sword, a pair of gloves. These last were peculiar, designed to cover the tops of the hands but expose the palms and fingertips. Perfect for a fireworker, she thought, pocketing them.

The notebook held mostly sketches—including several of the young woman—as well as a few scribbled notes and a travel ledger. Elsor was scrupulous, and by all evidence, he had indeed come alone. Several letters and slips were tucked into the notebook, and Lila studied his signature, practicing first with her fingers and then a stub of a pencil until she'd gotten it right.

She then began to empty the trunk, tossing the contents onto the bed one by one. A set of boxes near the bottom held an elongated hat that curled down over the brow, and a canvas that unfolded to reveal a set of toiletries.

And then, in a box at the back of the trunk, she found Elsor's mask.

It was carved out of wood, and vaguely resembled a ram, with horns that hugged the sides of one's head and curled against one's cheeks. The only real facial coverage was a nose plate. That wouldn't do. She returned it to the bottom of the chest, and closed the lid.

Next she tried on each piece of clothing, testing her measurements against Elsor's. As she'd hoped, they weren't too far off. An examination of a pair of trousers confirmed she was an inch or two shorter than the man, but wedging some socks in the heels of her boots gave her the extra measure of height.

Lastly, Lila took up the portrait from the sill, and examined the man's face. He was wearing a hat like the one discarded on the bed, and dark hair spilled out beneath it, framing his angled face with near-black curls.

Lila's own hair was several shades lighter, but when she doused it with water from the basin, it looked close. Not a permanent solution, of course, especially in winter, but it helped her focus as she drew out one of her knives.

She returned the portrait to the sill, studying it as she took up a chunk of hair and sawed at it with the blade. It had grown long in the months at sea, and there was something liberating about shearing it off again. Strands tumbled to the floor as she shortened the back and shaped the front, the abusive combination of cold and steel giving the ends a slight curl.

Digging through Elsor's meager supplies, she found a comb as well as a tub of something dark and glossy. It smelled like tree nuts, and when she worked it into her hair, she was relieved to see it hold the curl.

His charcoal coat lay on the bed, and she shrugged it on. Taking up the hat from the bed, she set it gingerly on her styled head, and turned toward her reflection. A stranger, not quite Elsor but certainly not Bard, stared back at her. Something was missing. The pin. She dug in the pockets of his coat and pulled out the iridescent collar pin, fastening it at her throat. Then she cocked her head, adjusting her posture and mannerisms until the illusion came into sharper focus.

Lila broke into a grin.

This, she thought, adding Elsor's short sword to her waist, *is* almost *as fun as being a pirate.*

"*Avan, ras Elsor,*" said a portly woman when she descended the stairs. The innkeeper.

Lila nodded, wishing she'd had a chance to hear the man speak. Hadn't Alucard said that Stross was from the same part of the empire? His accent had rough edges, which Lila tried to mimic as she murmured, "*Avan.*"

The illusion held. No one else paid her any mind, and Lila strode out into the morning light, not as a street thief, or a sailor, but a magician, ready for the *Essen Tasch.*

SEVEN

INTERSECTIONS

I

The day before the *Essen Tasch,* the Night Market roused itself around noon.

Apparently the lure of festivities and foreigners eager to spend money was enough to amend the hours. With time to kill before the Banner Night, Lila wandered the stalls, her coins jingling in Elsor's pockets; she bought a cup of spiced tea and some kind of sweet bun, and tried to make herself comfortable in her new persona.

She didn't dare go back to the Wandering Road, where she'd have to trade Elsor for Bard or else be recognized. Once the tournament began, it wouldn't matter. Identities would disappear behind personas. But today she needed to be seen. Recognized. Remembered.

It wasn't hard. The stall owners were notorious gossips—all she had to do was strike up conversation as she shopped, drop a hint, a detail, once or twice a name, purposefully skirt the topic of the tournament, leave a parcel behind so someone trotted after her calling out, "Elsor! Master Elsor!"

By the time she reached the palace edge of the market, the work was done, word weaving through the crowd. *Stasion Elsor. One of the competitors. Handsome fellow. Too thin. Never seen him before. What can he do? Guess we'll see.* She felt their eyes on her as she shopped, caught the edges of their whispered conversation, and tried to smother her thief's instinct to shake the gaze and disappear.

Not yet, she thought as the sun finally began to sink.

One thing was still missing.

"Lila," said Calla when she entered. "You're early."

"You didn't set a time."

The merchant stopped, taking in Lila's new appearance.

"How do I look?" she asked, shoving her hands in Elsor's coat.

Calla sighed. "Even less like a woman than usual." She plucked the hat off Lila's head and turned it over in her hands.

"This is not bad," said Calla, before noticing Lila's shorn hair. She took a piece between her fingers. "But what is *this*?"

Lila shrugged. "I wanted a change."

Calla tutted, but she didn't prod. Instead, she disappeared through a curtain, and emerged a moment later with a box.

Inside was Lila's mask.

She lifted it, and staggered at the weight. The interior had been lined with dark metal, so cleanly made and shaped that it looked poured instead of hammered. Calla hadn't disposed of the leather demon mask, not entirely, but she'd taken it apart and made something new. The lines were clean, the angles sharp. Where simple black horns had once corkscrewed up over the head, now they curled back in an elegant way. The brow was sharper, jutting forward slightly like a visor, and the bottom of the mask, which had once ended on her cheekbones, now dipped lower at the sides, following the lines of her jaw. It was still a monster's face, but it was a new breed of demon.

Lila slid the mask over her head. She was still wondering at the beautiful, monstrous thing when Calla handed her something else. It was made of the same black leather, and lined with the same dark metal, and it shaped a kind of crown, or a smile, the sides taller than the center. Lila turned it over in her hands, wondering what it was for, until Calla retrieved it, swept around behind her, and fastened the plate around her throat.

"To keep your head on your shoulders," said the woman, who then proceeded to clasp the sides of the neck guard to small, hidden hinges on the tapered sides of the mask. It was like a jaw, and when Lila looked at her reflection, she saw her features nested within the two halves of the monster's skull.

She broke into a devilish grin, her teeth glinting within the mouth of the helmet.

"You," said Lila, "are brilliant."

"*Anesh,*" said Calla with a shrug, though Lila could see that the merchant was proud.

She had the sudden and peculiar urge to *hug* the woman, but she resisted.

The hinged jaw allowed her to raise the mask, which she did, the demon's head resting on top of her own like a crown, the jaw still circling her throat. "How do I look?" she asked.

"Strange," said Calla. "And dangerous."

"Perfect."

Outside, the bells began to toll, and Lila's smile widened.

It was time.

🜋

Kell crossed to the bed and examined the clothes—a set of black trousers and a high-collared black shirt, both trimmed with gold. On top of the shirt sat the gold pin Rhy had given him for the royal reception. His coat waited, thrown over the back of a chair, but he left it there. It was a traveler's charm, and tonight he was confined to the palace.

The clothes on the bed were Rhy's choice, and they weren't simply a gift.

They were a message.

Tomorrow, you can be *Kamerov.*

Tonight, you are *Kell.*

Hastra had appeared earlier, only to confiscate his mask, on Rhy's orders.

Kell had been reluctant to relinquish it.

"You must be excited," Hastra had said, reading his hesitation, "about the tournament. Don't imagine you get to test your mettle very often."

Kell had frowned. "This isn't a game," he'd said, perhaps too sternly. "It's about keeping the kingdom safe." He felt a twinge of guilt as he watched Hastra go pale.

"I've sworn an oath to protect the royal family."

"I'm sorry then," said Kell ruefully, "that you're stuck protecting *me.*"

"It's an honor, sir." There was nothing in his tone but pure, simple truth. "I would defend you with my life."

"Well," said Kell, surrendering Kamerov's mask. "I hope you never have to."

The young guard managed a small, embarrassed smile. "Me too, sir."

Kell paced his room and tried to put tomorrow from his mind. First he had to survive tonight.

A pitcher and bowl sat on the sideboard, and Kell poured water into the basin and pressed his palms to the sides until it steamed. Once clean, he dressed in Rhy's chosen attire, willing to humor his brother. It was the least he could do—though Kell wondered, as he slipped on the tunic, how long Rhy would be calling in this payment. He could picture the prince a decade from now, telling Kell to fetch him tea.

"Get it yourself," he would say, and Rhy would tut and answer, "Remember Kamerov?"

Kell's evening clothes were tight, formfitting in the style Rhy favored, and made of a black fabric so fine it caught the light instead of swallowing it. The cut and fit forced him to stand at full height, erasing his usual slouch. He fastened the gold buttons, the cuffs and collar—saints, how many clasps did it take to clothe a man?—and lastly the royal pin over his heart.

Kell checked himself in his mirror, and stiffened.

Even with his fair skin and auburn hair, even with the black eye that shone like polished rock, Kell looked *regal*. He stared at his reflection for several long moments, mesmerized, before tearing his gaze away.

He looked like a prince.

🐍

Rhy stood before the mirror, fastening the gleaming buttons of his tunic. Beyond the shuttered balcony, the sounds of celebration were rising off the cold night like steam. Carriages and laughter, footsteps and music.

He was running late, and he knew it, but he couldn't seem to get his nerves under control, wrangle his fears. It was getting dark, and the darkness leaned against the palace, and against him, the weight settling on his chest.

He poured himself a drink—his third—and forced a smile at his reflection.

Where was the prince who relished such festivities, who loved nothing better than to be the contagious joy at the center of the room?

Dead, thought Rhy, drily, before he could stop himself, and he was glad, not for the first time, that Kell could not read his mind as well as feel his pain. Luckily, other people still seemed to look at Rhy and see what he'd been instead of what he was. He didn't know if that meant he was good at hiding the difference, or that they weren't paying attention to begin with. Kell looked, and Rhy was sure he saw the change, but he had the sense not to say anything. There was nothing to be said. Kell had given Rhy a life—*his* life—and it wasn't his fault if Rhy didn't like it as much as his own. He'd lost that one, forfeited by his own foolishness.

He downed the drink, hoping it would render him in better spirits, but it dulled the world without ever touching his thoughts.

He touched the gleaming buttons and adjusted his crown for the dozenth time, shivering as a gust of cold air brushed against his neck.

"I fear you haven't enough gold," came a voice from the balcony doors.

Rhy stiffened. "What are guards for," he said slowly, "when they let even pirates pass?"

The man took a step forward, and then another, silver on him ringing like muffled chimes. "*Privateer*'s the term these days."

Rhy swallowed and turned to face Alucard Emery. "As for the gold," he said evenly, "it is a fine balance. The more I wear, the more likely one is to try and rob me of it."

"Such a dilemma," said Alucard, stealing another stride. Rhy took him in. He was dressed in clothes that had clearly never seen the sea. A dark blue suit, accented by a silver cloak, his rich brown hair groomed and threaded with gems to match. A single sapphire sparkled over his right eye. Those eyes, like night lilies caught in moonlight. He used to smell like them, too. Now he smelled like sea breeze and spice, and other things Rhy could not place, from lands he'd never seen.

"What brings a rogue like you to my chambers?" he asked.

"A rogue," Alucard rolled the word over his tongue. "Better a rogue than a bored royal."

Rhy felt Alucard's eyes wandering slowly, hungrily, over him, and he blushed. The heat started in his face and spread down, through his collar, his chest, beneath shirt and belt. It was disconcerting; Rhy might not have magic, but when it came to conquests, he was used to holding the power—things happened at his whim, and at his pleasure. Now he felt that power falter, slip. In all of Arnes, there was only one person capable of flustering the prince, of reducing him from a proud royal to a nervous youth, and that was Alucard Emery. Misfit. Rogue. Privateer. And royal. Removed from the throne by a stretch of tangled bloodlines, sure, but still. Alucard Emery could have had a crest and a place in court. Instead, he fled.

"You've come for the tournament," said Rhy, making small talk.

Alucard pursed his lips at the attempt. "Among other things."

Rhy hesitated, unsure what to say next. With anyone else, he would have had a flirtatious retort, but standing there, a mere stride away from Alucard, he felt short of breath, let alone words. He turned away, fidgeting with his cuffs. He heard the chime of silver and a moment later, Alucard snaked an arm possessively around his shoulders and brought his lips to the prince's neck, just below his ear. Rhy actually *shivered.*

"You are far too familiar with your prince," he warned.

"So you confess it, then?" His brushed his lips against Rhy's throat. "That you are mine."

He bit the lobe of Rhy's ear, and the prince gasped, back arching. Alucard always did know what to say—what to do—to tilt the world beneath his feet.

Rhy turned to say something, but Alucard's mouth was already there on his. Hands tangled in hair, clutched at coats. They were a collision, spurred by the force of three years apart.

"You missed me," said Alucard. It was not a question, but there *was* a confession in it, because everything about Alucard— the tension in his back, the ways his hips pressed into Rhy's, the race of his heart and the tremor in his voice—said that the missing had been mutual.

"I'm a prince," said Rhy, striving for composure. "I know how to keep myself entertained."

The sapphire glinted in Alucard's brow. "*I* can be very entertaining." He was already leaning in as he spoke, and Rhy found himself closing the distance, but at the last moment Alucard tangled his fingers in Rhy's hair and pulled his head back, exposing the prince's throat. He pressed his lips to the slope below Rhy's jaw.

Rhy clenched his teeth, fighting back a groan, but his stillness must have betrayed him; he felt Alucard smile against his skin. The man's fingers drifted to his tunic, deftly unbuttoning his collar so his kisses could continue downward, but Rhy felt him hesitate at the sight of the scar over his heart. "Someone has wounded you," he whispered into Rhy's collarbone. "Shall I make it better?"

Rhy pulled Alucard's face back to his, desperate to draw his attention from the mark, and the questions it might bring. He bit Alucard's lip, and delighted in the small victory of the gasp it earned him as—

The bells rang out.

The Banner Night.

He was late. They were late.

Alucard laughed softly, sadly. Rhy closed his eyes and swallowed.

"*Sanct,*" he cursed, hating the world that waited beyond his doors, and his place in it.

Alucard was already pulling away, and for an instant all Rhy wanted to do was pull him back, hold fast, terrified that if he let go, Alucard would vanish again, not just from the room but from London, from *him,* slip out into the night and the sea as he'd done three years before. Alucard must have seen the panic in his eyes, because he turned back, and drew Rhy in, and pressed his lips to Rhy's one last time, a gentle, lingering kiss.

"Peace," he said, pulling slowly free. "I am not a ghost." And then he smiled, and smoothed his coat, and turned away. "Fix your crown, my prince," he called back as he reached the door. "It's crooked."

II

Kell was halfway down the stairs when he was met by a short *ostra* with a trimmed beard and a frazzled look. Parlo, the prince's shadow since the tournament preparations first began.

"Master Kell," he said, breathless. "The prince is not with you?"

Kell cocked his head. "I assumed he was already downstairs."

Parlo shook his head. "Could something be wrong?"

"Nothing's wrong," said Kell with certainty.

"Well then, it's about to be. The king is losing patience, most of the guests are here, and the prince has not yet made an entrance."

"Perhaps that's exactly what he's trying to make." Parlo looked sick with panic. "If you're worried, why don't you go to his room and fetch him?" The *ostra* paled even further, as if Kell had just suggested something unfathomable. Obscene.

"Fine," grumbled Kell, turning back up the stairs. "*I'll* do it."

Tolners and Vis were standing outside Rhy's room. Kell was a few strides shy of the chamber when the doors burst open and a figure came striding out. A figure that most certainly *wasn't* Rhy. The guards' eyes widened at the sight of him. The man obviously hadn't gone in that way. Kell pulled up short as they nearly collided, and even though it had been years—too few, in Kell's estimation—he recognized the man at once.

"Alucard Emery," he said coldly, exhaling the name like a curse.

A slow smile spread across the man's mouth, and it took all Kell's restraint not to physically remove it. "Master Kell," said Alucard, cheerfully. "What an unexpected pleasure, running into you here." His voice had a natural undercurrent of laughter in it, and Kell could never tell if he was being mocked.

"I don't see how it's unexpected," said Kell, "as *I* live here. What *is* unexpected is running into *you,* since I thought I made myself quite clear the last time we met."

"Quite," echoed Alucard.

"Then what were you doing in my brother's chambers?"

Alucard raised a single studded brow. "Do you want a detailed account? Or will a summary suffice?"

Kell's fingernails dug into his palms. He could feel blood. Spells came to mind, a dozen different ways to wipe the smug look from Emery's face.

"Why are you here?" he growled.

"I'm sure you've heard," said Alucard, hands in his pockets. "I'm competing in the *Essen Tasch.* As such, I was invited to the royal palace for the Banner Night."

"Which is happening downstairs, *not* in the prince's room. Are you lost?" He didn't wait for Alucard to answer. "Tolners," he snapped. The guard stepped forward. "Escort Master Emery to the Rose Hall. Make sure he doesn't wander."

Tolners motioned, as if to take hold of Alucard's sleeve, and found himself propelled suddenly backward into the wall. Alucard never took his hands from his pockets, and his smile never wavered as he said, "I'm sure I can find my way."

He set off in the direction of the stairs, but as he passed Kell, the latter caught his elbow. "Do you remember what I told you, before banishing you from this city?"

"Vaguely. Your threats all seem to run together."

"I said," snarled Kell through clenched teeth, "that if you

break my brother's heart a second time, I will cut yours out. I stand by that promise, Alucard."

"Still fond of growling, aren't you, Kell? Ever the loyal dog, nipping at heels. Maybe one day you'll actually bite." With that he pulled free and strode away, his silver blue cloak billowing behind him.

Kell watched him go.

The moment Alucard was out of sight, he slammed his fist into the wall, hard enough to crack the inlaid wooden panel. He swore in pain and frustration, and an echoing curse came from within Rhy's chambers, but this time, Kell didn't feel bad for causing his brother a little pain. Blood stained his palm where his nails had sliced into the skin, and Kell pressed it to the broken decoration.

"*As Sora*," he muttered. *Unbreak.*

The crack in the wood began to withdraw, the pieces of wood blending back together. He kept his hand there, trying to loosen the knot in his chest.

"Master Kell . . ." started Vis.

"What?" he snapped, spinning on the guards. The air in the hall churned around him. The floorboards trembled. The men looked pale. "If you see that man near Rhy's rooms again, arrest him."

Kell took a steadying breath, and was reaching for the prince's door when it swung inward to reveal Rhy, settling the gold band atop his head. When he saw the gathering of guards, and Kell at their center, he cocked his head.

"What?" he said. "I'm not *that* late." Before anyone else could speak, Rhy set off down the hall. "Don't just stand there, Kell," he called back. "We have a party to host."

❧

"You're in a mood," said the prince as they passed into the dignified splendor of the Rose Hall.

Kell said nothing, trying to salvage the man he'd seen earlier in his bedroom mirror. He scanned the hall, his attention snagging almost instantly on Alucard Emery, who stood socializing with a group of magicians.

"Honestly, Kell," chided Rhy, "if looks could kill."

"Maybe *looks* can't," he said, flexing his fingers.

Rhy smiled and nodded his head at a cluster of guests. "You knew he was coming," he said through set teeth.

"I didn't realize you'd be giving him such an intimate welcome," snapped Kell in return. "How could you be so foolish—"

"I didn't invite him in—"

"—after everything that's happened."

"*Enough,*" hissed the prince, loud enough to turn the nearest heads.

Kell would have shrunk from the attention, but Rhy spread his arms, embracing it.

"Father," he called across the hall, "if I may do the honors."

King Maxim lifted his glass in reply, and Rhy stepped lithely up onto the nearest stone planter, and the gathering fell quiet.

"*Avan!*" he said, voice echoing through the hall. "*Glad'ach. Sasors,*" he added to the guests from Vesk and Faro. "I am Prince Rhy Maresh," he continued, slipping back into Arnesian. "Maxim and Emira, the illustrious king and queen of Arnes, my father and mother, have given me the honor of hosting this tournament. And it *is* an honor." He lifted a hand, and a wave of royal servants appeared, carrying trays laden with crystal goblets, candied fruits, smoked meat, and a dozen other delicacies. "Tomorrow you shall be introduced as champions. Tonight, I ask you to enjoy yourselves as honored guests and friends. Drink, feast, and claim your sigil. In the morning, the Games begin!"

Rhy bowed, and the crowd of gathered magicians and royals applauded as he hopped down from his perch. The tide of people shifted, some toward the banquets, others toward the banner tables.

"Impressive," observed Kell.

"Come on," said Rhy without meeting his eye. "*One* of us needs a drink."

※

"Stop."

Lila had just started up the palace steps, the demon's mask beneath her arm, when she heard the order.

She stiffened, her fingers reaching reflexively for the knife at her back as a pair of guards in gleaming armor blocked her path. Her pulse pounded, urging her to fight or flee, but Lila forced herself to hold her ground. They weren't drawing weapons.

"I'm here for the Banner Night," she said, drawing Elsor's royal verification from her coat. "I was told to report to the palace."

"You want the Rose Hall," explained the first guard, as if Lila had a damn clue where *that* was. The other guard pointed at a second, smaller set of stairs. Lila had never noticed the other entrances to the palace—there were two, flanking the main steps, and both were tame by comparison—but now that they'd been pointed out, the flow of traffic up and around those steps compared to the empty grand entrance was obvious. As was the fact that the doors to the Rose Hall had been flung open, while the palace's main entrance was firmly shut.

"*Solase,*" she said, shaking her head. "I must be more nervous than I thought." The guards smiled.

"I will lead you," said one, as if she might honestly go astray a second time. The guard ushered her over to right set of stairs and up before handing her off to an attendant, who led her through the entryway and into the Rose Hall.

It was an impressive space, less ballroom than throne room, undoubtedly refined without being ostentatious—how far she'd come, she thought wryly, to find massive urns of fresh-cut flowers and sumptuous red and gold tapestries *restrained.*

A familiar captain stood near the mouth of the hall, dressed in silver and midnight blue. He saw Lila, and his face passed through several reactions before settling on cool appraisal.

"Master Elsor."

"Master Emery." Lila gave a flourish and a bow, stiffening her posture into angles.

Alucard shook his head. "I honestly don't know whether to be impressed or unnerved."

Lila straightened. "The two aren't mutually exclusive."

He nodded at the Sarows mask under her arm. "Do you *want* to be found out?"

Lila shrugged. "There are many shadows in the night." She caught sight of the mask tucked beneath his own arm. Made of dark blue scales, their edges tipped with silver, the mask ran from hairline to cheekbone. Once on, it would leave his charmer's smile exposed, and do nothing to tame the crown of brassy curls that rose above. The mask itself looked purely aesthetic, its scales offering neither anonymity nor protection.

"What are you supposed to be?" she asked in Arnesian. "A fish?"

Alucard made a noise of mock affront. "*Obviously,*" he said, brandishing the helmet, "I'm a dragon."

"Wouldn't it make more sense for you to be a fish?" challenged Lila. "After all, you do live on the sea, and you are rather slippery, and—"

"I'm a dragon," he interjected. "You're just not being very imaginative."

Lila grinned, partly in amusement, and partly in relief as they fell into a familiar banter. "I thought House Emery's sigil was a feather. Shouldn't you be a bird?"

Alucard rapped his fingers on the mask. "My family is full of birds," he said, the words laced with spite. "My father was a vulture. My mother was a magpie. My oldest brother is a crow. My sister, a sparrow. I have never really been a bird."

Lila resisted the urge to say he might have been a peacock. It didn't seem the time.

"But our house symbol," he went on, "it represents *flight,* and birds are not the only things that fly." He held up the dragon mask. "Besides, I am not competing for House Emery. I am competing for myself. And if you could see the rest of my outfit, you wouldn't—"

"Do you have wings? Or a tail?"

"Well, no, those would get in the way. But I do have more scales."

"So does a fish."

"Go away," he snapped, but there was humor in his voice, and soon they fell into an easy laugh, and then remembered where they were. *Who* they were.

"Emery!" called Jinnar, appearing at the captain's elbow.

His mask—a silver crown that curled like spun sugar, or perhaps a swirl of air—hung from his fingertips. His feet were firmly on the floor tonight, but she could practically feel the hum of energy coming off him, see it blur his edges. Like a hummingbird. How would she fight a hummingbird? How would she fight any of them?

"And who's this?" asked Jinnar, glancing at Lila.

"Why, Jinnar," said Alucard drolly, "don't you recognize our Master Elsor?"

The magician's silver eyes narrowed. Lila raised a challenging brow. Jinnar had met the *real* Stasion Elsor back in the tavern. Now his metallic eyes swept over her, confused, and then suspicious. Lila's fingers twitched, and Alucard's hand came to rest on her shoulder—whether it was to show solidarity or keep her from drawing a weapon, she didn't know.

"Master Elsor," said Jinnar slowly. "You look different tonight. But then again," he added, eyes flicking to Alucard, "the light was so low in the tavern, and I haven't seen you since."

"An easy mistake to make," said Lila smoothly. "I'm not overly fond of displays."

"Well," chimed in Alucard brightly. "I do hope you'll overcome that once we take the stage."

"I'm sure I'll find my stride," retorted Lila.

"I'm sure you will."

A beat of silence hung between them, remarkable considering the din of the gathering crowd. "Well, if you'll excuse me," said Alucard, breaking the moment, "I've yet to properly harass Brost, and I'm determined to meet this Kamerov fellow . . ."

"It was nice to meet you . . . again," said Jinnar, before following Alucard away.

Lila watched them go, then began to weave through the crowd, trying to keep her features set in resignation, as if mingling with dozens of imperial magicians was commonplace. Along one wall, tables were laden with swatches of fabric and pitchers of ink, and magicians turned through pages of designs as they declared their banners—a crow on green, a flame on white, a rose on black—pennants that would wave from the stands the following day.

Lila plucked a crystal goblet from a servant's tray, weighing it in her fingers before remembering she wasn't here as a thief. She caught Alucard's eye, and toasted him with a wink. As she lapped the hall, taking in the main floor and the gallery above and sipping sweet wine, she counted the bodies to occupy her mind and keep her composure.

Thirty-six magicians, herself included, twelve from each of the three empires, and all marked by a mask on top of their head or under their arm or slung over their shoulder.

Two dozen servants, give or take (it was hard to tell, dressed alike as they were, and always moving).

Twelve guards.

Fifteen *ostra,* judging by their haughty expressions.

Six *vestra,* going by their royal pins.

Two blond Veskans wearing crowns instead of masks, each with an entourage of six, and a tall Faroan with an expressionless face and an entourage of eight.

The Arnesian king and queen in splendid red and gold.

Prince Rhy in the gallery above.

And, standing beside him, Kell.

Lila held her breath. For once, Kell's auburn hair was swept back from his face, revealing both the crisp blue of his left eye and the glossy black of his right. He wasn't wearing his usual coat, in *any* of its forms. Instead he was dressed head to toe in elegant black, a gold pin over his heart.

Kell had told her once that he felt more like possession than a prince, but standing at Rhy's side, one hand around his glass and the other on the rail as he gazed down on the crowd, he looked like he belonged.

The prince said something, and Kell's face lit up in a silent laugh.

Where was the bloodied boy who'd collapsed on her bedroom floor?

Where was the tortured magician, veins turning black as he fought a talisman's pull?

Where was the sad, lonely royal who'd stood on the docks and watched her walk away?

That last one she could almost see. There, at the edge of his mouth, the corner of his eye.

Lila felt her body moving toward him, drawn as if by gravity, several steps lost before she caught herself. She wasn't Lila Bard tonight. She was Stasion Elsor, and while the illusion seemed to be holding well enough, she knew it would crumble in front of Kell. And in spite of that, part of her still wanted to catch his eye, relish his moment of surprise, watch it dissolve into recognition, and—hopefully—welcome. But she couldn't imagine he'd be glad to see her, not here, mingling with the throngs of competitors. And in truth, Lila savored the sensation of watching without being watched. It made her feel like a predator, and in a room of magicians, that was something.

"I don't believe we've met," came a voice behind her in accented English.

She turned to find a young man, tall and slender, with reddish brown hair and dark lashes circling grey eyes. He had a silver-white mask tucked beneath his arm, and he shifted it to his other side before extending a gloved hand.

"Kamerov," he said genially. "Kamerov Loste."

So this was the elusive magician, the one neither Jinnar nor Alucard had managed to find. She didn't see what all the fuss was about.

"Stasion Elsor," she answered.

"Well, Master Elsor," he said with a confident smile, "perhaps we will meet in the arena."

She raised a brow and began to move away.

"Perhaps."

III

"I took the liberty of designing your pennant," said Rhy, resting his elbows on the gallery's marble banister. "I hope you don't mind."

Kell cringed. "Do I even want to know what's on it?"

Rhy tugged the folded piece of fabric from his pocket, and handed it over. The cloth was red, and when he unfolded it, he saw the image of a rose in black and white. The rose had been mirrored, folded along the center axis and reflected, so the design was actually *two* flowers, surrounded by a coil of thorns.

"How subtle," said Kell tonelessly.

"You could at least pretend to be grateful."

"And you couldn't have picked something a little more . . . I don't know . . . imposing? A serpent? A great beast? A bird of prey?"

"A bloody handprint?" retorted Rhy. "Oh, what about a glowing black eye?"

Kell glowered.

"You're right," continued Rhy, "I should have just drawn a frowning face. But then everyone would *know* it's you. I thought this was rather fitting."

Kell muttered something unkind as he shoved the banner into his pocket.

"You're welcome."

Kell surveyed the Rose Hall. "You think anyone will notice

that I'm—well, that Kamerov Loste is missing from the festivities?"

Rhy took a sip of his drink. "I doubt it," he said. "But just in case . . ."

He nodded the drink at a lean figure moving through the crowd. Kell was halfway through a sip of wine when he saw the man, and nearly choked on it. The figure was tall and slim, with trimmed auburn hair. He was dressed in elegant black trousers and a silver high-collared tunic, but it was the mask tucked under his arm that caught Kell's eye.

A single piece of sculpted silver-white metal, polished to a high shine.

His mask. Or rather, *Kamerov*'s.

"Who on earth is *that*?"

"That, my dear brother, is Kamerov Loste. At least for tonight."

"Dammit, Rhy, the more people you tell about this plan, the more likely it is to fail."

The prince waved a hand. "I've paid our actor handsomely to play the part tonight, and as far as he's concerned it's because the real Kamerov doesn't care for public displays. This is the only event where all thirty-six competitors are expected to show their faces, Kamerov included. Besides, Castars is discreet."

"You *know* him?"

Rhy shrugged. "Our paths have crossed."

"Stop," said Kell. "Please. I don't want to hear about your romantic interludes with the man currently posing as me."

"Don't be obscene. I haven't been with him since he agreed to take up this particular role. And that right there is a testament to my respect for you."

"How flattering."

Rhy caught the man's eye, and a few moments later, having toured the room, the false Kamerov Loste—well, Kell supposed they were both false, but the copy of the copy—ascended the stairs to the gallery.

"Prince Rhy," said the man, bowing with a little more flourish than Kell would have used. "And Master Kell," he added reverently.

"Master Loste," said Rhy cheerfully.

The man's eyes, both grey, drifted to Kell. Up close, he saw that they were the same height and build. Rhy had been thorough.

"I wish you luck in the coming days," said Kell.

The man's smile deepened. "It is an *honor* to fight for Arnes."

"A bit over the top, isn't he?" asked Kell as the impostor returned to the floor.

"Oh, don't be bitter," said Rhy. "The important thing is that Kamerov has a *face*. Specifically a face that isn't *yours*."

"He doesn't have the coat."

"No, unfortunately for us, you can't pull coats *out* of that coat of yours, and I figured you'd be unwilling to part with it."

"You'd be right." Kell was just turning away when he saw the shadow moving across the floor, a figure dressed in black with the edge of a smirk and a demon's mask. It almost looked like the one he'd seen on Lila the night of Rhy's masquerade. The night Astrid had taken Kell prisoner, taken Rhy's body for her own. Lila had appeared like a specter on the balcony, dressed in black and wearing a horned mask. She'd worn it then, and later, as they fled with Rhy's dying body between them, and in the sanctuary room as Kell fought to resurrect him. She'd worn it in her hair as they stood in the stone forest at the steps of the White London castle, and it had hung from her bloody fingers when it was over.

"Who is that?" he asked.

Rhy followed his gaze. "Someone who clearly shares your taste for monochrome. Beyond that . . ." Rhy tugged a folded paper from his pocket, and skimmed the roster. "It's not Brost, he's huge. I've met Jinnar. Must be Stasion."

Kell squinted, but the resemblance was already fading. The hair was too short, too dark, the mask different, the smile replaced by hard lines. Kell shook his head.

"I know it's mad, but for a second I thought it was . . ."

"Saints, you're seeing her in everyone and everything now, Kell? There's a word for that."

"Hallucination?"

"Infatuation."

Kell snorted. "I'm not infatuated," he said. "I just . . ." He just wanted to see her. "Our paths crossed one time. Months ago. It happens."

"Oh yes, your relationship with Miss Bard is positively ordinary."

"Be quiet."

"Crossing worlds, killing royals, saving cities. The marks of every good courtship."

"We weren't courting," snapped Kell. "In case you forgot, she left."

He didn't mean to sound wounded. It wasn't that she left *him*, it was simply that she left. And he couldn't follow, even if he'd wanted to. And now she was *back*.

Rhy straightened. "When this is over, we should take a trip."

Kell rolled his eyes. "Not this again."

And then he saw Master Tieren's white robes moving through the hall below. All night—all week, all month—the *Aven Essen* had been avoiding him.

"Hold this," he said, passing the prince his drink.

Before Rhy could argue, Kell was gone.

❧

Lila slipped out before the crowd could thin, the demon mask hanging from one hand and her chosen pennant from the other.

Two silver knives crossed against a ground of black. She was in the foyer when she heard the sound of steps behind her. Not crisp boots on marble, but soft, well-worn shoes.

"Delilah Bard," said a calm, familiar voice.

She stopped mid-stride, then turned. The head priest of the London Sanctuary stood, holding a silver goblet in both hands, his fingers laced. His white robes were trimmed with gold, his silver-white hair groomed but simple around his sharp blue eyes.

"Master Tieren," she said, smiling even as her heart pounded in warning. "Is the *Aven Essen* supposed to drink?"

"I don't see why not," he said. "The key to all things, be they magical or alcoholic, is moderation." He considered the glass. "Besides, this is water."

"Ah," said Lila, cheating a step back, the mask behind her back. She wasn't entirely sure what to do. Normally her two options upon being cornered were turn and run or fight, but neither seemed appropriate when it came to Master Tieren. Some small part of her thrilled at being recognized, and she honestly couldn't imagine drawing a knife on Kell's mentor.

"That's quite an outfit you're wearing," observed the *Aven Essen,* advancing. "If you wanted an audience with Prince Rhy and Master Kell, I'm sure you could simply have called for one. Was a disguise really necessary?" And then, reading her expression, "But this disguise wasn't simply a way into the palace, was it?"

"Actually, I'm here as a competitor."

"No, you're not," he said simply.

Lila bristled. "How would you know?"

"Because I selected them myself."

Lila shrugged. "One of them must have dropped out."

He gave her a long, appraising look.

Was he reading her thoughts? *Could* he? That was the hardest part of being plunged into a world where magic was possible. It made you wonder if *everything* was. Lila was neither a skeptic nor a believer; she relied on her gut and the world she could see. But the world she could see had gotten considerably stranger.

"Miss Bard, what trouble have you gotten into now?" Before she could answer, he went on, "But that isn't the right question, is it? Judging by your appearance, the right question would be, where is Master Elsor?"

Lila cracked a smile. "He's alive and well," she said. "Well, he's alive. Or at least he was, the last time I checked." The priest let out a short exhale. "He's fine, Master Tieren. But he won't be able to make the *Essen Tasch,* so I'll be filling in."

There was another brief sigh, heavy with disapproval.

"You're the one who encouraged me," challenged Lila.

"I told you to tend your waking power, not cheat your way into an international tournament."

"You told me that I had magic in me. Now you don't think I have what it takes?"

"I don't *know* what you have, Lila. And neither do you. And while I'm glad to hear that your stay in our world has so far been fruitful, what you need is time and practice and a good deal of discipline."

"Have a little faith, Master Tieren. Some people believe that necessity is the key to flourishing."

"Those people are fools. And you have a dangerous disregard for your own life, and the lives of others."

"So I've been told." She cheated another step back. She was in the doorway now. "Are you going to try to stop me?"

He shot her a hard blue look. "Could I?"

"You could try. Arrest me. Expose me. We can make a show of it. But I don't think that's what you want. The real Stasion Elsor is on his way to Delonar, and won't be back in time to compete. Besides, this tournament, it's important, isn't it?" She drew a finger down the doorframe. "For diplomatic relations. There are people here from Vesk and Faro. What do you think they'd do if they knew where I really came from? What would that say about the doors between worlds? What would that say about *me*? It gets messy rather fast, doesn't it, Master Tieren? But more than that, I think you're curious to see what a Grey London girl can do."

Tieren fixed her with his gaze. "Has anyone ever told you that you're too sharp for your own good?"

"Too sharp. Too loud. Too reckless. I've heard it all. It's a wonder I'm still alive."

"Indeed."

Lila's hand fell from the door. "Don't tell Kell."

"Oh, trust me, child, that's the last thing I'll do. When you get caught, I plan on feigning ignorance about *all* of this." He lowered his voice, and added, mostly to himself, "This tournament will be the death of me." And then he cleared his throat. "Does he know you're here?"

Lila bit her lip. "Not yet."

"Do you plan to tell him?"

Lila looked to the Rose Hall beyond the priest. She did, didn't she? So what was stopping her? The uncertainty? So long as she knew and he didn't, she was in control. The moment he found out, the balance would shift. Besides, if Kell found out she was competing—if he found out what she'd *done* to compete—she'd never see the inside of an arena. Hell, she'd probably never see anything again but the inside of a cell, and even if she wasn't arrested, she'd certainly never hear the end of it.

She stepped out onto the landing, Tieren in her wake.

"How are they?" she asked, looking out at the city.

"The princes? They seem well enough. And yet . . ." Tieren sounded genuinely concerned.

"What is it?" she prompted.

"Things have not been the same since the Black Night. Prince Rhy is himself, and yet he isn't. He takes to the streets less often, and garners more trouble when he does."

"And Kell?"

Tieren hesitated. "Some think him responsible for the shadow that crossed our city."

"That's not fair," snapped Lila. "We saved the city."

Tieren gave a shrug as if to say, such is the nature of fear and doubt. They breed too easily. Kell and Rhy had seemed happy on that balcony, but she could see it, the fraying edges of the disguise. The darkness just beyond.

"You better go," said the *Aven Essen*. "Tomorrow will be . . . well, it will be something."

"Will you cheer for me?" she asked, forcing herself to keep her voice light.

"I'll pray you don't get yourself killed."

Lila smirked and started down the steps. She was halfway to the street when she heard someone say, "Wait."

But it wasn't Tieren. The voice was younger, one she hadn't heard in four months. Sharp and low, with a touch of strain, as if he were out of breath, or holding back.

Kell.

She hesitated on the stairs, head bowed, fingers aching where they gripped the helmet. She was about to turn around, but he spoke again, calling a name. It wasn't hers.

"Tieren," said Kell. "Please wait."

Lila swallowed, her back to the head priest and the black-eyed prince.

It took all of her strength to start walking again.

And when she did, she didn't look back.

🙙

"What is it, Master Kell?" asked Tieren.

Kell felt the words dry up in his throat. Finally, he managed a single petulant sentence. "You've been avoiding me."

The old man's eyes glittered, but he didn't deny the claim. "I have many talents, Kell," he said, "but believe it or not, deception has never been among them. I suspect it's why I've never won a game of Sanct. . . ."

Kell raised a brow. He couldn't picture the *Aven Essen* playing in the first place. "I wanted to thank you. For letting Rhy, and for letting me—"

"I haven't let you do anything," cut in Tieren. Kell cringed. "I simply haven't stopped you, because if I've learned one thing about you both, it's that if you want to do a thing, you'll do it, the world be damned."

"You think I'm being selfish."

"No, Master Kell." The priest rubbed his eyes. "I think you're being human."

Kell didn't know if that was a slight coming from the *Aven Essen,* who was supposed to think him *blessed.*

"I sometimes think I've gone mad."

Tieren sighed. "Truth be told, I think everyone is mad. I think Rhy is mad for putting this scheme together, madder still for planning it so well." His voice fell a measure. "I think the king and queen are mad for blaming one son above the other."

Kell swallowed. "Will they never forgive me?"

"Which would you rather have? Their forgiveness, or Rhy's life?"

"I shouldn't have to choose," he snapped.

Tieren's gaze drifted away to the steps and the Isle and the glittering city. "The world is neither fair nor right, but it has a way of balancing itself. Magic teaches us that much. But I want you to promise me something."

"What?"

That shrewd blue gaze swiveled back. "That you'll be careful."

"I'll do my best. You know I don't wish to cause Rhy pain, but—"

"I'm not asking you to mind Rhy's life, you stupid boy. I'm

asking you to mind your own." Master Tieren brought his hand to Kell's face, a familiar calm transferring like heat.

Just then, Rhy appeared, looking cheerfully drunk. "There you are!" he called, wrapping his arm around Kell's shoulders and hissing in his ear. "*Hide.* Princess Cora is hunting princes. . . ."

Kell let Rhy drag him back inside, casting one last glance at Tieren, who stood on the steps, his back to the palace and his eyes on the night.

IV

"What are we doing here?"

"Hiding."

"Surely we could have hidden in the palace."

"Really, Kell. You've no imagination."

"Is it going to sink?"

The bottle sloshed in Rhy's hand. "Don't be ridiculous."

"I think it's a valid question," retorted Kell.

"They told me it couldn't be done," Rhy said, toasting the arena.

"Couldn't, or shouldn't?" asked Kell, treading on the stadium floor as if it were made of glass. "Because if it's the latter—"

"You're such a nag—ow." Rhy stubbed his foot on something, a dull pain echoing through Kell's toes.

"Here," he grumbled, summoning a palmful of fire.

"No." Rhy lunged at him, forcing his hand closed and dousing the light. "We are sneaking. Sneaking is meant to be done in the dark."

"Well then, watch where you're going."

Rhy must have decided they'd gone far enough, because he slumped onto the polished stone floor of the arena. In the moonlight, Kell could see his brother's eyes, the circlet of gold in his hair, the bottle of spiced wine as he pulled out the stopper.

Kell lowered himself to the ground beside the prince and

rested against a something—a platform, a wall, a set of stairs? He tipped his head back and marveled at the stadium, what little he could see—the stands soon to be filled, the ruse soon to play out, and the idea that the whole thing could actually work.

"Are you sure about this?" asked Kell.

"A little late to change our minds," mused the prince.

"I'm serious, Rhy. There's still time."

The prince took a sip of wine and set the bottle down between them, clearly considering his answer. "Do you remember what I told you?" he asked gently. "After that night. About why I took the pendant from Holland."

Kell nodded. "You wanted strength."

"I still want it," Rhy whispered. "Every day. I wake up wanting to be a stronger person. A better prince. A worthy king. That want, it's like a fire in my chest. And then, there are these moments, these horrible, icy moments when I remember what I did . . ." His hand drifted to his heart. "To myself. To you. To my kingdom. And it hurts. . . ." His voice trembled. "More than dying ever did. There are days when I don't feel like I deserve this." He tapped the soul seal. "I deserve to be . . ." He trailed off, but Kell could feel his brother's pain, as though it were a physical thing.

"I guess what I'm trying to say," said Rhy, "is that I need this, too." His eyes finally found Kell's. "Okay?"

Kell swallowed. "Okay." He took up the bottle.

"That said, do try not to get us both killed."

Kell groaned, and Rhy chuckled.

"To clever plans," said Kell, toasting his brother. "And dashing princes."

"To masked magicians," said Rhy, swiping the wine.

"To mad ideas."

"To the *Essen Tasch*."

"Wouldn't it be amazing," murmured Rhy later, when the bottle was empty, "if we got away with it?"

"Who knows," said Kell. "We just might."

⅌

Rhy stumbled into his room, waving off Tolner's questions about where he'd been and shutting the door in the guard's face. It was dark, and he made it three unsteady strides before knocking his shin against a low table, and swearing roundly.

The room swam, a mess of shadows lit only by the pale light of the low-burning fire in the hearth and the candles in the corners, only half of which had been lit. Rhy retreated until his back found the nearest wall, and waited for the room to settle.

Downstairs, the party had finally dissipated, the royals retreating to their wings, the nobles to their homes. Tomorrow. Tomorrow the tournament would finally be here.

Rhy knew Kell's true hesitation, and it wasn't getting caught, or starting trouble; it was the fear of causing him pain. Every day Kell moved like Rhy was made of glass, and it was driving them both mad. But once the tournament started, once he saw that Rhy was fine, that he could take it, survive it—hell, he could survive *anything,* wasn't that the point?—then maybe Kell would finally let go, stop holding his breath, stop trying to protect him, and just *live.*

Because Rhy didn't need his protection, not anymore, and he'd only told a partial truth when he said they both needed this.

The whole truth was, Rhy needed it *more.*

Because Kell had given him a gift he did not want, could never repay.

He'd always envied his brother's strength.

And now, in a horrible way, it was his.

He was immortal.

And he *hated* it.

And he hated that he hated it. Hated that he'd become the thing he never wanted to be, a burden to his brother, a source of pain and suffering, a prison. Hated that if he'd had a choice, he would have said no. Hated that he was grateful he hadn't had a choice, because he wanted to live, even if he didn't deserve to.

But most of all, Rhy hated the way his living changed how *Kell* lived, the way his brother moved through life as if it were suddenly fragile. The black stone, and whatever lived inside it, and for a time in Kell, had changed his brother, woken something restless, something reckless. Rhy wanted to shout, to shake Kell and tell him not to shy away from danger on his account, but charge toward it, even if it meant getting hurt.

Because Rhy deserved that pain.

He could see his brother suffocating beneath the weight of it. Of him.

And he hated it.

And this gesture—this foolish, mad, dangerous gesture—was the best he could do.

The most he could do.

The room had steadied, and suddenly, desperately, Rhy needed another drink.

A sideboard stood along the wall, an ornate thing of wood and inlaid gold. Short glass goblets huddled beside a tray with a dozen different bottles of fine liquor, and Rhy squinted in the dimness, surveying the selection before reaching for the thin vial at the back, hidden by the taller, brighter bottles. The tonic in the vial was milky white, the stopper trailing a thin stem.

One for calm. Two for quiet. Three for sleep.

That's what Tieren said when he prescribed it.

Rhy's fingers trembled as he reached for the vial, jostling the other glasses.

It was late, and he didn't want to be alone with his thoughts. He could call for someone—he'd never had trouble finding company—but he wasn't in the mood to smile and laugh and charm. If Gen and Parrish were here, they'd play Sanct with him, help him keep the thoughts at bay. But Gen and Parrish were dead, and it was Rhy's fault.

You shouldn't be alive.

He shook his head, trying to clear the voices, but they clung.

You let everyone down.

"Stop," he growled under his breath. He hated the darkness, the wave of shadows that always caught up with him. He'd hoped the party would wear him down, help him sleep, but his tired body did nothing to quiet his raging thoughts.

You are weak.

He let three drops fall into an empty glass, followed by a splash of honeyed water.

A failure.

Rhy tossed back the contents (*Murderer*) and began to count, in part to mark the effects and in part to drown out the voices. He stood at the bar, staring down into the empty glass and measuring seconds until his thoughts and vision began to blur.

Rhy pushed away from the sideboard, and nearly fell as the room tipped around him. He caught himself against the bedpost and closed his eyes (*You shouldn't be alive*), tugging off his boots and feeling his way into bed. He curled around himself as the thoughts beat on: of Holland's voice, of the amulet, distorted now, twisting into memories of the night Rhy died.

He didn't remember everything, but he remembered Holland holding out the gift.

For strength.

He remembered standing in his chambers, slipping the pendant's cord over his head, being halfway down the hall, and then—nothing. Nothing until a searing heat tore through his chest, and he looked down to see his hand wrapped around the hilt of a dagger, the blade buried between his ribs.

He remembered the pain, and the blood, and the fear, and

finally the quiet and the dark. The surrender of letting go, of sinking down, away, and the shock of being dragged back, the force of it like falling, a terrible, jarring pain when he hit the ground. Only he wasn't falling down. He was falling up. Surging back to the surface of himself, and then, and then.

And then the tonic finally took hold, the memories silenced as the past and present both mercifully faded and Rhy slipped feverishly down into sleep.

V

White London.

Holland paced the royal chamber.

It was as vast and vaulting as the throne room, with broad windows to every side. Built into the castle's western spire, it over-looked the entire city. From here he could see the glow from the Sijlt dance like moonlight against the low clouds, see lamps burn pale but steady, diffused by windowpanes and low mist, see the city—*his* city—sleep and wake, rest and stir, and return to life.

His head snapped up as something landed on the sill— power surged reflexively to the surface—but it was just a bird. White and grey with a pale gold crest, and eyes that shone as black as Holland's. He exhaled.

A *bird*.

How long had it been since he'd seen one? Animals had fled with the magic long ago, rooting out the distant places where the world wasn't dying, burrowing down to reach the retreating life. Any creature foolish enough to stray within reach was slaughtered for sustenance or spellwork, or both. The Danes had kept two horses, pristine white beasts, and even those had fallen in the days after their deaths, when the city plunged into chaos and slaughter for the crown. Holland had missed those early days, of course. He'd spent them clinging to life in a garden a world away.

But here, now, was a bird.

He didn't realize he was reaching toward it until it ruffled and took wing, his fingertips grazing its feathers before it was out of reach.

A single bird. But it was a sign. The world was changing.

Osaron could summon many things, but not this. Nothing with a heartbeat, nothing with a soul. Holland supposed that was for the best. After all, if Osaron could make a body of his own, he would have no need for Holland. And as much as Holland needed Osaron's magic, the thought of the *oshoc* moving freely sent a shiver through him. No, Holland was not only Osaron's partner, he was Osaron's prison.

And his prisoner was growing restless.

More.

The voice echoed in his head.

Holland took up a book and began to read, but he was only two pages in when the paper shuddered, as if caught by a wind, and the whole thing—from parchment to cover—turned to glass in his hands.

"This is childish," he murmured, setting the ruined book aside and splaying his hands across the sill.

More.

He felt a tremor beneath his palms and looked down to find tendrils of fog sprawling over the stone and leaving frost, flowers, ivy, fire in their wake.

Holland wrenched his hands away as if burned.

"Stop this," he said, turning his gaze on the looking glass, a tall, elegant mirror between two windows. He looked at his reflection and saw Osaron's impatient, impetuous gaze.

We could do more.

We could be more.

We could have more.

We could have anything.

And instead . . .

The magic slithered forth, snaked out from Holland's own hands, a hundred wisp-thin lines that swept and arced around him, threading from wall to wall and ceiling to floor until he stood in the center of a cage.

Holland shook his head and dispelled the illusion. "This is my world," he said. "It is not a canvas for your whims."

You have no vision, sulked Osaron from the reflection.

"I have vision," replied Holland. "I have seen what happened to *your* world."

Osaron said nothing, but Holland could feel his restlessness. Could feel the *oshoc* pacing the edges of the *Antari*'s self, wearing grooves into his mind. Osaron was as old as the world, and as wild.

Holland closed his eyes and tried to force calm like a blanket over them both. He needed sleep. A large bed sat in the very center of the room, elegant but untouched. Holland didn't sleep. Not well. Athos had spent too many years carving—cutting, burning, breaking—the distrust of peace into his body. His muscles refused to unclench; his mind wouldn't unwind; the walls he'd built hadn't been built to come down. Athos might be dead, but Holland couldn't shake the fear that when his eyes closed, Osaron's might open. Couldn't bear the thought of surrendering control again.

He'd stationed guards beyond his room to make sure he didn't wander, but every time he woke, the chamber looked different. A spray of roses climbing the window, a chandelier of ice, a carpet of moss or some exotic fabric—some small change wrought in the night.

We had a deal.

He could feel the *oshoc*'s will warring with his own, growing stronger every day, and though Holland was still in control, he didn't know for how much longer. Something would have to be sacrificed. Or someone.

Holland opened his eyes, and met the *oshoc*'s gaze.

"I want to make a new deal."

In the mirror, Osaron inclined his head, waiting, listening.

"I will find you another body."

Osaron's expression soured. *They are too weak to sustain me. Even Ojka would crumble under my true touch.*

"I will find you a body as strong as mine," said Holland carefully.

Osaron looked intrigued. *An* Antari?

Holland pressed on. "*And* his world. To make your own. And in return, you will leave this world to me. Not as it was, but as it can be. Restored."

Another body, another world, mused Osaron. *So keen to be rid of me?*

"You want more freedom," said Holland. "I am offering it."

Osaron turned the offer over. Holland tried to keep his mind calm and clear, knowing the *oshoc* would feel his feelings and know his thoughts. *You offer me an* Antari *vessel. You know I cannot take such a body without permission.*

"That is my concern," said Holland. "Accept my offer, and you will have a new body and a new world to do with as you please. But you will not take *this* world. You will not ruin it."

Hmmm, the sound was a vibration through Holland's head. *Very well,* said the *oshoc* at last. *Bring me another body, and the deal is struck. I will take their world instead.*

Holland nodded.

But, added Osaron, *if they cannot be persuaded, I will keep your body as my own.*

Holland growled. Osaron waited.

Well? A slow smile crept over the reflection. *Do you still wish to make the deal?*

Holland swallowed, and looked out his window as a second bird soared past.

"I do."

EIGHT

THE *ESSEN TASCH*

I

Kell sat up, a scream still lodged in his throat.

Sweat traced the lines of his face as he blinked away the nightmare.

In his dreams, Red London was burning. He could still smell the smoke now that he was awake, and it took him a moment to realize that it wasn't simply an echo, trailing him out of sleep. The bedsheets were singed where he was gripping them—he had somehow summoned fire in his sleep. Kell stared down at his hands, the knuckles white. It had been years since his control had faltered.

Kell threw off the covers, and he was halfway to his feet when he heard the cascade of sound beyond the windows, the trumpets and bells, the carriages and shouts.

The tournament.

His blood hummed as he dressed, turning his coat inside out several times—assuring himself that Kamerov's silver jacket hadn't been swallowed up by the infinite folds of fabric—before returning it to its royal red and heading downstairs.

He put in a cursory appearance at breakfast, nodding to the king and queen and wishing Rhy luck as a flurry of attendants swirled around the prince with final plans, notes, and questions.

"Where do you think you're going?" asked the king as Kell palmed a sweet bun and turned toward the door.

"Sir?" he asked, glancing back.

"This is a royal event, Kell. You are expected to attend."

"Of course." He swallowed. Rhy shot him a look that said, *I've gotten you this far. Don't blow it now.* And if he did? Would Rhy have to call Castars back in to make another appearance? It would be too risky, trading the roles again in time for the fights, and Kell had a feeling Castars's charm wouldn't save him in the ring. Kell fumbled for an excuse. "It's just . . . I didn't think it wise for me to stand with the royal family."

"And why is that?" demanded King Maxim. The queen's gaze drifted in his direction, glancing off his shoulder, and Kell had to bite back the urge to point out that he *wasn't* actually a member of the royal family, as the last four months had made abundantly clear. But Rhy's look was a warning.

"Well," said Kell, scrambling for an explanation, "for the prince's safety. It's one thing to put me on display with dignitaries and champions in the company of royals, Your Highness, but you've said yourself that I'm a target." The prince gave a small, encouraging nod, and Kell pressed on. "Is it really wise to put me so close to Rhy in such a public forum? I was hoping to stake out a less conspicuous place, in case I'm needed. Somewhere with a good view of the royal podium, but not upon it."

The king's gaze narrowed in thought. The queen's gaze returned to her tea.

"Well thought," said Maxim grudgingly. "But keep Staff or Hastra with you at all times," he warned. "No wandering off."

Kell managed a smile. "There's nowhere I'd rather be."

And with that, he slipped out.

"The king *does* know about your role," said Hastra as they walked down the hall. "Doesn't he?"

Kell shot the young guard a glance. "Of course," he said, casually. And then, on a whim, he added, "But the queen does not. Her nerves couldn't handle the strain."

Hastra nodded knowingly. "She hasn't been the same, has she?" he whispered. "Not since that night."

Kell straightened, and quickened his step. "None of us have."

When they reached the steps into the Basin, Kell paused. "You know the plan?"

"Yes, sir," said Hastra. He flashed an excited smile and disappeared.

Kell shrugged off his coat and turned it inside out as he descended into the Basin, where he'd already drawn a shortcut on the glassy stone wall. His mask was sitting in its box atop the table, along with a note from his brother.

Keep this—and your head—on your shoulders.

Kell shrugged Kamerov's silver jacket on and opened the box. The mask waited within, its surface polished to mirror clarity, sharpening Kell's reflection until it looked like it belonged to someone else.

Beside the box sat a piece of rolled red fabric, and when Kell smoothed it out, he saw it was a new pennant. The two roses had been replaced by twin lions, black and white and lined with gold against the crimson ground.

Kell smiled and tugged the mask on over his head, his reddish hair and two-toned eyes vanishing behind the silvery surface.

"Master Kamerov," said Staff when he stepped out into the morning air. "Are you ready?"

"I am," he answered in Arnesian, the edges of his voice muffled and smoothed by the metal.

They started up the steps, and when they reached the top, Kell waited while the guard vanished, then reappeared a moment later to confirm the path was clear. Or rather, covered. The steps were sheltered by the palace's foundation, running from river to street, and market stalls crowded the banks, obstructing the path. By the time Kell stepped out of the palace's shadow, slipped between the tents and onto the main road, the *Antari* royal was left behind. Kamerov Loste had taken his place.

He might have been a different man, but he was still tall, lean, and dressed in silver, from mask to boot, and the eyes of the crowd quickly registered the magician in their midst. But after the first wave, Kell didn't cringe from the attention. Instead of trying to embody Rhy, he embodied a version of himself—one who didn't fear the public eye, one who had power, and nothing to hide—and soon he fell into an easy, confident stride.

As he made his way with the crowd toward the central stadium, Staff hung back, blending in with the other guards who lined the road at regular intervals and walked among the throngs of people.

Kell smiled as he mounted the bridge path from the banks to the largest of the three floating arenas. Last night he'd imagined feeling the ground move beneath him, but that might have been the wine, because this morning as he reached the archway to the arena floor, it felt solid as earth beneath his feet.

Half a dozen other men and women, all Arnesian, were already gathered in the corridor—the magicians from Faro and Vesk must be assembled in their own halls—waiting to make their grand entrance. Like Kell, they were decked out in their official tournament attire, with elegant coats or cloaks and, of course, helmets.

He recognized Kisimyr's coiled hair behind a catlike mask, Losen a step behind her, as if he were an actual shadow. Beside them was Brost's massive form, his features barely obscured by the simple strip of dark metal over his eyes. And there, behind a mask of scales trimmed in blue, stood Alucard.

The captain's gaze drifted over Kell, and he felt himself tense, but of course, where Kell saw a foe, Alucard would have seen only a stranger in a silver mask. And one who'd obviously introduced himself at the Banner Night, because Alucard tipped his head with an arrogant smile.

Kell nodded back, secretly hoping their paths might cross in the ring.

Jinnar appeared on a gust of wind against Kell's back, slipping past him with a breezy chuckle before knocking shoulders with Alucard.

More footsteps sounded in the tunnel, and Kell turned to see the last few Arnesians join the group, the dark shape of Stasion Elsor at the rear. He was long and lean, his face entirely hidden by a demon's mask. For an instant, Kell's breath caught, but Rhy was right: Kell was determined to see Lila Bard in every black-clad form, every smirking shadow.

Stasion Elsor's eyes were shadowed by the mask, but up close, the demon's face was different, the horns arcing back and a skeletal jawbone collaring mouth and throat. A lock of hair a shade darker than Lila's traced a line like a crack between the magician's shaded brown eyes. And though his mouth was visible between the demon's teeth, Stasion didn't smile, only stared at Kell. Kamerov.

"*Fal chas,*" said Kell. *Good luck.*

"And you," replied Stasion simply, his voice nearly swallowed by the sudden flare of trumpets.

Kell twisted back to the archways as the gate swung open, and the ceremonies began.

II

"See, Parlo?" said Rhy, stepping out onto the stadium's royal balcony. "I told you it wouldn't sink."

The attendant hugged the back wall, looking ill. "So far, so good, Your Highness," he said, straining to be heard over the trumpets.

Rhy turned his smile on the waiting crowd. Thousands upon thousands had piled into the central stadium for the opening ceremonies. Above, the canvas birds dipped and soared on their silk tethers, and below, the polished stone of the arena floor stood empty save for three raised platforms. Poles mounted on each hung massive banners, each with an empire's seal.

The Faroan Tree.

The Veskan Crow.

The Arnesian Chalice.

Atop each platform, twelve shorter poles stood with banners furled, waiting for their champions.

Everything was perfect. Everything was ready.

As the trumpets trailed off, a cold breeze rustled Rhy's curls, and he touched the band of gold that hugged his temples. More gold glittered in his ears, at his throat, at collar and cuff, and as it caught the light, Alucard's voice pressed against his skin.

I fear you haven't enough. . . .

Rhy stopped fidgeting. Behind him, the king and queen sat

enthroned on gilded chairs, flanked by Lord Sol-in-Ar and the Taskon siblings. Master Tieren stood to the side.

"Shall I, Father?"

The king nodded, and Rhy stepped forward until he was front and center on the platform, overlooking the arena. The royal balcony sat not at the very top of the stadium, but embedded in the center of one sloping side, an elegant box halfway between the competitors' entrances and directly across from the judge's own platform.

The crowd began to hush, and Rhy grinned and held up a gold ring the size of a bracelet. When he spoke, the spelled metal amplified his words. The same charmed rings—albeit copper and steel—had been sent to taverns and courtyards across the city so that all could hear. During the matches, commentators would use the rings to keep the city apprised on various victories and defeats, but at this moment, the city's attention belonged to Rhy.

"Good morning, to all who have gathered."

A ripple of pleased surprise went through the gathered crowd when they realized he was speaking Arnesian. The last time the tournament had been held in London, Rhy's father had stood above his people and spoken High Royal, while a translator on a platform below offered the words in the common tongue.

But this wasn't just an affair of state, as his father claimed. It was a celebration for the people, the city, the empire. And so Rhy addressed his people, his city, his empire, in *their* tongue.

He went a step further, too: the platform below, where the translators of not only Arnes but also Faro and Vesk were supposed to stand, was empty. The foreigners frowned, wondering if the absence was some kind of slight. But their expressions became buoyant when Rhy continued.

"*Glad-ach!*" he said, addressing the Veskans. "*Anagh cael tach.*" And then, just as seamlessly, he slid into the serpentine tongue of Faro. "*Sasors noran amurs.*"

He let the words trail off, savoring the crowd's reaction. Rhy had always had a way with languages. About time he put some of them to use.

"My father, King Maxim, has given me the honor of overseeing this year's tournament."

This time as he spoke, his words echoed from other corners of the stadium, his voice twisting into the other two neighboring tongues. An illusion, one Kell had helped him design, using a variety of voice and projection spells. His father insisted that strength was the *image* of strength. Perhaps the same was true for magic.

"For more than fifty years, the Element Games have brought us together through good sport and festival, given us cause to toast our Veskan brothers and sisters and embrace our Faroan friends. And though only one magician—one nation—can claim this year's title, we hope that the Games will continue to celebrate the bond between our great empires!" Rhy tipped his head and flashed a devilish smile. "But I doubt you're all here for the politics. I imagine you're here to see some *magic*."

A cheer of support went through the masses.

"Well then, I present to you your magicians."

A column of glossy black fabric unfurled from the base of the royal platform, the end weighted so it stretched taut. A matching banner unspooled from the opposite side of the arena.

"From Faro, our venerable neighbor to the south, I present the twins of wind and fire, Tas-on-Mir and Tos-an-Mir; the wave whisperer Ol-ran-Es; the unparalleled Ost-ra-Gal. . . ."

As Rhy read each name, it appeared in white script against the dark silk banner beneath him.

"From Vesk, our noble neighbors to the north, I present the mountainous Otto, the unmovable Vox, the ferocious Rul . . ."

And as each name was called, the magician strode forward across the arena floor, and took their place on the podium.

"And finally, from our great empire of Arnes, I present your champion, the fire cat, Kisimyr"—a thunderous cheer went through the crowd—"the sea king, Alucard; the windborne Jinnar . . ."

And as each magician took their place, their chosen banner unfurled above their head.

"And Kamerov, the silver knight."

It was a dance, elaborate and elegant and choreographed to perfection.

The crowd rumbled with applause as the last of the Arnesian pennants snapped in the cool morning air, a set of twin blades above Stasion Elsor.

"Over the next five days and nights," continued Rhy, "these thirty-six magicians will compete for the title and the crown." He touched his head. "You can't have this one," he added with a wink, "it's mine." A ripple of laughter went through the stands. "No, the tournament crown is something far more spectacular. Incomparable riches; unmatchable renown; glory to one's name, one's house, and one's kingdom."

All traces of writing vanished from the curtains of black fabric, and the lines of the tournament grid appeared in white.

"For the first round, our magicians have been paired off." As he said it, names wrote themselves into the outer edges of the bracket. Murmurs went through the crowd and the magicians themselves stirred as they saw their opponents' names for the first time.

"The eighteen victors," continued Rhy, "will be paired off again, and the nine that advance will be placed into groups of three, where they will face off one-on-one. From each group, only the one with the highest standing will emerge to battle in the final match. Three magicians will enter, and only one will leave victorious. So tell me," finished Rhy, twirling the golden ring between his fingers, "are you ready to see some magic?"

The noise in the stadium rose to a deafening pitch, and the prince smiled. He might not have been able to summon fire, or draw rain, or make trees grow, but he still knew how to make an impact. He could feel the audience's excitement, as if it were beating inside him. And then he realized it wasn't only their excitement he was feeling.

It was also Kell's.

All right, brother, he thought, balancing the gold ring on his thumb like a coin.

"The time has come to marvel, and cheer, and choose your champions. And so, without further delay . . ." Rhy flicked the gold circle up into the air, and as he did, fireworks exploded overhead. Each explosion of light had been paired with its own midnight blue burst of smoke, an illusion of night that reached only as far as the firework and set it off against the winter grey sky.

He caught the ring and held it up again, his voice booming over the fireworks and the crowd's cheers.

"Let the Games begin!"

III

Lila had lost her mind. That was the only explanation. She was standing on a platform, surrounded by men and women who practically shook with power, the explosion of fireworks above and the roar of the crowd to every side, wearing a stranger's stolen clothes and about to compete in a tournament in the name of an empire she didn't serve in a world she wasn't even from.

And she was grinning like a fool.

Alucard jostled her shoulder, and she realized the other magicians were descending the platform, filing back toward the corridor from which they'd entered.

She followed the procession out of the arena and across the bridge-tunnel framework—she honestly couldn't tell what was holding the stadium up, but whatever it was, she seemed to be walking on it—and back to the solid ground of the city's southern banks.

Once on land, the gaps between the magicians began to stretch as they walked at their own pace toward the tents, and Lila and Alucard found themselves with room to move and speak.

"You still look like a fish," whispered Lila.

"And you still look like a girl playing dress-up," snapped Alucard. A few silent strides later he added, "You'll be happy to know I had a small sum sent back to our friend's home, claiming it was a competitor's bonus."

"How generous," said Lila. "I'll pay you back with my *win-nings.*"

Alucard lowered his voice. "Jinnar will hold his peace, but there's nothing I can do about Master Tieren. You'd best avoid him, since he certainly knows what Stasion Elsor looks like."

Lila waved her hand. "Don't worry about that."

"You can't *kill* the *Aven Essen.*"

"I wasn't planning on it," she shot back. "Besides, Tieren already knows."

"*What?*" His storm-dark eyes narrowed behind his scaled mask. "And since when do you call the London *Aven Essen* by his first name? I'm pretty sure that's some kind of blasphemy."

Lila's mouth quirked. "*Master* Tieren and I have a way of crossing paths."

"All part of your mysterious past, I'm sure. No, it's fine, don't bother telling me anything useful, I'm only your captain and the man who helped you send an innocent man off into saints know what so you could compete in a tournament you're in no way qualified to be in."

"Fine," she said. "I won't. And I thought you weren't associating with Stasion Elsor."

Alucard frowned, his mouth perfectly exposed beneath the mask. He appeared to be sulking.

"Where are we going?" she asked to break the silence.

"The tents," said Alucard, as if that explained everything. "First match is in an hour."

Lila summoned the bracket in her mind, but it proved unnecessary, since every scrying board they passed seemed to be showing the grid. Every pairing had a symbol beside it marking the arena—a dragon for the east, a lion for the west, a bird for the one in the center—as well as an order. According to the grid, Kisimyr was set to face off against her own protégé, Losen, Alucard against a Veskan named Otto, Jinnar against a Faroan with a string of syllables. And Lila? She read the name across from Stasion's. *Sar Tanak*. A crow to the left of the name indicated that Sar was Veskan.

"Any idea which one is Sar?" asked Lila, nodding to the towering blond men and women walking ahead.

"Ah," said Alucard, gesturing to a figure on the other side of the procession. "*That* would be Sar."

Lila's eyes widened as the shape stepped forward. *"That?"* The Veskan stood six feet tall and was built like a rock slab. She was a woman, as far as Lila could tell, her features stony behind her hawkish mask, straw hair scraped into short braids that stuck out like feathers. She looked like the kind of creature to carry an ax.

What had Alucard said about Veskans worshipping mountains?

Sar *was* a mountain.

"I thought magic had nothing to do with physical size."

"The body is a vessel," explained Alucard. "The Veskans believe that the larger the vessel, the more power it can hold."

"*Great,*" Lila muttered to herself.

"Cheer up," said Alucard as they neared another scrying board. He nodded to their names, positioned on opposite sides of the grid. "At least our paths probably won't cross."

Lila's steps slowed. "You mean I have to beat all these people, just for the chance to take you on?"

He tipped his head. "You could have begged that privilege any night aboard the *Spire,* Bard. If you wanted a swift and humiliating death."

"Oh, is that so?"

They crossed in front of the palace as they chatted, and Lila discovered that, on the far side, in place of the gardens that usually ran from palace wall to copper bridge, stood three tents, great circular things sporting empire colors. Lila was secretly glad the tents weren't floating, too. She'd found her sea legs, of course, but had enough to worry about in the *Essen Tasch* without the prospect of drowning.

"And be glad you don't have Kisimyr in your bracket," continued Alucard as a guard held open the curtained flap that served as the main entrance of their tent. "Or Brost. You got off light."

"No need to sound so relieved. . . ." said Lila, trailing off as she took in the splendor of the Arnesian tent's interior. They were standing in a kind of common area at the center, the rest of the tent segmented into twelve pie-like wedges. Fabric billowed down from the peaked ceiling—just the way it did in the royal palace rooms—and everything was soft and plush and trimmed with gold. For the first time in her life, Lila's awe wasn't matched by the desire to pocket anything—she was either growing too accustomed to wealth or, more likely, had enough charges on her plate without adding theft.

"Believe it or not," Alucard whispered, "one of us would like to see you live."

"Maybe I'll surprise you."

"You always do." He looked around, spotting his banner on one of the twelve curtained rooms. "And now, if you'll excuse me, I have a match to prepare for."

Lila waved. "I'll be sure to pick up your pennant. It's the one with a fish on it, right?"

"Har har."

"Good luck."

❧

Lila unfastened her helmet as she passed into the private tent marked by a black flag with crossed knives.

"Bloody hell," she muttered as she tugged off the mask, the devil's jaw tangling in her hair. And then she looked up. And stopped. The room was many things—simple, elegant, softened by couches and tables and billowing fabric—but it was *not* empty.

A woman stood in the middle of the space, dressed in white and gold, holding a tray of tea. Lila jumped, fighting the urge to draw a weapon.

"*Kers la?*" she snapped, her helmet still resting on her head.

The woman frowned slightly. "*An tas arensor.*"

"I don't need an attendant," answered Lila, still in Arnesian, and still fighting with the helmet.

The woman set down the tray, came forward, and, in one effortless motion, disentangled the knot, freeing Lila from the devil's jaws. She lifted the helmet from Lila's head and set it on the table.

Lila had decided not to thank her for the unwarranted help, but the words still slipped out.

"You're welcome," answered the woman.

"I don't need you," repeated Lila.

But the woman held her ground. "All competitors are assigned an attendant."

"Well then," said Lila brusquely, "I dismiss you."

"I don't think you can."

Lila rubbed her neck. "Do you speak High Royal?"

The woman slid effortlessly into English. "It suits my station."

"As a servant?"

A smile nicked the corner of the woman's mouth. "As a priest." *Of course,* thought Lila. Master Tieren chose the competitors. It made sense that he would supply the attendants, too. "The prince insists that all competitors be provided an attendant, to see to their various needs."

Lila raised a brow. "Like what?"

The woman shrugged and gestured to a chair.

Lila tensed. There was a *body* in it. It had no head.

The woman crossed to the form, and Lila realized it wasn't a headless corpse after all, but a set of armor, not polished like

the kind worn by the royal guards, but simple and white. Lila
found herself reaching for the nearest piece. When she lifted it,
she marveled at its lightness. It didn't seem like it would do much
to protect her. She tossed it back onto the chair, but the attendant
caught it before it fell.

"Careful," she said, setting the piece down gently. "The plates
are fragile."

"What good is fragile armor?" asked Lila. The woman looked
at her as though she had asked a very stupid question. Lila
hated that kind of look.

"This is your first *Essen Tasch,*" she said. It wasn't an inquiry.
Without waiting for confirmation, the woman bent to a chest
beside the chair and drew out a spare piece of armor. She held
it up for Lila to see, and then threw it against the ground. When
it met the floor, the plate cracked, and as it did, there was a flash
of light. Lila winced at the sudden brightness; in the flare's wake,
the armor plate was no longer white, but dark grey.

"This is how they keep score," explained the attendant, re-
trieving the spent armor. "A full set of armor is twenty-eight
pieces. The first magician to break ten wins the match."

Lila reached down and took up the ruined plate. "Anything
else I should know?" she asked, turning it over in her hands.

"Well," said the priest, "you cannot strike blows with your
body, only your elements, but I'm sure you already knew that."

Lila hadn't. A trumpet sounded. The first matches were
about to begin.

"Do you have a name?" she asked, handing the plate back.

"Ister."

"Well, Ister . . ." Lila backed away toward the curtain. "Do
you just . . . stand here until I need you?"

The woman smiled and dug a volume from a pocket. "I have
a book."

"Let me guess, a religious text?"

"Actually," said Ister, perching on the low couch, "it's about pirates."

Lila smiled. The priestess was growing on her.

"Well," said Lila, "I won't tell the *Aven Essen*."

Ister's smile tilted. "Who do you think gave it to me?" She turned the page. "Your match is at four, Master Stasion. Don't be late."

🦢

"Master Kamerov," came a cheerful voice as Kell stepped into his tent.

"Hastra."

The young guard's armor and cape were gone, and in their place he wore a simple white tunic trimmed in gold. A scarf, marked with the same gold trim, wrapped loosely around his face and throat, masking all but his aquiline nose and warm brown eyes. A curl escaped the wrap, and when he pulled the scarf down around his neck, Kell saw that he was grinning.

Saints, he looked young, like a sanctuary novice.

Kell didn't bother removing his helmet. It was too dangerous, and not only because he could be recognized; the mask was a constant reminder of the ruse. Without its weight, he might forget who he was, and who he wasn't.

Reluctantly he shed the silver coat and left it on a chair while Hastra fitted the plates of armor over his long-sleeved tunic.

In the distance, trumpets sounded. The first three matches were about to begin. There was no telling how long the opening rounds would take. Some might last an hour. Others would be over in minutes. Kell was the third match in the western arena. His first opponent was a Faroan wind mage named Tas-on-Mir.

He went over these details in his mind as the plates of armor were fastened and tightened. He didn't realize Hastra had finished until the young guard spoke.

"Are you ready, sir?"

A mirror stood before one curtained wall, and Kell considered himself, heart pounding. *You must be excited,* Hastra had said, and Kell *was.* At first, he'd thought it madness—and honestly, if he thought about it too hard, he knew it was still madness—but he couldn't help it. Logic be damned, wisdom be damned, he was excited.

"This way," said Hastra, revealing a second curtained door at the outside edge of the private tent. It was almost as if the addition had been designed with Kell's deception in mind. Perhaps it *was.* Saints, how long had Rhy been planning this charade? Perhaps Kell hadn't given his wayward brother enough credit. And perhaps Kell himself wasn't paying enough attention. He *had* been spending too much time in his rooms, or in the Basin, and he had taken to assuming that just because he could sense Rhy's body, he also knew his brother's mind. Obviously, he was mistaken.

Since when are you so invested in empire politics?

I'm invested in my kingdom, Brother.

Rhy had changed, that much Kell *had* noticed. But he had only seen his brother's varying moods, the way his temper darkened at night. This was different. This was *clever.*

But just to be safe, Kell took up his knife, discarded along with his coat, and pulled back one of the tent's many tapestries. Hastra watched as he nicked the soft flesh of his forearm and touched his fingers to the welling blood. On the canvas wall, he drew a small symbol, a vertical line, with a small horizontal mark on top leading to the right, and another on the bottom, leading to the left. Kell blew on it until it was dry, then let the tapestry swing back into place, hiding the symbol from sight.

Hastra didn't ask. He simply wished him luck, then hung back in the tent as Kell left; within several strides, a royal guard—Staff—fell in step beside him. They walked in silence, the crowds on the street—men and women who cared less for the matches than the festivities surrounding them—parting around him. Here and there children waved banners, and Kell caught sight of tangled lions amid the other pennants.

"Kamerov!" shouted someone, and soon the chant was being carried on the air—*Kamerov, Kamerov, Kamerov*—the name trailing behind him like a cape.

IV

"Alucard! Alucard! Alucard!" chanted the crowd.

Lila had missed the beginning of the fight, but it didn't matter; her captain was winning.

The eastern arena was filled to capacity, the lower levels shoulder to shoulder, while the upper tiers afforded worse views but a little more air. Lila had opted for one of the highest tiers open to the public, balancing the desire to study the match with the need to maintain anonymity. Stasion's black hat perched on her brow, and she leaned her elbows on the railing and watched dark earth swirl around Alucard's fingers. She imagined she could see his smile, even from this height.

Prince Rhy, who'd appeared a few minutes before, cheeks flushed from traveling between the stadiums, now stood on the royal balcony and watched with rapt attention, the stern-looking Faroan noble at his shoulder.

Two poles rose above the royal platform, each bearing a pennant to mark the match. Alucard's was a silver feather—or a drop of flame, she couldn't tell—against a backdrop of dark blue. She held a copy in one hand. The other pennant bore a set of three stacked white triangles on forest green. Alucard's opponent, a Veskan named Otto, wore an ancient-looking helmet with a nose plate and a domed skull.

Otto had chosen fire to Alucard's earth, and both were now dancing and dodging each other's blows. The smooth stone of the arena floor was dotted with obstacles, rock formations offering cover as well as the chance for ambush, and they must have been warded, since Alucard never made them move.

Otto was surprisingly quick on his feet for a man nearly seven feet tall, but his skill was one of blunt force, while Alucard's was sleight of hand—Lila couldn't think of it any other way. Most magicians, just like most ordinary fighters, gave away their attack by moving in the same direction as their magic. But Alucard could stand perfectly still while his element moved, or in this case, could dodge one way and send his power another, and through that simple, effective method, had scored eight hits to Otto's two.

Alucard was a showman, adding flourish and flare, and Lila had been on the receiving end of his games enough times to see that he was now playing with the Veskan, shifting into a defensive mode to prolong the fight and please the crowd.

A cheer rose from the western arena, where Kisimyr was going up against her protégé, Losen, and moments later the words on the nearest bracket board shifted, Losen's name vanishing and Kisimyr's writing itself into the advancing spot. In the arena below, flames circled Otto's fists. The hardest thing about fire was putting force behind it, giving it weight as well as heat. The Veskan was throwing his own weight behind the blows, instead of using the fire's strength.

"Magic is like the ocean," Alucard had told her in her first lesson. "When waves go the same way, they build. When they collide, they cancel. Get in the way of your magic, and you break the momentum. Move with it, and . . ."

The air around Lila began to tingle pleasantly.

"Master Tieren," she said without turning.

The *Aven Essen* stepped up beside her. "Master Stasion," he said casually. "Shouldn't you be getting ready?"

"I fight last," she said, shooting him a glance. "I wanted to see Alucard's match."

"Supporting friends?"

She shrugged. "Studying opponents."

"I see. . . ."

Tieren gave her an appraising look. Or perhaps it was disapproving. He was a hard man to read, but Lila liked him. Not just because he didn't try to stop her, but because she could ask him questions, and he clearly didn't believe in protecting a person by keeping them in the dark. He'd entrusted her with a difficult task once, he'd kept her secrets twice, and he'd let her choose her own path at every turn.

Lila nodded at the royal box. "The prince seems keen on this match," she ventured, as down below Otto narrowly escaped a blow. "But who is the Faroan?"

"Lord Sol-in-Ar," said Tieren, "the older brother of the king."

Lila frowned. "Shouldn't being the eldest make *him* the king?"

"In Faro, the descent of the crown is not determined by the order of birth, but by the priests. Lord Sol-in-Ar has no affinity for magic. Thus, he cannot be king."

Lila could hear the distaste in Tieren's voice, and she could tell it wasn't for Sol-in-Ar, but for the priests who deemed him unworthy.

She didn't buy into all that nonsense about magic sorting the strong from the weak, making some kind of spiritual judgment. No, that was too much like fate, and Lila didn't put much stock in that. A person chose their path. Or they made a new one.

"How do you know so much?" she asked.

"I've spent my life studying magic."

"I didn't think we were talking about magic."

"We were talking about people," he said, his eyes following the match, "and people are the most variable and important component in the equation of magic. Magic itself is, after all, a constant, a pure and steady source, like water. People, and the world they shape—they are the conduits of magic, determining its nature, coloring its energy, the way a dye does water. You of all people should be able to see that magic changes in the hands of men. It is an element to be shaped. As for my interest in Faro and Vesk, the Arnesian empire is vast. It is not, however, the extent of the world, and last time I endeavored to check, magic existed beyond its borders. I'm glad of the *Essen Tasch,* if only for that reminder, and for the chance to see how magic is treated in other lands."

"I hope you've written this all down somewhere," she said. "For posterity and all."

He tapped the side of his head. "I keep it someplace safe." Lila snorted. Her attention drifted back to Sol-in-Ar. Men talked, and men at sea talked more than most. "Is it true what they say?"

"I wouldn't know, Master Elsor. I don't stay apprised."

She doubted he was half as naive as he seemed. "That Lord Sol-in-Ar wants to overthrow his brother and start a war?"

Tieren brought his hand down on her shoulder, his grip surprisingly firm. "Mind that tongue of yours," he said quietly. "There are too many ears for such careless remarks."

They watched the rest of the match in silence. It didn't last long.

Alucard was a blur of light, his helmet winking in the sun as he spun behind a boulder and around the other side. Lila watched, mesmerized, as he lifted his hands, and the earth around him shot forward.

Otto pulled his fire around him like a shell, shielding front and back and every side. Which was great, except he obviously couldn't *see* through the blaze, so he didn't notice the moment the earth changed direction and flew up into the air, pulling itself together into clods before it fell, not with ordinary force, but raining down in a blur. The crowd gasped, and the Veskan looked up too late. His hands shot skyward, and so did the fire, but not fast enough; three of the missiles found their mark, colliding with shoulder and forearm and knee hard enough to shatter the armor plates.

In a burst of light, the match was over.

An official—a priest, judging by his white robes—held a gold ring to his lips and said, "Alucard Emery advances!"

The crowd thundered with applause, and Lila looked up at the royal platform, but the prince was gone. She glanced around, already knowing that Tieren was, too. Trumpets sounded from the central arena. Lila saw that Jinnar had advanced. She scanned the list for the central arena's next match.

Tas-on-Mir, read the top name, and just below it, *Kamerov*.

❧

The magic sang in Kell's blood as the crowd roared in the arena above. Saints, had every single person in Red London turned up to witness the opening rounds?

Jinnar passed him in the tunnel on the way out of his match. It didn't even look like he'd broken a sweat.

"*Fal chas!*" called the silver-eyed magician, peeling off the remains of his armor. By the looks of it, he'd only broken three plates.

"*Rensa tav,*" answered Kell automatically as his chest hummed with nervous energy. What was he thinking? What was he doing here? This was all a mistake . . . and yet, his muscles and bones still ached for a fight, and beyond the tunnel, he could hear them calling the name—*Kamerov! Kamerov! Kamerov!*—and even though it wasn't his, it still sent a fresh burst of fire through his veins.

His feet drifted forward of their own accord to the mouth of the tunnel, where two attendants waited, a table between them.

"The rules have been well explained?" asked the first.

"And you are ready, willing, and able?" prompted the second.

Kell nodded. He'd seen enough tournament matches to know the way things worked, and Rhy had insisted on running through each and every one of them again, just to make sure. As the tournament went on, the rules would shift to allow for longer, harder matches. The *Essen Tasch* would become far more dangerous then, for Kell and Rhy both. But the opening rounds were simply meant to separate the good from the very good, the skilled from the masters.

"Your element?" prompted the first.

A selection of glass spheres sat on the table, much like the ones that Kell had once used to try to teach Rhy magic. Each sphere contained an element: dark earth, tinted water, colored dust to give the wind shape, and in the case of fire, a palmful of oil to create the flame. Kell's hand drifted over the orbs as he tried to decide which one he should pick. As an *Antari,* he could wield any of them. As Kamerov, he would have to choose. His hand settled on a sphere containing water, stained a vivid blue so it would be visible to the spectators once he entered the arena.

The two attendants bowed, and Kell stepped out into the arena, ushered forth on a wave of noise. He squinted up through his visor. It was a sunny winter day, the cold biting but the light bright, glinting off the arena's spires and the metallic thread in the banners that waved from every direction. The lions on Kell's pennant winked at him from all around the arena, while Tas-on-Mir's silver-blue spiral stood out here and there against its black ground (her twin sister, Tos-an-Mir, sported the inverse, black on silver-blue).

The drama and spectacle had always seemed silly from afar, but standing here, on the arena floor instead of up in the stands, Kell felt himself getting caught up in the show. The chanting, cheering crowd pulsed with energy, with magic. His heart thrummed, his body eager for the fight, and he looked up past the crowds to the royal platform where Rhy had taken his place beside the king, looking down. Their eyes met, and even though Rhy couldn't possibly see Kell's through his mask, he still felt the look pass between them like a taut string being plucked.

Do try not to get us both killed.

Rhy gave a single, almost imperceptible nod from the balcony, and Kell wove between the stone obstacles to the center of the arena.

Tas-on-Mir had already entered the ring. She was clothed, like all Faroans, in a single piece of wrapped fabric, its details lost beneath her armor. A simple helmet did more to frame her face than mask it, and silver-blue gems shone like beads of sweat along her brow and down her cheeks. In one hand, she held an orb filled with red powder. A wind mage. Kell's mind raced. Air was one of the easiest elements to move, and one of the hardest to fight, but force came easy, and precision did not.

A priest in white robes stood on a plinth atop the lowest balcony to officiate the match. He motioned, and the two came forward, nodded to the royal platform, and then faced each other, each holding out their sphere. The sand in Tas-on-Mir's orb began to swirl, while the water in Kell's sloshed lazily.

Then either silence fell across the stadium, or Kell's pulse drowned out everything—the crowds, the flapping pennants, the distant cheers from other matches. Somewhere in that void of noise, the spheres fell, and the first sound that reached Kell's ears was the crystalline sound of them shattering against the arena floor.

For an instant, the blood in Kell's veins quickened and the world around him slowed. And then, just as suddenly, it snapped back into motion. The Faroan's wind leaped up and began to coil around her. The dark water swirled around Kell's arms before pooling above his palms.

The Faroan jerked, and the red-tinted wind shot forth with spear-like force. Kell lunged back just in time to dodge one blow, and he missed the second as it smashed against his side, shattering a plate and showering the arena in light.

The blow knocked Kell's breath away; he stole a glance up at

Rhy in the royal box, and saw him gripping his chair and gritting his teeth. At a glance, it could have passed for concentration, but Kell knew it for what it was, an echo of his own pain. He uttered a silent apology, then dove behind the nearest mound of rock, narrowly escaping another hit. He rolled and came to his feet, grateful the armor was designed to respond only to attacks, not self-inflicted force.

Up above, Rhy gave him a withering look.

Kell considered the two pools of water still hovering above his hands, and imagined Holland's voice echoing around the arena, tangled in the wind. Taunting.

Fight.

Shielded by the rock, he held up one hand, and the watery sphere above his fingers began to unravel into two streams and then four, and then eight. The cords circled the arena from opposite sides, stretching thinner and thinner, into ribbons and then threads and then filaments, crisscrossing into a web.

In response, the red wind picked up, sharpening the way his water had, a dozen razors of air; Tas-on-Mir was trying to force him out. Kell winced as a sliver of wind nicked his cheek. His opponent's voice began to carry on the air from a dozen places, and to the rest of the arena it would look like Kell was fighting blind, but Kell could *feel* the Faroan—the blood and magic pulsing beneath her skin, the tension against the threads of water as he pulled them taut. Where . . . where . . . *there*. He spun, launching himself not to the side but *up*. He mounted the boulder, the second orb freezing the instant before it left his hand. It splintered as it hurtled toward Tas-on-Mir, who managed to summon a shield out of her wind before the shards could hit. But she was so focused on the attack from the front that she'd forgotten the web of water, which had reformed in the span of a second into a block of ice behind her. It crashed into her back, shattering the three plates that guarded her spine.

The crowd erupted as the Faroan fell forward to her hands and knees, and the water sailed back to Kell's side and twined around his wrists.

It had been a feint. The same one he'd used on Holland. But unlike the *Antari,* Tas-on-Mir didn't stay down. A moment later she was back on her feet, the red wind whipping around her as the broken plates fell away.

Three down, thought Kell. *Seven to go.*

He smiled behind his mask, and then they both became a blur of light, and wind, and ice.

※

Rhy's knuckles tightened on the arms of his chair.

Below, Kell ducked and dodged the Faroan's blows.

Even as Kamerov, he was incredible. He moved around the arena with staggering grace, barely touching the ground. Rhy had only seen his brother fight in scuffles and brawls. Was this what he'd looked like when he'd faced Holland? Or Athos Dane? Or was this the product of the months spent in the Basin, driven by his own demons?

Kell landed another hit, and Rhy found himself fighting back a laugh—at this, at the absurdity of what they were doing, at the very real pain in his side, at the fact that he couldn't make it stop. The fact that he wouldn't, even if he could. There was a kind of control in letting go, giving in.

"Our magicians are strong this year," he said to his father.

"But not *too* strong," said the king. "Tieren has chosen well. Let us hope the priests of Faro and Vesk have done the same."

Rhy's brow crinkled. "I thought the whole point of this was to show our strength."

His father gave him a chiding look. "Never forget, Rhy, that you are watching a *game.* One with three strong but equal players."

"And what if, one year, Vesk and Faro played to *win*?"

"Then we would know."

"Know what?"

The king's gaze returned to the match. "That war is near."

In the arena below, Kell rolled, then rose. The dark water swirled and swerved around him, slipping under and around the Faroan's wall of air before slamming into her chest. The armor there shattered into light with the blow, and the crowd burst into applause.

Kell's face was hidden, but Rhy knew he was smiling.

Show-off, he thought, just before Kell dodged too slowly and let a knifelike gust of wind get through, the blow slamming against his ribs. Light erupted in front of Rhy's eyes, and behind them as he caught his breath. Pain burned across his skin, and he tried to imagine he could draw it in, away from Kell, and ground it in himself.

"You look pale," observed the king.

Rhy sank back against the chair. "I'm fine." And he was. The pain made him feel alive. His heart pounded in his chest, racing alongside his brother's.

King Maxim got to his feet and looked around. "Where is Kell?" he asked. His voice had taken to hardening around the name in a way that turned Rhy's stomach.

"I'm sure he's around," he answered, gazing down at the two fighters in the ring. "He's been looking forward to the tournament. Besides, isn't that what Staff and Hastra are for? Keeping track of him?"

"They've grown soft in their duties."

"When will you stop punishing him?" snapped Rhy. "He's not the only one who did wrong."

Maxim's eyes darkened. "And *he's* not the future king."

"What does that have to do with it?"

"Everything," said his father, leaning close and lowering his voice. "You think I do this out of spite? Some ill-borne malice? This is meant to be a lesson, Rhy. Your people will suffer when you err, and you will suffer when your people do."

"Believe me," muttered Rhy, rubbing an echo of pain across his ribs. "I'm suffering."

Below, Kell ducked and spun. Rhy could tell the fight was coming to an end. The Faroan was outmatched—she'd been outmatched from the beginning—and her motions were slowing, while Kell's only grew faster, more confident.

"Do you really think his life's in danger?"

"It's not *his* life I'm worried about," said the king. But Rhy knew that wasn't true. Not entirely. Kell's power made him a target. Vesk and Faro believed that he was blessed, the jewel in the Arnesian crown, the source of power that kept the empire strong. It was a myth Rhy was pretty certain the Arnesian crown perpetuated, but the dangerous thing about legends was that some people took them to heart, and those who thought Kell's magic guarded the empire might also think that by eliminating him, they could hobble the kingdom. Others thought that if they could steal him, the strength of Arnes would be theirs.

But Kell wasn't some talisman . . . was he?

When they were children, Rhy looked at Kell and saw only his brother. As they grew older, his vision changed. Some days he thought he saw a darkness. Other times he thought he saw a god. Not that he would ever tell Kell that. He knew Kell hated the idea of being chosen.

Rhy thought there were worse things to be.

Kell took another hit down in the arena, and Rhy felt the nerves sing down his arm.

"Are you sure you're all right?" pressed his father, and Rhy realized his knuckles had gone white on the chair.

"Perfectly," he said, swallowing the pain as Kell delivered the final two blows, back to back, ending the match. The crowd erupted in applause as the Faroan staggered to her feet and nodded, the motion stiff, before retreating from the ring.

Kell turned his attention to the royal balcony and bowed deeply.

Rhy raised his hand, acknowledging the victory, and the figure in silver and white vanished into the tunnel.

"Father," said Rhy, "if you don't forgive Kell, you will lose him."

There was no answer.

Rhy turned toward his father, but the king was already gone.

V

People always said that waiting was the worst part, and Lila agreed. So much so, in fact, that she rarely waited for anything. Waiting left too much room for questions, for doubt. It weakened a person's resolve—which was probably why, as she stood in the tunnel of the western arena *waiting* for her match, she started to feel like she'd made a terrible mistake.

Dangerous.

Reckless.

Foolish.

Mad.

A chorus of doubt so loud her boots took a step back of their own accord.

In one of the other stadiums, the crowds cheered as an Arnesian emerged victorious.

Lila retreated another step.

And then she caught sight of the flag—*her* flag—in the stands, and her steps ground to a halt.

I am Delilah Bard, she thought. *Pirate, thief, magician.*

Her fingertips began to thrum.

I have crossed worlds and taken ships. Fought queens and saved cities.

Her bones shuddered and her blood raced.

I am one of a kind.

The summoning trumpets blared, and with them, Lila forced

herself forward through the archway, her orb hanging from her fingers. Iridescent oil sloshed inside, ready to be lit.

As soon as she took the field, the anxiety bled away, leaving a familiar thrill in its wake.

Dangerous.

Reckless.

Foolish.

Mad.

The voices started up again, but they couldn't stop her now. The waiting was over. There was no turning back, and that simple fact made it easier to go forward.

The stands let out a cheer as Lila entered the arena. From the balcony, the stadium had looked considerable. From the floor, it looked *massive*.

She scanned the crowd—there were so many people, so many eyes on her. As a thief in the night, Lila Bard knew that staying out of the light was the surest way to stay alive, but she couldn't help it, she *relished* this kind of trick. Standing right in front of a mark while you pocketed their coins. Smiling while you stole. Looking them in the eye and daring them to see past the ruse. Because the best tricks were the ones pulled off not while the mark's back was turned, but while they were watching.

And Lila wanted to be seen.

Then she saw the Veskan.

Sar entered the arena, crossing the wide space in a matter of strides before coming to a stop in the center. Standing still, she looked like she'd grown straight out of the stone floor, a towering oak of a woman. Lila had never thought of herself as short, but next to the Veskan, she felt like a twig.

The bigger they are, thought Lila, *the harder they fall. Hopefully.*

At least the armor plates were sized to fit, giving Lila a bigger target. Sar's mask was made of wood and metal twined together into some kind of beast, with horns and a snout and slitted eyes through which Sar's own blue ones shone through. In her hand hung an orb full of earth.

Lila's teeth clenched.

Earth was the hardest element—almost any blow would break a plate—but it was also given in the smallest quantity. Air was everywhere, which meant fire was, too, if you could wrangle it into shape.

Sar bowed, her shadow looming over Lila.

The Veskan's flag rippled overhead, a cloudless blue marked by a single yellow X. Between Sar's letter and Lila's knives, the crowd was a sea of crossed lines. Most were silver on black, but Lila thought that probably had less to do with rumors of Stasion Elsor's skill, and more to do with the fact he was Arnesian. The locals would always take the majority. Right now, their loyalty was by default. But Lila could earn it. She imagined an entire stadium of black and silver flags.

Don't get ahead of yourself.

The arena floor was dotted with obstacles, boulders and columns and low walls all made from the same dark stone as the floor, so that the competitors and their elements stood out against the charcoal backdrop.

The trumpets trailed off, and Lila's gaze rose to the royal balcony, but the prince wasn't there. Only a young man wearing a green cape and a crown of polished wood and threaded silver—one of the Veskan royals—and Master Tieren. Lila winked and, even though the *Aven Essen* probably couldn't see, his bright eyes still seemed to narrow in disapproval.

A tense quiet fell over the crowd, and Lila twisted back to see a man in white and gold robes on the judge's platform that cantilevered over the arena. His hand was up, and for a second she wondered if he was summoning magic, until she realized he was only summoning silence.

Sar held out her sphere, the earth rising and rattling inside with nervous energy.

Lila swallowed and lifted her own, the oil disturbingly still by comparison.

Tyger Tyger, burning bright . . .

Her fingers tightened on the orb, and the surface of the oil burst into flame. The effect was impressive, but it wouldn't last, not with so little air in the sphere. She didn't wait—the instant the man in white began to lower his hand, Lila smashed the orb against the ground, sending up a burst of air-starved flame. The force of it jolted Lila and surprised the audience, who seemed to think it was all in the spirit of spectacle.

Sar crushed her own orb between her hands, and just like that, the match was underway.

❧

"Focus," scolded Alucard.

"I am focusing,*" said Lila, holding her hands on either side of the oil.*

"You're not. Remember, magic is like the ocean."

"Yeah, yeah," grumbled Lila, "waves."

"When waves go the same way," he lectured, ignoring her commentary, "they build. When they collide, they cancel."

"Right, so I want to build the wave—"

"No," said Alucard. "Just let the power pass through you."

Esa brushed against her. The Spire *rocked slightly with the sea. Her arms ached from holding them aloft, a bead of oil in each palm. It was her first lesson, and she was already failing.*

"You're not trying."

"Go to hell."

"Don't fight it. Don't force it. Be an open door."

"What happened to waves?" muttered Lila.

Alucard ignored her. "All elements are inherently connected," he rambled on while she struggled to summon fire. "There's no hard line between one and the next. Instead, they exist on a spectrum, bleeding into one another. It's about finding which part of that spectrum pulls at you the strongest. Fire bleeds into air, which bleeds into water, which bleeds into earth, which bleeds into metal, which bleeds into bone."

"And magic?"

He crinkled his brow, as if he didn't understand. "Magic is in everything."

Lila flexed her hands, focusing on the tension in her fingers, because she needed to focus on something. "Tyger Tyger, burning bright . . ." Nothing.

"You're trying too hard."

Lila let out an exasperated sound. "I thought I wasn't trying hard enough!"

"It's a balance. And your grip is too tight."

"I'm not even touching it."

"Of course you are. You're just not using your hands. You're exerting force. But force isn't the same as will. You're seizing a thing, when you need only cradle it. You're trying to control the element. But it doesn't work like that, not really. It's more of a . . . conversation. Question and answer, call and response."

"Wait, so is it waves, or doors, or conversations?"

"It can be anything you like."

"You're a wretched teacher."

"I warned you. If you're not up to it—"

"Shut up. I'm concentrating."

"You can't glare magic into happening."

Lila took a steadying breath. She tried to focus on the way fire felt, imagined the heat against her palms, but that didn't work, either. Instead she drew up the memories of Kell, of Holland, of the way the air changed when they did magic, the prickle, the pulse. She thought of holding the black stone, summoning its power, the vibration between her blood and bones and something else, something deeper. Something strange and impossible, and at the same time, utterly familiar.

Her fingertips began to burn, not with heat, but something stranger, something warm and cool, rough and smooth and alive.

Tyger Tyger, burning bright, she whispered silently, *and an instant later, the fire came to life against her palms. She didn't need to see what she'd done. She could feel it—not only the heat, but the power swimming beneath it.*

Lila was officially a magician.

ॐ

Lila was still trying to wrangle the fire into shape when Sar's first ball of earth—it was basically a rock—slammed into her shoulder. The burst of light was sharp and fleeting as the plate broke. The pain lingered.

There was no time to react. Another mass came hurtling toward her, and Lila spun out of Sar's line of attack, ducking behind a pillar an instant before the earth shattered against it, raining pebbles onto the arena floor. Thinking she had time before the next attack, Lila continued around the pillar, prepared to strike, and was caught in the chest by a spear of earth, crushing the central plate. The blow slammed her back into a boulder, and her spine struck the rock with brutal force, two more plates shattering as she gasped and fell to her hands and knees.

Four plates lost in a matter of seconds.

The Veskan made a chuckling sound, low and guttural, and before Lila could even get upright, let alone retaliate, another ball of earth struck her in the shin, cracking a fifth plate and sending her back to her knees.

Lila rolled to her feet, swearing viciously, the words lost beneath the cheers and chants and snapping pennants. A puddle of fire continued to burn on the oil-slicked ground. Lila shoved against it with her will, sending a river of flame toward Sar. It barely grazed the Veskan, the heat licking harmlessly against the armor. Lila cursed and dove behind a barrier.

The Veskan said something taunting, but Lila continued to hide.

Think, think, think.

She'd spent all day watching the matches, making note of the moves everyone made, the way they played. She'd scraped together secrets, the chinks in a player's armor, the tells in their game.

And she'd learned one very important thing.

Everyone played *by the rules*. Well, as far as Lila could tell, there weren't that many, aside from the obvious: no touching. But these competitors, they were like performers. They didn't play dirty. They didn't fight like it really mattered. Sure, they wanted to win, wanted to take the glory and the prize, but they didn't fight like their *lives* were on the line. There was too much bravado, and too little fear. They moved with the confidence of knowing a bell would chime, a whistle would blow, the match would end, and they would still be safe.

Real fights didn't work that way.

Delilah Bard had never been in a fight that didn't matter.

Her eyes flicked around the arena and landed on the judge's platform. The man himself had stepped back, leaving the ledge open. It stood above the arena, but not by much. She could reach it.

Lila drew the fire in and tight, ready to strike. And then she turned, mounted the wall, and jumped. She made it, just barely, the crowd gasping in surprise as she landed on the platform and spun toward Sar.

And sure enough, the Veskan hesitated.

Hitting the crowds was clearly not allowed. But there was no rule about standing in front of them. That hitched moment was all Lila needed. Sar didn't attack, and Lila did, a comet of fire launching from each hand.

Don't fight it, don't force it, be an open door.

But Lila didn't feel like an open door. She felt like a magni-

fying glass, amplifying whatever strange magic burned inside her
so that when it met the fire, the force was its own explosion.

The comets twisted and arced through the air, colliding into
Sar from different angles. One she blocked. The other crashed
against her side, shattering the three plates that ran from hip to
shoulder.

Lila grinned like a fool as the crowd erupted. A flash of gold
above caught her eye. At some point, the prince had arrived to
watch. Alucard stood in the stands below him, and on her own
level, the judge in white was storming forward. Before he could
call foul, Lila leaped from the platform back to the boulder.
Unfortunately, Sar had recovered, both from her surprise and
the hit, and as Lila's foot hit the outcropping, a projectile of
earth slammed into her shoulder, breaking a sixth piece of armor and knocking her off the edge.

As she fell back, she flipped with feline grace and landed in
a crouch.

Sar braced herself for an attack as soon as Lila's boots struck
stone, which was why Lila launched the fire *before* she landed.
The meteor caught the Veskan's shin, shattering another plate.

Four to six.

Lila was catching up.

She rolled behind a barrier to recover as Sar stretched out her
thick fingers, and the earth strewn across the arena shuddered
and drew itself back toward her.

Lila saw a large clod of dirt and dropped to one knee,
fingers curling around the earth the moment before Sar's invisible force took hold and pulled, hard enough to draw the
element, and Lila with it. She didn't let go, boots sliding along
the smooth stone floor as Sar reeled her in without realizing it,
Lila herself still hidden by the various obstacles. The boulders
and columns and walls ended, and the instant they did, Sar
saw Lila, saw her let go of the ball of earth, now coated in flame.
It careened back toward the Veskan, driven first by her pull

and then by Lila's will, crashing into her chest and shattering two more plates.

Good. Now they were even.

Sar attacked again, and Lila dodged casually—or at least, she meant to, but her boot held fast to the floor, and she looked down to see a band of earth turned hard and dark as rock and fused to the ground. Sar's teeth flashed in a grin behind her mask, and it was all Lila could do to get her arms up in time to block the next attack.

Pain rang through her like a tuning fork as the plates across her stomach, hip, and thigh all shattered. Lila tasted blood, and hoped she'd simply bitten her tongue. She was one plate shy of losing the whole damn thing, and Sar was gearing up to strike again, and the earth that pinned her boot was still holding firm.

Lila couldn't pull her foot free, and her fire was scattered across the arena, dying right along with her chances. Her heart raced and her head spun, the noise in the arena drowning everything as Sar's ultimate attack crashed toward Lila.

There was no point in blocking, so she threw out her hands, heat scorching the air as she drew the last of her fire into a shield.

Protect me, she thought, abandoning poetry and spell in favor of supplication.

She didn't expect it to work.

But it did.

A wave of energy swept down her arms, meeting the meager flame, and an instant later, the fire *exploded* in front of her. A *wall* of flame erupted, dividing the arena and rendering Sar a shadow on the opposite side, her earthen attack burning to ash.

Lila's eyes widened behind her mask.

She'd never spoken to the magic, not directly. Sure, she'd cursed at it, and grumbled, and asked a slew of rhetorical questions. But she'd never commanded it, not the way Kell did with blood. Not the way she had with the stone, before she discovered the cost.

If the fire claimed a price, she couldn't feel it yet. Her pulse was raging in her head as her muscles ached and her thoughts raced, and the wall of flame burned merrily before her. Fire licked her outstretched fingers, the heat brushing her skin but never settling long enough to burn.

Lila didn't try to be a wave, or a door. She simply *pushed,* not with force, but with will, and the wall of fire shot forward, barreling toward Sar. To Lila, the whole thing seemed to take forever. She didn't understand why Sar was standing still, not until time snapped back into focus, and she realized that the wall's appearance, its transformation, had been the work of an instant.

The fire twisted in on itself, like a kerchief drawn through a hand, as it launched toward Sar, compressing, gaining force and heat and speed.

The Veskan was many things, but she wasn't fast—not as fast as Lila, and definitely not as fast as fire. She got her arms up, but she couldn't block the blast. It shattered every remaining plate across her front in a blaze of light.

Sar tumbled backward, the wood of her mask singed, and at last the earth crumbled around Lila's boot, releasing her.

The match was over.

And she had *won.*

Lila's legs went weak, and she fought the urge to sink to the cold stone floor.

Sweat streamed down her neck, and her hands were scraped raw. Her head buzzed with energy, and she knew that as soon as the high faded, everything would hurt like hell, but right now, she felt incredible.

Invincible.

Sar got to her feet, took a step toward her, and held out a hand that swallowed Lila's when she took it. Then the Veskan vanished into her tunnel, and Lila turned toward the royal platform to offer the prince a bow.

The gesture caught halfway when she saw Kell at Rhy's shoulder, looking windblown and flushed. Lila managed to finish the bow, one hand folded against her heart. The prince applauded. Kell only cocked his head. And then she was ushered out on a wave of cheers and the echo of "Stasion! Stasion! Stasion!"

Lila crossed the arena with slow, even steps, escaping into the darkened corridor.

And there she sank to her knees and laughed until her chest hurt.

VI

"You missed quite a match," said Rhy. Stasion Elsor had vanished, and the stadium began to empty. The first round was over. Thirty-six had become eighteen, and tomorrow, eighteen would become nine.

"Sorry," said Kell. "It's been a busy day."

Rhy swung his arm around his brother's shoulders, then winced. "Did you have to let that last blow through?" he whispered beneath the sounds of the crowd.

Kell shrugged. "I wanted to give the people a show." But he was smiling.

"You better put that grin away," chided Rhy. "If anyone sees you beaming like that, they'll think you've gone mad."

Kell tried to wrestle his features into their usual stern order, and lost. He couldn't help it. The last time he'd felt this alive, someone was trying to kill him.

His body ached in a dozen different places. He'd lost six plates to the Faroan's ten. It was far harder than he'd thought it would be, using only one element. Normally he let the lines between them blur, drawing on whichever he needed, knowing he could reach for any, and they would answer. In the end, it had taken half Kell's focus not to break the rules.

But he'd done it.

Rhy's arm fell away, and he nodded at the arena floor where

the Arnesian had been. "That one might give the others a run for their money."

"I thought the odds were in *Alucard*'s favor."

"Oh, they still are. But this one's something. You should see his next match, if you can find the time."

"I'll check my schedule."

A man cleared his throat. "Your Highness. Master Kell." It was Rhy's guard, Tolners. He led their escort out of the stadium, and Staff fell in step behind them on the way to the palace. It had only been hours since Kell left, but he felt like a different man. The walls weren't as suffocating, and even the looks didn't bother him as much.

It had felt so good to fight. The exhilaration was paired with a strange relief, a loosening in his limbs and chest, like a craving sated. For the first time in months, he was able to stretch his power. Not all the way, of course, and every moment he was constantly aware of the need for discretion, disguise, but it was *something*. Something he'd desperately needed.

"You're coming tonight, of course," said Rhy as they climbed the stairs to the royal hall. "To the ball?"

"Another one?" complained Kell. "Doesn't it get tiresome?"

"The politics are exhausting, but the company can be pleasant. And I can't hide you from Cora forever."

"Talk of exhausting," muttered Kell as they reached their hall. He stopped at his room, while Rhy continued toward the doors with the gold inlaid *R* at the end.

"The sacrifices we make," Rhy called back.

Kell rolled his eyes as the prince disappeared. He brought his hand to his own door, and paused. A bruise was coming out against his wrist, and he could feel the other places he'd been hit coloring beneath his clothes.

He couldn't wait for tomorrow's match.

He pushed open the door, and he was already shrugging out

of his coat when he saw the king standing at his balcony doors, looking out through the frosted glass. Kell's spirits sank.

"Sir," he said gingerly.

"Kell," said the king in way of greeting. His attention went to Staff, who stood in the doorway. "Please wait outside." And then, to Kell, "Sit."

Kell lowered himself onto a sofa, his bruises suddenly feeling less like victories, and more like traitors.

"Is something wrong?" asked Kell when they were alone.

"No," said the king. "But I've been thinking about what you said this morning."

This morning? This morning was years away. "About what, sir?"

"About your proximity to Rhy during the *Essen Tasch*. With so many foreigners flooding the city, I'd prefer if you kept to the palace."

Kell's chest tightened. "Have I done something wrong? Am I being punished?"

King Maxim shook his head. "I'm not doing this to punish you. I'm doing it to protect Rhy."

"Your Majesty, *I'm* the one who protects Rhy. If anything were to—"

"But Rhy doesn't need your protection," cut in the king, "not anymore. The only way to keep him safe is to keep *you* safe." Kell's mouth went dry. "Come, Kell," continued the king, "you can't care that much. I haven't seen you at the tournament all day."

Kell shook his head. "That's not the point. This isn't—"

"The central arena is visible from the palace balconies. You can watch the tournament from here." The king set a golden ring the size of his palm on the table. "You can even listen to it."

Kell opened his mouth, but the protests died on his tongue. He swallowed and clenched his hands. "Very well, sir," he said, pushing to his feet. "Am I banished from the balls, too?"

"No," said the king, ignoring the edge in Kell's voice. "We keep track of all those who come and go. I see no reason to keep you from those, so long as you are careful. Besides, we wouldn't want our guests to wonder where you were."

"Of course," murmured Kell.

As soon as the king was gone, Kell crossed into the small room off the main chamber and shut the door. Candles came to life on the shelf walls, and by their light he could see the back of the door, its wood marked by a dozen symbols, each a portal to another place in London. It would be so easy to go. They could not keep him. Kell drew his knife and cut a shallow line against his arm. When the blood welled, he touched his fingers to the cut, but instead of tracing an existing symbol, he drew a fresh mark on a bare stretch of wood: a vertical bar with two horizontal accents, one on top leading right, one on bottom leading left.

The same symbol he'd made in Kamerov's tent that morning.

Kell had no intention of missing the tournament, but if a lie would ease the king's mind, so be it. As far as breaking the king's trust, it didn't matter. The king hadn't trusted him in months.

Kell smiled grimly at the door, and went to join his brother.

VII

Ojka stood beneath the trees, wiping the blood from her knives.

She'd spent the morning patrolling the streets of Kosik, her old stomping ground, where trouble still flared like fire through dry fields. Holland said it was to be expected, that change would always bring unrest, but Ojka was less forgiving. Her blades found the throats of traitors and disbelievers, silencing their dissent one voice at a time. They didn't deserve to be a part of this new world.

Ojka holstered the weapons and breathed deeply. The castle grounds, once littered with statues, were now filled with trees, each blossoming despite the winter chill. For as long as Ojka could remember, her world had smelled like ash and blood, but now it smelled of fresh air and fallen leaves, of forests and raging fires, of life and death, of sweet and damp and clean, of promise, of change, of power.

Her hand drifted to the nearest tree, and when she placed her palm flat against the trunk she could feel a pulse. She didn't know if it was hers, or the king's, or the tree's. Holland had told her that it was the pulse of the world, that when magic behaved the way it should, it belonged to no one and everyone, nothing and everything. It was a shared thing.

Ojka didn't understand that, but she wanted to.

The bark was rough, and when she chipped away a piece with

her nail, she was surprised to see the wood beneath mottled with the silver threads of spellwork. A bird cawed overhead, and Ojka drew nearer, but before she could examine the tree, she felt the pulse of heat behind her eye, the king's voice humming through her head, resonant and welcome.

Come to me, he said.

Ojka's hand fell away from the tree.

❦

She was surprised to find her king alone.

Holland was sitting forward on his throne, elbows on knees and head bowed over a silver bowl, its surface brimming with twisting smoke. She held her breath when she realized he was in the middle of a spell. The king's hands were raised to either side of the bowl, his face a mask of concentration. His mouth was a firm line, but shadows wove through both of his eyes, coiling through the black of the left one before overtaking the green of the right. The shadows were alive, snaking through his sight as the smoke did in the bowl, where it coiled around something she couldn't see. Lines of light traced themselves like lightning through the darkness, and Ojka's skin prickled with the strength of the magic before the spell finished, the air around her shivered, and everything went still.

The king's hands fell away from the bowl, but several long moments passed before the living darkness retreated from the king's right eye, leaving a vivid emerald in its wake.

"Your Majesty," said Ojka carefully.

He did not look up.

"Holland."

At that, his head rose. For an instant his two-toned gaze was still strangely empty, his focus far away, and then it sharpened, and she felt the weight of his attention settle on her.

"Ojka," he said, in his smooth, reverberating way.

"You summoned me."

"I did."

He stood and gestured to the floor beside the dais.

That was when she saw the bodies.

There were two of them, swept aside like dirt, and to be fair, they looked less like corpses than like crumbling piles of ash, flesh withered black on bone frames, bodies contorted as if in pain, what was left of hands raised to what was left of throats. One looked much worse than the other. She didn't know what had happened to them. Wasn't sure she *wanted* to know. And yet she felt compelled to ask. The question tumbled out, her voice tearing the quiet.

"Calculations," answered the king, almost to himself. "I was mistaken. I thought the collar was too strong, but it is not. The people were just too weak."

Dread spread through Ojka like a chill as her attention returned to the silver bowl. "Collar?"

Holland reached inside the bowl—for an instant, something in him seemed to recoil, resist the motion, but the king persisted—and as he did, shadow spilled over his skin, up his fingers, his hands, his wrists, becoming a pair of black gloves, smooth and strong, their surfaces subtly patterned with spell-work. Protection from whatever waited in the dark.

From the depths of the silver bowl, the king withdrew a circlet of dark metal, hinged on one side, symbols etched and glowing on its surface. Ojka tried to read the markings, but her vision kept slipping, unable to find purchase. The space inside the circlet seemed to swallow light, energy, the air within turning pale and colorless and as thin as paper. There was something *wrong* with the metal collar, wrong in a way that bent the world around it, and that wrongness plucked at Ojka's senses, made her feel dizzy and ill.

Holland turned the circlet over in his gloved hands, as if inspecting a piece of craftsmanship. "It must be strong enough," he said.

Ojka braved a step forward. "You summoned me," she repeated, her attention flicking from the corpses to the king.

"Yes," he said, looking up. "I need to know if it works."

Fear prickled through her, the old, instinctual bite of panic, but she held her ground. "Your Majesty—"

"Do you trust me?"

Ojka tensed. Trust. Trust was a hard-won thing in a world like theirs. A world where people starved for magic and killed for power. Ojka had stayed alive so long by blade and trick and bald distrust, and it was true that things were changing now, because of Holland, but fear and caution still whispered warnings.

"Ojka." He considered her levelly, with eyes of emerald and ink.

"I trust you," she said, forcing the words out, making them real, before they could climb back down her throat.

"Then come here." Holland held up the collar as if it were a crown, and Ojka felt herself recoil. No. She had earned this place beside him. She had earned her power. Been strong enough to survive the transfer, the test. She had proven herself worthy. Beneath her skin, the magic tapped out its strong and steady beat. She wasn't ready to let go, to relinquish the power and return to being an ordinary cutthroat. *Or worse,* she thought, glancing at the bodies.

Come here.

This time the command rang through her head, pulled on muscle, bone, magic.

Ojka's feet moved forward, one step, two, three, until she was standing right before the king. *Her* king. He had given her so much, and he had yet to claim his price. No boon came without a cost. She would have paid him in deed, in blood. If this was the cost—whatever this was—then so be it.

Holland lowered the collar. His hands were so sure, his eyes so steady. She should have bowed her head, but instead, she held his gaze, and there she found balance, found calm. There she felt safe.

And then the metal closed around her throat.

The first thing she felt was the sharp cold of metal on skin. Surprise, but not pain. Then the cold sharpened into a knife. It slid under her skin, tore her open, magic spilling like blood from the wounds.

Ojka gasped and staggered to her knees as ice shot through her head and down into her chest, frozen spikes splaying out through muscle and flesh, bone and marrow.

Cold. Gnawing and rending, and then gone.

And in its wake—nothing.

Ojka's doubled over, fingers clamped uselessly around the metal collar as she let out an animal groan. The world looked wrong—pale and thin and empty—and she felt severed from it, from herself, from her king.

It was like losing a limb: none of the pain, but all of the wrongness, a vital piece of her cut away so fast she could feel the space where it had been, where it should be. And then she realized what it was. The loss of a sense. Like sight, or sound, or touch.

Magic.

She couldn't feel its hum, couldn't feel its strength. It had been everywhere, a constant presence from her bones to the air around her body, and it was suddenly, horribly . . . gone.

The veins on her hands were beginning to lighten, from black to pale blue, and in the reflection of the polished stone floor, she could see the dark emblem of the king's mark retreating across her brow and cheek, withdrawing until it was nothing but a smudge in the center of her yellow eyes.

Ojka had always had a temper, quick to flame, her power surging with her mood. But now, as panic and fear tore through her, nothing rose to match it. She couldn't stop shaking, couldn't drag herself from the shock and terror and fear. She was weak. Empty. Flesh and blood and nothing more. And it was *terrible*.

"Please," she whispered to the throne room floor while Holland stood over her, watching. "Please, my king. I have always . . . been loyal. I will always . . . be loyal. Please . . ."

Holland knelt before her and took her chin in his gloved hand, guiding it gently up. She could see the magic swirling in his eyes, but she couldn't feel it in his touch.

"Tell me," he said. "What do you feel?"

The word escaped in a shudder. "I . . . I can't . . . feel . . . anything."

The king smiled grimly then.

"Please," whispered Ojka, hating the word. "You chose me. . . ."

The king's thumb brushed her chin. "I chose you," he said, his fingers slipping down her throat. "And I still do."

An instant later, the collar was gone.

Ojka gasped, magic flooding back like air into starved veins. A welcome pain, bright and vivid and alive. She tipped her head against the cold stone.

"Thank you," she whispered, watching the mark trace its way through her eye, across her brow and cheek. "Thank you."

It took her several long seconds to get to her feet, but she forced herself up as Holland returned the horrible collar to its silver bowl, the gloves melting from his fingers into shadow around the metal.

"Your Majesty," said Ojka, hating the quiver in her voice. "Who is the collar for?"

Holland brought his fingers to his heart, his expression unreadable.

"An old friend."

If that is for a friend, she thought, *what does Holland do to enemies?*

"Go," he said, returning to his throne. "Recover your strength. You're going to need it."

NINE

COLLISION COURSE

I

When Lila woke up the next day, it took her a moment to remember where she was, and, more importantly, why everything hurt.

She remembered retreating to Elsor's room the night before, resisting the urge to collapse onto his bed still fully dressed. She'd somehow gotten back into her own clothes, her own room at the Wandering Road, though she didn't remember much of the journey. It was now well into morning. Lila couldn't recall the last time she'd slept so long, or so deeply. Wasn't sleep supposed to make you feel rested? She only felt exhausted.

Her boot was trapped beneath something that turned out to be Alucard's cat. Lila didn't know how the creature had gotten into her room. She didn't care. And the cat didn't seem to care about her either. She barely moved when Lila dragged her foot free, and sat up.

Every part of her protested.

It wasn't just the wear and tear of the match—she'd gotten in some bad fights before, but nothing felt like this. The only thing that even came close was the aftermath of the black stone. The talisman's repercussions had been hollowing and sudden, where this was subtle but deep. Proof that magic wasn't an inexhaustible resource.

Lila dragged herself off the cot, stifling a grunt of pain, grateful that the room was empty. She tugged off her clothes as gingerly as possible, wincing at the bruises that had started to blossom across her ribs. The thought of fighting again today made her cringe, and yet some part of her thrilled at the idea. Admittedly, it was a very small part of her.

Dangerous.

Reckless.

Foolish.

Mad.

The words were beginning to feel more like badges of pride than blows.

Downstairs, the main room was sparsely populated, but she spotted Alucard at a table along the wall. She crossed the room, boots scuffing until she reached him and sank into a chair.

He was looking over a paper, and he didn't look up when she put her head down on the table with a soft thud.

"Not much of a morning person?"

She grumbled something unkind. He poured her a cup of rich black tea, spices weaving through the steam.

"Such a useless time of day," she said, dragging herself upright and taking the cup. "Can't sleep. Can't steal."

"There *is* more to life."

"Like what?"

"Like eating. And drinking. And dancing. You missed quite a ball last night."

She groaned at the thought. It was too early to imagine herself as Stasion Elsor performing in an arena, let alone in a palace. "Do they celebrate *every* night?"

"Believe it or not, some people actually come to the tournament *just* for the parties."

"Doesn't it get tiresome, all that . . ." She waved her hand, as if the whole thing could be summed up with a single gesture. In truth, Lila had only been to one ball in her entire life, and that night had started with a demon's mask and a glorious new coat, and ended with both covered in a prince's blood and the stony remains of a foreign queen.

Alucard shrugged, offering her some kind of pastry. "I can think of less pleasant ways to pass a night."

She took the bread-thing and nibbled on the corner. "I keep forgetting you're a part of that world."

His look cooled. "I'm not."

The breakfast was reviving; her vision started to focus, and as it did, her attention narrowed on the paper in his hands. It was a copy of the bracket, the eighteen victors now paired off into nine new sets. She'd been so tired, she hadn't even checked. "What does the field look like today?"

"Well, *I* have the luxury of going up against one of my oldest friends, not to mention the best wind magician I've ever met—"

"Jinnar?" asked Lila, suddenly interested. That would be quite a match.

Alucard nodded grimly, "And you've only got to face . . ." He trailed his finger across the page. ". . . Ver-as-Is."

"What do you know about him?" she asked.

Alucard's brow furrowed. "I'm sorry, have you mistaken me for a comrade? The last time I checked we were on opposite sides of the bracket."

"Come on, Captain. If I die in this, you'll have to find your-self a new thief."

The words were out before she remembered she'd already lost her place aboard the *Night Spire*. She tried a second time. "My witty banter is one of a kind. You know you'll miss it when I'm gone." Again, it was the wrong thing to say, and a heavy silence settled in its wake. "Fine," she said, exasperated. "Two more questions, two more answers, in exchange for whatever you know."

Alucard's lips quirked. He folded the roster and set it aside, lacing his fingers with exaggerated patience. "When did you first come to our London?"

"Four months ago," she said. "I needed a change of scenery."

She meant to stop there, but the words kept coming. "I got pulled into something I didn't expect, and once it started, I wanted to see it through. And then it was over, and I was here, and I had a chance to start fresh. Not every past is worth holding onto."

That got a look of interest, and she expected him to continue down his line of inquiry, but instead he changed directions.

"What were you running from, the night you joined my crew?"

Lila frowned, her gaze escaping down to the cup of black tea. "Who said I was running?" she murmured. Alucard raised a brow, patient as a cat. She took a long, scalding sip, let it burn all the way down before she spoke. "Look, everyone talks about the unknown like it's some big scary thing, but it's the *familiar* that's always bothered me. It's heavy, builds up around you like rocks, until it's walls and a ceiling and a cell."

"Is that why you were so determined to take Stasion's spot?" he asked icily. "Because my company had become a burden?"

Lila set her cup down. Swallowed the urge to apologize. "You had your two questions, Captain. It's my turn."

Alucard cleared his throat. "Very well. Ver-as-Is. Obviously Faroan, and not a nice fellow, from what I've heard. An earth mage with a temper. You two should get along splendidly. It's the second round, so you're allowed to use a second element, if you're able."

Lila rapped her fingers on the table. "Water."

"Fire and water? That's an unusual pairing. Most dual magicians pick adjacent elements. Fire and water are on opposite sides of the spectrum."

"What can I say, I've always been contrary." She winked her good eye. "And I had such a good teacher."

"Flatterer," he muttered.

"Arse."

He touched his breast, as if offended. "You're up this afternoon," he said, pushing to his feet, "and I'm up soon." He didn't seem thrilled.

"Are you worried?" she asked. "About your match?"

Alucard took up his tea cup. "Jinnar's the best at what he does. But he only does one thing."

"And you're a man of many talents."

Alucard finished his drink and set the cup back on the table. "I've been told." He shrugged on his coat. "See you on the other side."

☙

The stadium was *packed*.

Jinnar's banner flew, sunset purple on a silver ground, Alucard's silver on midnight blue.

Two Arnesians.

Two favorites.

Two friends.

Rhy was up on the royal platform, but Lila saw no sign of the king or queen, or Kell for that matter, though she spotted Alucard's siblings on a balcony below. Berras scowled while Anisa clapped and cheered and waved her brother's pennant.

The arena was a blur of motion and light, and the entire crowd held its breath as the two favorites danced around each other. Jinnar moved like air, Alucard like steel.

Lila fidgeted with the sliver of pale stone—turning the White London keepsake over in her fingers as she watched, trying to keep up with the competitors' movements, read the lines of attack, predict what they would do, and understand how they did it.

It was a close match.

Jinnar was a thing of beauty when it came to wind, but Alucard was right; it was his only element. He could render it into a wall or a wave, use it to cut like a knife, and with its help he could practically fly. But Alucard held earth and water, and everything they made between them—blades as solid as metal, shields of stone and ice—and in the end, his two elements triumphed over Jinnar's one, and Alucard won, breaking ten plates of armor to Jinnar's seven.

The silver-eyed magician withdrew, a smile visible through the metal wisps of his mask, and Alucard tipped his scale-plated chin to the royal platform and offered a deep bow to the prince before disappearing into the corridor.

The audience started to file out, but Lila lingered. The walk to the arena had loosened her limbs, but she wasn't keen on moving again, not before she had to, so she hung back, watching the crowds ebb and flow as some left for other matches, and others came. The blue and silver pennants disappeared, replaced by a flaming red cat on a golden ground—that was Kisimyr's banner—and a pair of lions on red.

Kamerov.

Lila pocketed the shard of white stone and settled in. *This should be interesting.*

She had Kisimyr pinned as a fireworker, but the Arnesian champion came out—prowled, really, that mane of black hair spilling out in ropes below her feline mask—holding spheres of water and earth.

To the crowd's delight, Kamerov appeared with the same.

An equal match, then, at least as far the elements went. It wasn't even Lila's fight—thank god it wasn't her fight—but she felt her pulse tick up in excitement.

The orbs fell, and the match crashed into motion.

They were well paired—it took almost five full minutes for Kisimyr to land the first hit, a glancing blow to Kamerov's thigh. It took another eight for Kamerov to land the second.

Lila's eyes narrowed as she watched, picking up on something even before she knew what it was.

Kisimyr moved in a way that was elegant, but almost animal. But Kamerov . . . there was something *familiar* about the fluid way he fought. It was graceful, almost effortless, the flourishes tacked on in a way that looked unnecessary. Before the tournament, she'd truly only seen a handful of fights using magic. But it was like déjà vu, watching him down there on the arena floor.

Lila rapped her fingers on the rail and leaned forward.

Why did he seem so familiar?

🦋

Kell ducked, and rolled, and dodged, trying to pace his speed to Kisimyr's, which was hard because she was *fast*. Faster than his first opponent, and stronger than anyone he'd fought, save Holland. The champion matched him measure for measure, point for point. That first blow had been a mistake, clumsy, clumsy—but saints, he felt good. Alive.

Behind Kisimyr's mask, Kell caught the hint of a smile, and behind his own, he grinned back.

Earth hovered in a disk above his right hand, water swirling around his left. He twisted out from behind the shelter of a pillar, but she was already gone. Behind him. Kell spun, throwing the disk. Too slow. The two collided, attacked, and dove apart, as if they were fighting with swords instead of water and earth. Thrust. Parry. Strike.

A spear of hardened earth passed inches from Kell's armored cheek as he rolled, came up onto one knee, and attacked with both elements at the same time.

Both connected, blinding them in light.

The crowd went wild, but Kisimyr didn't even hesitate.

Her water, tinted red, had been orbiting her in a loop. Kell's attack had brought him close, into her sphere, and now she pushed hard against part of the circle, and it shot forward without breaking the ring, freezing as it did into an icy spike.

Kell jumped back, but not fast enough; the ice slammed into his shoulder, shattering the plate and piercing the flesh beneath.

The crowd gasped.

Kell hissed in pain and pressed his palm against the wound.
When he drew his hand away from his shoulder, blood stained
his fingers, jewel-red. Magic whispered through him—*As Travars.
As Orense. As Osaro. As Hasari. As Steno. As Staro*—and his lips
nearly formed a spell, but he caught himself just in time, wiped
the blood on his sleeve instead, and attacked again.

Lila's eyes widened.

The rest of the crowd was fixated on Kamerov, but she happened to look up right after the blow and saw Prince Rhy in the
royal box, his face contorted in pain. He hid it quickly, wiped
the tension from his features, but his knuckles gripped the
banister, head bowed, and Lila saw, and *understood*. She'd
been there that night, when the princes were bound together,
blood to blood, pain to pain, life to life.

Her attention snapped back to the arena.

It was suddenly obvious. The height, the posture, the fluid
motions, the impossible grace.

She broke in a savage grin.

Kell.

It was him. It had to be. She had met Kamerov Loste at the
Banner Night, had marked his grey eyes, his foxlike smile. But
she'd also marked his height, the way he moved, and there
was no question, no doubt in her mind—the man in the arena
wasn't the one who'd wished her luck in the Rose Hall. It was
the man she'd fought beside in three different Londons. The
one she'd stolen from and threatened and saved. It was Kell.

"What are you smiling about?" asked Tieren, appearing at her
side.

"Just enjoying the match," she said.

The *Aven Essen* made a small, skeptical hum.

"Tell me," she added, keeping her eyes on the fight. "Did you at least try to dissuade him from this madness? Or do you simply plan to feign ignorance with him, too?"

There was a pause, and when Tieren answered, his voice was even. "I don't know what you're talking about."

"Sure you don't, *Aven Essen*." She turned toward him. "I bet if Kamerov down there were to take off his helmet, he'd look like the man he was on the Banner Night, and not a certain black-eyed—"

"This kind of talk makes me wish I'd turned you in," said the priest, cutting her off. "Rumors are dangerous things, *Stasion,* especially when they stem from someone guilty of her own crimes. So I'll ask you again," he said. "What are you smiling about?"

Lila held his eyes, her features set.

"Nothing," she said, turning back to the match. "Nothing at all."

II

In the end, Kamerov won.

Kell won.

It had been a staggeringly close match between the reigning champion and the so-called silver knight. The crowd looked dizzy from holding its breath, the arena a mess of broken stone and black ice, half the obstacles cracked or chipped or in ruins.

The way he'd moved. The way he'd fought. Even in their short time together, Lila had never seen him fight like that. A single point—he'd won by a single point, unseated the champion, and all she could think was, *He's holding back.*

Even now he's holding back.

"Stasion! Stasion!"

Lila dragged her thoughts away from Kell; she had her own, more pressing concerns.

Her second match was about to begin.

She was standing in the middle of the western arena, the stands awash in silver and black, the Faroan's pale-green pennant only an accent in the crowd.

Across from her stood the man himself, Ver-as-Is, an orb of tinted earth in each palm. Lila considered the magician—he was lithe, his limbs long and thin and twined with muscle, his skin the color of char, and his eyes an impossibly pale green, the same as his flag. Set deep into his face, they seemed to glow. But it was the *gold* that most caught her interest.

Most of the Faroans she'd seen wore gems on their skin, but Ver-as-Is wore gold. Beneath his mask, which concealed only the top half of his head, beads of the precious metal traced the lines of his face and throat in a skeletal overlay.

Lila wondered if it was a kind of status symbol, a display of wealth.

But displaying your wealth was just *asking* to be robbed of it, and she wondered how hard it would be to remove the beads.

How did they stay on? Glue? Magic? No, she noticed the ornaments on Ver-as-Is hadn't been stuck in place, exactly—they'd been *buried,* each one embedded in the skin. The modification was expertly done, the flesh around the beads barely raised, creating the illusion that the metal had grown straight from his face. But she could see the faint traces of scarring, where flesh and foreign object met.

That would certainly make robbing difficult.

And messy.

"*Astal,*" said the judge in white and gold. *Prepare.*

The crowd stilled, holding its breath.

The Faroan lifted his orbs, waiting for her to do the same.

Lila held out her spheres—fire and water—said a quick prayer, and let go.

❧

Alucard filled two glasses from the decanter on the table.

The glass was halfway to Lila's lips when he said, "I wouldn't drink that if I were you."

She stopped and peered at the contents. "What is this?"

"Avise wine . . . mostly."

"Mostly," she echoed. She squinted, and sure enough, she could see particles of something swirling in the liquid. "What have you put in it?"

"Red sand."

"I assume you contaminated my favorite drink for a reason?"

"Indeed."

He set his own glass back on the table.

"Tonight, you're going to learn to influence two elements simultaneously."

"I can't believe you ruined a bottle of avise wine."

"I told you magic was a conversation—"

"You also said it was an ocean," said Lila. "And a door, and once I think you even called it a cat—"

"Well, tonight we're calling it a conversation. We're simply adding another participant. The same power, different lines."

"I've never been able to pat my head and rub my stomach at the same time."

"Well then, this should be interesting."

❧

Lila gasped for breath.

Ver-as-Is was circling, and her body screamed, still aching from the day before. And yet, tired as she was, the magic was there, under her skin, pulsing to get out.

They were even, six to six.

Sweat ran into her eyes as she ducked, dodged, leaped, struck. A lucky blow took out the plate on the Faroan's bicep. Seven to six.

Water spun before her in a shield, turning to ice every time Ver-as-Is struck. It shattered beneath his blows, but better the shield than her precious plates.

The ruse didn't work for long. After the second block, he caught on and followed up his first attack with another. Lila lost two more plates in a matter of seconds. Seven to eight.

She could feel her strength ebbing, and the Faroan only seemed to get stronger. Faster.

Fire and water was proving to be a wretched choice. They couldn't touch; every time they did, they canceled, turning to steam or smoke—

And that gave her an idea.

She maneuvered to the nearest boulder, one low enough to scale, and brought the two forces together in her hands. White smoke billowed forth, filling the arena, and in its cover she turned and vaulted up onto the rock. From above, she could see the swirl of air made by Ver-as-Is as he turned, trying to find her. Lila focused, and the steam separated; the water became mist and then ice, freezing around him, while her fire surged up into the air and then rained down. Ver-as-Is got his earth into an arcing shield, but not before she broke two of his plates. Nine to eight.

Before she could savor the advantage, a spike of earth shot through the air at her and she leaped backward off the boulder.

And straight into a trap.

Ver-as-Is was there, inside her guard, four earthen spears hurtling toward her. There was no way to avoid the blows, no *time*. She was going to lose, but it wasn't just about the match, not in this moment, because those spears were sharp, as sharp as the ice that had pierced Kell's shoulder.

Panic spiked through her, the way it had so many times when a knife came too close and she felt the balance tip, the kiss of danger, the brush of death.

No. Something surged inside her, something simple and instinctual, and in that moment, the whole world *slowed*.

It was magic—it had to be—but unlike anything she'd ever done. For an instant, the space inside the arena seemed to *change*, slowing her pulse and drawing out the fractions of time within the second, stretching the moment—not much, just long enough for her to dodge, and roll, and strike. One of Ver-as-Is's spears still grazed her arm, breaking the plate and drawing blood, but it didn't matter, because Ver-as-Is's body took an instant—that same, stolen instant—too long to move, and her ice hit him in the side, shattering his final plate.

And just like that, the moment snapped closed, and everything caught up. She hadn't noticed the impossible quiet of that suspended second until it collapsed. In its wake, the world was chaos. Her arm was stinging, and the crowd had exploded into cheers, but Lila couldn't stop staring at Ver-as-Is, who was looking down at himself, as if his body had betrayed him. As if he knew that what had just happened wasn't possible.

But if Lila had broken the rules, no one else seemed to notice. Not the judge, or the king, or the cheering stands.

"Victory goes to Stasion Elsor," announced the man in white and gold.

Ver-as-Is glowered at her, but he didn't call foul. Instead he turned and stormed away. Lila watched him go. She felt something wet against her lip, and tasted copper. When she reached her fingers through the jaws of her mask and touched her nose, they came away red. Her head was spinning. But that was all right; it had been a tough fight.

And she had won.

She just wasn't sure how.

III

Rhy was perched on the edge of Kell's bed, rubbing his collar while Hastra tried to wrap Kell's shoulder. It was healing, but not fast enough for a ball. "Suck it up, Brother," he chided the prince. "Tomorrow will be worse."

He'd won. It had been close—so close—and not just because beating Kisimyr by anything more than a hair would raise suspicions. No, she was good, she was excellent, maybe even the best. But Kell wasn't ready to stop fighting yet, wasn't ready to give up the freedom and the thrill and go back to being a trinket in a box. Kisimyr was strong, but Kell was desperate, and hungry, and he'd scored the tenth point.

He'd made it to the final nine.

Three groups of three, squaring off against each other, one at a time, only the holder of the highest points advancing. It wouldn't be enough to win. Kell would have to win by more than a single hit.

And he'd drawn the bad card. Tomorrow, he'd have to fight not one, but both matches. He pitied the prince, but there was no going back now.

Kell had told Rhy about the king's request that he keep to the palace. Of course, he'd told him *after* sneaking out to the match.

"He's going to have a fit if he finds out," Rhy warned.

"Which is why he won't," said Kell. Rhy looked unconvinced.

For all his rakish play, he'd never been good at disobeying his father. Up until recently, neither had Kell.

"Speaking of tomorrow," said Rhy from the bed, "you need to start losing."

Kell stiffened, sending a fresh jab of pain through his shoulder. "What? Why?"

"Do you have any idea how hard this was to plan? To pull off? It's honestly a miracle we haven't been found out—"

Kell got to his feet, testing his shoulder. "Well that's a vote of confidence—"

"And I'm not going to let you blow it by *winning.*"

"I have no intention of winning the tournament. We're only to the nines." Kell felt like he was missing something. The look on Rhy's face confirmed it.

"Top thirty-six becomes eighteen," said Rhy slowly. "Top eighteen becomes nine."

"Yes, I can do math," said Kell, buttoning his tunic.

"Top nine becomes three," continued Rhy. "And what happens to those three, wise mathematician Kell?"

Kell frowned. And then it hit him. "Oh."

"Oh," Rhy parroted, hopping down from the bed.

"The Unmasking Ceremony," said Kell.

"Yes, that," said his brother.

The *Essen Tasch* had few rules when it came to fighting, and fewer still when it came to the guises worn during those fights. Competitors were free to maintain their personas for most of the tournament, but the Unmasking Ceremony required the three finalists to reveal themselves to the crowds and kings, to remove their masks and keep them off for the final match, and the subsequent crowning.

Like many of the tournament's rituals, the origin of the Unmasking Ceremony was fading from memory, but Kell knew the story hailed from the earliest days of the peace, when an assassin tried to use the tournament, and the anonymity it afforded, to kill the Faroan royal family. The assassin slew the winning magician and donned his helmet, and when the kings and queens of the three empires invited him onto their dais to receive the prize, he struck, killing the Faroan queen and gravely wounding a young royal before he was stopped. The fledgling peace might have been shattered then and there, but no one was willing to claim the assassin, who died before he could confess. In the end, the peace between the kingdoms held, but the Unmasking Ceremony was born.

"You *cannot* advance beyond the nines," said Rhy, definitively.

Kell nodded, heart sinking.

"Cheer up, Brother," said the prince, pinning the royal seal over his breast. "You've still two matches to fight. And who knows, maybe someone will even beat you fairly."

Rhy went for the door, and Kell fell in step behind him.

"Sir," said Hastra, "a word."

Kell stopped. Rhy paused in the doorway and looked back. "Are you coming?"

"I'll catch up."

"If you don't show, I'm likely to do something foolish, like throw myself at Aluc—"

"I won't miss the stupid ball," snapped Kell.

Rhy winked and shut the door behind him.

Kell turned to his guard. "What is it, Hastra?"

The guard looked profoundly nervous. "It's just . . . while you were competing, I came back to the palace to check on Staff. The king was passing through, and he stopped and asked me how you'd spent the day. . . ." Hastra hesitated, leaving the obvious unspoken: the king wouldn't have asked such a thing if he'd known of Kell's ruse. Which meant he didn't.

Kell stiffened. "And what did you say?" he asked, bracing himself.

Hastra's gaze went to the floor. "I told him that you hadn't left the palace."

"You lied to the king?" asked Kell, his voice carefully even.

"It wasn't really a lie," said Hastra slowly, looking up. "Not in the strictest sense."

"How so?"

"Well, I told him that *Kell* didn't leave the palace. I said nothing about *Kamerov*. . . ."

Kell stared at the young man in amazement. "Thank you, Hastra. Rhy and I, we shouldn't have put you in that position."

"No," said Hastra, with surprising firmness, and then quickly, "but I understand why you did."

The bells started ringing. The ball had begun. Kell felt a sharp pain in his shoulder, and strongly suspected Rhy of making a point.

"Well," he said, heading for the door, "you won't have to lie much longer."

That night, Lila had half a mind to go to the ball. Now that she knew the truth, she wanted to see Kell's face without the mask, as if she might be able to see the deception written in the lines of his frown.

Instead, she ended up wandering the docks, watching the ships bob up and down, listening to the hush of water against their hulls. Her mask hung from her fingertips, its jaws wide.

The docks themselves were strangely empty—most of the sailors and dockworkers must have ventured to the pubs and parties, or at least the Night Market. Men at sea loved land more than anyone on shore, and they knew how to make the best of it.

"That was quite a match today," said a voice. A moment later Alucard appeared, falling in step beside her.

She thought of their words that morning, of the hurt in his voice when he asked why she'd done it, stolen Elsor's identity, put herself—put them *all*—at risk. And there it was again, that treacherous desire to apologize, to ask for her place back on his ship, or at least in his graces.

"Following me again?" she asked. "Shouldn't you be celebrating?"

Alucard tipped his head back. "I had no taste for it tonight. Besides," he said, his gaze falling, "I wanted to see what you did that was so much better than balls."

"You wanted to make sure I didn't get into trouble."

"I'm not your father, Bard."

"I should hope not. Fathers shouldn't try to seduce their daughters to learn their secrets."

He shook his head ruefully. "It was *one time.*"

"When I was younger," she said absently, "I used to walk the docks back in London—my London—looking at all the ships that came in. Some days I imagined what mine would look like. Other days I just tried to imagine one that would take me away." Alucard was staring at her. "What?"

"That's the first time you've ever volunteered a piece of information."

Lila smiled crookedly. "Don't get used to it."

They walked in silence for a few moments, Lila's pockets jingling. The Isle shone red beside them, and in the distance, the palace glowed.

But Alucard had never been good with silence. "So this is what you do instead of dancing," he said. "Haunt the docks like some sailor's ghost?"

"Well, only when I get bored of doing *this.*" She pulled a fist from her pocket and opened it to reveal a collection of jewelry, coins, trinkets.

Alucard shook his head, exasperated. "Why?"

Lila shrugged. Because it was familiar, she might say, and she was good at it. Plus, the contents of people's pockets were far more interesting in *this* London. She'd found a dream stone, a fire pebble, and something that looked like a compass, but wasn't. "Once a thief, always a thief."

"What's this?" he asked, plucking the sliver of white stone from amid the tangle of stolen gems.

Lila tensed. "That's mine," she said. "A souvenir."

He shrugged and dropped the shard back onto the pile. "You're going to get caught."

"Then I better have my fun while I still can," she said, pocketing the lot. "And who knows, maybe the crown will pardon me, too."

"I wouldn't hold your breath." Alucard had begun rubbing his wrists and, realizing it, stopped and smoothed his coat. "Well, you may content yourself with haunting docks and robbing passersby, but I'd rather have a hot drink and a bit of finery, so . . ." He gave a sweeping bow. "Can I trust you to stay out of trouble, at least until tomorrow?"

Lila only smirked. "I'll try."

Halfway back toward the Wandering Road, Lila knew she was being followed.

She could hear their steps, smell their magic on the air, feel her heart pick up in that old familiar way. So when she glanced back and saw someone in the narrow road, she wasn't surprised.

She didn't run.

She should have, should have cut onto a main road when she first noticed them, put herself in public view. Instead, Lila did the one thing she'd promised Alucard she'd try not to do.

She found trouble.

When she reached the next turn in the road, an alley, she took it. Something glinted at the far end, and Lila took a step toward it before she realized what it was.

A knife.

She twisted out of the way as it came sailing toward her. She was fast, but not quite fast enough—the blade grazed her side before clattering to the ground.

Lila pressed her palm against her waist.

The cut was shallow, barely bleeding, and when her gaze flicked back up, she saw a man, his edges blurring into the dark. Lila spun, but the entrance to the alley was being blocked by another shape.

She shifted her stance, trying to keep her eyes on both at once. But as she stepped into the deeper shadow of the alley wall, a hand grasped her shoulder and she lurched forward as a third figure stepped out of the dark.

Nowhere to run. She took a step toward the shape at the alley's mouth, hoping for a drunken sailor, or a thug.

And then she saw the gold.

Ver-as-Is wasn't wearing his helmet, and without it she could see the rest of the pattern that traced up above his eyes and into his hairline.

"Elsor," he hissed, his Faroan accent turning the name into a serpentine sound.

Shit, thought Lila. But all she said was, "You again."

"You cheating scum," he continued in slurring Arnesian. "I don't know how you did it, but I saw it. I *felt* it. There was no way you could have—"

"Don't be sore," she interrupted. "It was just a ga—"

She was cut off as a fist connected with her wounded side and she doubled over, coughing. The blow hadn't come from Ver-as-Is, but one of the others, their gemmed faces masked by dark cloth. Lila's grip tightened on the metal-lined mask in her hand and she struck, slamming the helmet into the nearest man's forehead. He cried out and staggered back, but before Lila could strike again, they were on her, six hands to her two, slamming her into the alley wall. She stumbled forward as one wrenched her arm behind her back. Lila dropped to one knee on instinct and rolled, throwing the man over her shoulder, but before she could stand a boot cracked across her jaw. The darkness exploded into shards of fractured light, and an arm wrapped around her throat from behind, hauling her to her feet.

She scrambled for the knife she kept against her back, but the man caught her wrist and twisted it viciously up.

Lila was trapped. She waited for the surge of power she'd felt in the arena, waited for the world to slow and her strength to return, but nothing happened.

So she did something unexpected—she laughed.

She didn't feel like laughing—pain roared through her shoulder, and she could barely breathe—but she did it anyway, and was rewarded by confusion spreading like a stain across Ver-as-Is's face.

"You're pathetic," she spat. "You couldn't beat me one-on-one, so you come at me with three? All you do is prove how weak you really are."

She reached for magic, for fire or earth, even for bone, but nothing came. Her head pounded, and blood continued to trickle from the wound at her side.

"You think yours are the only people who can spell metal?" Ver-as-Is hissed, bringing the knife to her throat.

Lila met his gaze. "You're really going to kill me, just because you lost a match."

"No," he said. "Like for like. You cheated. So will I."

"You've already lost!" she snapped. "What's the fucking point?"

"A country is not a man, but a man is a country," he said, and then, to his men, "Get rid of him."

The other two began to drag her toward the docks.

"Can't even do it yourself," she chided. If the jab landed, he didn't let it show, just turned and began to walk away.

"Ver-as-Is," she called after him. "I'll give you a choice."

"Oh?" He glanced back, pale-green eyes widening with amusement.

"You can let me go right now, and walk away," she said, slowly. "Or I will kill you all."

He smiled. "And if I let you go, I suppose we will part as friends?"

"Oh no," she said, shaking her head. "I'm going to kill *you* either way. But if your men let me go now, I won't kill them as well."

For a moment, she thought she felt the arm at her throat loosen. But then it was back, twice as tight. *Shit,* she thought, as Ver-as-Is came toward her, spinning the knife in his hand.

"If only words were weapons . . ." he said, bringing the blade down. The handle crashed against her temple, and everything went black.

IV

Lila woke like a drowning person breaking the surface of water.

Her eyes shot open, but the world stayed pitch-black. She opened her mouth to shout, and realized it was already open, a cloth gag muffling the sound.

There was a throbbing ache in the side of her head that sharpened with every motion, and she thought she might be sick. She tried to sit up, and she quickly discovered that she couldn't.

Panic flooded through her, the need to retch suddenly replaced by the need to breathe. She was in a box. A very small box.

She went still, and she exhaled shakily when the box didn't shift or sway. As far as she could tell, she was still on land. Unless, of course, she was *under* it.

The air felt suddenly thinner.

She couldn't tell if the box was *actually* a coffin, because she couldn't see the dimensions. She was lying on her side in the darkness. She tried again to move and realized why she couldn't—her hands and feet had both been tied together, her arms wrenched behind her back. Her wrists ached from the coarse rope that circled them, her fingers numb, the knots tight enough that her skin was already rubbing raw. The slightest attempt to twist free caused a shudder of needle-sharp pain.

I will kill them, she thought. *I will kill them all.* She didn't say the words aloud because of the gag . . . and the fact that there wasn't much air in the box. The knowledge made her want to gasp.

Stay calm.

Stay calm.

Stay calm.

Lila wasn't afraid of many things. But she wasn't fond of small, dark spaces. She tried to survey her body for knives, but they were gone. Her collected trinkets were gone. Her shard of stone was gone. Anger burned through Lila like fire.

Fire.

That's what she needed. *What could go wrong with fire in a wooden box?* she wondered drily. Worst case, she would simply burn herself alive before she could get out. But if she was going to escape—and she *was* going to escape, if only to kill Ver-as-Is and his men—then she needed to be free of the rope. And rope burned.

So Lila tried to summon fire.

Tyger Tyger, burning bright . . .

Nothing. Not even a spark. It couldn't be the knife wound; that had dried, and the spell dried with it. That was how it worked. *Was* that how it worked? It seemed like it should work that way.

Panic. More panic. Clawing panic.

She closed her eyes, and swallowed, and tried again.

And again.

And again.

❦

"Focus," said Alucard.

"Well it's a little hard, considering." Lila was standing in the middle of his cabin, blindfolded. The last time she'd seen him, he

was sitting in his chair, ankle on knee, sipping a dark liquor. Judging by the sound of a bottle being lifted, a drink being poured, he was still there.

"Eyes open, eyes shut," he said, "it makes no difference."

Lila strongly disagreed. With her eyes open, she could summon fire. And with her eyes shut, well, she couldn't. Plus, she felt like a fool. "What exactly is the point of this?"

"The point, Bard, is that magic is a sense."

"Like sight," she snapped.

"Like sight," said Alucard. "But not sight. You don't need to see it. Just feel it."

"Feeling is a sense, too."

"Don't be flippant."

Lila felt Esa twine around her leg, and resisted the urge to kick the cat. "I hate this."

Alucard ignored her. "Magic is all and none. It's sight, and taste, and scent, and sound, and touch, and it's also something else entirely. It is the power in all powers, and at the same time, it is its own. And once you know how to sense its presence, you will never be without it. Now stop whining and focus."

&

Focus, thought Lila, struggling to stay calm. She could feel the magic, tangled in her pulse. She didn't need to see it. All she needed to do was reach it.

She squeezed her eyes shut, trying to trick her mind into thinking that the darkness was a choice. She was an open door. She was in control.

Burn, she thought, the word striking like a match inside her. She snapped her fingers and felt the familiar heat of fire licking the air above her skin. The rope caught, illuminating the dimensions of the box—small, very small, too small—and when she turned her head, a grisly face stared back at her, which resolved into the demon's mask right before Lila was thrown by searing pain. When the fire hovered above her fingers, it didn't hurt, but now, as it ate through the ropes, it *burned*.

She bit back a scream as the flame licked her wrists before finally snapping the rope. As soon as her hands were free, she rolled over the fire, plunging herself back into darkness. She tugged the gag off and sat up to reach her ankles, smacking her head against the top of the box and swearing roundly as she fell back. Maneuvering carefully, she managed to reach the ropes at her feet and unknot them.

Limbs free, she pushed against the lid of the box. It didn't budge. She swore and brought her palms together, a tiny flame sparking between them. By its light she could see that the box had no latches. It was a cargo crate. And it was nailed shut. Lila doused the light, and let her aching head rest against the floor of the crate. She took a few steadying breaths—*Emotion isn't strength,* she told herself, reciting one of Alucard's many idioms—and then she pressed her palms to the wooden walls of the crate, and *pushed.*

Not with her hands, but with her *will.* Will against wood, will against nail, will against air.

The box shuddered.

And *exploded.*

Metal nails ground free, boards snapped, and the air within the box shoved everything *out.* She covered her head as debris rained back down on her, then got to her feet, dragging in air. The flesh of her wrists was angry and raw, her hands shaking from pain and fury as she fought to get her bearings.

She'd been wrong. She was in a cargo hold. On a ship. But judging by the boat's steadiness, it was still docked. Lila stared down at the remains of the crate. The irony of the situation wasn't lost on her; after all, she'd tried to do the same thing to Stasion Elsor. But she liked to believe that if she'd actually put him in a crate, she would have given him air holes.

The devil's mask winked at her from the wreckage, and she

dug it free, pulling it down over her head. She knew where Ver-as-Is was staying. She'd seen his crew at the Sun Streak, an inn on the same street as the Wandering Road.

"Hey," called a man, as she climbed to the deck. "What do you think you're doing?"

Lila didn't slow. She crossed the ship briskly and descended the plank to the dock, ignoring the shouts from the deck, ignoring the morning sun and the distant sound of cheers.

Lila had warned Ver-as-Is what would happen.

And she was a girl of her word.

꙳

"What part of *you need to lose* don't you understand?"

Rhy was pacing Kell's tent, looking furious.

"You shouldn't be here," said Kell, rubbing his sore shoulder.

He hadn't meant to win. He'd just wanted it to be a good match. A close match. It wasn't his fault that 'Rul the Wolf' had stumbled. It wasn't his fault that the nines favored close combat. It wasn't his fault that the Veskan had *clearly* had a little too much fun the night before. He'd seen the man fight, and he'd been brilliant. Why couldn't he have been brilliant *today*?

Kell ran a hand through his sweat-slicked hair. The silver helmet sat, cast off, on the cushions.

"This is not the kind of trouble we need, Kell."

"It was an accident."

"I don't want to hear it."

Hastra stood against the wall, looking as if he wanted to disappear. Up in the central arena, they were still cheering Kamerov's name.

"Look at me," snapped Rhy, pulling Kell's jaw up so their eyes met. "You need to start losing *now*." He started pacing again, his voice low even though he'd had Hastra clear the tent. "The nines is a point game," he continued. "Top score in your group advances. With any luck, one of the others will take their match by a landslide, but as far as you're concerned, Kamerov is going *out.*"

"If I lose by too much, it will look suspicious."

"Well you need to lose by *enough,*" said Rhy. "The good news is, I've seen your next opponent, and he's good enough to beat you." Kell soured. "Fine," amended Rhy, "he's good enough to beat *Kamerov.* Which is exactly what he's going to do."

Kell sighed. "Who am I up against?"

Rhy finally stopped pacing. "His name is Stasion Elsor. And with any luck, he'll slaughter you."

🜂

Lila locked the door behind her.

She found her knives in a bag at the foot of the bed, along with the trinkets and the shard of stone. The men themselves were still asleep. By the looks of it—the empty bottles, the tangled sheets—they'd had a late night. Lila chose her favorite knife, the one with the knuckled grip, and approached the beds, humming softly.

How do you know when the Sarows is coming?
(Is coming is coming is coming aboard?)

She killed his two companions in their beds, but Ver-as-Is she woke, right before she slit his throat. She didn't want him to beg; she simply wanted him to see.

A strange thing happened when the Faroans died. The gems that marked their dark skin lost their hold and tumbled free. The gold beads slid from Ver-as-Is's face, hitting the floor like rain. Lila picked up the largest one and pocketed it as payment before she left. Back the way she'd come with her coat pulled tight and her head down, fetching the mask from the bin where she'd stashed it. Her wrists still burned, and her head still ached, but she felt much better now, and as she made her way toward the Wandering Road, breathing in the cool air, letting sunlight warm her skin, a stillness washed over her—the calm that came from taking control, from making a threat and following through. Lila felt like herself again. But underneath it all was a twinge, not of guilt or regret, but the nagging pinch that she was forgetting something.

When she heard the trumpets, it hit her.

She craned her neck, scouring the sky for the sun, and finding only clouds. But she knew. Knew it was late. Knew *she* was late. Her stomach dropped like a stone, and she slammed the helmet on and *ran*.

🐉

Kell stood in the center of the arena, waiting.

The trumpets rang out a second time. He squared his shoulders to the opposite tunnel, waiting for his opponent to emerge.

But no one came.

The day was cold, and his breath fogged in front of his mask. A minute passed, then two, and Kell found his attention flicking to the royal platform where Rhy stood, watching, waiting. Behind him, Lord Sol-in-Ar looked impassive, Princess Cora bored, Queen Emira lost in thought.

The crowd was growing restless, their attention slipping.

Kell's excitement tensed, tightened, wavered.

His banner—the mirrored lions on red—waved above the podium and in the crowd. The other banner—crossed knives on black—snapped in the breeze.

But Stasion Elsor was nowhere to be found.

🐉

"You're very late," said Ister as Lila surged into the Arnesian tent.

"I know," she snapped.

"You'll never—"

"Just *help me,* priest."

Ister sent a messenger to the stadium and enlisted two more attendants, and the three rushed to get Lila into her armor, a flurry of straps and pads and plates.

Christ. She didn't even know who she was set to fight.

"Is that blood?" asked one attendant, pointing to her collar.

"It's not mine," muttered Lila.

"What happened to your wrists?" asked another.

"Too many questions, not enough work."

Ister appeared with a large tray, the surface of which was covered in weapons. No, not weapons, exactly, only the hilts and handles.

"I think they're missing something."

"This is the nines," said Ister. "You have to supply the rest." She plucked a hilt up from the tray and curled her fingers around it. The priest's lips began to move, and Lila watched as a gust of wind whipped up and spun tightly around and above the hilt until it formed a kind of blade.

Lila's eyes widened. The first two rounds had been fought at a distance, attacks lobbed across the arena like explosives. But weapons meant hand-to-hand combat, and close quarters were Lila's specialty. She swiped two dagger hilts from the tray and slid them underneath the plates on her forearms.

"*Fal chas,*" said Ister, just before the trumpets blared in warning, and Lila cinched the demon's jaw and took off, the final buckles on her mask still streaming behind her.

❧

Kell cocked his head at Rhy, wondering what the prince would do. If Elsor didn't show, he would be forced to forfeit. If he was forced to forfeit, Kell would have the points to advance. Kell *couldn't* advance. He watched the struggle play out across Rhy's face, and then the king whispered something in his ear. The prince seemed to grow paler as he raised the gold ring to his mouth, ready to call the match. But before he could speak, an attendant appeared at the edge of the platform and spoke rapidly. Rhy hesitated, and then, mercifully, the trumpets rang.

Moments later Stasion hurried into the stadium looking . . . disheveled. But when he saw Kell, he broke into a smile, his teeth shining white behind his devil's mask. There was no warmth in that look. It was a predator's grin.

The crowds burst into excited applause as Kamerov Loste and Stasion Elsor took their places at the center of the arena.

Kell squinted through his visor at Elsor's mask. Up close it was a nightmarish thing.

"*Tas renar*," said Kell. *You are late.*

"I'm worth the wait," answered Stasion. His voice caught Kell off guard. Husky and smooth, and sharp as a knife. And yet, undeniably female.

He knew that voice.

Lila.

But this wasn't Lila. This *couldn't* be Lila. She was a human, a Grey-worlder—a Grey-worlder unlike any other, yes, but a Grey-worlder all the same—and she didn't know how to do magic, and she would definitely never be crazy enough to enter the *Essen Tasch.*

As soon as the thought ran through his head, Kell's argument crumbled. Because if anyone was bullheaded enough to do something this stupid, this rash, this suicidal, it was the girl who'd picked his pocket that night in Grey London, who'd followed him through a door in the worlds—a door she should never have survived—and faced the black stone and the white royals and death itself with a sharpened smile.

The same sharpened smile that glinted now, between the lips of the demon's face.

"*Wait*," said Kell.

The word was a whisper, but it was too late. The judge had already signaled, and Lila let go of her spheres. Kell dropped his own an instant later, but she was already on the attack.

Kell hesitated, but she didn't. He was still trying to process her presence when she iced the ground beneath his feet, then struck out at close range with a dagger made of flame. Kell lunged away, but not far enough, and a moment later he was on his back, light bursting from the plate across his stomach, and Lila Bard kneeling over him.

He stared up into her mismatched brown eyes.

Did she know it was him behind the silver mask?

"Hello," she said, and in that one word, he knew that she did. Before he could say anything, Lila pushed herself off again. Kell quickly rolled backward, leveraging himself into a fighting crouch.

She had two knives now (of *course* she had chosen the blades—one made of fire, one made of ice), and she was twirling them casually. Kell had chosen nothing. (It was a bold move, one Kamerov would make, and one designed to sink him. But not this fast.) He lashed his water into a whip and struck, but Lila rolled out of reach and threw her icy blade. Kell dodged, and in that distracted moment she tried to strike again, but this time his earth caught hold of her boot and his whip lashed out. Lila got her fire knife up to block his blow, the water whip breaking around the blade, but the whip's end managed to find her forearm, shattering a plate.

Lila was still pinned in place, but she was smirking, and an instant later her ice blade hit Kell from behind. He staggered forward as a second plate broke and he lost his hold on her foot.

And then the real fight began.

They sparred, a blur of elements and limbs, hits marked only by a flare of light. They came together, lunged apart, matching each other blow for blow.

"Have you lost your mind?" he growled as their elements crashed together.

"Nice to see you, too," she answered, ducking and spinning behind him.

"You have to stop," he ordered, narrowly dodging a fireball.

"You first," she chided, diving behind a column.

Water slashed, and fire burned, and earth rumbled.

"This is madness."

"I'm not the only one in disguise." Lila drew near, and he thought she'd go in for a strike, but at the last second she changed her mind, touched the fire blade to her empty palm, and *pushed*.

For an instant, the air around them faltered. Kell saw pain flash across Lila's face behind the mask, but then a wall of flame *erupted* toward him, and it was all he could do to will his water up into a wave over his head. Steam poured forth as the two elements collided. And then Lila did something completely unexpected. She reached out and froze the water over Kell's head. *His* water.

The audience gasped, and Kell swore, as the sheet of ice cracked and splintered and came crashing down on top of him. It wasn't against the rules—they'd both chosen water—but it was a rare thing, to claim your opponent's element for yourself, and overpower them.

A rarer thing still, to be overpowered.

Kell could have escaped, could have drawn the fight out another measure, maybe two. But he had to lose. So he held his ground and let the ceiling of ice fall, shattering the plates across his shoulders and back, and sending up flares of light.

And just like that, it was over.

Delilah Bard had won.

She came to a stop beside him, offered him her hand.

"Well played, *mas vares*," she whispered.

Kell stood there, dazed. He knew he should bow to her, to the crowd, and go, but his feet wouldn't move. He watched as Lila tipped her mask up to the stands, and the king, then watched as she gave him one last devilish grin and slipped away. He gave a rushed bow to the royal platform and sprinted after her, out of the stadium and into the tents, throwing open the curtain marked by the two crossed blades.

An attendant stood waiting, the only figure in an otherwise empty tent.

"Where is she?" he demanded, even though he knew the answer.

The devil's mask sat on the cushions, discarded along with the rest of the armor.

Lila was already gone.

V

Lila leaned back against Elsor's door, gasping for air.

She'd caught him off guard, that much was sure, and now Kell knew. Knew she'd been in London for days, knew she'd been there, right beside him, in the tournament. Her heart was pounding in her chest; she felt like a cat who'd finally caught its mouse, and then let it go. For now.

The high began to settle with her pulse. Her head was throbbing, and when she swallowed, she tasted blood. She waited for the wave of dizziness to pass, and when it didn't, she let her body sink to the wooden floor, Kell's voice ringing in her ears.

That familiar, exasperated tone.

This is madness.

So superior, as if they weren't *both* breaking all the rules. As if he weren't playing a part, just like her.

You have to stop.

She could picture his frown behind that silver mask, the crease deepening between those two-toned eyes.

What would he do now?

What would *she* do?

Whatever happened, it was worth it.

Lila got to her knees, frowning as a drop of blood hit the wooden floorboards. She touched her nose, then wiped the streak of red on her sleeve and got up.

She began to strip off Elsor's clothes, ruined from Ver-as-Is's assault and the subsequent match. Slowly she peeled away the weapons, and the fabric, then stared at herself in the mirror, half clothed, her body a web of fresh bruises and old scars.

A fire burned low in the hearth, a basin of cold water on the chest. Lila took her time getting clean and dry and warm, rinsing the darkening grease from her hair, the blood from her skin.

She looked around the room, trying to decide what to wear.

And then she had an idea.

A novel, dangerous idea, which was, of course, her favorite kind.

Maybe it's time, she thought, *to go to a ball.*

🐉

"Rhy!" called Kell, the crowd parting around him. He'd shed the helmet and switched the coat, but his hair was still slicked with sweat, and he felt breathless.

"What are you doing here?" asked the prince. He was walking back to the palace, surrounded by an entourage of guards.

"It was her!" hissed Kell, falling in step beside him.

All around them, people cheered and waved, hoping to get so much as a glance or a smile from the prince. "Who was her?" Rhy asked, indulging the crowd.

"Stasion Elsor," he whispered. "It was *Lila.*"

Rhy's brow furrowed. "I know it's been a long day," he said, patting Kell's shoulder, "but obviously—"

"I know what I saw, Rhy. She spoke to me."

Rhy shook his head, the smile still fixed on his mouth. "That makes no sense. Tieren selected the players weeks ago."

Kell looked around, but Tieren was conveniently absent. "Well, he didn't select me."

"No, but *I* did." They reached the palace steps, and the crowd hung back as they climbed.

"I don't know what to tell you—I don't know if she *is* Elsor, or if she's just posing as him, but the person I just fought back

V. E. SCHWAB

there, that wasn't some magician from the countryside. That was Delilah Bard."

"Is that why you lost so easily?" asked the prince as they reached the top of the steps.

"You told me to lose!" snapped Kell as the guards held open the doors. His words echoed through the too-quiet foyer, and Kell's stomach turned when he glanced up and saw the king standing in the center of the room. Maxim took one look at Kell and said, "Upstairs. *Now.*"

"I thought I made myself clear," said the king when they were in his room.

Kell was sitting in his chair beside the balcony, being chastised like a child while Hastra and Staff stood silently by. Rhy had been told to wait outside and was currently kicking up a fuss in the hall.

"Did I not instruct you to stay within the palace walls?" demanded Maxim, voice thick with condescension.

"You did, but—"

"Are you deaf to my wishes?"

"No, sir."

"Well I obviously didn't make myself clear when I asked you as your father, so now I command you as your *king.* You are hereby *confined* to the palace until further notice."

Kell straightened. "This isn't *fair.*"

"Don't be a child, Kell. I wouldn't have asked if it wasn't for your own good." Kell scoffed, and the king's eyes darkened. "You mock my command?"

He stilled. "No. But we both know this isn't about what's good for *me.*"

"You're right. It's about what's good for our kingdom. And if you are loyal to this crown, and to this family, you will confine yourself to this palace until the tournament is over. Am I understood?"

Kell's chest tightened. "Yes, sir," he said, his voice barely a whisper.

The king spun on Staff and Hastra. "If he leaves this palace again, you will both face charges, do you understand?"

"Yes, Your Majesty," they answered grimly.

With that the king stormed out.

Kell put his head in his hands, took a breath, then swiped everything from the low table before him, scattering books and shattering a bottle of avise wine across the inlaid floor.

"What a waste," muttered Rhy, sagging into the opposite chair.

Kell sank back and closed his eyes.

"Hey, it's not so bad," pressed Rhy. "At least you're already out of the competition."

That sank Kell's spirits even lower. His fingers drifted to the tokens around his neck, as he struggled to suppress the urge to *leave. Run.* But he couldn't, because whatever the king believed, Kell *was* loyal, to his crown, to his family. To *Rhy.*

The prince sat forward, seemingly oblivious to the storm in Kell's head. "Now," he said, "what shall we wear to the party?"

"Hang the party," grumbled Kell.

"Come now, Kell, the party never did anything to you. Besides, what if a certain young woman with a penchant for cross-dressing decides to show? You wouldn't want to miss that."

Kell dragged his head up off the cushions. "She shouldn't be competing."

"Well, she made it this far. Maybe you're not giving her enough credit."

"I let her win."

"Did everyone else do the same?" asked Rhy, amused. "And I have to say, she looked like she was holding her own."

Kell groaned. She *was.* Which made no sense. Then again, nothing about Lila ever did. He got to his feet. "Fine."

"There's a good sport."

"But no more red and gold," he said, turning his coat inside out. "Tonight I'm wearing black."

🜂

Calla was humming and fastening pins in the hem of a skirt when Lila came in.

"Lila!" she said cheerfully. "*Avan*. What can I help you with this night? A hat? Some cuffs?"

"Actually . . ." Lila ran her hand along a rack of coats, then sighed, and nodded at the line of dresses. "I need one of those." She felt a vague dread, staring at the puffy, impractical garments, but Calla broke into a delighted smile. "Don't look so surprised," she said. "It's for Master Kell."

That only made the merchant's smile widen. "What is this occasion?"

"A tournament ball." Lila started to reach for one of the dresses, but Calla rapped her fingers. "No," she said firmly. "No black. If you are going to do this, you are going to do it right."

"What is wrong with black? It's the perfect color."

"For hiding. For blending into shadows. For storming castles. Not for balls. I let you go to the last one in black, and it has bothered me all winter."

"If that's true, you don't have enough things to worry about."

Calla *tsk*ed and turned toward the collection of dresses. Lila's gaze raked over them, and she cringed at a yolk-yellow skirt, a velvety purple sleeve. They looked like pieces of ripe fruit, like decadent desserts. Lila wanted to look powerful, not *edible*.

"Ah," said Calla, and Lila braced herself as the woman drew a dress from the rack and presented it to her. "How about this one?"

It wasn't black, but it wasn't confectionary either. The gown was a dark green, and it reminded Lila of the woods at night, of slivers of moonlight cutting through leaves.

The first time she had fled home—if it could be called that—she was ten. She headed into St. James's Park and spent the whole night shivering in a low tree, looking up through the limbs at the moon, imagining she was somewhere else. In the morning she dragged herself back and found her father passed out drunk in his room. He hadn't even bothered looking for her.

Calla read the shadows in her face. "You don't like it?"

"It's pretty," said Lila. "But it doesn't suit me." She struggled for the words. "Maybe who I was once, but not who I am now."

Calla nodded and put the dress back. "Ah, here we go."

She reached for another gown and pulled it from the rack. "What about this?" The dress was . . . hard to describe. It was something between blue and grey, and studded with drops of silver. Thousands of them. The light danced across the bodice and down the skirts, causing the whole thing to shimmer darkly.

It reminded her of the sea and the night sky. It reminded her of sharp knives and stars and freedom.

"That," breathed Lila, "is perfect."

She didn't realize how complicated the dress was until she tried to put it on. It had resembled a pile of nicely stitched fabric draped over Calla's arm, but in truth it was the most intricate contraption Lila had ever faced.

Apparently the style that winter was structure. Hundreds of fasteners and buttons and clasps. Calla cinched and pulled and straightened and somehow got the dress onto Lila's body.

"*Anesh,*" said Calla when it was finally done.

Lila cast a wary glance in the mirror, expecting to see herself at the center of an elaborate torture device. Instead, her eyes widened in surprise.

That bodice transformed Lila's already narrow frame into something with curves, albeit modest ones. It supplied her with a waist. It couldn't help much when it came to bosom, as Lila didn't have anything to work with, but thankfully the winter trend was to emphasize shoulders, not bust. The dress came all the way up to her throat, ending in a collar that reminded Lila vaguely of her helmet's jawline. The thought of the demon's mask gave her strength.

That's all this was, really: another disguise.

To Calla's dismay, Lila insisted on keeping her slim-cut pants on beneath the skirts, along with her boots, claiming no one would be able to tell.

"Please tell me this is easier to take off than it was to put on."

Calla raised a brow. "You do not think Master Kell knows how?"

Lila felt her cheeks burning. She should have disabused the merchant of her assumption months ago, but that assumption—that Kell and Lila were somehow . . . engaged, or at least entangled—was the reason Calla had first agreed to help her. And matters of pride aside, the merchant was dreadfully handy.

"There is the release," said Calla, tapping two pins at the base of the corset.

Lila reached back, fingering the laces of the corset, wondering if she could hide one of her knives there.

"Sit," urged the merchant.

"I honestly don't know if I can."

The woman *tsk*ed and nodded to a stool, and Lila lowered herself onto it. "Do not worry. The dress won't break."

"It's not the dress I'm worried about," she grumbled. No wonder so many of the women she stole from seemed faint; they obviously couldn't breathe, and Lila was fairly certain their corsets hadn't been *nearly* as tight as this one.

For god's sake, thought Lila. *I've been in a dress for five minutes and I'm already whining.*

"You close your eyes."

Lila stared, skeptical.

"*Tac,* you must trust."

Lila had never been good at trust, but she'd come this far, and now that she was in the dress, she was committed to following through. So she closed her eyes and let the woman dab some-thing between lash and brow and then against her lips.

Lila kept her eyes closed as she felt a brush running through her hair, fingers tousling the strands.

Calla hummed as she worked, and Lila felt something in her sag, sadden. Her mother had been dead a very long time, so long she could barely remember the feeling of her hands smoothing her hair, the sound of her voice.

Tyger Tyger, burning bright.

Lila felt her palms begin to burn and, worried that she'd ac-cidentally set fire to her dress, pressed them together and opened her eyes, focusing on the rug of the tent and the faint pain of pins sliding against her scalp.

Calla had set a handful of the hairpins in Lila's lap. They were polished silver, and she recognized them from the chest she'd brought ashore.

"These you bring back," said Calla as she finished. "I like them."

"I'll bring it all back," said Lila, getting to her feet. "I have no use for a dress like this beyond tonight."

"Most women believe that a dress need only matter for one night."

"Those women are wasteful," said Lila, rubbing her wrists. They were still chafed raw from the ropes that morning. Calla saw, and said nothing, only fastened broad silver bracelets over both. *Gauntlets,* thought Lila, even though the first word to come to mind was *chains.*

"One final touch."

"Oh for god's sake, Calla," she complained. "I think this is more than enough."

"You are a very strange girl, Lila."

"I was raised far away."

"Yes, well, that will explain some of it."

"Some of what?" asked Lila.

Calla gestured at her. "And I suppose where you were raised, women dressed as men and wore weapons like jewelry."

". . . I've always been unique."

"Yes, well, it is no wonder you and Kell attract. Both unique. Both . . . a bit . . ." Suddenly, conveniently, the language seemed to fail her.

"Mean?" offered Lila.

Calla smiled. "No, no, not mean. Guard up. But tonight," she said, fastening a silver brim-veil into Lila's hair, "you bring his guard down."

Lila smiled, despite herself. "That's the idea."

VI

White London.

The knife glinted in Ojka's hand.

The king stood behind her, waiting. "Are you ready?"

Her fingers tightened on the blade as fear hummed through her. Fear, and power. She had survived the marking, the blood fever, even that collar. She would survive this.

"*Kosa,*" she said, the answer barely a whisper. *Yes.*

"Good."

They were standing in the castle courtyard, the gates closed and only the statues of the fallen twins bearing witness as the king's gaze warmed her spine and the winter wind bit at her face. Life was returning to the city, coloring it like a bruise, but the cold had lingered at the edges. Especially at night. The sun was warm, and things grew beneath it, but when it sank, it took all the heat with it. The king said that this was normal, that a healthy world had seasons of warmth and light, and others of shadow.

Ojka was ready for heat.

That was the first thing she had felt, back when the blood fever came. Glorious heat. She'd seen the burnt-up shells of her failed predecessors, but she'd welcomed the fire.

She'd believed, then, in Holland's power. In her potential.

She'd still believed, even when the king's collar had closed around her throat.

And now, he was asking her to believe again. Believe in his magic. In the magic he had given her. She had done the blood spells. Summoned ice and fire. Mended some things and broken others. Drawn doors within her world. This would be no different. It was still within her reach.

She stared down at the knife, hilt against one palm, edge pressed to the other. She had her orders. And yet she hesitated.

"My king," she said, still facing the courtyard wall. "It is not cowardice that makes me ask, but . . ."

"I know your mind, Ojka," said Holland. "You wonder why I ask this errand of you. Why I do not go myself. The truth is, I cannot."

"There is nothing you cannot do."

"All things come at a cost," he said. "To restore this world— *our* world—I had to sacrifice something of myself. If I left now, I am not certain I would be able to return."

So that was where the power came from. A spell. A deal. She had heard the king speaking to himself as if to someone else, had seen what lurked in the shadow of his eye, even thought she'd seen his reflection move when he did not.

How much had Holland sacrificed already?

"Besides . . ." She felt his hands come to rest on her shoulders, heat and magic flaring through her with his touch. "I gave you power so you could use it."

"Yes, my king," she whispered.

Her right eye pulsed as he folded his broad frame around her narrower one, shaping his body to hers. His arms shadowed her own, tracing from shoulders to elbows to wrists, his hands coming to rest against hers. "You will be fine, Ojka, so long as you are strong enough."

And if I am not?

She didn't think she'd said the words aloud, but the king heard her either way.

"Then you will be lost, and so will I." The words were cold, but not the way he said them. His voice was as it always was, a stone worn smooth, with a weight that made her knees weaken. He brought his lips to her ear. "But I believe in you." With that, he guided her knife hand with his own, dragging the blade against her skin. Blood welled, dark as ink, and he pressed something against her bloody palm. A coin, as red as her hair, with a gold star in the center.

"You know what I ask of you," he said, guiding her wounded hand and the coin within to the cold stone wall. "You know what you must do."

"I will not let you down, my king."

"I hope not," said Holland, withdrawing from her, taking the heat with him.

Ojka swallowed and focused on the place where her searing palm met the cold stones as she said the command, just as he'd taught her. *"As Travars."*

Her marked eye sang in her skull, her blood shuddering with the words. Where her hand met stone, shadow blossomed out into a door. She meant to step forward, step through, but she never had the chance.

The darkness ripped her forward. The world tore. And so did she.

A rending in her muscles. A breaking in her bones.

Her skin burned and her blood froze and everything was pain.

It lasted forever and an instant, and then there was nothing.

Ojka crumpled to her knees, shuddering with the knowledge that somehow she had failed. She wasn't strong enough. Wasn't worthy. And now she was gone, ripped away from her world, her purpose, her king. This calm, this settling feeling, this must be death.

And yet.

Death was not supposed to have edges, and this did. She

could feel them, even with her eyes closed. Could feel where her body ended, and the world began. Could death be a world unto itself? Did it have music?

Ojka's eyes drifted open, and she drew in a breath when she saw the cobbled street beneath her, the night sky tinged with red. Her veins burned darkly across her skin. Her eye pulsed with power. The crimson coin still dug into her palm, and her knife glinted on the stones a few feet away.

And the understanding hit her in a wave.

She'd done it.

A sound escaped her throat, something tangled up in shock and triumph as she staggered to her feet. Everything hurt, but Ojka relished the pain. It meant she was alive, she had *survived*. She had been tried, tested, and found able.

My king? she thought, reaching through the darkness of space and the walls between worlds. Worlds that *she* had crossed.

For a long moment, there was no answer. Then, incredibly, she heard his voice, paired with the thrumming of her pulse in her head.

My messenger.

It was the most beautiful sound. A thread of light in the darkness.

I am here, she thought, wondering where exactly *here* was. Holland had told her about this world. That red glow, that must be the river. And that beacon of light, the palace. She could hear the sounds of people, feel their energy as she readjusted her pale cloak and shifted her red hair in front of her marked eye. *What now?*

There was another pause, and when the king's voice came again, it was smooth and even.

Find him.

TEN

CATASTROPHE

I

Red London.

The city glittered from the palace steps, a stretch of frost and fog and magic.

Lila took it in, and then turned and presented Elsor's invitation. The stairs were filled with foreigners and nobles, and the guards didn't bother to look at the name on the slip, simply saw the royal seal and ushered her inside.

It had been four months since she'd last set foot in the heart of the royal palace.

She had seen the Rose Hall, of course, before the tournament, but that had been separate, impersonal. The palace itself felt like a grand house. A royal *home*. The entry hall was once again lined with heaping flower bouquets, but they had been arranged into a path, ushering Lila left through the foyer and past another set of large doors that must have been shut before, but were now thrown open, like wings. She stepped through into a massive ballroom of polished wood and cut glass, a honeycomb of light.

They called this one the Grand Hall.

Lila had been in another ballroom, the night of the Masquerade—the Gold Hall—and it was impressive, with its stonework and metal. This had all of the splendor, the opulence, and then something *more*. Dozens of chandeliers hung from the vaulted ceiling several stories up and lit the space with refracted candlelight. Columns rose from the oak floor, adorned with spiral staircases that broke off onto walkways and led to galleries and alcoves set into the walls overhead.

In the center of the ballroom, raised on a dais, a quartet of musicians played. Their instruments varied, but they were all made from polished wood and strung with golden wire, and the players themselves were brushed with gold. They stood perfectly still, save for only the most necessary movements of their fingers.

What had Jinnar said about Prince Rhy? A flair for drama.

Lila scanned the cavernous ballroom, and caught sight of the prince moving between tables on the opposite side of the hall. There, by the balcony doors, she saw Alucard, bowing to a lovely Faroan in purple silk. Flirt.

She skirted the room, wondering how long it would take her to spot Kell in such a crowd. But within moments, she saw him, not on the dance floor or mingling among the tables, but over-head. He stood alone on one of the lower balconies, his lanky form draped over the rail. His tousled auburn hair glinted be-neath the chandeliers, and he rolled a glass between his palms, seeming troubled. From this angle, she couldn't see his eyes, but she imagined she could see the crease between them.

He looked as though he were looking for someone.

And Lila had a feeling that someone was *her*.

She retreated into the safety of the column's shadow, and for a few moments, she watched Kell watch the crowd. But she hadn't put on a dress for the sake of wearing it, so she finally finished her drink, set the empty glass on the nearest table, and stepped out into the light.

As she did, a girl appeared at Kell's side. The princess from Vesk. Her hand touched Kell's shoulder, and Lila frowned. Was she even old enough to flirt like that? Christ, she looked like a *child*. Slim but round-faced, pretty but dimpled—s*oft*—with a wreath of wood and silver atop her straw-blond braid.

Kell gave the princess a look, but he didn't recoil from the touch, and she must have taken his stillness as an invitation, because she slipped her arm through his, and rested her head against his shoulder. Lila found her fingers itching for a knife, but then to her surprise, Kell's gaze drifted past the girl, down to the ballroom, and landed on *her*.

Kell tensed visibly.

So did Lila.

She watched as he said something to the princess and drew his arm free. The girl looked put out, but he didn't give her a second glance—didn't take his gaze from Lila—as he descended the stairs and came toward her, eyes dark, fists clenched at his side.

He opened his mouth, and Lila braced herself for an attack. But instead of yelling, Kell exhaled, held out his hand, and said, "Dance with me."

It wasn't a question. It was barely a request.

"I don't know how to dance," she said.

"I do," he said simply, as if the act didn't require two. But he was standing there, waiting, and eyes were beginning to turn their way, so she took his hand, and let him lead her out onto the shadowed edge of the ballroom floor. When the music kicked up, Kell's fingers tightened around hers, his other hand found her waist, and they began to move; well, Kell began to move, and Lila moved with him, forcing herself to follow his lead, to trust in it.

She hadn't been this close to him in months. Her skin hummed where he touched her. Was that normal? If magic coursed through everyone and everything, was this what it felt like when it found itself again?

They danced in silence for several long moments, spinning together and apart, a slower version of their cadence in the ring. And then, out of nowhere, Lila asked, "Why?"

"Why what?"

"Why did you ask me to dance?"

He *almost* smiled. A ghost. A trick of the light. "So you couldn't run away again before I said hello."

"Hello," said Lila.

"Hello," said Kell. "Where have you been?"

Lila smirked. "Why, did you miss me?"

Kell opened his mouth. Closed it. Opened it again before finally managing to answer, "Yes."

The word was low, and the sincerity caught her off guard. A blow beneath her ribs. "What," she fumbled, "the life of a royal no longer to your tastes?" But the truth was, she'd missed him, too. Missed his stubbornness and his moods and his constant frown. Missed his eyes, one crisp blue, the other glossy black.

"You look . . ." he started, then trailed off.

"Ridiculous?"

"Incredible."

Lila frowned. "You don't," she said, seeing the shadows under his eyes, the sadness in them. "What's wrong, Kell?"

He tensed slightly, but he didn't let go. He took a breath, as if formulating a lie, but when he exhaled, the truth came out. "Ever since that night, I haven't felt . . . I thought competing would help, but it only made it worse. I feel like I'm suffocating. I know you think it's madness, that I have everything I need, but I watched a king wither and die inside a castle." He looked down, as if he could see the problem through his shirt. "I don't know what's happening to me."

"Life," she said, as they spun around the floor. "And death."

"What do you mean?"

"Everyone thinks I have a death wish, you know? But I don't want to die—dying is easy. No, I want to *live,* but getting close to death is the only way to feel alive. And once you do, it makes you realize that everything you were doing before wasn't *actually* living. It was just making do. Call me crazy, but I think we do the best living when the stakes are high."

"You're crazy," said Kell.

She laughed softly. "Who knows? Maybe the world's gone crooked. Maybe you're still possessed. Or maybe you just got a taste of what it really means to be alive. Take it from someone who's had her fair share of close calls. You almost died, Kell. So now you know what it feels like to *live*. To fear for that life. To fight for it. And once you know, well, there's no going back."

His voice was unsteady. "What do I do?"

"I'm the wrong person to ask," she said. "I just run away."

"Running sounds good."

"Then run," she said. He stifled a laugh, but she was serious. "The thing about freedom, Kell? It doesn't come naturally. Almost no one has it handed to them. I'm free because I fought for it. You're supposed to be the most powerful magician in all the worlds. If you don't want to be here, then go."

The music picked up, and they came together, drew apart.

"I made Rhy a promise," said Kell as they turned, carried along by the dance. "That I would stand at his side when he was king."

She shrugged. "Last time I checked, he's not on the throne yet. Look, I stay here because I have nothing to go back to. There's no reason that once you leave, you can't return. Maybe you simply need to stretch your legs. Live a little. See the world. Then you can come back and settle down, and you and Rhy can live happily ever after."

He snorted.

"But, Kell . . ." she said, sobering, ". . . don't do what I did."

"You're going to have to be more specific."

She thought of Barron, the silver watch in the bottom of her coat. "If you decide to leave—when you decide to leave—don't do it without saying good-bye."

The music struck its final notes, and Kell spun Lila into his arms. Their bodies tangled, and both held their breath. The last time they'd embraced, they were bruised and bloody and about to be arrested. That had felt real; this felt like a fantasy.

Over Kell's shoulder, Lila saw the Princess of Vesk at the edge of the room, surrounded by gentlemen, and staring daggers at *her*. Lila flashed a smile and let Kell lead her off the floor, between a pair of columns.

"So, Kamerov?" she said as they found a quiet place to talk.

His grip tightened on her. "No one knows. They *can't*."

She shot him a withering look. "Do I really strike you as the telling type?" she asked. Kell said nothing, only examined her with that strange two-toned gaze, as if he expected her to disappear. "So . . ." she said, plucking a glass of sparkling wine from a passing tray, "did you kill the real Kamerov?"

"What? Of course not. He's a fiction." His brow furrowed. "Did *you* kill the real Elsor?"

Lila shook her head. "He's on a boat headed for Denolar. Or was it Delo—"

"*Delonar*?" snapped Kell, shaking his head. "Saints, what were you thinking?"

"I don't know," she said, honestly. "I don't understand what I am, how I'm alive, what I can do. I guess I just wanted to see."

"You didn't have to enter the most visible tournament in the three empires to test your fledgling abilities."

"But it's been fun."

"Lila," he said softly, and for once, his voice didn't sound angry. Tense, yes, but not mad. Had he ever said her name like that? It sounded almost like longing.

"Yes?" she asked, her breath tight.

"You have to withdraw."

And just like that, the warmth between them shattered, replaced by the Kell she remembered, stubborn and righteous.

"No, I don't," she said.

"You can't possibly continue."

"I've made it this far. I'm not dropping out."

"Lila—"

"What are you going to do, Kell? Have me arrested?"

"I should."

"But I'm not Stasion Elsor," she said, gesturing down to the ball gown. "I'm Delilah Bard." Truth really was the best disguise. His frown deepened. "Come on, don't be a sore loser."

"I threw the match," he snapped. "And even if I hadn't, you *can't* move on."

"I can, and I will."

"It's too dangerous. If you defeat Rul, you'll be in the final three. You'll be unmasked. This ruse of yours might work from a distance, but do you honestly think no one will notice who you are—and who you're not—if you show your face? Besides, I saw you in the ring today—"

"When I *won*?"

"When you *faltered*."

"I've made it this far."

"I felt your power slip. I saw the pain written on your face."

"That had nothing to do with our match—"

"What happens if you lose control?"

"I won't."

"Do you remember the cardinal rule of magic?" he pressed. *"Power in Balance, Balance in Power."* He lifted her hand, frowning at the veins on the back. They were darker than they should have been. "I don't think you're balancing. You're taking and using, and it's going to catch up with you."

Lila stiffened with annoyance. "Which is it, Kell? Are you angry at me, or worried about me, or happy to see me? Because I can't keep up."

He sighed. "I'm all of those things. Lila, I . . ." But he trailed off as he caught sight of something behind her. She watched the light go out of his eyes, his jaw clench.

"Ah, there you are, Bard," came a familiar voice, and she turned to see Alucard striding over. "Saints, is that a *dress* you're in? The crew will never believe it."

"You've got to be kidding me," growled Kell.

Alucard saw him, and stopped. He made a sound halfway between a chuckle and a cough. "Sorry, I didn't mean to interrupt—"

"It's fine, Captain," said Lila at the same time Kell growled, "Go away, Emery."

Lila and Kell looked at each other, confused.

"You *know* him?" demanded Kell.

Alucard straightened. "Of course she does. Bard works for me aboard the *Night Spire*."

"I'm his best thief," said Lila.

"Bard," chided Alucard, "we don't call it thieving in the presence of the crown."

Kell, meanwhile, appeared to be losing his mind. "No," he muttered, running a hand through his copper hair. "No. No. There are *dozens*."

"Kell?" she asked, moving to touch his arm.

He shook her off. "*Dozens* of ships, Lila! And you had to climb aboard *his*."

"I'm sorry," she shot back, bristling, "I was under the impression that I was free to do as I pleased."

"To be fair," added Alucard, "I think she was planning to steal it and slit my throat."

"Then why didn't you?" snarled Kell, spinning on her. "You're always so eager to slash and stab, why couldn't you have stabbed *him*?"

Alucard leaned in. "I think she's growing fond of me."

"*She* can speak for herself," shot Lila. She twisted toward Kell. "Why are you so upset?"

"Because Alucard Emery is a worthless noble with too much charm and too little honor, and you chose to go with *him*." The words cut through the air as Rhy rounded the corner.

"What on earth are you all shouting about . . ." The prince trailed off as he saw Kell, Lila, and Alucard huddled there.

"Lila!" he said cheerfully. "So you aren't a figment of my brother's imagination after all."

"Hello, Rhy," she said with a crooked smile. She turned toward Kell, but he was already storming out of the ballroom.

The prince sighed. "What have you done now, Alucard?"

"Nothing," said the captain, innocently.

Rhy turned to go after Kell, but Lila stepped ahead of him. "I'll take care of it."

❧

Kell shoved open a pair of patio doors. For a moment he just stood there, letting the icy air press against his skin. And then, when the biting cold wasn't enough to douse his frustration, he plunged out into the winter night.

A hand caught his as he stepped onto the balcony, and he knew without turning back that it was hers. Lila's fingertips burned with heat, and his skin caught the spark. He didn't look back.

"Hello," she said.

"Hello," he said, the word a rasp.

He continued forward onto the balcony, her hand loosely twined with his. The cold wind stilled around them as they reached the edge.

"Of all the ships, Lila."

"Are you going to tell me why you hate him?" she asked.

Kell didn't answer. Instead he looked down at the Isle. After a few moments, he said, "The House of Emery is one of the oldest families in Arnes. They have long ties with the House of Maresh. Reson Emery and King Maxim were close friends. Queen Emira is Reson's cousin. And Alucard is Reson's second son. Three years ago, he left, in the middle of the night. No word. No warning. Reson Emery came to King Maxim for help finding him. And Maxim came to me."

"Did you use your blood magic, the way you did to find Rhy, and me?"

"No," said Kell. "I told the king and queen that I couldn't locate him, but the truth was, I never tried."

Lila's brow furrowed. "Why on earth not?"

"Isn't it obvious?" said Kell. "Because I'm the one who told him to go. And I wanted him to stay gone."

"Why? What did he do to you?"

"Not *me,*" said Kell, jaw clenched.

Lila's eyes brightened in understanding. "Rhy."

"My brother was seventeen when he fell for your *captain*. And then Emery broke his heart. Rhy was devastated. I didn't need a magical tattoo to know my brother's pain on that front." He ran his free hand through his hair. "I told Alucard to disappear, and he did. But he didn't stay gone. No, he turned up a few months later when he was dragged back to the capital for crimes against the crown. Piracy, of all things. The king and queen turned the charge over, as a favor to the house of Emery. Gave Alucard the *Night Spire,* installed him in the name of the crown, and sent him on his way. And I told him that if he *ever* set foot in London again, I would kill him. I thought this time he would actually listen."

"But he came back."

Kell's fingers tightened around hers. "He did." Her pulse beat against his, strong and steady. He didn't want to let go. "Alucard has always been careless when it comes to precious things."

"I didn't choose him," she said, drawing Kell back from the edge. "I just chose to run."

She started to let go, but he wasn't ready. He pulled her toward him, their bodies nested against the cold. "Do you think you'll ever stop running?"

She tensed against him. "I don't know how."

Kell's free hand drifted up her bare arm to the nape of her neck. He tipped his head and rested his forehead against hers.

"You could just . . ." he whispered, "stay."

"Or you could go," she countered, "with me."

The words were a breath of fog against his lips, and Kell found himself leaning in to her warmth, her words.

"Lila," he said, the name aching in his chest.

He wanted to kiss her.

But she kissed him first.

The last time—the only time—it had been nothing but a ghost of lips against his, there and gone, so little to it, a kiss stolen for luck.

This was different.

They crashed into each other as if propelled by gravity, and he didn't know which of them was the object and which the earth, only that they were colliding. This kiss was Lila pressed into a single gesture. Her brazen pride and her stubborn resolve, her recklessness and her daring and her hunger for freedom. It was all those things, and it took Kell's breath away. Knocked the air from his lungs. Her mouth pressed hard against his, and her fingers wove through his hair as his sank down her spine, tangling in the intricate folds of her dress.

She forced him back against the railing, and he gasped, the shock of icy stone mixing with the heat of her body against him. He could feel her heart racing, feel the energy crackling through her, through him. They turned, caught up in another dance, and then he had her up against the frost-laced wall. Her breath hitched, and her nails dug into his skull. She sank her teeth into his bottom lip, drawing blood, and gave a wicked laugh, and still he kissed her. Not out of desperation or hope or for luck, but simply because he wanted to. Saints, he wanted to. He kissed her until the cold night fell away and his whole body sang with heat. He kissed her until the fire burned up the panic and the anger and the weight in his chest, until he could breathe again, and until they were both breathless.

And when they broke free, he could feel her smile on his lips.

"I'm glad you came back," he whispered.

"Me, too," she said. And then she looked him in the eyes, and added, "But I'm not dropping out of the tournament."

The moment cracked. Shattered. Her smile was fixed and sharp, and the warmth was gone.

"Lila—"

"Kell," she mimicked, pulling free.

"There are consequences to this game."

"I can handle them."

"You're not listening," he said, exasperated.

"No," she snapped. *"You're* not." She licked the blood from her lips. "I don't need saving."

"Lila," he started, but she was already out of reach.

"Have a little faith," she said as she opened the door. "I'll be fine."

Kell watched her go, hoping she was right.

II

Ojka crouched on the palace patio, tucked into the shadow where the balcony met the wall, her hood up to hide her crimson hair. Inside this strange river castle, they appeared to be having some kind of celebration. Light danced across the stones, and music seeped through the doors. The cold air bit at Ojka's skin, but she didn't mind. She was used to cold—*real* cold—and the winter in this London was gentle by comparison.

Beyond the frosted glass, men and women ate and drank, laughed and spun around an ornate dance floor. None of them had markings. None of them had scars. All across the hall, magic was being used in petty ways, to light braziers and sculpt ice statues, to enchant instruments and entertain guests.

Ojka hissed, disgusted by the waste of power. A fresh language rune burned against her wrist, but she didn't need to speak this tongue to know how much they took for granted. Squandering life while her people starved in a barren world.

Before Holland, she reminded herself. Things were changing now; the world was mending, flourishing, but would it ever look like *this*? Months ago it would have been impossible to imagine. Now it was simply difficult. Hers was a world being slowly roused by magic. This was a world long graced.

Could a polished rock ever truly resemble a jewel?

She had the sudden, pressing urge to set fire to something.

Ojka, came a gentle chiding voice in her head, soft and teasing as a lover's whisper. She brought her fingers to her eye, the knot in the tether between her and her king. Her king, who could hear her thoughts, feel her desires—could he feel them *all?*—as if they were one.

I would not do it, Your Highness, she thought. *Not unless it pleased you. Then I would do anything.*

She felt the line between them slacken as the king drifted back into his own mind. Ojka turned her attention back to the ball.

And then she saw him.

Tall and thin, dressed in black, circling the floor with a pretty girl done up in green. Beneath a circlet of silver and wood, the girl's hair was fair , but Kell's was red. Not as red as Ojka's, no, but the copper still caught the light. One of his eyes was pale, the other as black as hers, as Holland's.

But he was *nothing* like her king. Her king was beautiful and powerful and perfect. This *Kell* was nothing but a skinny boy.

And yet, she knew him at first sight, not only because Holland knew him, but because he shone to her like a flame in the dark. Magic radiated like heat off the edges of his form, and when his dark eye drifted lazily across the bank of windows, past shadow and snow and Ojka, she *felt* the gaze. It rippled through her, and she braced herself, sure he would see her, feel her, but he didn't even notice. She wondered if the glass was mirrored instead of clear, so that everyone inside saw only themselves. Smiles reflecting back again and again while outside, the darkness waited, held at bay.

Ojka adjusted her balance on the balcony's rail. She'd made it this far by a series of ice steps forged on the palace wall, but the building itself must have been warded against intrusion; the one and only time she'd tried to slip inside through a pair of upstairs doors, she'd been rebuffed, not loudly, or painfully, but *forcefully.* The spellwork was fresh, the magic strong.

The only way in appeared to be the front doors, but Holland had warned her not to make a scene.

She pulled on the tether in her mind, and felt him take hold of the rope.

I have found him. She didn't bother explaining. She simply looked. She was the king's eyes. What she saw, so would he. *Shall I force him out?*

No, came the king's voice in her head. It hummed so beautifully in her bones. *Kell is stronger than he looks. If you try to force him and fail, he will not come. He must come. Be patient.*

Ojka sighed. *Very well.* But her mind was not at ease, and her king could tell. A soothing calm passed through her with his words, his will.

You are not only my eyes, he said. *You are my hands, my mouth, my will. I trust you to behave as I say I would.*

I will, she answered. *And I will not fail.*

III

"You look like hell."

Alucard's words rang through her head, the only thing he'd said that morning when she wished him luck.

"You say the sweetest things," she'd grumbled before escaping into her own tent. But the truth was, Lila *felt* like hell. She hadn't been able to find sleep in Elsor's room, so she'd gone back to the Wandering Road, with its cramped quarters and familiar faces. But every time she closed her eyes, she was back in that damn crate, or on the balcony with Kell—in the end she'd spent most of the night staring up at the candlelight as it played across the ceiling, while Tav and Lenos snored (who knew where Vasry was) and Kell's words played over and over in her head.

She closed her eyes, felt herself sway slightly.

"Master Elsor, are you well?"

She jerked back to attention. Ister was fitting the last of the armor plates on her leg.

"I'm fine," she muttered, trying to focus on Alucard's lessons.

Magic is a conversation.

Be an open door.

Let the waves through.

Right now, she felt like a rocky coastline.

She looked down at her wrist. The skin was already healing where the ropes had cut, but when she turned her hands over, her veins were dark. Not black, like the Dane twins, but not as light as they should be, either. Concern rippled through her, followed swiftly by annoyance.

She was fine.

She would be fine.

She'd come this far.

Delilah Bard was *not* a quitter.

Kell had beat the Veskan, Rul, by only two points, and lost to her by four. He was out of the running, but Lila could lose by a point and still advance. Besides, Alucard had already won his second match, securing his place in the final three alongside a magician named Tos-an-Mir, one of the famous Faroan twins. If Lila won, she'd finally get a chance to fight him. The prospect made her smile.

"What is that?" asked Ister, nodding down at the shard of pale stone in her hand. Lila had been rubbing it absently. Now she held it up to the tent's light. If she squinted, she could almost see the edge of Astrid's mouth, frozen in what could be a laugh, or a scream.

"A reminder," said Lila, tucking the chipped piece of statue into the coat slung over a cushion. It was a touch morbid, perhaps, but it made Lila feel better, knowing that Astrid was gone, and would stay gone. If there *was* a kind of magic that could bring back an evil queen turned to stone, she hoped it required a full set of pieces. This way, she could be certain that one was missing.

"Of what?" asked Ister.

Lila took up the dagger hilts and slid them into her forearm plates. "That I'm stronger than my odds," she said, striding out of the tent.

That I have crossed worlds, and saved cities.

She entered the stadium tunnel.

That I have defeated kings and queens.

She adjusted the helmet and strode out into the arena, awash in the cheers.

That I have survived impossible things.

Rul stood in the center of the floor, a towering shape.

That I am Delilah Bard . . .

She held out her spheres, her vision blurring for an instant before she let them go.

And I am unstoppable.

🜚

Kell stood on the balcony of his room, the gold ring on the rail between his hands, the sounds of the stadium reverberating through the metal.

The eastern arena floated just beside the palace, its ice dragons bobbing in the river around it, their bellies red. With the help of a looking scope, Kell could see down into the stadium, the two fighters like spots of white against the dark stone floor. Lila in her dark devil's mask. Rul with the steel face of a canine, his own wild hair jutting out like a ruff. His pennant was a blue wolf against a white ground, but the crowd was awash of silver blades on black.

Hastra stood behind him in the balcony doors, and Staff by the ones in the bedroom.

"You know him, don't you?" asked Hastra. "Stasion Elsor?"

"I'm not sure," murmured Kell.

Far below, the arena cheered. The match had started.

Rul favored earth and fire, and the elements swirled around him. He'd brought a handle and hilt into the ring; the earth swirled around the handle, hardening into a rock shield, while the fire formed a curving sword. Lila's own daggers came to life as they had the day before, one fire and the other ice. For an instant the two stood there, sizing each other up.

Then they collided.

Lila landed the first blow, getting in under Rul's sword, then spinning behind him and driving the fire dagger into the plate on the back of his leg. He twisted around, but she was already up and out, readying another strike.

Rul was taller by at least a foot, and twice as broad, but he was faster than a man his size had any right to be, and when she tried to find her way beneath his guard again, she failed, losing two plates in the effort.

Lila danced backward, and Kell could imagine her sizing the man up, searching for an in, a weakness, a chink. And somehow she found one. And then another.

She didn't fight like Rul, or Kisimyr, or Jinnar. She didn't fight like anyone Kell had ever seen. It wasn't that she was *better*—though she was certainly fast, and clever—it was just that she fought in the ring the way he imagined she did on the streets back in Grey London. Like everything was on the line. Like the other person was the only thing standing between her and freedom.

Soon she was ahead, six to five.

And then, suddenly, Rul struck.

She was rushing toward him, mid-stride when he turned the rock shield and threw it like a disk. It caught Lila in the chest, hard enough to throw her back into the nearest column. Light burst from the shattered plates on her stomach, shoulders, and spine, and Lila crumpled to the stone floor.

The crowd gasped, and the voice in the gold ring announced the damage.

Four plates.

"*Get up,*" growled Kell as he watched her stagger to her feet, one hand gripping her ribs. She took a step and nearly fell, obviously shaken, but Rul was still on the attack. The massive disk flew back into his hand, and in a single fluid move he spun and launched it again, adding momentum to the force of magic.

Lila must have seen the attack, noticed the stone careening toward her, yet to Kell's horror, she didn't dodge. Instead she dropped both daggers and threw her *hands* up instead of her forearms to block the blow.

It was madness.

It wouldn't work—couldn't work—and yet, somehow the rock shield *slowed*.

Shock went through the crowd as they realized Stasion Elsor wasn't a dual magician after all. He had to be a *triad*.

The shield dragged through the air, as if fighting a current, and came to a stop inches from Lila's outstretched hands. It hovered there, suspended.

But Kell knew it wasn't simply hanging.

Lila was *pushing* against it. Trying to overpower Rul's element the way she had with his. But he'd let her then, he'd *stopped* fighting; Rul, momentarily stunned, now redoubled his efforts. Lila's boots slid back along the stone ground as she pushed on the disk with all her force.

The arena itself seemed to tremble, and the wind picked up as the magicians fought will to will.

Between Lila and Rul, the earthen disk shuddered. Through the looking scope, Kell could see her limbs shaking, her body curved forward with the strain.

Let go! He wanted to shout. But Lila kept pushing.

You stubborn fool, he thought as Rul summoned a burst of strength, lifted his fiery sword, and threw it. The blade went wide, but the flame must have snagged Lila's attention because she faltered, just enough, and the still-suspended rock shield stuttered forward and caught her in the leg. A glancing blow, but hard enough.

The tenth plate shattered.

The match was over.

The crowd erupted, and Rul let out a howl of victory, but Kell's attention was still on Lila, who stood there, arms at her side, head tipped back, looking strangely peaceful.

Until the moment she swayed, and collapsed.

IV

Kell was already moving through his room when the judge's voice spilled through the ring, calling for a medic.

He'd warned her. Over and over, he'd warned her.

Kell had his knife in his hand before he reached the door to the second chamber, Hastra on his heels. Staff tried to block the way, but Kell was faster, stronger, and he was in the alcove before the guards could stop him.

"*As Staro,*" he said, sealing the door shut behind him and drawing the symbol while Staff pounded on the wood.

"*As Tascen.*"

The palace fell away, replaced by the tournament tent.

"*The victory goes to Rul,*" announced the judge as Kell surged out of Kamerov's quarters and into Lila's. He got there as two attendants lowered her onto a sofa, a third working to undo her helmet. They started at the sight of him and went pale.

"Out," said Kell. "All of you."

The first two retreated instantly, but the third—a female priest—ignored him as she freed the hinged pieces of the demon's mask from Lila's head and set them aside. Beneath, her face was ghostly white, dark veins tracing her temples and twin streams of blackish red running from her nose. The priest rested a hand against her face, and a moment later her eyes fluttered open. A dozen oaths bubbled up, but Kell held his tongue. He held it as she drew a stilted breath and dragged herself into a sitting position, held it as she rolled her head and flexed her fingers, and lifted a cloth to her nose.

"You can go, Ister," she said, wiping away the blood.

Kell held his tongue as long as he could, but the moment the priest was gone, he lost it.

"I warned you!" he shouted. Lila winced, touching a hand to her temple.

"I'm fine," she muttered.

Kell made a stifled sound. "You collapsed in the ring!"

"It was a hard match," she said getting to her feet, trying and failing to hide her unsteadiness.

"How could you be so stupid?" he snapped, his voice rising. "You're bleeding black. You play with magic as if it were a game. You don't even understand the rules. Or worse, you decide there are none. You go stomping through the world, doing whatever the hell you please. You're careless. Senseless. Reckless."

"Keep it down, you two," said Rhy, striding in, Vis and Tolners at his back. "Kell, *you* shouldn't be here."

Kell ignored him and addressed the guards. "Lock her up."

"For what?" growled Lila.

"Calm down, Kell," said Rhy.

"For being an impostor."

Lila scoffed. "Oh, you're one to tal—"

Kell slammed her back into the tent pole, crushing her mouth with his hand. "Don't you *dare*." Lila didn't fight back. She went still as stone, mismatched eyes boring into him. There was a wildness to them, and he thought she might actually be afraid, or at least shocked. And then he felt the knife pressed against his side.

And the look in her eyes said that if it weren't for Rhy, she would have stabbed him.

The prince held up his hand. "*Stasion,*" he said, addressing Lila as he took Kell's shoulder. "Please." She lowered the knife, and Rhy wrenched Kell backward with Tolners' help.

"You never listen. You never *think*. Having power is a responsibility, Lila, one you clearly don't deserve."

"Kell," warned Rhy.

"Why are you defending her?" he snapped, rounding on his brother. "Why am I the only one in this fucking world to be held accountable for my actions?"

They just stared at him, the prince and the guards, and Lila, she had the nerve to smile. It was a grim, defiant smile, marred by the dark blood still streaking her face.

Kell threw up his hands and stormed out.

He heard the sound of Rhy's boots on the cobbles coming after him, but Kell needed space, needed air, and before he knew what he was doing, he had the knife free from its sheath, the coins free from his collar.

The last thing he heard before he pressed his bloody fingers to the nearest wall was Rhy's voice calling for him to stop, but then the spell was on Kell's lips, and the world was falling away, taking everything with it.

V

One moment Kell was there, and the next he was gone, nothing but a dab of blood on the wall to mark his passing.

Rhy stood outside the tent, staring at the place where his brother had been, his chest aching not from physical pain but the sudden, horrible realization that Kell had purposefully gone where Rhy couldn't follow.

Tolners and Vis appeared like shadows behind him. A crowd was gathering, oblivious to the quarrel in the tent, oblivious to everything but the presence of a prince in their midst. Rhy knew he should be wrestling his features into form, fixing his smile, but he couldn't. He couldn't tear his eyes from the streak of blood.

Maxim strode into sight, Kell's guards on his heels. The crowd parted around the king, who smiled and nodded and waved even as he took Rhy's arm and guided him back toward the palace, talking about the final round and the three champions and the evening events, filling the silence with useless chatter until the doors of the palace closed behind them.

"What happened?" snapped the king, dragging him into a private chamber. "Where is Kell?"

Rhy slumped into a chair. "I don't know. He was in his rooms, but when he saw the match go south, he went down to the tents. He was just worried, Father."

"About what?" *Not about what,* Rhy thought. *Who.* But he

couldn't exactly tell the king about the girl parading as Stasion Elsor, the same girl who'd dragged the Black Night across the city at Kell's side (and saved the world, too, of course, but that wouldn't matter), so instead he simply said, "We had a fight."

"Where is he now?"

"I don't know." Rhy put his head in his hands, fatigue folding over him.

"Get up," ordered his father. "Go get ready."

Rhy dragged his head up. "For what?"

"Tonight's festivities, of course."

"But Kell—"

"Is *not here*," said the king, his voice as heavy as a stone. "He may have abandoned his duties, but you have not. You *will* not." Maxim was already heading for the door. "When Kell returns, he will be dealt with, but in the meantime, you are still the Prince of Arnes. And as such, you will act like it."

෪

Kell sagged back against the cold stone wall as the bells of Westminster rang out the hour.

His heart pounded frantically with what he'd done.

He'd *left*. Left Red London. Left Rhy. Left Lila. Left a city— and a mess—in his wake.

All of it only a step away. A world apart.

If you don't want to be here, then go.

Run.

He hadn't meant to—he'd just wanted a moment of peace, a moment to *think*—and now he was here, fresh blood dripping to the icy street, his brother's voice still echoing in his head. Guilt pulled at him, but he shoved it away. This was no different from the hundreds of trips he'd made abroad, each and every one placing him out of reach.

This time it had simply been *his* choice.

Kell straightened and set off down the street. He didn't know where he was going, only that the first step had not been enough; he needed to keep moving before the guilt caught up. Or the cold. Grey London's winter had a bitter dampness to it, and he pulled his coat tight, and bent his head, and walked.

Five minutes later, he was standing outside the Five Points.

He could have gone anywhere, but he always ended up there. Muscle memory, that was the only real explanation. His feet carried him along the paths worn into the world, the cosmic slope, a gravitational bend drawing things of mass and magic to the fixed point.

Inside, a familiar face looked up from behind the bar. Not Barron's wide brow and dark beard, but Ned Tuttle's large eyes, his long jaw, his broad, surprised, *delighted* smile.

"Master Kell!"

At least the young Enthusiast didn't launch himself over the counter when Kell came in. He only dropped three glasses and knocked over a bottle of port. The glasses Kell let fall, but the port he stopped an inch above the floor, the gesture lost on all but Ned himself.

He slid onto a stool, and a moment later a glass of dark whisky appeared before him. Not magic, just Ned. When he finished the first glass in a single swig, the bottle appeared at his elbow.

The Enthusiast pretended to busy himself with the handful of other patrons while Kell drank. On the third glass, he slowed down; after all, it wasn't his body alone he was trashing. But how many nights had Kell borne Rhy's drinking; how many mornings had he woken with the stale taste of wine and elixirs coating his tongue?

Kell tipped a little more into his tumbler.

He could feel the eyes of the patrons drifting toward him, and he wondered if they were being drawn by magic or rumor. Could they feel the pull, the tip of gravity, or was it simply word of mouth? What had Ned told them? Anything? Everything?

Right then, Kell didn't care. He just wanted to smother the feelings before they could smother him. Blot out the image of Lila's bloody face before it ruined the memory of her mouth against his.

It was only a matter of time before Ned reappeared, but when he did, it wasn't with questions or mindless chatter. Instead, the lanky young man poured himself a drink from the same bottle, folded his arms on the edge of the counter, and set something down in front of Kell. It glinted in the lamplight.

A Red London lin.

The coin Kell had left behind on his last visit.

"I believe this is yours," he said.

"It is."

"It smells like tulips."

Kell tilted his head; the room tilted with it. "The King of England always said roses."

Ned gaped. "George the fourth said that?"

"No, the third," said Kell absently, adding, "the fourth is an ass."

Ned nearly choked on his drink, letting out a simple, startled laugh. Kell flicked his fingers, and the Red London lin leaped up onto its side and began to spin in lazy circles. Ned's eyes widened. "Will I ever be able to do that?"

"I hope not," said Kell, glancing up. "You shouldn't be able to do anything."

The man's narrow features contorted. "Why's that?"

"A long time ago, this world—your world—had magic of its own."

Ned leaned in, a child waiting for the monster in the story. "What happened?"

Kell shook his head, the whisky muddling his thoughts. "A lot of very bad things." The coin made its slow revolutions. "It's all about balance, Ned." Why couldn't Lila understand? "Chaos needs order. Magic needs moderation. It's like a fire. It doesn't have self-control. It feeds off whatever you give it, and if you give it too much, it burns and burns until there's nothing left.

"Your world had fire, once," said Kell. "Not much—it was too far from the source—but enough to burn. We cut it off before it could, and what was left began to dwindle. Eventually, it went out."

"But how do you know we would have burned?" asked Ned, eyes fever bright.

Kell knocked the coin over with a brush of his fingers. "Because too little of something is just as dangerous as too much." He straightened on his stool. "The point is, magic shouldn't exist here anymore. It shouldn't be *possible*."

"Impossibility is a thing that begs to be disproven," said Ned brightly. "Perhaps it hasn't been possible for years, perhaps it's not even possible right now, but that doesn't mean it *can't* be. It doesn't mean it *won't* be. You say the magic guttered, the flame went out. But what if it simply needed to be stoked?"

Kell poured himself another drink. "Maybe you're right."

But I hope you're wrong, he thought. *For all our sakes.*

❧

Rhy was *not* in the mood.

Not in the mood to be at the ball.

Not in the mood to play host.

Not in the mood to smile and joke and pretend that everything was all right. His father cast warning looks his way, and his mother stole glances, as if she thought he would break. He wanted to yell at both of them, for driving his brother away.

Instead, he stood between the king and queen while the three champions cast off their masks.

First came the Veskan, Rul, his rough hair trailing down his jaw, still preening from his victory over Elsor.

Then Tos-an-Mir, one half of the favored Faroan twins, her gems tracing fiery patterns from brow to chin.

And of course, Alucard Emery. Rogue, rake, royal, and re-newed darling of the Arnesian empire.

Rhy congratulated Lord Sol-in-Ar and Prince Col on the excellent showing, marveled aloud at the balanced field—an Arnesian, a Faroan, and a Veskan in the finals! What were the odds?—and then retreated to a pillar to drink in peace.

Tonight's festivities were being held in the Jewel Hall, a ball-room made entirely of glass. For a place so open, it made Rhy feel entombed.

All around him, people drank. People danced. Music played.

Across the ballroom, Princess Cora flirted with half a dozen Arnesian nobles, all while casting glances in search of Kell.

Rhy closed his eyes and focused on his brother's pulse, the echo of his own; he tried to reach through that beat and convey . . . what? That he was angry? That he was sorry? That he couldn't do any of this without Kell? That he didn't blame him for leaving? That he *did*?

Come home, he thought selfishly. *Please.*

Refined applause rang through the glass chamber, and he dragged his eyes open and saw the three champions returning in fresh attire, their masks tucked under their arms, their faces on display.

The wolfish Rul went straight for the nearest table of food, where his Veskan comrades were already deep in their cups.

Tos-an-Mir maneuvered the crowd, trailed by her sister, Tas-on-Mir, the first magician to fall to Kell. Rhy could only tell them apart by the gems set into their dark skin, Tos-an-Mir's a fiery orange where Tas-on-Mir's were pearlescent blue.

Alucard was the center of his own private universe. Rhy watched as a pretty *ostra* brought her painted lips to Alucard's ear to whisper something, and felt his grip tighten on his glass.

Someone slouched against the pillar beside him. A slim figure dressed in black. Lila looked better than she had that afternoon: still drawn, with shadows like bruises beneath her eyes, and yet spry enough to swipe two fresh glasses from a passing tray. She offered one to Rhy. He took it absently. "You came back."

"Well," she said, tipping her drink toward the ballroom, "you do know how to throw a party."

"To London," clarified Rhy.

"Ah," she said. "That."

"Are you all right?" he asked, thinking of her match that afternoon.

She swallowed, kept her eyes on the crowd. "I don't know."

A silence formed around them, a raft of quiet in the sea of sound.

"I'm sorry," she said at last, the words so soft Rhy almost didn't hear.

He rolled his shoulder toward her. "For what?"

"I don't really know. It seemed like the right thing to say."

Rhy took a long drink and considered this strange girl, her sharp edges, her guarded face. "Kell only has two faces," he said.

Lila raised a brow. "*Only* two? Don't most people have one?"

"On the contrary, Miss Bard—and you are Bard again, judging by your clothes? I assume Stasion has been left somewhere to recuperate? Most people have far more than two. I myself have an entire wardrobe." He didn't smile when he said it. His gaze drifted past his parents, the Arnesian nobles, Alucard Emery. "But Kell has only two. The one he wears for the world at large, and the one he wears for those he loves." He sipped his wine. "For us."

Lila's expression hardened. "Whatever he feels for me, it isn't love."

"Because it isn't soft and sweet and doting?" Rhy rocked back, stretching against the pillar. "Do you know how many times he's nearly beat me senseless out of love? How many times I've done the same? I've seen the way he looks at those he hates . . ." He shook his head. "There are very few things my brother cares about, and even fewer people."

Lila swallowed. "What do you think he's doing?"

Rhy considered his wine. "Judging by the way this is going to my head," he said, lifting the glass, "I'd say he's drowning his feelings, just like me."

"He'll come back."

Rhy closed his eyes. "I wouldn't."

"Yes," said Lila, "you would."

🦋

"Ned," said Kell in the early hours of the morning, "you wanted to give me something, the last time I was here. What was it?"

Ned looked down and shook his head. "Oh, it was nothing."

But Kell had seen the excitement in the man's eyes, and even though he couldn't take whatever it was, he still wanted to know. "Tell me."

Ned chewed his lip, then nodded. He reached beneath the counter and drew out a carved piece of wood. It was roughly the length of a hand, from palm to fingertip, the length etched with a pattern and the end pointed.

"What is it?" asked Kell, curious and confused.

Ned dragged the Red London lin toward him and balanced the point of the carved stick on top. When he let go, the wood didn't fall. It stood, perfectly upright, the carved point balancing on the coin.

"Magic," said Ned with a tired smile. "That's what I thought, anyway. I know now it's not really magic. A clever trick with magnets, that's all." He nudged the wood with his finger and it wavered, then righted. "But when I was young, it made me believe. Even when I found out it was a trick, I still *wanted* to believe. After all, just because this wasn't magic, that didn't mean nothing was." He plucked the stick from its perch and set it on the counter, stifling a yawn.

"I should go," said Kell.

"You can stay." It was very late—or very early—and the Five Points had long since emptied.

"No," said Kell simply. "I can't."

Before Ned could insist—before he could offer to keep the tavern open, before he could give Kell the room at the top of the stairs—the one with the green door and the wall still warped from his first encounter with Lila, when he'd pinned her to the wood, the one marked by Kell's finding spell and stained with Barron's blood—Kell got to his feet and left.

He turned up the collar of his coat, stepped out into the dark, and began to walk again. He walked the bridges and the streets of Lila's London, the parks and the paths. He walked until his muscles hurt and the pleasant buzz of whisky burned off and he was left with only that stubborn ache in his chest and the nagging pressure of guilt, of need, of duty.

And even then, he walked.

He couldn't stop walking. If he stopped, he would think, and if he thought too hard, he would go home.

He walked for hours, and only when his legs felt like they would give way unless he stopped, did he finally sink onto a bench along the Thames and listen to the sounds of Grey London, similar to and yet so different from his own.

The river had no light. It was a stretch of black, turning purple with the first hints of morning.

He turned the options over in his mind like a coin.

Run.

Run home.

Run.

Run home.

Run.

VI

Red London.

Ojka paced the palace shadows, furious with herself.

She'd lost him. She didn't know how he'd gotten away, only that he had. She'd spent the day searching for him in the crowds, waiting for night to fall, had returned to her post on the balcony, but the ballroom was dark, the celebration somewhere else. A steady stream of men and women poured up and down the steps, vanished and emerged, but none of them were Kell.

In the thickest hours of the night she saw a pair of guards, men in splendid red and gold, leaning in the shadow of the palace steps, talking softly. Ojka drew her blade. She couldn't decide if she should cut their throats and steal their armor, or torture them for information. But before she could do either, she heard a name pass between them.

Kell.

As she drew close, the language rune began to burn against her skin, and their words took shape.

". . . saying he's gone . . ." continued one.

"What do you mean, *gone*? As in taken?"

"Run off. Glad, too. Always gave me the creeps. . . ."

Ojka hissed, retreating down the banks. He wasn't gone. He couldn't be *gone*.

She knelt on the cold earth and drew a piece of parchment

from her pocket, spreading it over the ground. Next she dug her fingers into the dirt and ripped up a clod, crushing it in her palm.

This wasn't blood magic. Just a spell she'd used a hundred times in Kosik, hunting down those who owed her coin, or life.

"*Køs øchar,*" she said as the earth tumbled onto the parchment. As it fell, it traced the lines of the city, the river, the streets.

Ojka dusted off her hands.

"*Køs Kell,*" she said. But the map didn't change. The earth didn't stir. Wherever Kell was, he wasn't in London. Ojka clenched her teeth, and stood, dreading her king's reaction even as she drew upon the bond.

He is gone, she thought, and a moment later she was met by Holland—not only his voice, but his displeasure.

Explain.

He is not in this world, she said. *He is gone.*

A pause and then, *Did he go alone?*

Ojka hesitated. *I believe so. The royal family is still here.*

The silence that followed made her ill. She imagined Holland sitting on his throne, surrounded by the bodies that had failed him. She would not be one of those.

At last, the king spoke.

He will come back.

How do you know? asked Ojka.

He will always come home.

❧

Rhy was a wreck. He'd stayed up through the night, through the darkness, through the memories, resisting the urge to take something to bring sleep without knowing where Kell was, and what might happen to his brother if he did. Instead the prince had tossed and turned for half the night before throwing the blankets off and pacing the room until dawn finally broke over the city.

The final match of the *Essen Tasch* was mere hours away. Rhy didn't care about the tournament. He didn't care about Faro and Vesk and politics. He only cared about his brother.

And Kell was still gone.

Still gone.

Still gone.

The darkness swarmed in Rhy's head.

The palace was coming to life around him. Soon he'd have to don the crown, and the smile, and play prince. He ran his hands through his hair, wincing in pain as a dark curl snagged on one of his rings. Rhy cursed. And then stopped pacing.

His eyes danced across the room—pillows and blankets and sofas, so many *soft* things—before landing on the royal pin. He'd cast it off with his tunic after the ball, and now it glinted in the first of the morning's light.

He tested the tip against his thumb, biting his lip as it drew blood. Rhy watched the bead well and spill down his palm, his heart racing. Then he brought the pin to the crook of his arm.

Maybe it was the lingering alcohol. Or maybe it was the gnawing panic of knowing that he couldn't reach Kell, or the guilt of understanding just how much his brother had given up, or the selfish need for him to give up more, to come back, to come home, that made Rhy press the point of the pin into the smooth flesh on the inside of his forearm, and begin to write.

᪥

Kell hissed at the sudden burning in his skin.

He was used to dull aches, shallow pains, echoes of Rhy's various mishaps, but this was sharp and bright, deliberate in a way that a glancing blow to the ribs or a banged knee never was. The pain dragged itself along the inside of his left arm, and he forced up the sleeve, expecting to see blood staining his tunic, angry red marks across his skin, but there was nothing. The pain stopped, and then started again, drawing itself down his arm in waves. No, *lines*.

He stared down at the skin, trying to make sense of the searing pain.

And then, suddenly, he understood.

He couldn't see the lines, but when he closed his eyes, he could feel them trace their way over his skin the way Rhy used to trace letters with his fingertip, writing out secret messages on Kell's arm. It was a game they'd played when they were young, stuck side by side at some event or a boring dinner.

This wasn't a game, not now. And yet Kell could feel the letters blazing down his arm, marked with something far sharper than a fingernail.

S

S-O

S-O-R

S-O-R-R

S-O-R-R-Y.

Kell was on his feet by the second *R,* cursing at himself for leaving as he drew the coins from around his throat and abandoned the ashen dawn of one London for the vibrant morning of another.

As he made his way to the palace, he thought of everything he wanted to say to the king, but when he climbed the grand stairs and stepped into the foyer, the royal family was already there. So were the Veskan prince and princess, the Faroan lord.

Rhy's gaze met Kell's, and his expression blazed with relief, but Kell kept his guard up as he stepped forward. He could feel the storm coming, the energy in the air thick with everything unsaid. He was braced for the fight, the harsh words, the accusations, the orders, but when the king spoke, his voice was warm. "Ah, there he is. We were about to leave without you."

Kell couldn't hide his surprise. He'd assumed he would be bound to the palace, perhaps indefinitely. Not welcomed back without the slightest reprimand. He hesitated, meeting the king's gaze. It was steady, but he could see the warning in it.

"Sorry I'm late," he said, straining to keep his voice airy. "I was on an errand, and I lost track of time."

"You're here now," said the king, bringing a hand to Kell's shoulder. "That is what matters." The hand squeezed, hard, and for an instant Kell thought he wouldn't let go. But then the procession set out, and Maxim's hand fell away, and Rhy came to Kell's side, whether out of solidarity or desperation, he didn't know.

The central arena was filled to capacity, onlookers spilling out into the streets despite the early hour. In a clever touch, the dragons of the eastern arena and the lions of the western one had been moved, and were now converging on the central stadium, icy beasts in the river, lions posted on the stone supports, and the central's birds in flight overhead. The stadium floor was a tangle of obstacles, columns and boulders and rock shelves, and the stands above swarmed with life and color; Alucard's pennant with its silver feather waved from every side, dotted here and there with Rul's blue wolf, and Tos-an-Mir's black spiral.

When the three magicians finally emerged from their respective tunnels and took their places in the center of the floor, the roar was deafening; Kell and Rhy both cringed at the noise.

In the broad light of morning, the prince looked terrible (Kell could only assume he looked the same). Dark circles stood out beneath Rhy's pale eyes, and he held his left arm gingerly, shielding the letters freshly scarred into his skin. To every side, the stadium was alive with energy and noise, but the royal box was perilously quiet, the air heavy with things unsaid.

The king kept his eyes on the arena floor. The queen finally shot a glance at Kell, but it was laced with scorn. Prince Col seemed to sense the tension, and watched it all with hawkish blue eyes, while Cora seemed oblivious to the dangerous mood, still sulking from Kell's subtle rebuff.

Only Lord Sol-in-Ar appeared immune to the atmosphere of dissent. If anything his mood had improved.

Kell scanned the masses below. He didn't realize he was searching for Lila, not until he found her in the crowd. It should have been impossible in such a massive space, but he could feel the shift of gravity, the pull of her presence, and his eyes found hers across the stadium. From here he couldn't see her features, couldn't tell if her lips were moving, but he imagined them forming the word *hello.*

And then Rhy stepped forward, managing to muster a shadow of his usual charm as he brought the gold amplifier to his lips.

"Welcome!" he called out. "*Glad'ach! Sasors!* What a tournament it has been. It is only fitting that our three great empires find themselves here, represented equally by three great champions. From Faro, a twin by birth, without equal in the ring, the fiery Tos-an-Mir." Whistles filled the air as the Faroan bowed, her gold mask winking in the light. "From Vesk, a beast of a fighter, a wolf of a man, Rul!" In the arena, Rul himself let out a howl, and the Veskans in the crowd took up the call. "And of course, from our own Arnes, the captain of the sea, the prince of power, Alucard!"

The applause was thunderous, and even Kell brought his hands together, albeit slowly, and without much noise.

"The rules of this final round are simple," continued Rhy, "because there are few. This is no longer a game of points. A magician's armor is composed of twenty-eight plates, some broad targets, others small and hard to hit. Today, the last one with plates unbroken wins the crown. So cheer your three magicians, because only one will leave this ring the champion!"

The trumpets blared, the orbs fell, and Rhy retreated into the platform's shadow as the match began

Below, the magicians became a blur of elements: Rul's earth and fire; Tos-an-Mir's fire and air; Alucard's earth, air, and water. *Of course he's a triad,* thought Kell grimly.

It took less than a minute for Alucard to land the first blow on Rul's shoulder. It took more than five for Rul to land the second on Alucard's shin. Tos-an-Mir seemed content to let the two men strike each other from the books, until Alucard landed an icy blow to the back of her knees, and then she joined the fray.

The air in the royal booth was suffocating. Rhy was silent, slumped tiredly in the shadow of the balcony's awning, while Kell stood vigilantly beside the king, whose gaze never wavered from the match.

Below, Tos-an-Mir moved like a gold-masked shadow, dancing on the air, while Rul loped and lunged in his predatory lupine way. Alucard still moved with a noble's poise, even as his elements arced and crashed around him in a storm. The sounds of the fight were lost beneath the swell of cheers, but every point was marked by an explosion of light, a burst of brightness that only drove the crowd to a higher pitch.

And then, mercifully, the tension in the royal booth began to ease. The mood lightened, like the air after a storm, and Kell felt dizzy with relief. Attendants brought tea. Prince Col made a joke, and Maxim laughed. The queen complimented Lord Sol-in-Ar's magician.

By the end of the hour, Rul was out of plates, sitting on the stone floor looking dazed while Alucard and Tos-an-Mir danced around each other, crashing together like swords before breaking apart. And then, slowly but surely, Alucard Emery began to lose. Kell felt his spirits lift, though Rhy knocked his shoulder when he went so far as to cheer for one of Tos-an-Mir's hits. He rallied, closing the gap, and they fell into a stalemate.

At last, she got behind Alucard and under his guard. She moved to shatter the last of the his plates with a knifelike gust, but at the last instant, he twisted out of its path and a lash of water split her final piece of armor.

And just like that, it was over.

Alucard Emery had officially won.

Kell let out a groan as the stadium erupted into noise, raining down cheers and roses and silver pennants, and filling the air with a name.

"Alucard! Alucard! Alucard!"

And even though Rhy had the good taste not to whoop and shout like the rest of the crowd, Kell could see him beaming proudly as he stepped forward to formally announce the victor of the *Essen Tasch*.

Sanct, thought Kell. Emery was about to become even more insufferable.

Lord Sol-in-Ar addressed Tos-an-Mir and the crowd in Faroan, Princess Cora praised Rul and the gathered Veskans, and at last Prince Rhy dismissed the stands with promise of parties and closing ceremonies, the rest of the day a cause for celebration.

The king smiled and even clapped Kell on the back as the Maresh family made their way back to the palace, a train of cheerful subjects in their wake.

And as they climbed the palace stairs, and stepped inside the flower-strewn hall, it seemed as if everything would be all right.

And then Kell saw the queen hold Rhy back on the landing with a word, a question, and by the time he turned back to see why they'd stopped, the doors were swinging shut, blocking out the morning light and the sounds of the city. In the dim foyer, Kell caught the glint of metal as the king shed the illusion of kindness and said only two words, not even directed at Kell, but at the six guards that were circling loosely.

Two words that made Kell wish he'd never come back.

"Arrest him."

VII

Lila lifted her glass with the rest of the *Night Spire* as they toasted their captain.

The crew was gathered around on table and chair in the Wandering Road, and it was like they were back on the ship after a good night's take, laughing and drinking and telling stories before she and the captain retreated below.

Alucard Emery was bruised, bloody, and undoubtedly exhausted, but that didn't stop him from celebrating. He was standing atop a table in the center of the room, buying drinks and giving speeches about birds and dragons, Lila didn't really know, she'd stopped listening. Her head was still pounding and her bones ached with every motion. Tieren had given her something to soothe the pain and restore her strength, insisting as well on a diet of solid food and real sleep. Both of which seemed about as likely as getting out of London without a price on her head. She'd taken the tonic, made vague promises about the rest.

"Balance," he'd instructed, pressing the vial into her hand, "is not solely about magic. Some of it is simply common sense. The body is a vessel. If it's not handled carefully, it will crack. Everyone has limits. Even you, Miss Bard."

He'd turned to go, but she'd called him back.

"Tieren." She had to know, before she gave up another life. "You told me once that you saw something in me. Power."

"I did."

"What is it?" she'd asked. "What am I?"

Tieren had given her one of his long, level looks. "You are asking whether or not I believe you to be an *Antari*."

Lila had nodded.

"That I cannot answer," said Tieren simply. "I do not know."

"I thought you were supposed to be wise," she'd grumbled.

"Whoever told you that?" But then his face turned sober. "You are *something*, Delilah Bard. As to what, I cannot say. But one way or another, I imagine we'll find out."

Somewhere a glass shattered, and Lila's attention snapped back to the tavern, and Alucard up on the table.

"Hey, Captain," called out Vasry. "I have a question! What are you planning to do with all those winnings?"

"Buy a better crew," said Alucard, the sapphire winking again at his brow.

Tav swung an arm around Lila's shoulders. "Where you been, Bard? Hardly seen you!"

"I get enough of you all aboard the *Spire*," she grumbled.

"You talk tough," said Vasry, eyes glassy from drink, "but you're soft at heart."

"Soft as a knife."

"You know, a knife's only a bad thing if you're on the wrong side."

"Good thing you're one of us."

Her chest tightened. They didn't know—about her ruse, about the real Stasion Elsor somewhere on the sea, about the fact that Alucard had cut her from the crew.

Her eyes found Lenos across the table, and there was something in that look of his that made her think *he* knew. Knew she was leaving, at least, even if he didn't know the why of it.

Lila got to her feet. "I need some air," she muttered, but when she made it out the door, she didn't stop.

She was halfway to the palace before she realized it, and then she kept going until she climbed the steps and found Master

Tieren on the landing and saw in his eyes that something was wrong.

"What is it?" she asked.

The *Aven Essen* swallowed. "It's Kell."

ৡ

The royal prison was reserved for special cases.

At the moment, Kell appeared to be the only one. His cell was bare except for a cot and a pair of iron rings set into the wall. The rings were clearly meant to hold chains, but at present there were none, only the cuffs clamped around his wrists, the bindings cold and cut with magic. Every piece of metal in the cell was incised with marks, enchanted to dull and dampen power. He should know. He'd helped to spell them.

Kell sat on the cot, ankles crossed, his head tipped back against the cold stone wall. The prison was housed in the base of the palace, one pillar over from the Basin where he trained, but unlike the Basin the walls were reinforced, and none of the river's red light seeped through. Only the winter chill.

Kell shivered slightly; they'd taken his coat, along with the traveling tokens around his neck, hung them on the wall beyond the cell. He hadn't fought the men off. He'd been too stunned to move as the guards closed in, slamming the iron cuffs around his wrists. By the time he believed what was happening, it was too late.

In the hours since, Kell's anger had cooled and hardened.

Two guards stood outside the cell, watching him with a mixture of fear and wonder, as if he might perform a trick. He closed his eyes, and tried to sleep.

Footsteps sounded on the stairs. Who would it be?

Tieren had already come. Kell had only one question for the old man.

"Did you know about Lila?"

The look in Tieren's eyes told him all he needed to know.

The footsteps drew closer, and Kell looked up, expecting the king, or Rhy. But instead Kell beheld the queen.

Emira stood on the opposite side of the bars, resplendent in her royal red and gold, her face a careful mask. If she was glad to see him caged—or saddened at all by the sight—it didn't show. He tried to meet her eyes, but they escaped to the wall behind his head.

"Do you have everything you need?" she asked, as if he were a guest in a plush palace wing, and not a cell. A laugh tried to claw its way up Kell's throat. He swallowed it and said nothing.

Emira brought a hand to the bars, as if testing their strength. "It shouldn't have come to this."

She turned to go, but Kell sat forward. "Do you hate me, my queen?"

"Kell," she said softly, "how could I?" Something in him softened. Her dark eyes finally found his. And then she said, "You gave me back my son."

The words cut. There had been a time when she insisted that she had two sons, not one. If he had not lost all her love, he had lost that.

"Did you ever know her?" asked Kell.

"Who?" asked the queen.

"My real mother."

Emira's features tightened. Her lips pursed.

A door crashed open overhead.

"Where is he?" Rhy came storming down the stairs.

Kell could hear him coming a mile away, could feel the prince's anger twining through his own, molten hot where Kell's ran cold. Rhy reached the prison, took one look at Kell behind the cell bars, and blanched.

"Let him out *now*," demanded the prince.

The guards bowed their heads, but held their places, gauntleted hands at their sides.

"Rhy," started Emira, reaching for her son's arm.

"Get off me, Mother," he snapped, turning his back on her. "If you won't let him out," he told the guards, "then I order you to let me in."

Still they did not move.

"What are the charges?" he snarled.

"Treason," said Emira, at the same time the guard answered, "Disobeying the king."

"I disobey the king all the time," said Rhy. "You haven't arrested *me*." He offered up his hands. Kell watched them bicker, focusing on the cold, letting it spread like frost, overtaking everything. He was so tired of caring.

"This will not stand." Rhy gripped the bar, exposing his gold sleeve. Blood had soaked through, dotting the fabric where he'd carved the word.

Emira paled. "Rhy, you're hurt!" Her eyes immediately went to Kell, so full of accusation. "What—"

More boots sounded on the stairs and a moment later the king was there, his frame filling the doorway. Maxim took one look at his wife and son, and said, "Get out."

"How could you do this?" demanded Rhy.

"He broke the law," said the queen.

"He is my brother."

"He is not—"

"*Go*," bellowed the king. The queen fell silent, and Rhy's hands slumped back to his side as he looked to Kell, who nodded grimly. "Go."

Rhy shook his head and went, Emira a silent specter in his wake, and Kell was left to face the king alone.

❧

The prince stormed past Lila in a blur.

A few seconds later she heard a crash, and she turned to see Rhy gripping the nearest sideboard, a shattered vase at his feet. Water wicked into the rug and spread across the stone floor, flowers strewn amid the broken glass. Rhy's crown was gone, his curls wild. His shoulders were shaking with anger, and his knuckles were white on the shelf.

Lila knew she should probably go, slip away before Rhy noticed her, but her feet were already carrying her toward the prince. She stepped over the mess of petals, the shards of glass.

"What did that vase ever do to you?" she asked, tipping her shoulder against the wall.

Rhy looked up, his amber eyes rimmed with red.

"An innocent bystander, I'm afraid," he said. The words came out hollow, humorless.

He ducked his head and let out a shuddering sigh. Lila hesitated. She knew she should probably bow, kiss his hand, or swoon—at the very least explain what she was doing there, in the private palace halls, as close to the prison as anyone would let her—but instead she flicked her fingers, producing a small blade. "Who do I need to kill?"

Rhy let out a stifled sound, half sob, half laugh, and sank onto his haunches, still gripping the wooden edge of the table. Lila crouched beside him, then shifted gingerly and put her back to the sideboard. She stretched out her legs, scuffed black boots sinking into the plush carpet.

A moment later, Rhy slumped onto the carpet beside her. Dried blood stained his sleeve, but he folded his forearm against his stomach. He obviously didn't want to talk about it, so she didn't ask. There were more pressing questions.

"Did your father really arrest Kell?"

Rhy swallowed. Nodded.

"Christ," she muttered. "What now?"

"The king will let him go, when his temper cools."

"And then?"

Rhy shook his head. "I honestly don't know."

Lila let her head fall back against the sideboard, then winced.

"It's my fault, you know," said the prince, rubbing his bloodied arm. "I asked him to come back."

Lila snorted. "Well, I told him to leave. I guess we're both at fault." She took a deep breath and shoved herself up to her feet. "Come on?"

"Where are we going?"

"We got him in there," she said. "We're going to get him out."

🜸

"This isn't what I wanted," said the king.

He took up the keys and unlocked Kell's cell, then stepped inside and unfastened the iron cuffs. Kell rubbed his wrists but made no other move as the king retreated through the open cell door, pulled up a chair, and sat down.

Maxim looked tired. Wisps of silver had appeared at his temples, and they shone in the lantern light. Kell crossed his arms and waited for the monarch to meet his eye.

"Thank you," said the king.

"For what?"

"For not leaving."

"I did."

"I meant here."

"I'm in a cell," said Kell drily.

"We both know it wouldn't stop you."

Kell closed his eyes, and heard the king slump back in his chair.

"I will admit I lost my temper," said Maxim.

"You had me *arrested*," growled Kell, his voice so low the king might have missed it, had there been any other noises in the cell. Instead the words rang out, echoed.

"You disobeyed me."

"I did." Kell forced his eyes open. "I have been loyal to this crown, to this family, my entire life. I have given everything I have, everything I am, and you treat me like . . ." His voice faltered. "I can't keep doing this. At least when you treated me like a son, I could pretend. But now . . ." He shook his head. "The queen treats me as a traitor, and you treat me as a prisoner."

The king's look darkened. "You made this prison, Kell. When you tied your life to Rhy's."

"Would you have had him die?" snapped Kell. "I saved his life. And before you go blaming me for putting it in danger, we both know he managed that much himself. When will you stop punishing me alone for a family's worth of fault?"

"You both put this *whole kingdom* in danger with your folly. But at least Rhy is trying to atone. To prove that he deserves my trust. All you've done—"

"*I brought your son back from the dead!*" shouted Kell, lunging to his feet. "I did it knowing it would bind our lives, knowing what it would mean for me, what I would become, knowing that the resurrection of his life would mean the end of mine, and I did it anyway, because he is my brother and your son and the future King of Arnes." Kell gasped for breath, tears streaming down his face. "What more could I possibly do?"

They were both on their feet now. Maxim caught his elbow and forced him close. Kell tried to pull free, but Maxim was built like a tree, and his massive hand gripped the back of Kell's neck.

"I can't *keep atoning*," Kell whispered into the king's shoulder. "I gave him my life, but you cannot ask me to stop living."

"Kell," he said, voice softening. "I am sorry. But I cannot let you go." The air lodged in Kell's chest. The king's grip loosened, and he tore free. "This is bigger than you and Rhy. Faro and Vesk—"

"I do not care about their superstitions!"

"You should. People *act* on them, Kell. Our enemies scour the world for another *Antari*. Our allies would have you for themselves. The Veskans are convinced you are the key to our kingdom's power. Sol-in-Ar thinks you are a weapon, an edge to be turned against foes."

"Little do these people know I'm just a *pawn*," spat Kell, retreating from the king's grip.

"This is the card you've been dealt," said Maxim. "It is only a matter of time before someone tries to take you for themselves, and if they cannot have your strength, I believe they will try to snuff it out. The Veskans are right, Kell. If you die, so does Arnes."

"I am not the key to this kingdom!"

"But you are the key to my son. My heir."

Kell felt ill.

"Please," begged Maxim. "Hear reason." But Kell was sick of reason, sick of excuses. "We all must sacrifice."

"No," snarled Kell. "I am done making sacrifices. When this is over, and the lords and ladies and royals are all gone, I am *leaving*."

"I cannot let you go."

"You said it yourself, Your Majesty. You do not have the power to stop me." And with that, Kell turned his back on the king, took his coat from the wall, and walked out.

❧

When Kell was a child, he used to stand in the royal courtyard, with its palace orchard, and close his eyes and listen—to the music, to the wind, to the river—and imagine he was somewhere else.

Somewhere without buildings, without palaces, without people.

He stood there now, among the trees—trees caught in the throes not only of winter, but of spring, summer, fall—and squeezed his eyes shut, and listened, waiting for the old sense of calm to find him. He waited. And waited. And—

"Master Kell."

He turned to see Hastra waiting a few paces back. Something was off, and at first Kell couldn't place it; then he realized that Hastra wasn't wearing the uniform of a royal guard. Kell knew it was because of him. One more failure to add to the stack. "I'm sorry, Hastra. I know how much you wanted this."

"I wanted an adventure, sir. And I've had one. It's not so bad. Rhy spoke to the king, and he's agreed to let me train with Master Tieren. Better the sanctuary than a cell." And then his eyes widened. "Oh, sorry."

Kell only shook his head. "And Staff?"

Hastra grimaced. "Afraid you're stuck with him. Staff's the one who fetched the king when you first left."

"Thank you, Hastra," he said. "If you're half as good a priest as you were a royal guard, the *Aven Essen* better watch his job."

Hastra broke into a grin, and slipped away. Kell listened to the sounds of his steps retreating across the courtyard, the distant sound of the courtyard doors closing, and turned his attention back to the trees. The wind picked up, and the rustling of the leaves was almost loud enough to drown out the sounds of the palace, to help him forget the world that waited back inside the doors.

I am leaving, he thought. *You do not have the power to stop me.*

"Master Kell."

"What now?" he asked, turning back. His brow furrowed. "Who are you?"

A woman stood there, between two of the trees, hands clasped behind her back and head bowed as if she'd been waiting for some time, though Kell hadn't even heard her approach. Her red hair floated like a flame above her crisp white cape, and he wondered why she felt so strange and so familiar at the same time. As if they'd already met, though he was sure they hadn't.

And then the woman straightened and looked up, revealing her face. Fair skin, and red lips, and a scar beneath two different-colored eyes, one yellow and the other impossibly black.

Both eyes narrowed, even as a smile passed her lips.

"I've been looking everywhere for you."

VIII

The air caught in Kell's chest. An *Antari*'s mark was confined to the edges of one's eye, but the black of the woman's iris spilled over like tears down her cheek, inky lines running into her red hair. It was unnatural.

"Who are you?"

"My name," she said, "is Ojka."

"*What* are you?" he asked.

She cocked her head. "I am a messenger." She was speaking Royal, but her accent was thick, and he could see the language rune jutting from her cuff. So she was from White London.

"You're an *Antari*?" But that wasn't possible. Kell was the last of those. His head spun. "You can't be."

"I am only a messenger."

Kell shook his head. Something was wrong. She didn't *feel* like an *Antari*. The magic felt stranger, darker. She took a step forward, and he found himself stepping back. The trees thickened overhead, from spring to summer.

"Who sent you?"

"My king."

So someone had clawed his way to the White London throne. It was only a matter of time.

She stole another slow step forward, and Kell kept his distance, slipping from summer to fall.

"I'm glad I found you," she said. "I've been looking."

Kell's gaze flicked past her, to the palace doors. "Why?"

She caught the look, and smiled. "To deliver a message."

"If you have a message for the crown," he said, "deliver it yourself."

"My message is not for the crown," she pressed. "It is for *you*."

A shiver went through him. "What could you have to say to me?"

"My king needs your help. My city needs your help."

"Why me?" he asked.

Her expression shifted, saddened. "Because it's all your fault."

Kell pulled back, as if struck. "What?"

She continued toward him, and he continued back, and soon they stood in winter, a nest of bare branches scratching in the wind. "It *is* your fault. You struck down the Danes. You killed our last true *Antari*. But *you* can help us. Our city needs you. Please come. Meet with my king. Help him rebuild."

"I cannot simply leave," he said, the words automatic.

"Can't you?" asked the messenger, as if she'd heard his thoughts.

I am leaving.

The woman—Ojka—gestured to a nearby tree, and Kell noticed the spiral, already drawn in blood. A door.

His eyes went to the palace.

Stay.

You made this prison.

I cannot let you go.

Run.

You are an Antari.

No one can stop you.

"Well?" asked Ojka, holding out her hand, the veins black against her skin. "Will you come?"

"What do you mean he's been released?" snapped Rhy.

He and Lila were standing in the royal prison, staring past a guard at the now empty cell. He'd been ready to storm the men and free Kell with Lila's help, but there was no Kell to free. *"When?"*

"King's orders," said the guard. "Not ten minutes ago. Can't have gotten far."

Rhy laughed, a sick, hysterical sound clawing up his throat, and then he was gone again, racing back up the stairs to Kell's rooms with Lila in tow.

He reached Kell's room and flung open the doors, but the chamber was empty.

He fought to quell the rising panic as he backed out into the hall.

"What are you two doing?" asked Alucard, coming up the stairs.

"What are *you* doing here?" asked Rhy.

"Looking for you," said Alucard at the same time Lila asked, "Have you seen Kell?"

Alucard raised a brow. "We make a point of avoiding each other."

Rhy let out an exasperated sound and surged past the captain, only to collide with a young man on the stairs. He almost didn't recognize the guard without his armor. "Hastra," he said, breathlessly. "Have *you* seen Kell?"

Hastra nodded. "Yes, sir. I just left him in the courtyard."

The prince wilted with relief. He was about to start off down the stairs again when Hastra added, "There's someone with him now. I think. A woman."

Lila prickled visibly. "What kind of woman?"

"You think?" asked Alucard.

Hastra looked a little dazed. "I . . . I can't remember her face." A crease formed between his brows. "It's strange, I've always been so good with faces. . . . There was something about her face though . . . something off . . ."

"Hastra," said Alucard, his voice tense. "Open your hands."

Rhy hadn't even noticed that the young guard's hands were clenched at his sides.

Hastra looked down, as if he hadn't noticed, either, then held them out and uncurled his fingers. One hand was empty. The other clutched a small disk, spellwork scrawled across its surface.

"Huh," said the guard. "That's odd."

But Rhy was already tearing down the hall, Lila a stride behind him, leaving Alucard in their wake.

🦢

Kell reached out and took Ojka's hand.

"Thank you," she said, voice flooding with happiness and relief as her fingers tightened around his. She pressed her free hand to the blood-marked tree.

"*As Tascen,*" she said, and a moment later, the palace courtyard was gone, replaced by the streets of Red London. Kell looked around. It took him a moment to register where they were . . . but it wasn't where they *were* that mattered, but where they *would* be.

In this London, it was only a narrow road, flanked by a tavern and a garden wall.

But in White London, it was the castle gate.

Ojka pulled a trinket from beneath her white cloak, then pressed her still-bloody hand to the winter ivy clinging to the wall stones. She paused and looked to Kell, waiting for his permission, and Kell found himself glancing back through the streets, the royal palace still visible in the distance. Something rippled through him—guilt, panic, hesitation—but before he could pull back, Ojka said the words, and the world folded in around them. Red London disappeared, and Kell felt himself stepping forward, out of the street, and into the stone forest that stood before the castle.

Only it wasn't a stone forest, not anymore.

It was just an ordinary one, filled with trees, bare winter branches giving way to a crisp blue sky. Kell started—since when did White London have such a color? This wasn't the world he remembered, wasn't the world she'd spoken of, one damaged and dying.

This world wasn't broken at all.

Ojka stood near the gate, steadying herself against the wall. When she looked up, a feline smile curled across her face.

Kell had only a moment to process the changes—the grass beneath his feet, the sunlight, the sound of birds—and to realize he'd made a terrible mistake, before he heard footsteps, and spun to find himself face to face with the *king*.

He stood across from Kell, shoulders back and head high, revealing two eyes: one emerald, and the other black.

"Holland?"

The word came out as a question, because the man in front of him bore almost no resemblance to the Holland Kell had known, the one he had fought—had defeated, had cast into the abyss—four months ago. The last time Kell had seen Holland, he had been a few dragging pulses from death.

That Holland couldn't be standing here.

That Holland could never have survived.

But it *was* Holland before him, and he hadn't just survived.

He'd been *transformed*.

There was healthy color in his cheeks, the glow that only came in the prime of life, and his hair—which, despite his age, had always been a charcoal grey—was now straight and black and glossy, carving sharp lines where it fell against his temples and brow. And when Kell met Holland's gaze, the man— magician—king—*Antari*—actually *smiled,* a gesture that did more to transform his face than the new clothes and the aura of health.

"Hello, Kell," said Holland, and a small part of him was relieved to find that the *Antari*'s voice, at least, was still familiar. It wasn't loud, had never been loud, but it was commanding, edged by that subtle gravel that made it sound like he'd been shouting. Or screaming.

"You shouldn't be here," said Kell.

Holland raised a single, black brow. "Neither should you."

Kell felt the shadow at his back, the shift of weight just before a lunge. He was already reaching for his knife, but he was too late, and his fingers only found the hilt before something cold and heavy clamped around his throat, and the world exploded in pain.

🜏

Rhy burst through the courtyard doors, calling his brother's name. There was no sign of him before the line of trees, no answer but the echo of Rhy's own voice. Lila and Alucard were somewhere behind him, the pounding of boots lost beneath his raging pulse.

"Kell?" he called out again, surging into the orchard. He dug his nails into the wound at his arm, the pain a tether he tried to pull on as he passed the line of spring blossoms.

And then, halfway between the lines of summer green and autumn gold, Rhy collapsed with a scream.

One moment he was on his feet, and the next he was on his hands and knees, crying out in pain as something sharp and jagged tore through him.

"Rhy?" came a voice nearby as the prince folded in on himself, a sob tearing its way free.

Rhy.

Rhy.

Rhy.

His name echoed through the courtyard, but he was drowning in his own blood; he was sure he would see it painting the stones. His vision blurred, sliding out of focus as he fell, the way he had so many times when the darkness came, bringing forth the memories and the dreams.

This was a bad dream.

His mouth was filling with blood.

It had to be a bad dream.

He tried to get to his feet.

It—

He collapsed again with a scream as the pain ripped through his chest and buried itself between his ribs.

"Rhy?" shouted the voice.

He tried to answer, but his jaw locked. He couldn't breathe. Tears were streaming down his face and the pain was too real, too familiar, a blade driven through flesh and muscle, scraping against bone. His heart raced, and then stuttered, skipped a beat, and his vision went black and he was back on the cot in the sanctuary again, falling through darkness, crashing down into—

෯

Nothing.

Lila had run straight for the courtyard wall, sprinting through the strange orchard and out the other side. But there was no sign of them, no blood on the stones, no mark. She backed away, trying to think of where else to look. Then she heard the scream.

Rhy.

She found the prince on the ground, clawing at his chest. He was sobbing, pressing his arm to his ribs as if he'd been stabbed, but there was no blood. Not here. It hit her like a blow.

Whatever was happening to Rhy wasn't happening to Rhy at all.

It was happening to *Kell.*

Alucard appeared, and went ashen at the sight of the prince. He called to the guards before folding to his knees as Rhy let out another sob. "What's happening to him?" asked Alucard.

Rhy's lips were stained with blood, and Lila didn't know if he'd bitten them through, or if the damage was worse.

"Kell . . ." gasped the prince, shuddering in pain. "Something's . . . wrong . . . can't . . ."

"What does Kell have to do with this?" asked the captain.

Two royal guards appeared, the queen behind them, looking pale with fear.

"Where is Kell?" she cried as soon as she saw the prince.

"Get back!" called the guards when a handful of nobles tried to come near.

"Call for the king!"

"Hold on," pleaded Alucard, talking to Rhy.

Lila backed away as the prince curled in on himself.

She started searching the trees for a sign of Kell, of the woman, of the way they had gone.

Rhy rolled onto his side, tried to rise, failed, and began coughing blood onto the orchard ground.

"Someone find Kell!" demanded the queen, her voice on the edge of hysteria.

Where had he gone?

"What can I do, Rhy?" whispered Alucard. "What can I do?"

❧

Kell surfaced with the pain.

He was breaking into pieces, some vital part being torn away. Pain radiated from the metal collar at his throat, cutting off air, blood, thought, power. He tried desperately to summon magic, but nothing came. He gasped for air—it felt as if he were drowning, the taste of blood pooling in his mouth even though it was empty.

The forest was gone, the room around him barren. Kell

shivered—his coat and shirt were gone—the bare skin of his
back and shoulders pressed against something cold and metal.
He couldn't move; he was standing upright, but not by his own
strength. His body was being held in a kind of frame, his arms
forced wide to either side, his hands bound to the vertical bars
of the structure. He could feel a horizontal bar against his shoulders, a vertical one against his head and spine.

"A relic," said an even voice, and Kell dragged his vision into
focus and saw Holland standing before him. "From my predecessors."

The *Antari*'s gaze was steady, his whole form still, as if sculpted
from stone instead of flesh, but his black eye swirled, silvery
shadows twisting through it like serpents in oil.

"What have you done?" choked Kell.

Holland tipped his head. "What *should* I have done?"

Kell set his teeth, forced himself to think beyond the collar's
icy pain. "You should . . . have stayed in Black London. You
should . . . have died."

"And let my people die, too? Let my city plunge into yet
another war, let my world sink farther and farther toward
death, knowing I could save it?" Holland shook his head.
"No. My world has sacrificed enough for yours."

Kell opened his mouth to speak, but the pain knifed through
him, sharpening over his heart. He looked down and saw the
seal fracturing. No. *No.*

"Holland," he gasped. "Please. You have to take this collar
off."

"I will," said Holland slowly. "When you agree."

Panic tore through him. "To what?"

"When I was in Black London—after *you* sent me there—I
made a deal. My body for *his* power."

"His?"

But there could be only one thing waiting in that darkness to
make a deal. The same *thing* that had crushed a world, that had

tried to escape in a shard of stone. The same thing that had torn a path through his city, tried to devour Kell's soul.

"You *fool*," he snarled. "You're the one . . . who told me that to let dark magic in was to lose . . ." His teeth were chattering. "That you were either the master . . . or the servant. And look . . . what you've done. You may be free of Athos's spell . . . but you've just traded one master for another."

Holland took Kell by the jaw and slammed his head back against the metal beam. Pain rang through his skull. The collar tightened, and the seal above his heart cracked and split.

"Listen to me," begged Kell, the second pulse faltering in his chest. "I know this magic."

"You knew a shadow. A sliver of its power."

"That power destroyed one world already."

"And healed another," said Holland.

Kell couldn't stop shaking. The pain was fading, replaced by something worse. A horrible, deadening cold. "Please. Take this off. I won't fight back. I—"

"You've had your perfect world," said Holland. "Now I want *mine*."

Kell swallowed, closed his eyes, tried to keep his thoughts from fraying.

Let me in.

Kell blinked. The words had come from Holland's mouth, but the voice wasn't his. It was softer, more resonant, and even as it spoke, Holland's face began to change. Shadow bled from one eyes into the other, consuming the emerald green and staining it black. A wisp of silver smoke curled through those eyes, and someone—something—looked out, but it wasn't Holland.

"*Hello,* Antari."

Holland's expression continued to shift, the features of his face rearranging from hard edges into soft, almost gentle ones. The lines of his forehead and cheeks smoothed to polished stone, and his mouth contorted into a beatific smile. And when the creature spoke, it had two voices; one filling the air, a smoother version of Holland's own, while the other echoed in Kell's head, low and rich as smoke. That second voice twined behind Kell's eyes, and spread through his mind, searching.

"*I can save you,*" it said, plucking at his thoughts. "*I can save your brother. I can save everything.*" The creature reached up and touched a strand of Kell's sweat-slicked hair, as if fascinated. "*Just let me in.*"

"You are a monster," growled Kell.

Holland's fingers tightened around Kell's throat. "*I am a god.*" Kell felt the creature's will pressing against his own, felt it forcing its way into his mind with icy fingers and cold precision.

"Get out of my head." Kell slammed forward against the binds with all his strength, cracking his forehead against Holland's. Pain lanced through him, hot and bright, and blood trickled down his nose, but the thing in Holland's body only smiled.

"*I am in everyone's head,*" it said. "*I am in everything. I am as old as creation itself. I am life and death and power. I am inevitable.*"

Kell's heart was pounding, but Rhy's was slipping. One beat for every two. And then three. And then—

The creature flashed its teeth. "*Let me in.*"

But Kell couldn't. He thought of his world, of setting this creature loose upon it wearing his skin. He saw the palace crumble and the river go dark, saw the bodies fall to ash in the streets, the color bleed out until there was only black, and saw himself standing at the center, just as he had in every nightmare. Helpless.

Tears streamed down his face.

He couldn't. He couldn't do that. He couldn't *be* that.

I'm sorry, Rhy, he thought, knowing he'd just damned them both.

"No," he said aloud, the word scraping his throat.

But to his surprise, the monster's smile widened. "*I was hoping you would say that.*"

Kell didn't understand the creature's joy, not until it stepped back and held up its hands. *"I like this skin. And now that you have refused me, I get to keep it."*

Something shifted in the creature's eyes, a pulse of light, a sliver of green, flaring, fighting, only to be swallowed again by the darkness. The monster shook its head almost ruefully. *"Holland, Holland . . ."* it purred.

"Bring him back," demanded Kell. "We are not done." But the creature kept shaking its head as it reached for Kell's throat. He tried to pull away, but there was no escape.

"You were right, Antari," it said, running its fingertips along the metal collar. *"Magic is either a servant or a master."*

Kell fought against the metal frame, the cuffs cutting into his wrists. "Holland!" he shouted, the word echoing through the stone room. "Holland, you bastard, fight back!"

The demon only stood and watched, its black eyes amused, unblinking.

"Show me you're not weak!" screamed Kell. "Prove you're not still a slave to someone else's will! Did you really come all the way back to lose like this? Holland!"

Kell sagged back against the metal frame, wrists bloody and voice hoarse as the monster turned and walked away.

"Wait, demon," choked Kell, straining against the pressing darkness, the cold, the fading echo of Rhy's pulse.

The creature glanced back. *"My name,"* it said, *"is Osaron."*

Kell fought against the metal frame as his vision blurred, refocused, and then began to tunnel. "Where are you going?"

The demon held something up for him to see, and Kell's heart lurched. It was a single crimson coin, marked by a gold star in its center. A Red London lin.

"No," he pleaded, twisting against the cuffs until they shredded his skin and blood streamed down his wrists. "Osaron, you can't."

The demon only smiled. "But who will stop me now?"

IX

Lila paced the orchard.

She had to do something.

The courtyard was brimming with guards, the palace in a frenzy. Tieren was trying to coax answers from Hastra, and several rows away, Alucard was still curled over Rhy, murmuring something too soft for her to hear. It sounded like a soothing whisper. Or a prayer. She had heard men praying at sea, not to God, but to the world, to magic, to anything that might be listening. A higher power, a different name. Lila hadn't believed in God for a very long time—she'd given up praying when it was clear that no one would answer—and while she was willing to admit that magic *existed,* it didn't seem to listen, or at least, it didn't seem to care. Lila took a strange pleasure in that, because it meant the power was her own.

God wasn't going to help Rhy.

But Lila could.

She marched back through the orchard.

"Where are you going?" demanded Alucard, looking up from the prince.

"To fix this," she said. And with that she took off, sprinting through the courtyard doors. She didn't stop, not for the attendants or the guards who tried to bar her way. She ducked and spun, surging past them and through the palace doors and down the steps.

Lila knew what she had to do, though she had no idea if it would work. It was madness to try, but she didn't have a choice. That wasn't true. The old Lila would have pointed out that she always had a choice, and that she'd live a hell of a lot longer if she chose herself.

But when it came to Kell, there was a debt. A bond. Different from the one that bound him and Rhy, but just as solid.

Hold on, she thought.

Lila pressed through the crowded streets and away from the festivities. In her mind she tried to draw a map of White London, what little she'd seen of it, but she couldn't remember much besides the castle, and Kell's warning to never cross over exactly where you wanted to be.

When she finally found herself alone, she pulled the shard of Astrid Dane from her back pocket. Then she rolled up her sleeve and withdrew her knife.

This is madness, she thought. *Sheer and utter madness.*

She knew the difference between elemental and *Antari.* Yes, she had survived before, but she had been with Kell, under the protection of his magic. And now she was alone.

What am I? she'd asked Tieren.

What am I? she'd wondered every night at sea, every day since she'd first found herself here in this city, in this world.

Now Lila swallowed and drew the knife's blade across her forearm. It bit into flesh, and a thin ribbon of red rose and spilled over. She smeared the wall with her blood and clutched the shard of stone.

Whatever I am, she thought, pressing her hand to the wall, *let it be enough.*

APPENDIX

GLOSSARY

ANTARI

As Anasae: blood command to *dispel.*

As Athera: blood command to *grow.*

As Besara: blood command to *take.*

As Hasari: blood command to *heal.*

As Herena: blood command to *give.*

As Illumae: blood command to *light.*

As Isera: blood command to *freeze.*

As Narahi: blood command to *quicken.*

As Orense: blood command to *open.*

As Pyrata: blood command to *burn.*

As Staro: blood command to *seal.*

As Steno: blood command to *break.*

As Tascen: blood command to *transfer.*

As Tosal: blood command to *confine.*

As Travars: blood command to *travel.*

ARNESIAN NUMBERS

1: on
2: sessa
3: ris
4: tal
5: nissa
6: son
7: vis
8: volo
9: ossa
10: non

ARNESIAN WORDS

An: a flexible word in Arnesian language, it can mean *I, a,* or
   no, depending on context
Anos: (adj.) eternal
Anoshe: (n., excl.) the closest thing to a farewell
Arensor: (n.) attendant, assistant
Arna: (n.) mistress, madam, term of respect
Ast: (n.) sun
Astal: (v.) to rise, prepare
Av: (n.) day(s)
Aven: (adj.) blessed
Ayes: (n.) fields, pasture

Cas: (adj.) hot
Casero: (n.) captain

Casnor: (v.) setting, descending
Cason: (n.) to take
Choser: (n.) giants
Cryssac: (n.) gems, specifically elemental ones

Er: (pro.) much like *an,* a flexible word meaning *that*, *it*, or *this*
Eran: (adj.) best
Erase: (v.) to come
Es: (conj.) or
Essen: (n. or adj.) balance, stability, purity,
Essen Tasch: (n.) Element Games
Essenir: (n.) essential items, primarily in the execution of
   spells

Fera: (adj.) dark
Ferase: (v.) to go

Gast: (n.) thief
Gosar: (n.) banner

Hals: (n.) land
Hosna: (n.) ghost

Ir: (prep.) in
Ira: (n.) eye
Is: (art.) the

Kir: (adj.) a vibrant red

Lin: (n.) a unit of coin, akin to a shilling
Lish: (n.) an order of coinage higher than lin (ten lin make one lish)

Marist: (n.) pleasure
Merst: (n.) market

Nas: (adv.) a formal refusal
Nes: (pro.) them
Noche: (n.) night

Onase: (n.) head, as in head of house; the highest position in an
    organization
Ostra: (n.) London's elite

Pilse: (n.) a foul epithet
Postran: (n.) wardrobe
Priste: (n.) power

Rachenast: (n.) splendor
Ranes: (n.) copper
Rast: (n.) heart
Renache: (adj.) away, elsewhere
Renar: (adj.) late
Rosin: (v.) to give

Sanct: (n. or interj.) a game of cards; also an exclamation of dis-
    may or anger
Sarenach: (imp.) surrender
Saren Noche: (n.) Night Spire
Sarows: (n.) a mythical spirit the haunts ships at sea
Sasenroche: (n.) a black market where the three empires meet
Sensan: (v.) sinking
Sha: (n.) the slums, though the word is also used as a slang akin
    to "cool!"

Shast: (n.) a road, or a soul

Soner: (adj.) beating, steady

Stran: (n.) thread

Stras: (n.) waters, rivers

Strast: (n.) guard

Tes: (adj.) a diminutive, little

Tessane: (n.) a hot herbal tea favored in the market

Tol: (n.) steel, or brother

Van: (v.) to tell

Vares: (n.) prince; both a title and a common word, depending on the usage

Vasar: (v.) to kill

Vasken: (v.) to pirate

Vesnara: (v.) wandering

Vestra: (adj.) belonging to one of the royal families

Viris: (adj.) foolish

Vitari: (n., proper n., v.) magic, Magic, or the act of creating magic

Arnesian Phrases and Sayings:

Alos mas en: Let me in

An: No

An esto: I'm coming

Anesh: A word of accord, akin to "sure"

Anoshe: Until next time

As esher tan ves: an idiomatic expression meaning "I hope you are well"

As esta narash: All things are

Avan: Good evening or Hello

Fal chas: Good luck

Ir chas: Literally "in faith," an expression used to seal deals
Ir chas era: Literally "in faith lost," an idiomatic expression meaning "sore loser"
Ise av eran: An idiomatic expression meaning "to each their secrets"

Kers?: What?
Kers la?: What's this?
Kes ile?: Don't you agree? Akin to the French "*N'est-ce pas?*"

Mas aven: My goodness
Mas marist: My pleasure

Priste ir Essen. Essen ir Priste: Power in Balance. Balance in Power

Ras al!: Conventionally "watch out," though literally it means "good see"
Rensa tav: Thank you
Res naster: Good sir/gentleman

Ser asina gose: You sound good
Sha!: Cool!
Skan: Nothing
Solase: Apologies
Stas reskon: Chasing danger

Tac: A sound of scorn
Tas enol: After you

Tosa!: Help!

Vas ir: "In peace," an idiomatic expression used as a casual good-bye

A KISIMYR VASRIN
SHORT STORY

by V. E. Schwab

THE CONSEQUENCE
OF TRIUMPH

Kisimyr shuddered, her lungs straining.

A drop of sweat ran down her face and fell from her chin, only to be caught before it hit the ground, drawn into the coil of water that wove around her hands, twisting over and back on itself in the air between palm and wrist, tendrils snaking between fingers.

Few magicians could wield any element with so much precision.

Fewer still could wield *two*.

But Kisimyr Vasrin was the best magician in three empires. She had the laurels—and her weight in gold—to prove it. And so, even as the water coiled in the air, the ground beneath her feet hovered several inches above the rest of the courtyard, a disc of earth bound and raised by nothing more than her will.

Her muscles ached from the effort, pain tracing its way beneath her skin.

She'd been training since midday, and now the sun was plunging toward the highest spire of the royal palace where it arced on the Isle. Kisimyr's own estate, on a rise two short streets off the northern banks, afforded a perfect view. The house, like so many other things, had been purchased with the victory chest, one more token of her triumph.

Most champions had taken their winnings and retired, content to spend the rest of their days enjoying their fame and fortune.

But Kisimyr had never been *content,* never understood the pleasure that came with being *done.*

It had been more than two years since she was crowned Champion of the *Essen Tasch,* which meant there was less than an year until the stadiums sprang up again, this time in her own city. Thanks to Kisimyr's victory, the Element Games were coming to London. Thanks to her—and she had no intention of sitting them out, reclining in a nice chair in some esteemed box, put on display like a relic at twenty-eight.

Twenty-eight, and stronger than she'd been the year she'd won. Twenty-eight, and ready to claim a new title—the first champion to ever win *twice.*

The sun finally dipped beneath the palace, and Kisimyr let out a shuddering breath and released her grip on the elements.

The water lost its shape and fell from her hands, and the ground beneath her gave way, crumbling back into loose dirt as it rained down onto the courtyard a foot below.

Kisimyr dropped, too, her bare feet sinking into the damp earth before she buckled forward, hands plunging in up to the elbows.

She crouched there for a moment, too unsteady to rise.

At least the view was something to enjoy. The courtyard looked out onto the Isle River, with its constant crimson glow—the pulse of London, a current in every magician's bones. Her estate sat on the northern bank, a mansion with rooms she hardly used, and luxuries Fallori enjoyed far more than Kisimyr did.

But she certainly enjoyed the having of them.

After all, how many years had Kisimyr spent dreaming of a view like this? How many years spent looking up at mansions like this one, longing to look down from their balconies instead of up from the streets?

"Why must you train so much?" came a voice from the patio.

Kisimyr turned her back on the Isle and found Fallori leaning in the doorway. The river light cast a reddish glow over the woman's high cheeks, found the places where she let her silk robe part to show bare skin.

"You are already the best," she said. "Isn't that enough?"

But it wasn't.

"Becoming the best is one thing," said Kisimyr. "*Staying* the best is another."

Fallori tilted her head thoughtfully. She had her arms crossed beneath her chest, accentuating her bosom, which she knew was Kisimyr's favorite feature. Along with her face. And her legs. And the curve of her hip. And her voice.

Kisimyr checked the sky—it was getting dark now, and she was expected at the Rosec estate by half eight. But she had trained hard, had earned this small reward.

She crossed to Fallori, fingers already rising to cup the woman's face, but Fallori caught Kisimyr's hand, nose crinkling.

"You're filthy, Kis," she chided, a smile playing at the edge of her mouth. "You need a bath."

Kisimyr looked down. She *was* dirty—soaked with sweat, shins and forearms slicked with damp earth. The hand so close to Fallori's skin was still coated in grime, and when she swallowed she tasted salt, sweat.

"I suppose I do." She ran the back of a dirt-caked hand over her cheek, leaving a streak of mud behind for good measure.

"And someone to help make me clean. Now, where might I find such a—"

But Fall was already drawing her through the door and down the tiled hall, and into the steam-filled chamber where the grand bath waited, glass and gold tiles lining the deep pool in the floor.

Fallori slid out of her robe and sank one foot onto the step, gasping a little at the heat before descending the steps.

It took Kisimyr a measure longer to undress, prying off the training garments, unlacing the various bracers and weights she wore to simulate the gear she wore in the arena. She left a trail of sweat-stained clothes behind her as she went.

The bath, when she finally reached it, was blessedly hot, scented with citrus and mint. Her skin prickled from the initial, almost painful heat, but as she continued down, Kisimyr nearly groaned in pleasure as the water rose over her tired body.

A goblet sat waiting on the bath's edge, surface sweating from the steam, and Kisimyr washed the taste of training from her mouth, replaced it with the sweet, crisp taste of summer wine.

Fallori stood waiting against the bath's back wall, her arms stretched out along the tile rim to either side. She was watching Kisimyr through lidded eyes, and by the time Kis reached her, the bath's subtle current had peeled away the dirt, its spelled surface collecting the grime and drawing it away like a curse.

Kisimyr's hand followed the path it had started in the courtyard, cupping Fallori's cheek before sliding behind her neck, nesting in her dark curls. She meant to pull Fall in for a kiss, but Fall was already there, her mouth on hers, lips guiding hers open, stealing the kiss before it could be given.

Fall's hands moved down Kisimyr's bare body, followed the

lean muscles over her ribs before trailing down her back, nails digging lightly into the curve of her ass as she pulled Kis closer.

She was trying to take control, but Kisimyr wasn't ready to yield just yet. She pressed Fallori back against the tile wall, her leg sliding between Fall's, eliciting a small gasp of pleasure, one that deepened as Kisimyr's hand drifted down under the water, found the heat of Fall's body amid the warmth of the bath.

Fallori was a master of pleasure. Perhaps that was why Kisimyr took such delight in pleasuring *her*. In taking control, coaxing delight from the curves of her body, the soft places the other woman knew so well.

Fallori moved against her, cheeks flushing. Her head fell forward, teeth grazing Kisimyr's collar.

"I'm supposed to be pleasing *you*," breathed Fall.

"This does please me," said Kis, her hand quickening its rhythms until Fallori's back arched, breath catching at Kisimyr's private kind of magic.

🐉

Kisimyr stood before the mirror.

The bath had done her well, scrubbed the salt and earth from her skin, released the tension in her back. But in its place, there had been left a deep fatigue. Her limbs still ached as she dressed, and the bed at her back was a temptress, as was the woman lying in it.

Kisimyr resisted the urge to sit, knowing she would lack the will to rise again. Instead, she stood before the glass, twisting gold rings into the dark ropes of her hair. Dusting gold along the dark skin of her cheeks and throat, painting lines of black and gold around her lashes to reflect the mottling in her eyes, the flecks in the cloth of her tunic and cloak. She was more comfortable dressing for the arena, but this, she told herself, was another kind of armor. More subtle, perhaps, but then, so were the weapons.

"If I had known you intended to leave so soon," said Fallori, rising to slide her arms around Kisimyr's waist, "I would have drained the bath and left you dirty."

Amazing; they'd bathed in the same water, but Fallori smelled not only clean but sweet as summer wine. Intoxicating.

Kis met her gaze in the mirror. "You could come with me."

"You could stay here," countered Fall.

"I'd love nothing more."

"Then *stay*," she said, burrowing her face to Kisimyr's back. "Don't indulge the Vestran wolves. They don't deserve you."

Kis sighed. "It comes with the job."

"They just want to put you on display."

"You could give them something better to stare at."

Fallori clicked her tongue and pulled free, turning back toward the bed. "Flattery."

"Truth," said Kis, plucking her mask from the table. Once gold and black, the feline helmet she'd worn in the last *Essen Tasch* had seen its share of damage. Scorch marks licked up one side, the paint and gilt was worn away, and a crack ran down through the right eye.

Her next one, she'd decided, would be solid gold.

Fallori slumped, sulking, amid the sheets.

"You know," she said, "I'm beginning to think you have another lover."

"As if anyone could hold a candle to you."

Kisimyr tied the mask around her throat, but didn't raise it yet to cover her face. Instead, she spun it so the feline grin hung between her shoulders, just one more ornament. The message was simple, but clear: Kisimyr was more than a single victor's mask. And soon enough, she would prove it.

"Perhaps not," said Fall, plucking a piece of fruit from the bowl by the bed, "except for the *magic*." She rolled the round fruit thoughtfully along her palm. "You spend more time with it than me." She bit spitefully into the fruit, splitting its skin.

Kisimyr turned toward the woman in her bed.

"Magic bought the fruit in your hand," she said, approaching the mound of cushions. "And the silk under your perfect ass," she said, running her hand up Fallori's leg. "And the bath we just shared," she continued, bowing her face toward Fall's. "And don't forget, my love," whispered, lips brushing Fallori's mouth, "magic bought *you*."

And with that, Kisimyr turned her face toward the fruit in Fall's hand, and took a bite. But as she began to pull away, Fallori's fingers caught her, drew her close. Kis curled her fingers in the sheets to keep from falling.

Fallori looked into her eyes, her own pensive, dark.

"What can I do to make you happy?"

The question was a knife, short but sharp, a grazing cut. "I *am* happy."

Fallori sighed dramatically. "But not satisfied."

Kisimyr managed a wan smile. "Satisfaction is the death of ambition. I hope I am never satisfied."

Fallori's face fell. "How sad," she said, slipping closer. She lifted enough to kiss the tender skin beneath Kisimyr's jaw. "Don't *I* satisfy you?" she breathed.

Kis caught her chin, guiding Fallori's face up. "You *please* me. Isn't that better?"

Fallori gave a petulant sigh. "Why must you make every-thing hard?"

"If I were Goster, I'd say something salacious."

Fallori rolled her eyes, and fell back among the sheets, and Kisimyr forced herself away from the woman and the bed be-fore she lost her will.

"I won't be late," she called over her shoulder.

"I won't be waiting," countered Fall, as the door to their bedroom swung shut.

✣

Of the five noble families in London, the Rosecs were hardly Kisimyr's favorite—she had a soft spot for the Maresh, truly—but they did know how to throw a party. Their mansion glit-tered on the eastern rise, traced with light, the lanterns along the walk enchanted to burn the colors of the house Rosec, silver and violet.

The late autumn air was heady with the scents of sugar, wine, and spice, the front walk crowded with carriages. Kisimyr ran her hand along a horse's pale flank as she wove between them to the broad front steps, garlanded with vines and vibrant flow-ers, their petals tipped with silver.

Goster and Marro were waiting on the front steps, Goster's black hair slicked back, the tips of each strand flecked with gold, while Marro's long locks were braided with metallic rib-bons. The two were decked out in sharp adornments designed to match Kisimyr's own, to mark the man and woman as mem-bers of her personal entourage.

The two were quarreling over something—they were always quarreling—but it didn't stop Marro from reaching out and snapping her fingers to light the taper clutched between Goster's teeth.

He inhaled, and blew a ring of white smoke.

"No way," he was saying.

"I'm telling you," insisted Marro. "Ten lin says he shows up on the list this turn."

Kisimyr knew what list they were referring to—the tournament roster—and knew it wouldn't go up for another month. What she *didn't* know was who they were talking about.

Goster turned to Kisimyr.

"Marro, tell Kis here what you just told me."

She held up hands. "I'm only passing on the words, I didn't conjure them."

"And the words are?" prompted Kisimyr,

"That *Alucard Emery* is going to compete."

That *would* be a magic trick, considering the infamous—and infamously disowned—younger son of the House Emery hadn't set foot on London soil for the better part of three years after running off to become, of all things, a privateer.

Kisimyr plucked the taper from Goster's mouth and took a long drag, savoring the rich herbs, the way they eased her shoulders, loosened her chest. "Where did you hear that?"

Marro shrugged. "People like to tell me secrets. I have that kind of face. Word is that Alucard's little sister applied on his behalf."

"Well," said Kis, stubbing out the last of the taper. "I suppose we'll find out soon enough."

He *would* be a worthy competitor—if there was truth to the rumor.

Kisimyr turned her attention up to the polished bronze doors, each blazoned with the Rosec's crest—a tree, with high branches and deep roots—and sighed.

"Shall we?"

§

The party was in full swing.

Kisimyr couldn't remember if it was a feast day, an anniversary, a birth, or if the Rosecs, like all nobles, simply loved to flaunt their wealth and station.

It didn't really matter.

The invitation had summoned her.

And so she had come.

Kisimyr Vasrin was their favorite kind of trophy. A commoner from the streets of London, raised to fame by glory. As champion of the latest *Essen Tasch,* she was something to be put on display, paraded about for the *vestra* and *ostra* to appreciate and enjoy. A testament, not to her own strength, apparently, but to the strength of her empire. The prize of Arnes.

She moved through rooms of silver and stone, flanked by Goster and Marro, their stark attire set off against the pale colors popular that season.

Murmurs followed her, glasses raised in toast even as heads bowed to whisper.

She hated these nobles, hated herself for craving their attention, their respect. But, she thought, plucking a glass from a passing tray, they had good taste in wine. And she had no qualms about drinking it.

Kisimyr kept her head high as she moved through the crowd, her smile fastened to her face, and if there was the faintest curl to the edge of it, a glint in the corner of her eye, well, no one noticed.

"Look who's here," observed Marro.

Kisimyr followed her gaze, and spotted the princes across the room, each, in their own way, impossible to miss. The crown prince, Rhy, was radiant, his dark skin set off by gold silk, his smile broad, his manner easy. His brother, by contrast, was tall and slim, a somber figure in a crimson coat, his red hair dancing like a flame over his pale face.

"He *is* quite handsome," said Marro, sipping her wine.

Goster raised a brow. "Which one?"

"Prince Rhy, obviously."

"Really? I've always preferred the ghost," said Goster, nodding toward Kell.

"Too moody for me," said Marro. "But the eyes are a sight."

Kisimyr cleared her throat. "I thought you were meant to be *my* admirers."

"Of course, my champion," said Marro with exaggerated reverence.

Goster caught her hand and bowed to kiss it. "We have eyes only for you."

"Fuck off," said Kisimyr, her attention drifting back to the princes.

The *Antari* trailed behind Rhy like a shadow, stiff-backed and stoic. They were so different, not just in coloring, but in temper. Rhy Maresh seemed perfectly at home, while Kell seemed to chafe at the attention, one hand gripping his wine as if it were a shield.

He looked as though he felt as out of place as she did.

The crowd parted around him the way it did around her, a mixture of awe and discomfort. As if each of them were weapons, beautiful, but sharp, dangerous to touch.

The difference, of course, was that Kisimyr was expected to

be grateful for the attention paid her, to be happy for her place here, or at the very least to pretend, to smile.

The only person *Kell* seemed to smile for was his brother, and even then, it stole across his mouth like a secret. What she wouldn't give to face *him* in the tournament, to test her skills against the royal *Antari,* for whom magic came so naturally.

As if he could feel her watching, Kell's eyes flicked toward her, one radiant blue, and other pitch black. She resisted the urge to look away.

"Kisimyr Vasrin," teased Marro. "Do *you* have eyes for the *Antari*?"

She blinked, wrenching her attention away.

"He's not my type," she said, draining her glass, and abandoning it on the nearest shelf.

Kisimyr released Goster and Marro to their own affairs, and walked back to her house alone, sometime after midnight. She could have called a carriage, but the night was nice, the walk sobering, and if she did run into any trouble, she was quite certain she could take it. Truth be told, she found herself almost wishing for the chance to spar with someone. She did cut a pretty purse, covered as she was in gold, but she was also on the north bank, and no one took the bait, and shortly before one, she arrived home entirely unchallenged and unscathed.

Kisimyr looked up at the glass windows of her house, let her eyes linger on the balcony that led to her bedroom, and hoped that Fallori would be there, wrapped in silk and sleep. Her own bones groaned, begging for sleep, but instead of mounting the front steps, she passed through the gates into the courtyard, the marks of her last training session still visible in the dark.

She unfastened the mask from her collar and stripped off the cloak, tossing both into the grass. Water pooled in a shallow basin at the center of the lawn, and Kisimyr drew her palm over the surface, calling the liquid up around her hand. She reached out the other, summoning earth from the mound where it lay disturbed. A ribbon peeled away, came to call at her fingers where it collapsed itself into a ball and spun.

It wasn't enough to be the best.

You had to *stay* the best.

And as she stood there, magic rolling through tired muscles, the first beads of sweat bricking on her gold-flushed skin, she stared out at the Isle, at the palace, at her city, London, host to the next *Essen Tasch*. And as the elements turned through the air around her, Kisimyr Vasrin smiled.

She would be the first magician to win the tournament *twice*.

ACKNOWLEDGMENTS

Here we are again. The end of another book. I'm always surprised to have made it this far. It might have taken you days, or weeks, or even months to read *A Gathering of Shadows,* but it took me years to write, edit, and see this book to publication. That duration renders this moment surreal. Even harder is remembering who to thank.

To my mother and father, for telling me I could be whatever I wanted, whether that was a designer, an interrogator, or a fantasy author.

To my editor, Miriam, for being a killer editor, a stalwart champion, and an ace GIF user. And for being a friend and companion on this particularly wondrous adventure.

To my agent, Holly, for proving time and again that you are magic.

To my former publicist, Leah, and my new publicist, Alexis, and to Patty Garcia, for keeping me afloat.

To art director Irene Gallo and cover designer Will Staehle, for making things look so fierce.

To my beta reader, Patricia, for sticking with me through thick and thin and strange and dark.

To my Nashville crew, especially Courtney and Carla, Ruta,

Paige, Lauren, Sarah, Ashley, Sharon, David, and so, so many more, for being the warmest community in all the land.

To my wee Scottish flatmate, Rachel, for being an utter delight, and not making fun of me when I talked to myself or vanished for long stretches into the deadline pit.

To my new housemate, Jenna, because you have no idea what you're in for.

To my readers, who are, without question, the best readers in the entire world (sorry everyone else's readers).

To everyone else: So many of you have stood at my side, championed my work, cheered on good days and been present on bad, and taken this journey with me stride for stride. I can never thank you all, but please know that if you're reading this, you matter. You've made an impact on my life and my series, and for that, I'm incredibly grateful.

(I also want to point out that I made it nine books without invoking the dreaded cliffhanger.)